The Witch Chronicles: Unraveled

Maggie Frost

Editing: Arianna Fox

Cover design: E.W. Stark

Dedication:
To my mom and dad. Thank you for raising me right and supporting me in all that I do. I love you both so much.

Daddy, I wish you could be here with me and see how far I've come. But God had other plans. And I know you are looking down on me from the stars, smiling; happy I could achieve one of my dreams that you inspired me so much in. I miss you.

Maggie Frost

Table of Contents

Pronunciation Guide

Names

Almira: Al-meer-uh

Brianna: Bree-ann-uh

Eira: Ur-uh

Flores: Floor-ez

Haven: Hey-ven

Qiu: Chee-ooo

Rai: Ray

Zira: Zur-uh

Spells

Apairago: uh-pair-uh-goh

Breyonio: bur-ay-own-ee-oh

Canoro lentaran: can-or-oh len-tar-ann

Conwe: con-way

Crairto forcan: cr-air-toe for-can

Flordra garifiolte: floor-druh gahr-if-ee-ol-tay

Fuhian: foo-hon

Grana maukino: gr-on-uh mah-key-no

Gwynocha brunori: gwyn-ah-cuh broo-nor-ee

Ineldig: in-el-dig

Leneradu forcan: len-ur-ah-doo for-can

Lyrache: lie-rah-chee

Mecola: mel-cola

Monis decantio: mon-iss dee-can-tee-oh

Peionasu: fee-on-ass-su

Reobicar: ree-oh-bic-air

Soruziar: soar-rue-zee-are

Sceldir: sc-el-dar

Telepras: tell-ee-prass

Teleprasportio: tell-ee-prass-por-tee-oh

Whiari: why-are-ee

Spanish

Adiós, para siempre: ah-dyohs, pah-rah syehm-preh

Así es: ah-see ehs

Ay, mija: ay, mee-hah

Bienvenida a casa: byehm-beh-nee-duh ah kah-sah

Bienvenidos, hijos de puta: byehm-beh-nee-dohs, ee-hohs dee poo-tah

Bienvenidos: byehm-beh-nee-dohs

Bien, supongo: byehn, soo-pon-go

Buenos días: bweh-nohs dee-ahs

Cálmate: kahl-mah-teh

Cariña: kuh-ri-nuh

Cariñita: kuh-ri-nee-tuh

Cavar en: kah-bahr ehn

Cena: seh-nah

Claro: klah-roh

¿Cómo dormiste?: koh-moh dohr-mees-teh

Cuídate: kwee-dah-teh

De nada: deh nah-dah

Disculpe, ¿dónde está el baño?: dees-kool-peh, dohn-deh ehs-tah ehl bah-nyoh

Dos: dohs

En serio: ehn seh-ryoh

Entra: ehn-truh

Español: esh-pah-nyohl

Gracias: grah-syahs

¡Hasta luego!: ahs-tah lweh-goh

Hermana: ehr-mah-nah

Hermanito: ehr-mah-nee-toh

Hijita: ee-hee-tah

Hola: oh-lah

Inglés: eeng-glehs

Justo al final del pasillo a la derecha: hoos-toh ahl fee-nahl dehl pah-see-yoh ah lah deh-reh-chah

The Witch Chronicles: Unraveled

La comida: lah coh-mee-dah

La verdad es que: lah behr-dahd ehs keh

Lo sé: loh seh

Lo siento: loh syehn-toh

Mamá: mah-mah

Mami: mah-mee

Me encanta mi casa: meh ehng-kahn-tah mee kah-sah

Me encantaría: meh ehng-kahn-tah-ree-ah

Mi amor: mee ah-mohr

Mierda: myehr-dah

Mi hogar: mee oh-gahr

Mija: mee-hah

Mijita: mee-hee-tah

Mi niñita: mee neen-yee-tah

Mira: mee-rah

Mi reina: mee rrey-nah

Mi vida: mee bee-dah

Mucho gusto: moo-choh goos-toh

No me asustes así: noh meh ah-soo-stehs ah-see

Papi: pah-pee

Princesa: preen-seh-sah

Por favor vuelve a casa, mi princesa: pohr-fah-bohr buel-beh uh kah-sah, mee preen-seh-sah

Querida familia: keh-ree-dah fah-mee-lyah

Sígueme: see-gyeh-meh

Sí: see

Son tus amigas: sohn toos ah-mee-gohs

Suena bien: sweh-nah byehn

Tamales: tah-mah-lyehs

Te quiero: teh kyeh-roh

Tortas ahogadas: tor-tahz ah-oh-gah-dahs

Tres: trehs

Todo está bien: toh-doh ehs-tah byehn

Uno: oo-noh

Vamos: bah-mohs

Vaya: bah-yah

Ven aquí: behn ah-kee

French

Étincelles: ee-tah-cells

Je l'adore: jey luh-door

Papillon: pah-pee-yon

Irish

Aishling: ash-ling

Tá fáilte romhat: taw foyle-cha roh-ot

Hawaiian

'Ae: eye

Welsh

Y mae: uh my

Translation to English Guide

Spanish

Adiós, para siempre: Goodbye, forever

Así es: That's right

Ay, mija: Oh, my daughter

Bienvenida a casa: Welcome home

Bienvenidos, hijos de puta: Welcome motherfuckers

Bienvenidos: Welcome

Bien, supongo: Fine, I suppose

Buenos días: Good morning

Cálmate: Calm down

Cariña: Honey (term of endearment)

Cariñita: Little honey (term of endearment)

Cavar en: Dig in

Cena: Dinner

Claro: Of course

¿Cómo dormiste?: How did you sleep?

Cuídate: Take care

De nada: You're welcome

Disculpe, ¿dónde está el baño?: Excuse me, where's the bathroom?

Dos: Two

En serio: Seriously

Entra: Enter

Español: Spanish

Gracias: Thank you

¡Hasta luego!: See you later!

Hermana: Sister

Hermanito: Little brother

Hijita: Little daughter

Hola: Hello

Inglés: English

Justo al final del pasillo a la derecha: Just at the end of the hallway on the right

La comida: The food

La verdad es que: The truth is that

Lo sé: I know

Lo siento: I'm sorry

Mamá: Mom

Mami: Mommy

Me encanta mi casa: I love my home

Me encantaría: I'd love to

Mi amor: My love

Mierda: Crap

Mi hogar: My home

Mija: My daughter

Mijita: My little daughter

Mi niñita: My little girl

Mira: Look

Mi reina: My queen

Mi vida: My life

Mucho gusto: Nice to meet you

No me asustes así: Don't scare me like that

Papi: Daddy

Princesa: Princess

Por favor vuelve a casa, mi princesa: Please come home, my princess

Querida familia: Dear family

Sígueme: Follow me

Sí: Yes

Son tus amigas: They're your friends

Suena bien: Sounds good

Tamales: Tamales, a common Mexican dish

Te quiero: I love you

Tortas ahogadas: Tortas ahogadas, a Mexican dish

Tres: Three

Todo está bien: Everything is okay

Uno: One

Vamos: Let's go

Vaya: Whoa

Ven aquí: Come here

French

Étincelles: Sparkles

Papillon: Butterfly

Je l'adore: I love it

Hawaiian

'Ae: Yes

Irish

Aisling: A vision or dream

Tá fáilte romhat: You're welcome

Welsh

Y mae: Yes

<u>Spell Guide</u>

Apairago: Reverses "ineldig" and makes the objects visible again.

Breyonio: Berries. Berry is the same just minus the last "o."

Canoro lentaran: Slows time down for a few seconds. Only the caster will be unaffected.

Conwe: Can freeze any liquid.

Crairto forcan: Creates harmless fire that can be used for heating and lighting purposes.

Flordra garifiolte: Makes a small, solid, translucent square the caster can control. The color of the square will be the color of the caster's magic.

Fuhian: Creates fire.

Grana maukino: Creates a circle that makes everything in it soft.

Gwynocha brunori: A knowledge spell of the Witchery language. Whomever it's cast on will know the Witchery language almost completely.

Ineldig: Can turn any object invisible to the non-magical eye.

Leneradu forcan: Causes the fire made by "crairto forcan" to grow.

Lyrache: Milk.

Mecola: Mixes potion ingredients together.

Monis decantio: Brings heat into the caster's hand(s).

Peionasu: A failsafe for when a Witch or Warlock needs a potion to end before it automatically runs out.

Reobicar: Can make anyone remember a specific memory, usually what the cast-tee is thinking of at the time.

Sceldir: Can melt any frozen liquid.

Soruziar: Fixes simple electronic problems.

Telepras: Teleports object of choice.

Teleprasportio: Teleportation spell for humans.

Whiari: Creates ice on an object.

Prologue

Origins

Zira groaned as she slowly opened her eyes, heaviness weighing on her heart once again. She rubbed her face and got out of bed, heading for the bathroom.

She squirted toothpaste onto her green toothbrush and turned on the faucet, letting the water run smoothly down into the sink. As the tap continued to run, her heart lightened a little. The sound comforted her. It always had. After a few moments, however, she saw something that made her nearly drop her toothbrush. The faucet handle moved, and the flow of water stopped.

Fear seized her chest, and she froze. Looking down at the handle, Zira wasn't sure if she wanted to turn it back on or pack her things and move to some remote city in Mexico. She was leaning toward the second option.

However, she took a deep breath and turned the tap back on. Option one was a success. The water ran smoothly just as it did before, and Zira exhaled in exhausted relief. *I was probably just imagining things.* That likely would've been the case if it didn't happen again.

This time, Zira dropped her toothbrush and backed up against the door.

"What is going on?" she whispered with a hint of panic in her tone. Maybe her dad was playing a trick on her? No, he was a man of simple humor. Maybe it was just a result of exhaustion? No, not if she saw it twice. *A ghost?* The concept didn't make logical sense, but Zira wasn't the most logical person. Either it was a ghost or she was completely losing it.

After a while of carefully watching the now unmoving faucet, she decided to try again. Cautiously grabbing her toothbrush out of the sink, she turned the water back on. This time, she stared at it fixedly while brushing her teeth. Nothing happened.

So far, so good. Zira breathed one last sigh of relief, and then cleaned her toothbrush under the running water. As she went to turn off the tap, her right hand lit up a deep lavender color along with the sink handle, silver and white sparkles floating around both.

Zira could feel the panic explode in her before she even fully registered what was going on. The purple glow moved the sink handle down, and the eleven-year-old froze in place.

Thoughts were running through her head like a swarm of active bees. *What was that? Why did my hand glow? This isn't a fantasy book; stuff like this doesn't happen!* One thought,

28

however, ruled dominant above all the rest. *But what if it does? What if I have powers?*

Her fear began to take over. *Wait—me? Have powers?* She tried to assess the situation logically, but all she could recognize inside of her was anxiety.

But after a moment, as if she was compelled by some outside force, she put her toothbrush down, and placed both hands around the sink handle, palms facing it.

She willed the purple light to come back to her palms, and then she felt it: the raw energy coursing through her veins as her hands and the faucet began to glow.

A line of sweat formed on her forehead as she struggled to control the energy. It almost felt like another appendage that wasn't attached to her body— and yet somehow, she could still control it.

Well, somewhat control it.

Zira forced the handle up as much as she could, and a small stream of water trickled out of the spigot. She had successfully controlled her newfound telekinesis.

She let go of her grip on the energy, panting from the exertion, and looked at her hands in amazement.

"What...am I?"

"*You're a Witch,*" a deep male voice echoed in her mind.

"Ah!" Zira screamed, taking cover.

The voice laughed. "*There's no need to be frightened, child. I am your guiding voice. All Witches and Warlocks get one if they can't have an in-person mentor.*"

Zira was still crouched down, her eyes squeezed shut and her hands on her head. "This is impossible!"

"*You just used telekinesis. How is a person talking in your head impossible?*" There was a certain playfulness in his voice which was slightly comforting.

Zira opened her eyes and sat up slowly, putting her arms down. "But...but this is just too weird! Who are you? *Where* are you? Why can't I have an in-person mentor? Where did I even get these powers?"

"*It's okay. I'm here to help,*" the voice said gently. "*My name is Lynn; I'm in a library right now; you can't have an in-person mentor because no one close to you has magic; and I don't know how you got these powers, but we'll figure that out together—I promise.*"

Zira slowly stood, swaying as she did. She leaned on the sink for support. "Lynn, I'm scared. I don't understand what's going on. Why are you in my head? Why do I need a mentor?"

"*You need a mentor to teach you the ways of Witchery. Er, that's the type of magic you have. And I'm in your head because I can't be with you physically. I'm sorry about that, but I know we can make the best with what we have. Do you have any other questions?*"

"Why do I have powers?" Zira asked. "Am I supposed to fight someone, or something? That happens in a lot of books I read."

"*Well, I can't say for certain that you must fight someone, but I also can't say that you won't. Magic is a tricky thing,*" Lynn said, seeming to be lost in thought.

They remained silent for a while. Zira allowed herself to think. Eventually, she spoke.

"Well, I guess this is something to do now that my sister is at college. And having powers could be fun! It usually is—in the books I read."

Lynn chuckled. "*You're a funny one.*"

Zira smiled. "So, what do we do first? Are there any other reasons I could have these powers besides being destined to stop some evil?"

"*There is much to learn, little one. I told you I don't know how you* got *these powers, but I do* know *why* you have these powers. They're your destiny.*"

"My destiny," Zira repeated in a whisper, goosebumps covering her skin. "Okay, so, where do we start? What do we start with? How does this magic even work?"

Lynn laughed. "*Let's start with something small: What is your name?*"

"Zira," she answered. "Z-I-R-A. But it's pronounced 'zur-uh,' not 'z-eye-ruah' or 'zeer-uh.' Got it?"

"*Got it, Zira. I am looking forward to getting to know you. Now, shall we start our first lesson?*"

She smiled.

"So, how do you think I have these powers, Lynn?" Zira asked him the following day, sitting on her bed.

"*Witchery can be genetically inherited, but there are other ways to gain the ability. For instance, if you touch a magical object and the magic finds you worthy, it can transfer itself into you and become a part of your very being. But I'm guessing you haven't touched anything out of the ordinary?*"

"Not that I can think of. Lionfield County is pretty normal." Zira looked down. "What if my parents are magical? Do you think I inherited my powers from one of them?"

"*If that were the case, I would not have been called by your magic to be your guiding voice. Your parents would be able to train you. But since they can't, I am here. Like I said, magic is a tricky thing, and it rather has a mind of its own. The important thing to remember is that you control the power; the power does not control you. It will help you and guide you on your journey, but it is not its own person. Understand?*"

Zira sat up straight and nodded. "Yes, sir."

Lynn burst out laughing. "*There's no need to call me 'sir.' We are equals. I am just your mentor, here to guide you in Witchery. Now, want to learn your first potion?*"

Zira grinned and nodded eagerly. "Yes."

"*Then it's time to get mixy.*"

"Like this?" Zira asked, putting the front of her wrists together while her arms were somewhat outstretched above her.

"*Hmmm, not quite. Leave a good amount of space between your hands and lower your arms. Also, your wrists shouldn't be connected. Put your hands more upright.*"

Zira moved her hands away from each other, adjusting the angle, and then let her arms fall a few inches.

"Is this it?"

"*Yes! You've got it. Now, activate your magic. Light yourself up and say the words I taught you.*"

Zira took a deep breath and let the energy flowing through her body light up her hands. As soon as the raw power began to take form, she began to manipulate it and cover herself in its glow.

"*Gwynocha brunori.*"

As soon as she said the words, she regretted it.

Fire engulfed her mind and she let out a small scream, collapsing to her knees. As the painful burning overcame her head, her blue irises changed to a deep lavender—the same color as her magic—and glowed.

The intense feeling faded as quickly as it came. After a few moments, the pain in her head disappeared and her eyes reverted to their normal, deep blue color.

Zira panted, gripping her chest firmly. "What was that?"

"*It was a knowledge spell,*" he answered cheerfully. "*Now you know the Witchery language, so I don't need to teach you the words anymore. It'll be second nature, just like Spanish and English already are to you.*"

Zira's mouth formed into a smile, and she stood up. "So...I know *every* spell now?"

He laughed. "*Not quite. There are still many you don't know, but you have what you need. Just trust your instincts with the words. They will come to you when you need them.*" Lynn severed their connection after that, the buzzing energy in Zira's mind vanishing.

"So long, Lynn," she whispered. "Until next time."

It had been a month since she gained powers and met Lynn. He felt like a member of the family now. He never led her astray and always seemed to say the right thing. He reminded her a bit of her older sister, Destiny, who had left for college the week before Zira got magic. Her heart ached to see her again, but at least they still talked on the phone once a week.

Now that Lynn was gone and magic practice was over for the day, Zira stood in her room, staring mindlessly at the wall. She snapped out of her daze and could already feel the happiness inside her fading. She exited her room and went down some stairs, turning on the small landing to go down some more. She entered the connecting living room and kitchen.

"*Hola*, Zira," her mom greeted from the kitchen. "Did you finish your homework?"

Zira forced a smile. "*Sí, Mamá.* What's for dinner?"

"Leek soup." Her mom gestured to the pot she was stirring with a wooden spoon.

"Great," Zira said, walking into the living room and slumping on the couch. "Is it almost done?"

Her mom turned the stove to "low" and came to sit beside her daughter. "I just finished."

Zira gave her a small, tired smile, but her face returned to its usual melancholy expression.

Her mom put an arm around her and brushed the bangs out of Zira's eyes. "*Mira,* I know it's been hard since Destiny left...and starting a new school in a new place. But you can't stay sad forever. Eventually, things will get brighter. Right?"

Zira looked up at her mom, genuinely smiling this time as her mind flashed to Lynn. "Yeah, I know. But I still miss Destiny."

"And there's nothing wrong with that—but she won't be gone forever. Just try to stay positive. You never know when something good might happen."

Zira snuggled close to her and closed her eyes. "Thanks, *Mami.*"

Her mom kissed the top of her head and gave her a quick squeeze. "You're welcome, *mija.* Now come on. Let's go have some dinner."

Her mom walked away and she followed, holding on to the love she felt in that moment, even if the sadness was just as great.

Zira walked down the school hallway, her eyes darting in different directions. Her heart pounded inside her, and she felt the all-too-familiar ball of anxiety in her stomach.

She reached her locker and opened it, putting her books inside. When she grabbed her science book and swung the locker door closed, a familiar boy's face behind it startled her.

Zira turned and tried to book it, but he grabbed onto the back of her shirt, causing her to gag.

"Hey, no running in the halls," he scolded, narrowing his eyes at her. "But who the hell cares? Definitely not us."

The two boys behind him chuckled.

"It's time for you to pay up," he said, letting Zira go with a jerk.

She turned around, her eyes trained on the floor. "But Tom..."

"No buts. Remember last week? You said you would have something for me. Hand it over."

Zira gulped and looked up at his scowling face. The two goons behind him smirked evilly. She pulled a fifty-dollar bill out of her pocket and handed it to him.

"Is... Is that all?"

Tom shoved it in his pocket. "No, you forgot your tip." He kicked Zira in the shin.

She whimpered, slowly sliding to the floor as she grabbed her left leg, tears pricking her eyes. The three bullies laughed.

"Alright, we're done—for now. See you at recess. I suggest staying away from the swings."

They walked away laughing, leaving Zira on the floor in pain.

Once they were out of sight, she let the tears fall as she hugged her legs, hiding her face from the rest of the school. Not that they cared, anyway. No one here cared about Zira. She was just their dummy—someone to take their aggressions out on.

As Zira silently cried into her knees, someone tapped her on the shoulder.

"Hey, um, you're in front of my locker."

Rage ignited inside Zira, and she shot the boy an ugly look. "Some of us have bigger problems."

"But...my books. I need them for class."

"Oh, you need your books for class? Well, I need a life that doesn't suck! Go be a waste of space somewhere else, you entitled fish."

The boy's mouth gaped open. He turned and sprinted down the hallway, not bothering to look back.

Zira stared after him. *What... What did I just do? And why did it feel kind of good?*

Two Years Later...

Zira closed her locker and shared a laugh with her best friend Ember. "I can't believe Arianna decided to wear that today! She looks like a total dork."

Ember nodded. "I know, right? What an idiot!"

They laughed again and started striding down the crowded school hallway, students parting down the middle as they passed. While walking, they saw a girl rapidly approaching. She had a braid crowning her head like a headband, and the rest of her light brown hair was in a tight, low bun. As she drew nearer, she confidently adjusted the ruffles of a pink, knee-length dress which was worn over jeans. *Jeans.* Zira and Ember were not about to let that slide.

They moved to the side of the hallway by the lockers and called her over as she passed them. "Hey, Katy!"

"Yes?" she asked as she walked over to them, a sparkle of expectancy in her eyes.

Zira put her hand on her chin. "Katy, your outfit looks so... so... How do I put this? Dumb. Why did you wear such a nice dress over jeans? That's such a stupid fashion choice."

Ember nodded her head in agreement.

"But—but my hairstyle is so cool!" Katy protested, frowning. "You complimented someone on the same style just last week. Why do you always pay attention to the bad?"

Zira shook her head with a smirk. "Because if there's anything bad, it ruins the good."

She started walking away and bumped into Katy with her hip, knocking her leftward. Ember did the same on the other side, and it moved their victim back into her original spot. Katy's eyes filled with tears, and she darted down the hall.

"Can you believe that?" Zira asked her red-headed friend with a laugh. "Who thinks they can have cool hair with dumb clothes? What a loser."

"I know, right?" Ember rolled her bluish-green eyes. "She needs to get a brain."

"Yeah, no kidding."

They both giggled. As they kept walking, they found two girls standing together outside of their next class.

"Hey, queen," the raven-haired girl greeted. "You're looking mighty fine today. How are you?"

Zira glanced at her dark-blue peek-a-boo shoulder shirt and her white-striped black skirt. "Thank you, Mal. And today has been a good day. We just busted a girl for wearing a dress over jeans."

"Can you believe girls still wear that style?" the other girl—Aurora— asked, her hazel eyes widened dramatically. "I'm so glad you put a stop to it."

Zira beamed. "Just doing my job."

They all laughed as they walked into the next classroom, where the teacher gave them a friendly wave.

"Hey, girls. Having fun?"

"Yes, Mr. Zadison," Ember answered for the group.

He nodded at them, and they took their usual seats in the back.

"So, how's your puppy, Aurora?" Zira asked.

"She's doing amazing. And she's so cute! When I come home, she always comes right to me with her tail wagging, and then we go on a long walk together. It's so fun being a dog owner—minus the cleanup when she uses the floor as a bathroom...and having to watch her a lot. But I really do love the rest of it."

"I bet it's nice," Mal added, "having someone at home with you."

"It is," Aurora answered. "I know you're lonely, M. But your parents will come around eventually."

Mal gave her a weak smile. "Thanks for the optimism, but they won't. And it's okay. I still have you guys."

They all smiled at her.

The rest of the students filed in and took their seats. The teacher closed the door, and took his place in front of his desk. "So, today, we're learning about..."

This is where most of the students blocked him out—but not Zira. She listened with full attention and answered as many questions as she could. She didn't particularly like math, but she liked getting good grades. It made her parents happy, which meant they praised her—and Zira loved the attention.

After math class, Zira had French. Only one of her friends had this class with her, so they walked there together.

"So," the black girl said hesitantly, "have you ever had a crush on someone?"

Zira stopped in her tracks. "A *crush*? *You* have a crush?"

She looked down. "Y—yes...?"

"Raven Duncan has a crush," Zira said with a wide smile, putting her hands on her face in shock. "I can't believe you, out of all of my friends, have a crush." She let out a squeal, and a few people turned their heads in her direction. She scowled at them, causing them to quickly turn away.

Raven rushed to grab Zira's wrists and shush her. "You can't let anyone know."

"Of course I won't," Zira said as she shook Raven off. "But why did you tell me?"

Raven looked down again. "I wanted your advice. Should I tell him? And if I do, how should I go about it?"

"Okay, okay, you have my full attention. But we need to get to class, so let's walk and talk."

Raven agreed, following Zira.

"So where did you meet him?" Zira asked. "Is he here?!"

"No, I met him at my church youth group. He's super sweet and always tries to stay with me the whole time. I only saw him as a friend at first, but a few weeks ago...that changed."

Zira was practically skipping. "Eee! I'm so happy for you, Raven! What's his name?"

"Mark," she answered. "I...really don't want to ruin my friendship with him, Z. But I might if I tell him how I feel. Please help me."

"Okay. I'm no love expert, but I think giving him a simple gift along with a straightforward love confession would be so romantic. Or maybe a note would be even cuter!"

Raven thought for a moment. "I could give one of those a try. Our next youth group meeting is this Friday, so I'll think about what I want to say." She paused for a second. "Or if I want to say anything at all." She buried her face in her hands.

"Raven, you're a queen. Any boy would be beyond lucky to call you his girlfriend."

Raven looked over at Zira. "You mean it?"

"Of course I mean it. And if he does reject your love confession, you can always just spread gossip and ruin his reputation."

"Oh, yeah, that's right," she said, pretending like she didn't remember.

They both snickered as they arrived at the classroom.

Zira's last class was English: one of her least favorites. She made her way down the hall with Ivy, another one of the girls from her group.

Everyone cleared a path for them as usual. The chatter between the two girls was never-ending and rapid-fire as they commented on anything and anybody they could.

"Why a hat indoors?"

"I can't believe you wore your socks *over* your leggings. Ugh!"

"Why carry so many books? We have lockers for a reason, idiot."

"Are you colorblind? Because that burgundy shirt and those teal jeans don't match at all."

"Your hair is a mess today, Jenna. Did you even brush it?"

Ivy and Zira giggled at each other's creative insults. When they turned the corner, they saw a familiar face sitting on the floor, raking through the items in her locker, a headset over her ears.

The two girls shared a look and approached the girl.

"Hey, *Salmon,* where are you headed to?" Zira asked sarcastically, using the nickname she came up with for the freckled girl, which reminded the Witch of a salmon's pattern.

The brunette looked up nervously. "S-Science, Zira."

"Oh, really? 'Cause I thought it was 'How to be Clumsy.' Are you sure you checked your schedule right? Or did you get confused because of your *problem*?"

The girl swallowed, closing her locker and standing while her eyes remained fixed on the ground. "I—I'm sure I checked it right. But, um, thank you, Zira."

Zira tilted her head to the side. "You're welcome. So, I see you haven't been taking my advice about wearing makeup. I can still see your freckles, and they still make you look like a fish." She took a step forward and lifted the girl's face up with her hand, revealing her Caribbean blue eyes. "But your hair seems shinier. Did you use the blow dryer technique I told you about, or did you just forget to shower this morning?"

Ivy and Zira laughed and high-fived each other.

"I—I, um, just... I have to go." She took a shaky step away, but Zira grabbed her shoulder.

"You don't leave until we tell you to leave," Zira said darkly, her eyes piercing into her victim's. "So, are you going to your stupid drama club today?"

"N-no," she answered, her head hanging lower.

"Oh, but I thought you wrote the musical this year. Aren't you the next Stephen Sondheim?"

Ivy cackled at this remark.

"I may have helped write the musical, but everyone still ignores me," the brunette muttered.

"As they should." Zira responded, followed by a moment of silence. "All right, I've had enough of your...existence for today. You may go." She let go of the girl's shoulder.

"Thank you," she managed to say, speedily walking away.

Zira turned to Ivy. "Don't you just love our other *friends*?"

Ivy nodded. "Oh, yes. They are most...interesting."

The two girls laughed and continued down the hallway to their English class.

44

A Cold Heart

"I'm home!" Zira announced.

"*Hola, princesa,*" her dad greeted from the breakfast bar, his eyes on his laptop. "How was school today?"

"*Hola, Papi.* Today was a good day. No surprise tests or anything." Zira walked to the fridge. "How was your day?"

"It was good. I got to enjoy some me time at the movies and then I finished the book I was reading." He glanced at the kitchen clock. "I started working about two hours ago. And I take it you have some work of your own to do as well?" He winked.

Zira froze while taking a sip of water. "Yeah, I'll get right on it—after a quick snack."

Her father laughed.

While she got baby carrots and ranch out of the fridge, her dad groaned.

She turned to face him. "What's wrong, *Papi?*"

45

"My computer glitched out. If I don't get it back on, I can't send this stuff to my boss. You know he doesn't like it when I'm late." He cringed.

Zira walked over to him and slid the computer in front of her. "Let me take a look."

Her father smiled. "You're always trying to help out, Z. It's one of the things I love most about you."

Zira blushed. She pretended to click buttons in a strategic manner, but in actuality, she was thinking of a spell that would turn it back on. She lit up her hands and the side of the laptop her dad was *not* on.

Soruziar, she said in her head while mouthing it, careful to hold back the wave of power that swept over her whenever she cast a spell.

The laptop flashed back to life, the start screen lighting up victoriously.

"*Vaya, princesa,* you're amazing! You always know just what to do." He put a hand on her shoulder.

Zira smiled sheepishly, blushing. "*Gracias, Papi.* I'm glad I could help."

A moment later, Zira got to the stairs with her bowl of ranch-covered carrots in hand. She turned around and sighed contentedly. Her dad's laptop was now fully functioning. There would be no delay, and his boss would be happy—and it was all because of her.

I love having magic.

46

Zira sat at her desk, working on history homework. As she read, she mindlessly twisted her hand in the air, which was glowing the customary deep lavender color with silver and white sparkles floating around it. The fact that this familiar magic—this comforting source of energy—was unusual only a couple years ago was difficult to believe.

She levitated a carrot, its orange color partially overpowered by the purple glow and sparkles that her magic caused. It floated effortlessly to her mouth, and she took a bite.

A knock on the door interrupted her reading.

"Come in," Zira yelled, hastily grabbing the floating carrot from the air.

"Hey, honey," her mom said as she entered the room. "I'm home early."

"Oh, hey, *Mami*! How was work today?"

"Not too bad. But I want to know how *your* day was, *mijita*." Her mom smiled. "Your brother said his was rough school wise, but good friend wise. I was curious if yours was similar."

"It was pretty good. My friends and I played two truths and a lie at lunch, and we had no surprise tests."

"Well, that sounds like fun. I'm glad it was a good day." Her mom's smile faded. "That's more than I can say for myself...."

Zira frowned. "What happened? Did a patient have a gross rash or something?"

"I'm pretty sure you don't want to know the details. Some things are best left undescribed." Her mother shivered; her face twisting into a grimace.

Zira chuckled awkwardly. "Maybe it's better you don't tell me, then."

"*Así es.* Anyway, I'll let you get back to your homework. Gotta keep those grades up, right?" She patted Zira's thigh, beaming at her. "I'm so proud of how well you're doing in school, *Mija.* Just don't overwork yourself, okay? I'll call you for dinner."

Zira watched her mom leave, then turned back to her homework with a bright smile. Her heart swelled at her mother's praise. *It's good to be me. Queen of the school, proud parents, and amazing powers. What could be better?*

She returned to studying history and eating floating carrots, filled to the brim with happiness.

The next day at school, Zira took a seat next to Ember and her friends as she put her tray down.

"You guys, you'll never believe what I saw during PE."

"Oh my gosh, what?" Ember asked, leaning her head against her hand.

"We were playing basketball outside, and Chilly was on my team. She got the ball and ran to dunk it in the net. When she jumped, she tried to do a fancy three-sixty move, but she totally miscalculated her spin and missed the basket. She fell flat on her face. It was so embarrassing!"

"What did you do about it?" asked the blonde girl with double-braided hair across from Zira.

"Oh, you know, just told her she needed to get her act together or else she was going to get it," Zira responded as she took a bite of an apple slice.

"Good for you," Ember said. "No one gets to embarrass my girl like that."

Zira smiled slyly. "Exactly."

After a moment, the blonde spoke up. "So, are any of you trying out for the upcoming musical?"

"Oh, I am!" Aurora exclaimed, raising her hand.

"Same." Ember leaned back a bit, smirking.

"I might help out with costumes or another department." Raven shrugged. "I'm not sure what yet, but I'm excited to try something new." She beamed.

"I'll probably just stick to the side and observe," Zira said. "School plays are so not my thing. Besides, I'm pretty busy with homework."

"Not surprising—but I think you'd be really good in a play, Z," Sara—the blonde with the braids—told her genuinely.

"Meh, it's just not my thing," Zira responded, not making eye contact.

Sara shrugged. "Suit yourself."

Zira walked down the hall, heading to her health class. As usual, she observed her fellow students to see if anyone was doing or wearing anything stupid—and, of course, they were.

"Hazel, why would you put your hair up?"

"Remember what I told you about acne cover-up, Johnny."

"Are you seriously doing a magic trick in the hallway? Loser."

She turned around and began walking backwards to face another student. "Eliza, I can't believe you wore baggy cargo pants with that below-the-knee dress. Does your mom—Woah!"

Since she was walking backwards, Zira didn't see the book that lay on the floor directly behind her. She stepped on it, causing the book to slide under her weight, and she fell on her behind.

"Ow!"

The people around her couldn't help but laugh.

"Stop that!" Zira shouted, her face reddening. "Whose book was that?" She stood up, brushing herself off.

A short girl with pale skin and freckles shyly stepped forward while taking her headset off. "It—it was mine, Zira."

Zira shot a glare straight at the girl's Caribbean blue eyes. "And how did it get on the floor, Salmon?"

The girl gulped. "I—I tripped, and all my books fell out of my hands."

"And why didn't you pick it up?" Zira asked through clenched teeth, holding back the buzzing energy that was trying to break loose.

"I—I didn't have time before you stepped on it and fell."

"Oh, you didn't have time? What if I hurt myself?"

"I'm sorry; I didn't mean to trip. It was an accident." Now the girl had tears welling up in her eyes.

"Well, you need to be more careful," she snapped, anger and energy coursing through her veins. The Witch was on a rampage, and she wasn't about to stop. "Watch where you're going next time. Oh, that's right; you can't, can you? You're just a blind little bat."

Tear after tear streamed down the girl's red face. "I—I'm sorry. Let me make it up to you."

"It's too late for that. You've done enough damage. Do me a favor and fly back into the cave you came from. I've had enough of your existence to last a lifetime—and then some."

Zira violently slapped the books out of the girl's hands. "Bitch," she said, walking away.

Everyone stood with mouths agape, stunned at what had occurred. This was the reason Zira ruled the school. Though she had a heart, it was often a cold one, and she was not afraid to show it.

The girl who had just been a victim of Zira's outrage was frozen in fear and humiliation. She hyperventilated as more tears poured down her face. Her eyes were filled with pleading desperation as she glanced around, but no one who had watched the scene came to help her. Now she simply stared into space, paralyzed like a goat who had just been frightened.

At last, a passing student came and snapped her out of her gaze. "Are you okay?"

She ignored the tall, tan boy, only grabbing her books off the floor and darting down the hall.

Seek The Truth

A few days later, after dinner, the Flores family was relaxing in the living room. Zira was snuggled up in a chair reading a particularly good book, her brother was drawing a comic on the coffee table, her mom was sitting on the couch looking at her laptop, and her dad was also reading.

"David," Zira's mom said, her tone flecked with concern, "would you please take Patrick to the basement? There's something I need to discuss with Zira. In private."

"Okay. Come on, Patrick. *¡Vamos!*" He put his book face-down on the coffee table, careful not to lose his page.

Patrick put his marker down and stood, following his father as he walked to the hallway. "What are they going to talk about?"

"Don't worry about it right now," he said, closing the door behind them.

Zira put her bookmark in her book and shut it. Something was very wrong; she knew it the moment her mom kicked the boys out. A pit formed in her stomach as she sat next to her.

"What is it, *Mami*?"

Her mother put her laptop to the side and looked her daughter straight in the eyes, her own blue ones misty. "One of your classmates died a few days ago."

Zira's eyes widened. "What? Who?"

A few tears streamed down her mother's face as she grabbed the laptop and handed it to Zira. "I'll let you read the email."

Zira glanced over the words, searching for the girl's name. When she found it, her heart heavied. *Salmon....*

"Oh, um, o-okay." Zira handed her mom the laptop.

"Are you okay, *mija*?" she asked as she took Zira's hand.

The teenager's head was down. "I...I think so. I didn't know her too well. But...she was in my history class. It's just...I don't know. I need some time to think about this."

Zira fled to the comfort of her canopy bed upstairs, putting the book on her nightstand as she sat.

She stared at her cream-colored carpet, countless emotions swirling inside of her. Yes, there was sadness and confusion — what one would expect after hearing someone they knew died — but there was also a familiar sharp feeling Zira couldn't name. *Anger? No.... Disappointment? No, why would I be disappointed?*

"Whatever. It's not important." She tried to shrug it off and went back to reading her book, but all she could do was stare at the page as her mind went to the girl and that horrible feeling she couldn't name. "What is it? Why do I feel this way? I didn't even know her that well!"

Zira sighed and closed her book, moving to lay on her side. "What is it about that girl?"

53

The next Monday morning, Zira went back to school. The feeling was still present in every recess of her mind and body, pounding in her head and churning in her gut. No matter how hard she tried to figure it out, it remained, haunting her like a shadow, making the buzzing of her magic grow.

Did I know her from somewhere else? Were we in the same club before? She mindlessly walked down the halls, not caring to insult anybody.

I mean, she did humiliate me, and I told her off like I should've. Maybe that's it? Maybe I just feel weird because of that. As she arrived at her locker, Zira shook her head. *Whatever. It doesn't matter. Time to rule the school, just like I always do.*

It had only been a few minutes of transferring books from her locker to her backpack when a tall, tan boy showed up behind the locker door.

Zira glanced at him. "What do you want?"

"I want you to look at me," he responded sternly.

Zira flinched at the harshness in his voice. She closed her locker and turned to face him. "What is it, Sun-Boy?"

Tears formed in his eyes. "You...you killed her."

Zira's face softened and that pit in her stomach returned with a vengeance.

"What are you talking about? Who is 'she'?"

"M-my cousin. You yelled at her a few days ago and then—" He took a harsh breath, his body starting to shake. He hugged himself. "And then she was gone that night. She killed herself because of you."

Zira's breathing quickened. "Wha... What? You mean...Salmon...committed suicide...." A fresh layer of tears unwillingly misted her eyes.

"Don't call her that!" he shouted, immediately recoiling. "Her death is your fault. She would still be here if it wasn't for you."

Zira stared; her mind fuzzy. *No....*

"No!" she said out loud. "I have no reason to believe you. You just hate me because of what I did to her. Well...she deserved it! Now, if you'll excuse me, I have a class to get to. Bye-bye, Sun-Boy!"

Zira darted off, heading down the hall toward homeroom. She pushed what the boy had said to the back of her mind. He was just being overdramatic.

But something in her gut kept nagging at her.

"It's not my fault," she whispered aloud to combat the voice that seemed to say it was. "I just did what needed to be done. I didn't do anything wrong. It's my job to keep people in their place."

She rushed into her homeroom class and sat down next to Aurora.

"Hey, Zira!" she chirped. "Did you see the— Are you okay?"

Zira bit her lip. "Yeah, I'm okay. Sundown just said something weird to me in the hallway. It's fine. I'm sure he's lying."

"Since when do you worry about what he thinks? You're the queen of the school. If he lied to you, you need to correct his mistake." She nodded her head, causing her wavy blonde hair to bounce.

Zira forced herself to stop chewing on her lip. "You're right, Aurora. I am the queen of the school, and he will pay for lying to me."

Aurora smiled. "See? That's the Zira I know." She resumed doodling in her notebook.

Zira took a few deep breaths and forced her body to be still, but as the teacher entered and started talking, she couldn't stop her leg from bouncing up and down. Sundown's words replayed violently in her mind. *"She would still be here if it wasn't for you."*

Later that night, Zira entered the dining room and took her seat at the square table, her father and brother on both sides of her.

"So, how was school today, *princesa?*" her dad asked, squirting some dressing onto his salad.

Zira stared at her food. "It was...okay."

"Why is that?" her mother asked, using tongs to put salad on her plate.

A bolt of panic shot through Zira. *Crap, I let my guard down.*

"Um...because...because *she* wasn't there. The teacher called her absent. I guess they're waiting to announce it to the school."

Her mom grimaced. "Well, let's hope she's in a better place."

"Yeah, let's hope so." There was silence for a moment before Zira added, "Let's just eat. I'm tired."

Her parents exchanged worried looks.

"Okay but let us know if you need to talk. We're always here for you, *mija*."

That would usually make Zira smile, but not today. She slowly picked up her fork and poked at her food, Sundown's words still echoing in her mind.

"She would still be here if it wasn't for you."

The Flores family fell into silence, the only noise being metal scratching against plates.

Eventually, Patrick spoke up. "I'm...sorry about what happened, Zira." He shot an attempt at light-hearted consolation as he added, "Hey, if you need me for anything, I'm only a short walk from your room."

Zira didn't reply.

"Zira, *en serio*, are you okay?" Patrick asked, putting a hand on her arm.

Zira pushed him away. "Yes, I'm fine! Okay? Why does this whole conversation have to be about me? It's not like I knew the girl. I barely spoke to her."

"*Zira, cálmate,*" her mother said, firmer than before. "Patrick's just concerned. We all are."

"Why? I'm not the one who lost her! Go worry about her cousin; he's the one who's upset! I'm perfectly fine!" Her shouts rang in the dining room as she slammed her hands on the table, able to feel the energy in her veins more clearly.

Silence filled the air. Zira looked at the shocked faces of her family and a bolt of panic shot through her.

"I...I just... I need some time to think. May I be excused? I'm not very hungry anyway."

"Go ahead," her dad said.

"*Gracias,*" Zira responded, pushing her chair out and leaving the room. When she was sure no one could see her, she darted up the stairs and into her bedroom. After shutting the door gently behind her, she dove into her bed.

"What's wrong with me? I didn't do anything to that girl. She chose her path. It's not my fault she had problems." After a moment, Zira sighed and sat up. "I can't shake this feeling, though. I need to find *proof* I had nothing to do with her death—or else I'll feel miserable for the rest of my life."

The teenager sat in silence, letting her mind wander. An idea popped into her head. "If she...committed suicide...then there would be a note, right? Maybe I can find it and read why she killed herself. That way, I'll know for sure it wasn't my fault."

Or that it was my fault.

Zira's heart rate increased at the thought. "No! No. There's no way I had anything to do with it. But because my stupid feelings won't believe me, I'm finding that note. I will prove I didn't hurt that girl. Or else...I may never find peace again."

With Power Comes Responsibility

The next morning, Zira was focused. On her walk to school, she brainstormed ways to get Salmon's suicide note, and the best plan she had was to ask Sundown how he *knew* she had contributed to his cousin's demise. She hoped with all her heart he had no proof—that he was only attacking her as a way to cope with his grief; that would be so much easier to believe. But truthfully, she was full of doubt, and it didn't help that Sundown's voice seemed permanently lodged in her brain.

"She would still be here if it wasn't for you."

Zira growled at herself as she entered Crystal Sky Middle School. *Stop feeling bad. You have no idea if you were involved in that girl's death, okay? So, until you do, drop it!*

She made her way down the wide hallways to her locker. She quickly swapped books and stormed down the hall to find Sundown. She knew *exactly* where his locker was.

Once he came into sight, unease filled her. Did she really want to know? What if she *had* hurt that girl?

No, I didn't! And I'm proving it once and for all.

She marched up to him. "Hey, Sundown."

59

"Hello, witch," he said blankly. "What do you want? More cousins to torture?"

She glared at him. "How do you know I hurt your cousin? Did she tell you that?"

Sundown took a deep breath. "It was in her...her note."

Zira's breath escaped her. *Wait—no. Don't believe him until he has proof.*

"Do you have this note?"

Sundown looked at the floor. "I...I have a picture of it on my phone."

Zira raised her eyebrows. "Can I see it?"

"Why?"

Don't tell him the truth. "I...I just need to see it. And if you don't let me see it, I will *destroy* your reputation around here, Basketball Boy. No one will ever talk to you again. Especially your own team."

He looked affected for a moment, but his face quickly hardened. "You know what—why not? It's not like you'll feel any better after reading it." He put his backpack on the floor and opened it, pulling out a black flip phone. He pressed a few buttons and handed it to Zira, the picture of the note glowing hauntingly on the screen.

Zira stared at it, her expression as nonchalant as she could make it, but her heart was secretly pounding in her chest at an alarming rate. "Can...can I read it in the bathroom?" She hated how weak she sounded.

"No, read it here. I don't trust you with my phone."

Zira took a breath in an attempt to steady her nerves and started reading.

It has come to my attention that I am not needed here. All my siblings ignore me, and I have no friends. I do nothing at drama club, and at school, I'm constantly ignored—at best.

After my parents divorced two years ago, nothing has been the same. Mom's always at work, and Dad moved to another state. I don't blame them, though. Who would want to be around such a disappointment of a child anyway?

At school today, the queen bee helped me see the answer to my problem. All I need to do is take my life and remove my horrible self from this planet. I'd be doing everyone else a favor. Honestly, I probably should've done it a long time ago. Oh, well—you live, and you learn. And trust me; I've learned.

Tears blurred Zira's vision. *I did hurt her. I didn't even use my magic this time. I'm dangerous with* and *without it. I am a monster.*

"Zira?" Sundown waved his hand in front of her face. "My phone?"

She shot her head up at him. "Oh, you want your phone? Take it! I can't believe you!" She shoved his phone at him and put her hands on her head, squeezing her eyes shut as the adrenaline and energy coursed through her. Her thoughts came in pellets like a hailstorm.

Why did you become so mean? Why did you yell at that girl? Why couldn't you just be nice to everyone instead? Why would you be such a jerk? Ugh, you're disgusting!

"Zira?" Sundown asked, pulling her from her thoughts.

"What?" she shouted, causing other students to turn their heads. "What do you want from me?! It's your fault I feel this way. Why did you have to tell me about your cousin? Everything was perfect the way it was!"

No, it wasn't, her mind combated.

"*Me?* You're the one who constantly picked on her. Maybe if you hadn't, she would still be here!"

"What? I was trying to help her, unlike you. You were her cousin, and you didn't even know what she was going through. What kind of family is that?" Energy pumped through her, fueling her every word...though her thoughts were entirely different.

You never tried to help her; you hurt her. She was going through so much, and you just added to that. Lynn was right to leave you. You don't deserve anyone. Tears streamed mercilessly down her face.

"I always tried to help her," Sundown defended, his tone frantic. "*She* rejected me! But honestly, Zira, what kind of a person finds out they caused someone's death, *asks for more details*, then blames the one who told them? You really are a *monster.*"

Her eyes widened and her mouth gaped. *"You really are a monster."*

The energy inside her increased exponentially, her face now completely red with suppressed rage. At last, the volcano of hatred and anger erupted inside of her. She yelled at the top of her lungs, balling her hands into fists, then turned toward the lockers and moved her right fist back. As her arm went forward, the energy inside her darted to her hand, and her fist faintly glowed purple.

She squeezed her eyes shut and screamed as her knuckles collided with the locker. The metal crumpled and bent, a large dent forming.

Silence reigned for a moment. It was as if she had gone to sleep for a microsecond. When Zira opened her eyes, her fist was still in the locker, and people were beginning to whisper around her. As panic took hold of her emotions, she quickly removed her hand and backed away, looking around at her fellow students. Some made eye contact, but most averted their gazes.

She looked back at the locker and her misty eyes widened in realization.

They were afraid—of *her*.

Zira grabbed her right wrist and looked down at her hand. *What...have I become?* She looked up at Sundown and the rest of the kids. Before any of them could move, however, she bolted for the girls' bathroom. Ignoring the gawking students, she made it to the handicapped stall, locking it behind her.

The Witch stumbled back and fell onto the toilet, putting her hands in her hair.

"Who even *am* I?" She whispered amidst racking sobs, shutting her eyes and letting the tears fall.

"How is your hand not broken, Zira?" the school nurse asked as she examined the teenager's right hand, amazed. "It feels perfectly intact."

"I...I don't know. I just got really mad and punched the locker. I guess pure rage protected me."

"Well, in all my years of working at the ER back in California, I've never seen 'pure rage' protect anyone," she said skeptically, walking over to the counter, her long ponytail swaying. "And how on earth did you destroy that locker?"

Zira shrugged sheepishly. "Am I getting punished?"

"Well, normally you would, but based off what the bystanders said, you and Sundown were...talking about the recent death." She sighed. "I'm going to miss her. She was such a sweet girl. I just wish I could've helped her more."

A spike of anxiety shot through the teenager. "You knew her?"

"Mhm. She came by for asthma treatment every day. Anyway, you can return to your classes. Your hand seems to be fine. But if you feel any pain at all, let me know, okay?"

Zira nodded. "Yes, ma'am." She hopped off the examination chair and grabbed her bag, slumping it onto her shoulder. "Bye."

"Zira," the nurse added, "don't take her death too hard. We'll be okay. And there will be counselors here tomorrow if you need someone to talk to."

"Thanks. But...I don't think so. Goodbye, Nurse Luz."

"Goodbye," Luz said with a small smile, but Zira could still see the sadness in her eyes.

Great. Someone else's pain I'm responsible for. She left the room and slowly walked down the hallway. *I hurt that girl, and I hurt the nurse.* Unstoppable tears filled her deep blue eyes. *I've hurt my friends. I've hurt teachers...and I've hurt everyone in this school.* Her cheeks were now drenched with tears. *How did I get here? When did I become such a jerk?* Small whimpers escaped her mouth, her body shaking slightly.

"I really am a monster."

Zira stopped walking and stood parallel with the lockers, leaning against them and sinking to the floor. She hid her face with her knees, hugging her legs.

I'm not the person I thought I was.

"Hey, Zira, how was school today?" her dad asked, sitting beside her on the couch.

Zira shrugged weakly. "Meh."

"I know today was rough, *princesa,*" he said, placing a hand on her shoulder, "but it will be okay. The three of us are here for whatever you need."

"Thanks, *Papi.* But I really need some space right now, so if you'll excuse me, I'm gonna head to my room." She hurried to the stairs.

"Of course, *mija.* Have a good night," he said, watching his daughter disappear behind the wall. He rubbed his face, exasperated.

"I know how you feel," his wife said as she sat down next to him.

"I can't believe she punched a locker and crumpled it. How does a thirteen-year-old girl even do that?"

"I don't know, David. But...Zira's clearly been under a lot of stress after her classmate's death. Maybe her adrenaline kicked in?"

"Maybe. I just wish there was something we could do for her, Estelle. I feel so helpless just waiting for her grief to pass."

Estelle squeezed her husband's hand. "There is. We can be there for her when she needs us." Her expression darkened. "But, *la verdad es que*...well, I'm worried too. She wasn't even this bad when Destiny left for college. Or after they had their fight."

"Hey, she moved on from that after a while. Maybe this will be the same." David intertwined his hand with Estelle's.

She gave him a tired smile, then relaxed into him and let his warmth overtake her, the sweet smell of his cologne filling her nose.

He snuggled into her, and a sense of peace overcame them both.

"I hope you're right, David," she said, her eyes now closed.

"I'm sure I am. Zira's a tough girl. She'll come through— eventually."

"I trust you, honey."

"You'd better. I didn't marry you for nothing," he said with a smirk.

Estelle shot up in mock surprise. "Oh, *¿así es?* That's how you want to play tonight?" She grabbed a red pillow and hit him in the face.

"Now it's on," he said dramatically, then lunged to tickle her.

The area downstairs quickly became filled with laughter, while the area upstairs was filled with a much different emotion. Zira was in her room, currently sobbing her heart and soul onto her pillow.

Every time she tried to calm herself down, Salmon's face came back to her. That wide-eyed, freckled face. That ash brown hair....and those bright blue eyes full of fear. Fear of her.

How had she been so blind? She spread fear everywhere she went in that school. No wonder the students laughed at her when she fell. They enjoyed seeing *her* make a mistake for once, because she would never hesitate at the opportunity to tease others for theirs. If she hadn't been so self-absorbed, maybe she would have noticed what she did to those people.

But she had been, and nothing could change that. That was what hurt Zira the most: All the damage she had done was irreversible. Sure, maybe they would get over it in a few years, but sometimes there was no going back. And that's exactly what happened to that girl.

The only thing Zira could think to do in her honor was mentally torment herself for the rest of her life. And...reform. She could change her ways and leave people alone for once.

The idea didn't lessen her sadness, and it didn't bring any joy or excitement. But she knew she had to do it for the sake of that girl—and for the sakes of all the people's lives she had ruined. It was the right thing to do. It had *always* been the right thing to do. It just took someone's *death* for her to see it.

"Never again," she whispered, her voice cracking. "I'm gonna do it right this time and never hurt people again."

Zira's body shuddered as she continued to sob. Thinking about this didn't make her feel any better, but she didn't care. As long as she wasn't hurting others, nothing else mattered.

Into The Light

The next morning was a particularly cloudy Wednesday. Zira went to school like she did nearly every day of the week, but this Wednesday was different. It was the first Wednesday she dressed in all black. It was the first Wednesday she wouldn't be a bully in almost two years. And it was the first Wednesday she knew that girl wouldn't be in her history class.

Before classes started, the principal morosely announced the girl's death. Some people knew and others didn't, but everyone in that room shared the same feeling: grief.

Zira tried to keep the tears at bay, but it was impossible. All she wanted to do was stand up and shout that it was her fault the girl died. Maybe everyone in the room would punish her by screaming in her face, telling her *she* was a blind little bat and that *she* should fly back into the cave she came from. Zira hoped they would. She didn't deserve any mercy. She was a snake for causing the girl and everyone else in the room all that pain.

Zira looked around at the listeners; grief and depression were written on their faces in various shades. Sundown, in particular, looked miserable. All students wore similar expressions of pity when he burst into a sobbing fit after the principal said Salmon's real name. He was so upset that two teachers had to remove him from the room.

It was her fault that he was so upset, and it was her fault that everyone was sitting in this auditorium and reacting to the distressing news.

If I just hadn't screamed at her, none of this would be happening! Zira tried to keep it in, but her heart was so heavy that she couldn't help but break out in quiet sobs, her magical energy increasing along with her sorrow.

A teacher came over and escorted her out. "Do you need to see one of our counselors?"

Zira shook her head. "No, I need her back!"

"All right, I'm going to take you to a counselor."

He ushered Zira to the principal's office, where he gestured for her to sit in a chair in the corner. She stayed there, sobbing into her hands.

My magic is the reason for all of this. If I hadn't gotten my stupid powers, I would never have become so full of myself. I wish my magic would hurt me for once! The powerful buzz of her magic along with her severe regret caused her whole body to shake. She didn't want to talk to a counselor. That couldn't happen. He would ask how she was feeling about all of this, and she would be forced to lie about what really occurred. She didn't need any more guilt on her conscience.

Although her head said to run, Zira couldn't move. All she could do was sit there and drown in her own tears.

She probably drowned in her own tears too. All because of you.

Zira's body couldn't take it anymore.

She let the buzzing energy flow to her hands and lit up the back of her head. *Inconshibodol,* she mouthed, and the purple light faded from her. In one swift movement, her vision went black, and her body fell to the floor.

"Zira?" a voice whispered. "Zira, honey, please wake up. Please."

Zira's head throbbed in pain. She felt the dim buzzing of her magic, but her eyes were sore and her whole body was limp. When she slowly opened her eyes, she could barely make anything out except for the natural light coming in through the closed curtains.

"What happened?" she asked, her words slurred and her throat scratchy.

"You passed out, *cariña*," her mother spoke gently as she helped her sit up.

"How long was I out?" Zira grimaced and rubbed her head with her hand. Then it all came back to her: the announcement. Sundown screaming. Her breaking. She looked at her surroundings and realized she was in her room, sitting on her canopy bed. "How did I get here?"

"Honey, after you passed out, the principal called us to come pick you up. They were able to wake you, but you were still very much out of it. You collapsed on your bed when you got home. That was two hours ago."

Zira's mouth gaped open. "What?"

"I know; I know. Shh. It's a lot to take in. But you need to calm down. *Todo está bien.*"

"No, it's not okay, *Mamá*! I passed out because...because I was so distressed after they announced the girl's death."

Estelle sat next to her daughter and put her arm around her in a side hug. "It's okay, *mija*. It's okay. Shhh."

"I told you, it's *not* okay. It's my fault that girl died. If I wouldn't have yelled at her, she would still be here!" Zira's body shook, and the magical buzzing got stronger.

You just revealed your biggest secret to your mom, her mind said. *I don't care! I'm done hiding from my family,* Zira yelled back in her thoughts, squeezing her eyes shut.

Her mom's mouth gaped open. "*What?* Why did you yell at her?"

Zira took a deep, shaky breath. "Because she dropped her books, and I slipped on one of them. It's the stupidest, pettiest thing I could've done; I know. But...that's who I was at school—who I am. I'm the most feared kid at Crystal Sky Middle School."

Now Estelle's eyes misted up. "Why? What did you do?"

Zira wiped the tears off her warm face. "I...made it that way. I would tell kids they looked horrible. I would make fun of people for tripping or for getting bad grades. If anyone disrespected me, I would yell at them. And that's what I did to the girl. She tripped, and all her books went flying on the floor. I

71

was distracted telling a girl her outfit looked dumb, and then I slipped and fell. Some kids laughed at me, and then I found out who dropped the book—one of my main targets. I yelled at her so much for—for no reason. Congratulations, I slipped. *Who cares?* That girl paid for it with her life. And there's nothing I can do about it anymore!"

Zira turned and sobbed into her mother's shoulder.

Estelle sat there in complete awe. She started to say something but stopped, and instead rubbed Zira's back, attempting to whisper words of comfort to her daughter. "It's okay. You…didn't know what the girl was going through. It's not entirely your fault."

"But it *is* my fault, Mom. I read her note, and she specifically said that the queen bee helped her see she shouldn't be here anymore! If it's not my fault, why would she say that?"

Zira's body trembled as she sobbed harder, and Estelle hugged her tighter, tears of her own now streaming down her face.

She held onto her mother like her life depended on it, afraid if she let go her mother would realize what a horrible person she truly was.

Zira lay on her bed, her face still red and puffy. Her mom had left the room when her brother came home. Shortly after that, her dad came home, and her parents hadn't come to see her yet. She figured they were discussing her punishment.

Well, I deserve whatever they give me. I probably deserve double that. Or triple.

A knock on her door pulled her from her thoughts.

"Come in," she said, her voice congested.

Both parents entered and sat down in front of her. She thought it best to get the difficult part out of the way first, so she folded her hands, sniffled, and asked. "So, what's my punishment?"

The parents glanced at each other in surprise.

"Why would we punish you?" her father asked.

"Because I lied to you guys for almost two years, bullied my entire middle school, and caused someone's death. That's why." Tears filled her eyes again. *How many times am I going to cry today?*

Estelle scooted closer to her and grabbed her hand. "Honey, are we disappointed you lied and picked on the kids at your school? Of course. But we aren't going to punish you. You've clearly learned your lesson and won't do something like that again."

"We came in here to ask you why you even became mean in the first place," Zira's father said, looking directly into her eyes.

I can't mention that I'm afraid of myself. They'll ask why and I'll have to beat around the bush to avoid mentioning my powers. Besides, they would be afraid of me if they knew—and I promised Lynn I'd keep it a secret.

"Because...kids were bullying me when I started going there. They wouldn't leave me alone. And then I yelled at someone because I was angry. I realized I could be the one in charge instead of the bullies, so I told them off until they left me alone.

73

But...I liked the way telling people off made me feel. So, I kept doing it to other kids, and eventually, I became the queen bee. It felt like everyone was finally getting what they deserved—including myself."

Zira sighed. "But I wasn't doing what I thought I was. I thought I was helping people, whether that meant picking on them until they stood up for themselves or telling them what to wear so they would look 'cooler.' I didn't understand it then, but I was hurting them. And it took death—a death *I* caused—for me to see it." Tears fought for another opportunity to glisten in her eyes, but this time, Zira was determined not to have another breakdown. She took her hand out of her mom's and wiped her tears away, taking a deep breath.

"Thank you for telling us the truth. We appreciate it." Estelle smiled warmly and looked into her daughter's tormented blue eyes.

"And you have to understand," her father added firmly, "what you did—bullying people—is *not* okay by any means. You... You did contribute to that girl's problems, but that does not make you responsible for her choices. Her suicide is not on your hands, but your hands aren't completely clean either."

"I understand, *Papi*. I know what I did was wrong. I'm not going to do something like that ever again. I promise."

He gave her a nod. "We all make mistakes. However, we can grow from those mistakes. You'll never be able to take back what you did, but that doesn't mean you can't do better now."

Zira smiled at her parents. She felt as if a huge weight had been lifted off her shoulders and she could finally breathe fresh air. "I'm so glad I told someone what was going on inside my head. It feels good to let that out."

"I'm glad you told us too, Zira," her mom said.

"And thanks...for always being there for me. For being amazing, understanding parents that most kids don't have. I know how lucky I am."

Estelle and David had loving smiles on their faces as they encased Zira in a hug.

A warm, fuzzy feeling filled up her chest, and she felt she could spend an eternity like this. She would always be safe as long as she was in her parents' arms.

Betrayal

Zira stayed home from school the next day. She needed time alone to come to terms with who she was and what happened. She knew she couldn't stay home forever, even if she really wanted to, but one day was all she needed to sort things out.

While sitting on her bed thinking, a subject came up that planted a new fear in her. *What are you going to do about your friends?* She didn't want to leave them—they had their good moments, of course—but she knew she would have to take some action if they continued down the path Zira was now so narrowly trying to avoid.

Let's not think about that right now. I'll deal with that on Monday.

With some effort, she pushed the thought to the back of her mind. It was only about ten seconds, though, before another uncomfortable thought replaced its predecessor.

What am I going to do about my magic?

The question made her shiver. After burning Patrick almost two years ago, and Lynn leaving her because of it, she had promised to never use more powerful Witchery again. The only things she allowed herself to do were make potions, perform telekinesis, and cast easy spells that she got on her first try. Anything else was deemed too dangerous.

The question of magic was soon trumped by another even more frightening thought. *If you killed someone without your magic, how much more damage would your untamed magic cause?* She had already destroyed a locker in her rage; what was next? Punching someone with added power? Accidentally setting the house or the school on fire? The only reason she made that promise was to protect people. If she couldn't protect people with that promise, what was the point? The least she could do to make up for the damage she caused was to learn how to truly control her magic. That would keep people safe. Not shoving it away and using her words to hurt people.

After grabbing some snacks and a water bottle, Zira returned to her room and set up her practice station.

As she stood in the middle of her bedroom, staring at the fold-up desk in front of her, she could feel the adrenaline and energy flowing through her body. This was the first time she would train without Lynn.

Tears pricked her eyes, but she blinked them back. *No*, she told herself, *I'm going to do this for him. He left me because I was dangerous, and he was right. But I can listen to him now; I can take responsibility for my powers.*

Zira took a gulp of water from a bottle and put it back on her desk, turning to face the fold-up one, her bed little ways in front of it on the raised part of the room. The usually brightly lit room was dim with unnatural light, both windows' curtains closed so no one could see what she was doing.

Zira took a deep breath, and then held out her right hand to the cup of water on the fold-up desk. She activated her magic, the energy rushing to her palm. She used it to light up the cup.

"*Conwe*," Zira whispered, her voice choked up with emotion. The water inside the plastic cup froze into a solid state, the outside of the cup forming a layer of frost.

She put her hand down and let out a breath of relief. *I did it.*

After letting the initial panic subside, she lifted her hand back up and did the same as before. "*Sceldir.*" The ice melted.

Zira smiled; she had successfully done a freezing and melting spell. They weren't that complicated—probably some of the easiest spells out there—but at least she didn't mess up. It made her happy, feeling like she was good at something for once. It gave her much-needed confidence.

Zira continued doing simple spells, building her way up to intermediate ones. She had tried some of these only once before, and that was with Lynn guiding her. Just the idea of doing them alone made her insides churn.

She pushed away the feeling and decided on a spell that could create fire and spread it around without burning anything it touched, being useful only for lighting purposes or tricking purposes.

Zira put both hands out this time. She closed her eyes and generated all the energy she could into her hands, making her palms glow brighter than usual, then made the top of the fold-up desk glow also and spoke the incantation. "*Crairto forcan.*"

Her irises changed, glowing a deep lavender like her magic.

Her vision blurred slightly, but that didn't scare her. This had happened with harder spells before. Ignoring it, she tried to focus on the desk, where she could clearly see a glowing flame about the size of a peach atop it.

She blinked her eyes a few times and continued the spell. "*Leneradu forcan.*" She moved her hands apart, controlling the energy that was coursing through and out of her hands. The fire spread slowly across the fold-up desk, and then down the metal legs. From there, it blazed onto her cream carpet. She decided to rejoin the separate flames into one and use both hands to control the singular path of fire. The flames did her bidding and moved toward her as a sense of pride swelled in her chest. *Hey, not bad.*

Her blurred vision began to increase, however, making it hard to distinguish the fire from the floor. She shook her head and tried to continue the spell, but after a second, she could feel the grip on her energy slipping, causing the flames to crackle and burn outside of her control.

Zira panicked and spoke the spell that would stop it. The flames went out, and so did she. With shaky breaths, she fell onto her knees and then her stomach, drained of energy.

When she opened her eyes a few minutes later, exhaustion and nausea cascaded over her. She stayed on the floor; certain she didn't have the strength to push herself up. All she needed to do was patiently wait for her strength to return...like Lynn had taught her.

After a while, the weight in Zira's arms felt lighter and she pushed herself up, swaying slightly. Once she was balanced, she assessed the state of the slightly burnt carpet and perfectly intact fold-up desk.

Not much damage. Zira was impressed it wasn't worse. She had rarely felt like that before. She was still ablaze with energy, but the buzzing her magic often caused felt slightly dimmed this time, and easier to keep inside. She didn't even realize how strong it was before.

"What if it had consumed me?" she whispered. The teenager looked down at the hands that would glow purple whenever she used her magic.

Purple, she pondered, letting her thoughts wander. Truly, she had no idea why her magic was purple. It was just that color when her powers showed up one morning. She'd never forget that morning....

She shook the memory away. Now was not the time for reminiscence. She got up, straightened out her skirt, and headed for her closet.

A potion should do the trick. She opened her closet and knelt, grabbing a shoebox on the floor. Opening it, she found bottles full of colorful neon glowing liquids and sparkling dust. This was one of Zira's most prized possessions: her potion collection.

She grabbed a bottle half full of orange dust. Putting down the box, she strode over to the burnt carpet and knelt beside it. She uncorked the bottle and poured some in her palm, rubbing it into the burn mark.

After a few seconds, the glittering orange potion and black scorch mark started fading, and then it disappeared completely. Zira smirked. Potions were a lot safer than spells, so she hardly restricted herself from making them—and at this moment, she was thankful she didn't.

After putting the potion away, Zira moved the desk back to where it belonged and threw away the cup in the kitchen. She looked at the clock: *1:04.* No one would be home for at least three more hours.

She looked around the connecting kitchen and living room. *Now what?* More magic practice was out of the question since she was too exhausted.

I guess I could make a practice plan. The more Zira thought about it, the smarter she realized that idea was. If she could stick to a schedule for practicing magic, she'd get her powers under control in no time.

Zira raced back to her room and found a brand-new journal, a magician's wand on the purple cover with sparkles coming out of the top of it. She sat on her bed and grabbed a pencil off her side table.

This was going to be so much fun.

Half an hour later, Zira had her magic schedule planned out for the rest of the year. She would practice every other day and whenever she was home alone. It seemed like the perfect plan, and the Witch felt very content with herself.

Once again, Zira found herself standing in the entryway wondering what to do. She eyed the TV; a movie seemed like a good idea. As she began to watch it, however, exhaustion took hold of her, and she could feel her eyelids slowly closing.

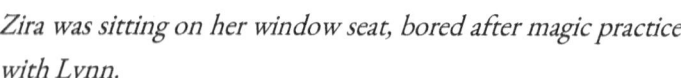

Zira was sitting on her window seat, bored after magic practice with Lynn.

She had been practicing magic for about five months now, and she was loving every moment of it. Lynn was impressed how quickly she learned, and Zira was impressed she was still alive.

The new Witch assumed that after getting her magic some evil was going to come after her and she would need to use her powers to defend herself—but nothing had happened, which meant the tween was bored.

Zira lifted her right hand and let the energy flow to her palm, causing it to glow purple.

"Monis dectantio," she spoke, causing a small reddish-yellow light to appear in the center of her palm. She let the purple fade away.

Zira sighed happily. "I love having magic. It's so cool."

She spoke the deactivation words and put her hand down, standing up and making her way to find her younger brother.

Zira hadn't been talking to him much. Without Destiny, it only made her feel lonely. Their trio was now down to a duo, and it just didn't feel the same. Plus, with her new powers and new school—not to mention bullies—Zira had become fairly reserved, keeping both things from her family.

Zira walked down the stairs and found Patrick sitting at the breakfast bar, an open binder in front of him.

"Hola, hermanito. Whatcha up to?"

She walked to him and subconsciously placed a hand on his arm. He immediately screamed in pain and brought it to his chest.

"What's wrong?!"

"You hurt me!" he yelled, tears streaming down his face.

She had hurt her little brother? But how?

Before she could say anything, her father ran out from his office and rushed to Patrick's side. "¿Qué pasó?"

"Zira burned me!" Patrick screamed, showing his father the damage. The part of his arm that she had touched was red and blistered.

Realization hit Zira; she hadn't activated her magic when she said the deactivation words for her heat spell. Lynn, help me, please.

"Zira, what did you do?" David asked sternly.

She stood there awkwardly, opening her mouth to speak but quickly closing it, uncertain of what excuse she could use. "I'm— I'm not sure."

Her father's eyebrows knitted together, a frown still lining his face. "How are you not sure? Your brother is clearly burned and he says you did it, but you're not sure what happened?"

Zira nodded her head. She really needed to come up with a good lie before he punished her. But shouldn't she be punished? She had recklessly forgotten to deactivate her magic. That deserved punishment, didn't it? She had hurt her brother. She didn't even want to imagine how much damage a more powerful spell could have done

You're a monster, *her mind whispered. And Zira believed it.*

"I'll figure this out later," David said. *"Patrick needs treatment. I'm going to run his arm under some cold water; just...go to your room for now."*

Zira did as she was told, careful not to touch anything on the way upstairs. Before she entered her room, she lit up her right hand and quietly spoke the spell deactivation words.

After watching the red glow fade from her palm, she opened the door and walked in, sitting on her bed. Tears stung her eyes, and she tried to hold them in as she opened her connection to Lynn.

Lynn? Are you there?

Sielnce.

Hello? Lynn? I really need you right now. I... forgot to light up my hands before I spoke the deactivation words for the heating hand spell you just taught me. I touched my brother and now he's hurt! What do I do, Lynn? How can I fix it? Do I deserve to be punished? Am I a bad person?

"Zira, I need— talk— you!" he exclaimed.

"Lynn! Is there anyway—"

"Shush— brother— stop— waited— never— imagined— you— couldn't— better—"

Zira froze, panic forming inside her. Lynn?

"Powerful— magic— practice—only way—leaving—get it together—"

Though Zira was only getting every other word, she knew what he was saying. Her breathing quickened. Lynn, I know you're angry, but please, I can do better. Give me—

"No— won't—" he stammered out, "Farewell— I'll— forget you."

84

"Lynn?" she whispered, her voice breaking.

Minutes later, Zira's unfocused vision went black, and the scene slipped away, her memory turning into a dream. She found herself standing in a pitch-black void.

Before she could figure out what was happening, a red version of herself with glowing white eyes appeared before her, and she froze.

"You killed her," she screamed in Zira's face.

"I—I know. I'm sorry!" Zira exclaimed. "I didn't mean to...."

"You think because you didn't mean to, that makes it all okay?" Red-Zira's size grew, and her voice got deeper. Soon she was a twenty-foot-tall giant, and Zira was practically an ant.

"No! No. Of course not! I just..." Zira didn't know what to say. No words could change the situation. Tears streamed down her face and her heart rate increased, the guilt and fear crashing down on her like a tidal wave.

"Why did you even yell at her anyway?" Red-Zira asked pointedly, unrelenting in her attacks.

"I don't know why I yelled at her, okay?! I just did. I didn't realize the effect my words could have on another person. I'm sorry!" Zira screamed the last words at the top of her lungs, her voice raspy and her hands on her head. "I feel horrible about it already. The guilt hasn't stopped eating me alive!"

"Good. You deserve all the pain in the world. She's not even the only one you've hurt, is she?"

Zira tried to answer, but her body wouldn't allow her to speak.

"Is she, Witch?" Red-Zira asked again, this time louder.

"She isn't!" Zira yelled back, sobbing with no restraint as she fell to her knees.

"You've been hurting people since the day you got your powers!" More red people appeared behind Red-Zira. She walked over to the first person in the row. "You burned our brother when you were eleven and didn't even take the blame for it." She continued down the row, gesturing to each person as she spoke about them. "You broke our best friend's heart when you never responded to her birthday invitation. You hurt our little cousins when you wouldn't play with them on Thanksgiving. You cause our parents pain whenever you lie to them. You've hurt everyone at our middle school since the day you walked through those doors."

Zira's hands were now on her face as she bawled. She sat there on her knees and let Red-Zira's words sink in, because deep down, she knew she was right. Zira had been hurting everyone since the day she got her powers. Those powers weren't her destiny; they were a curse.

The other people disappeared, and Red-Zira shrunk down to normal size, crouching to meet Zira's eyes. She grabbed her face tightly.

"And, most importantly, you caused someone's death," she spat.

Zira froze and submitted to her own self's power, her body now limp in shame and her weight only held up by Red-Zira's grip.

"You killed someone, Zira Flores. Her blood will always be on your hands, and I will always be in your head, causing every waking minute of your life to be miserable and sad. You don't *deserve a happy life, and you certainly don't deserve anyone's mercy." She violently flung Zira backwards and walked off as she faded into dust and floated away, leaving Zira sobbing on the floor.*

Zira bolted up as consciousness returned to her. Her heart was racing, and her hair was matted with sweat and tears. She looked around the room, panting.

She was momentarily relieved that burning Patrick and Lynn leaving was only a memory relived in her dreams, but the relief was quickly replaced with guilt and despair at what Purple-Zira had told her. That may have been a dream, but what that giant had said was real. Zira scrunched up into a ball, her breaths ragged and uneven.

"It's my fault she's gone," she whispered weakly, "and she's never—coming—back."

"I'm—a—monster," Zira hiccuped between breaths. "I—hurt people—wherever I go. All—because of—my stupid—powers!" She let out another sob. "I wish you were still here, Lynn. I'm sorry I made you leave."

The more she sat still, the more her demons could squeeze their taloned grip on her, filling every inch of her body with a creepy, dreadful sensation that began to drive her insane. She got to her knees and screamed at the top of her lungs, then fell over to the other side of the couch. After bawling with every last bit of energy she had, she finally calmed down enough to crawl her way to the end of the couch. Before she could hide her face, a picture on the nearby side table made her freeze. It was Destiny on her graduation day.

It brought Zira a moment of relief, but sadness and longing quickly took its place.

She reached over and grabbed the picture, sitting up as she did. Holding it close to her chest, the last sobs she had left in her came painfully. "I wish—you—were here— big— sister."

All Zira could do was think of the times she had with Destiny before she left, but those memories didn't bring any comfort. All they brought was the fiery sensation of anger.

And a gripping feeling of betrayal.

Te Quiero, Hermanito

Zira was lying on her bed when she heard the front door open and close downstairs. *Patrick.*

Dread filled her gut at the prospect of having to interact with one of her family members after the day she had. He hadn't called her name yet, though, so maybe he would leave her alone.

That idea went out the window when Zira heard a knock on her door a few minutes later.

A spark of annoyance shot through her, and she resisted the urge to yell for Patrick to go away like she usually did when he came to see her.

After a few moments, another knock sounded. "Zira?"

The temptation to tell him off was getting stronger by the second, but she resisted, knowing that's what her old self would've done.

Patrick broke the silence. "Zira, please let me in. I just want to make sure you're okay."

Zira sighed. "Come in."

She heard him open the door and close the door, then she felt the left of her mattress sink, knowing he had sat on the edge of it.

"Hey, Z. You okay?"

"Not really."

"You wanna talk about it? I know this girl's death was hard on you. Were you guys close?"

"Nope," Zira said simply. "I barely even knew her name. Now it's engraved into my mind."

"What was it?" Patrick asked.

"I don't wanna talk about it, okay?" she said, her voice raised. She turned to look at him and saw the fear in his eyes, guilt immediately flooding in. "I'm sorry, Patrick. I'm just...so, so done with all of this. Why did she have to die?"

She sat up and hugged her knees.

"I—I don't know. *Mami* and *Papi* told me you confessed to being the cause of her suicide...but they said that wasn't entirely true. They said you didn't mean to hurt her."

"I didn't. But it's still my fault," Zira said, annoyed. "I wish I could take back what I said to her."

"What did you say to her?"

Zira grimaced. "You don't want to know. But it wasn't good."

"Then why did you say it?"

"Because I slipped on her book and felt humiliated. I took it out on her. I wanted to punish her for what she did to me...." Zira looked into Patrick's eyes, surprised to see no fear this time, only concern. "So, I yelled at her and called her names. I'm the most feared kid in Crystal Sky Middle School, Patrick. And I can't change that."

Patrick remained silent for a moment. "Why can't you?"

Zira popped up straight. "What?"

"Why can't you change being the most feared kid at your school? I mean, I know it will take time for people to trust you, but you can change. You can be nice and show people who you really are." Patrick had the most innocent smile on his face, and it made Zira want to cry tears of *happiness* for once.

"Well— Well, I guess I *could* do that. I mean, I don't want to be a jerk anymore. Why not be helpful instead, right?" For the first time in years, Zira genuinely smiled. "Thanks, *hermanito.*"

She hugged him, and he returned the embrace. She could feel his muscles relax, and she let hers do the same.

"Of course," Patrick said as he retreated. "I'm your brother. What else do brothers do besides be helpful?"

Zira's eyebrows knitted together, a playful look of skepticism forming across her face. "You mean besides be annoying, and butting in on things that are none of their business?"

Patrick's mouth gaped open. "How could you say I'm annoying? I just helped you!"

Zira burst into laughter. "I'm kidding, Patrick. Of course you aren't annoying...at least, most of the time."

"Oh." Patrick looked down with an awkward smile. "And you aren't annoying most of the time either." His smile faded. "I mean, it's not like I see you much. You're usually in your room, or with your friends."

91

It dawned on Zira that he was right. She didn't spend much time with her family at all.

"I'm so sorry. I *should* spend more time with you. What can I do to make it up to you?"

"Well...since you offered, we could do something now if you're not busy."

Zira smirked. "Like a...tickle fight?" She jumped forward on the last words and tickled her little brother as much as she could. His laughter filled the room.

"Stop— Please— I can't take it!" He tried to fight back, but Zira was surprisingly strong for a thirteen-year-old girl.

"Never!"

Zira continued to tickle him until her arms got tired and she had to stop. They both panted a little, and once they had a drink of water, Patrick got an idea. He grabbed one of Zira's pillows and hit her on the head with it. Her dirty blonde hair instantly became frizzy, and the Saturn clip holding her long bangs was falling out.

After a moment of processing the injustice that Patrick had just done to her, she knew it was time to retaliate. She grabbed a pillow of her own, her expression showing fierce determination.

With his pillow, Patrick ran to the end of the room by the window seat and took a fighting stance, a long bookshelf full of books on his left. Zira followed and stood near the end of her bed, passed the drop in the floor, the other window on her left. "*Uno...*"

"*Dos...*" Patrick continued.

"*¡Tres!*" They both yelled, then ran slowly to the center of the room, beginning to hit each other with their pillows.

As the battle wore on, the laughter became consistent and contagious. Pillows flew and hand-to-hand tactics were soon put in use; and all the while, Zira felt her heart bubbling with contentment. Maybe letting Patrick into her room was a good idea after all.

Beginning With An End

The following Monday, Zira went back to school.

Her heart raced as she walked, and her breathing was shallow. Every instinct told her to run, but she pushed through. Arriving in front of the school with the raised flower beds, Zira hesitated to go in. She stared up at the big, blue letters that read, "*Crystal Sky Middle School.*"

She couldn't look at the school without thinking of all the people she had caused pain to, especially Salmon. A wave of regret hit her. *Why did I ever think making fun of people was okay?* An image of a freckled girl with brown hair and bright blue eyes flashed in her mind, causing tears to sting her eyes, but she held it back. *No. I'm not going to mope around like a sad sack anymore. I have to move forward and make up for my mistakes.*

She took a deep breath. *I'm changing my ways. And I think signing up to help with your musical is the right first step. I wish I could've seen how talented you were before this.*

Putting a hand on her chest in an attempt at quelling the pounding, she made her way to the dreaded building.

Once Zira was inside, she noticed that the halls seemed to have a new meaning. They weren't the halls she owned anymore; they were just halls. They were everyone's halls. The only one who could say they owned them was the government.

As she turned the corner to her locker, she spotted her friend group. *Oh, great.* She approached them with a serious face, but it felt as though her insides were turning to mush.

"Hi, guys."

"Zira! How are you? I love the outfit. A flowy black skirt, deep purple shirt, and royal blue sweater—it's totally cool. But of course, you already know that, or you wouldn't have worn it."

The other girls chuckled at Ember's statement, but Zira didn't.

"Ember, I don't care if my outfit is cool or not. I like it and it's my style, but that doesn't mean it's everyone's." Zira's eyes dropped to the floor. She had never realized before how difficult it was to disagree with one's best friends.

Ember's smile faded and her eyebrows knitted together. "What are you talking about, Z? Of course it's everyone's style. They just don't see it yet."

"Ember, no!" Zira's voice raised against her will. She took a deep breath, trying to calm her shaking body. "I'm sorry. It's just...it's *not* everyone's style. It's probably not even half of yours. Remember how we met? Most of you were so scared of me you decided to join me. I didn't see it at the time, but I do now. It's wrong to make fun of people—and I was wrong to make you guys believe it was okay."

95

They gaped in shock for a solid few seconds before exchanging looks.

"What are you saying, Z?" Aurora asked.

"I'm saying...we're done. At least I am. I'm done picking on people. They have a right to dress any way they want, and they have a right to *live* however they want. I'm no longer going to let myself be a part of the problem. And if you still want to take part in all that...then we can't be friends anymore."

They exchanged looks again. "Just a moment," Mal said, forming into a huddle with the rest of her friends as they murmured amongst themselves. Zira simply stood and waited.

Eventually, Ivy stepped forward. "Why are you doing this? We're all best friends. We've been through so much together."

"I know, but I can't be best friends with you guys if you're going to pick on others. I can't...keep hurting people." Zira's eyes dropped to the floor. She didn't want them to see the shame in her eyes.

"Is this because of that Sundown kid who yelled at you last week?" Ember added in an almost exasperated tone. "Oh, please, Zira. You didn't hurt his cousin; she had her own problems to deal with. You know, she probably had no friends because they didn't like her face. I mean, you were right: She needed makeup *badly*—"

"Shut up!" Zira slammed her fist into her closed locker door, once again attracting all eyes. "You will never speak of her like that again!"

Ember narrowed her eyes at her best friend. "Geez, it's not like I said anything that wasn't true. Calm down, Z—"

"Stop calling me Z," Zira burst out. "That nickname is for my family and real friends only. Never call me that again."

Ember's eyes collected a thin layer of mist. "What are you saying?"

"I'm saying...we're done, Ember. The rest of you are welcome to join me if you want, but whatever you choose, just know I'm done with being mean." She looked at her other friends, her expression unchanging.

"I don't know, Zira," Ivy said. "You were pretty mean to Ember just now. I'm not sure you know what being not-mean is." She put her arms around Ember, and they turned and rushed past their other friends down the hall.

"What about the rest of you?" Zira asked, tears forming in her eyes.

"I don't think so," Aurora said quickly.

"Yeah, no way," Mal agreed, rolling her eyes.

"Not a chance, *prima donna*," Sara barked with a scowl.

Everyone looked to Raven for the last decision.

"Raven...?" Zira stared into her deep brown eyes, and she instantly recognized what she saw in them: fear and a desperate sadness.

She's afraid of me. Zira looked at the others, perceiving the same familiar gaze of fear across all faces, not to mention the furrowed brows characteristic of anger and hurt. *I am a monster.*

Raven closed her eyes and put her head down. "I'm sorry, Zira, but I can't go with you either."

They all turned and quickly walked to catch up with Ember and Ivy. The other students around Zira stared at her, and she heard a boy whisper to his friend, "What just happened?" She wanted to tell him about her new plan for goodness, but she couldn't. He was likely still afraid of her, and on top of that, she didn't know him. She didn't know *anyone*. Other than her family, Zira was all alone.

Zira stood in front of a table with a wooden box. It had a slit in the top for slipping in papers.

The teenager took a deep breath. *Well, I wanted to do good, right? And this is how I'm going to do it.* She stepped forward and shoved a folded white sheet of paper into the box. *Helping with her musical is the best way to make up for what I did to her—at least, the best way I can think of. Although, nothing will ever truly make up for it...but this is the best way to start becoming a better person. I can use my talents for something good instead of evil.*

She sighed and wiped her tears away. She looked at the bulletin board above the table and read the musical audition information. *I like the main character.... I wish I could be like her. Instead, I'm like the villain. We already have two things in common: We're both evil and Witches. If I tried out, I'd probably get cast as her before I even did anything. They'd be able to see right through me.* Her eyes trailed to the floor. *But I'm not trying out. So, there's no reason to think about that.*

Zira pushed auditions to the back of her mind and looked back at the box. She stared at it for a moment and a smile tugged at her lips. She turned around and headed to her next class, a small bit of relief and peace overcoming her.

After school, Zira made her way home. She wondered if anyone else would sign up for props for the play. If no one else was helping, she would have to do it alone, and she wasn't sure how she felt about that. She'd never done a school activity alone. If this was going to help her atone, however, she couldn't back out of it. She had to try to make a positive difference, even if it meant discomfort.

Zira arrived at her house, the dark green shutters and tannish gray walls coming into view. She made it to the small porch, reached into the front pocket on her galaxy-themed backpack, and pulled out the front door keys. As she entered, her gaze landed on the blender and the image of a refreshing smoothie popped into her head. She licked her lips as she imagined the tantalizing flavor. She threw her bag by the door and went to the kitchen, lighting up her magic. "*Telepras Breyonio.*" Purple flashed inside the blender, and frozen berries appeared inside.

"*Telepras Lyrache,*" Zira spoke, causing another flash of purple inside the blender. White liquid appeared in a splash.

She completed the rest of the process effortlessly, her magic facilitating each step until she finally poured herself a glass and took a sip. Her features relaxed as the tangy flavor of raspberry, blueberry, and blackberry overcame her taste buds. She eyed the leftover smoothie. *I should give Patrick the rest. I owe it to him.* She poured her brother a glass and put it in the fridge, then magically cleaned up her mess, grabbed her items, and went to her room to start homework.

Sitting at her white desk, she put down her smoothie and pulled out her folder of math homework.

"I do not feel like thinking right now," the Witch said as she slumped back in her chair and stared at the ceiling, letting her foggy thoughts become clear. *I left my friends. I'm never going to find out if Mal gets a pet, or if Raven ends up with Mark, or if Ember's relationship with her brother will improve.*

Tears fell from her eyes. Zira had no idea where her life was going. She lost all her friends. *I guess that's the punishment I was waiting for.*

Zira's heart felt as though it were suppressed by leaden weights. She knew she deserved everything she was feeling. It was her fault that girl was gone. It was her fault she had destroyed school property. It was her fault her brother felt left out. And it was *her* fault all her friends were bullies in the first place. If she hadn't become the queen of the school, none of this would've happened.

"I hate myself!" she screamed into the silent house, breaking down once more into sobs.

All Zira felt inside was a massive and heavy pit of despair, not a glimmer of hope in sight.

To Be Understood

The next day, Zira went to school begrudgingly. She didn't want to see her old friends again. They were walking reminders of how alone she was—but this was her new life. She needed to learn how to live in it.

While in science class, Mal kept tossing bunched-up balls of paper at her. Zira did her best to ignore them. She assumed there were notes written inside, but she didn't dare look at them during class since she was trying to pay attention. Although Mal tossed a note any chance she got, making that persistently difficult.

After class, Zira picked up all the notes, uncrumpled them, and took them with her as she left the classroom. She walked to the nearest empty spot in the hallway and read the one on top, her heart breaking as she finished it.

Zira, I can't believe you would abandon your friends like that yesterday. You upset Ember to the point that she cried. You are SUCH A JERK.

There were now tears in her eyes. What Mal said did sting her heart, but she *knew* she did the right thing. *I'm in a better place now. I might have been too harsh on Ember, though.*

She sighed and looked at the next one. It said more harsh and accusatory things about her, but she continued reading them. She *needed* to punish herself for what she had done. Zira knew she deserved the pain.

She only made it through three before the tears were streaming down her face.

Fighting against her blurred vision, Zira folded up the notes and shoved them into her backpack which she swung over her shoulder. She wiped her face as she walked down the hallway.

Once she reached her locker, she took out the notes and her science book and threw them in. Zira reached for her history book and froze, Salmon's face flashing in her mind again without warning. Although she was angry and hurt, there was nothing that could make her forget her former history classmate. *Nothing.*

More tears formed in her eyes, and she quickly wiped them away, her body now trembling with anger. Zira grabbed the book and slammed her locker shut, storming down the hall toward the bathroom. She tried to push away the building anxiety as the image of a girl with long brown hair, a face full of freckles, and Caribbean blue eyes became lodged in her mind. Pushing away the anxiety only made it grow, however, and her vision faltered as she swayed, overcome with heat and nausea.

Zira frantically stuffed her history book into her bag, then ran as quickly as she could to the bathroom. She pushed the door open and found only one girl looking at herself in the mirror. Zira did her best to ignore her as she rushed to a stall, stumbling a little on her way there and somehow managing to lock the door.

Zira threw her bag off and kneeled over the toilet, panting. Her mind couldn't stop returning to the girl, which increased the burning feeling inside, causing more nausea and dizziness.

Her body couldn't take it anymore. Her breathing stopped as a big lump went up her throat, causing her to retch and finally vomit into the toilet.

Burning shot through her throat and she continued to pant, sweat running down her forehead as she waited to see if more vomit would come up.

"Are you okay?" a semi-raspy, feminine voice asked.

Zira's voice was barely more audible than a whisper. "Yeah, I'm— I'm fine." The burning in the teen's body spiked as she slurred her words.

"Are you sure? Do you...need the nurse?"

Zira attempted to take a deep breath, but her body wouldn't allow it; she only continued to hyperventilate. "Yeah...I'm good. No... No need to worry." It felt as if something was blocking air from entering her lungs, and this increased her panic all the more.

What is happening to me?

Her vision now became blotched and spotty. "Oh, no."

"What?" the girl asked, her voice tinged with concern.

"I think... I think I'm gonna..." She trailed off, her vision going black and her body hitting the floor with a thud.

Zira slowly opened her eyes, blinking in the bright light. She slurred, "What happened?"

"You passed out in the bathroom," answered the nurse. "Haven found you and told a student to come get me."

Luz handed Zira a glass of water which she gulped down in an instant, not realizing how thirsty she was. She handed the cup back to the tan nurse, who then walked to the sink.

Zira watched her rinse out the cup, but a figure in her peripheral vision caught her eye. She looked to her left and saw a short-haired brunette wearing a burgundy sweatshirt and jeans.

"You were the one talking to me in the bathroom, right?"

Haven nodded. "That would be correct."

"Well, thank you for helping me." Zira smiled at her, but it was quickly replaced with a grimace as she put her hand on her head.

"What's wrong?" Nurse Luz asked, rushing back to her.

"I just feel a little dizzy."

"That should go away in a bit. Now, do you know why you passed out again? This is the second time it's happened in a week, and this time you vomited."

"Um, I think I was...emotionally overwhelmed." Zira looked down at her lap.

"Well, that's nothing to be ashamed of. But if this is the second time you've passed out from being emotionally overwhelmed, you may need some counseling to help manage your emotions."

Zira's eyes widened. "Um, yeah, maybe. I'll think about that." She looked up at the nurse. "Can I go back to my classes now?"

"Are you sure you're ready? You may want to go home."

Zira shook her head. "No, thanks, Miss Luz. I think I'll be okay."

She gave her an uncertain look. "Okay. Just be sure to drink lots of water throughout the rest of the day. I'll give you a bottle now."

Zira slowly got off the bed and took the water Luz got her. She picked up her bag and went to the door, Haven following behind. "*Gracias.*"

The nurse nodded with a smile. "*De nada.*"

When both students entered the hallway, they found it empty. Zira turned around to face the short-haired girl. "Why did you stay with me?"

Haven shrugged. "Because I was worried, and you seemed like you needed someone. I'm...glad you're okay, Zira."

The Witch's eyes widened at her name. "You know my name? That means you know how mean I am!" Tears filled her dry eyes. "Why would you stay with someone like me?"

"Because...I was never sure if you were actually mean. My gut told me something else was going on. And after I heard the conversation between you and your crew yesterday, I knew you had changed for the better." Haven smiled at Zira's incredulity. "Did something happen between you and S—"

"Don't say her name," Zira said in a panicked tone. "I'm not worthy to say or hear it ever again."

"So, something did happen between you guys... Do you want to talk about it?"

Zira looked at the floor and shook her head. "No."

"That's all right. Just know I'm here for you, Zira. I'm not going anywhere." Their eyes locked, and Haven's expression became serious. "Believe that."

Zira nodded, slightly uncomfortable. "Well...I should get to class."

Her fellow student nodded and turned left toward her own class.

"Haven, wait," Zira said, causing the tawny-skinned girl to turn around. "Thank you."

Haven smiled. "You're welcome."

They held each other's gaze for a few seconds, and then parted ways without saying another word.

Zira knew she had just made a friend—a real friend. Someone who seemed to understand her for a change.

My Fault

Later that day, Zira was in her room preparing for a funeral—a funeral she caused.

The witch stared at herself in the bathroom mirror. She had changed into a black, long-sleeved knitted dress and leggings. A plain black bow held up her bangs directly above her reddened and puffy eyes. She could barely move or think without internally blaming herself and breaking down into tears.

When she came downstairs, she saw her family dressed in all black too.

"*Vamos, mija,*" Estelle said somberly, offering Zira her hand. She took it and followed her family out to the car.

As David pulled out of the driveway, her mother asked, "How are you doing, *cariña*?"

"About as well as you would expect."

The parents exchanged a glance.

"Well, just know we're here for you," her father said softly.

"I know."

When they arrived at the church, they found the parking lot packed. Zira hitched a breath. *I'm the reason they're all here.*

They all got out of the car and walked to the building, David opened the heavy wooden door for them. They made it to the area where the service was being held, and Zira saw with horror and dread that every row was filled. Some had to stand on the sides because of how crowded it was.

Zira looked around at all the attendees. She spotted Sundown in one of the front rows, his arm around his younger sister. His parents were looking down, but she could still see their tear-stained faces.

Guilt came crashing down on Zira. *I...I did that. That family is grieving because of me.* Her hands trembled in her lap, and she could barely hold back the emotion brewing up inside of her.

A bell rang, signaling the start of the service, and a woman dressed in a black suit came up to the microphone.

"Good evening, everyone. Today, we celebrate the life of..." Zira purposely made her mind blank as the woman spoke the girl's name. Whenever she heard it, the anxiety built up inside her, ready to burst. She didn't deserve to hear it.

"And we mourn her loss," the woman continued. "Now, if you would join me in singing 'Amazing Grace'..."

The piano music started, and everyone joined in. Zira wanted so badly to sing too, but she couldn't. Her heart was too heavy, and her mind was too loud. Whenever she opened her mouth and tried, a strange noise not far off from a sob came out. So, she just stood there, paralyzed like a fly caught in honey.

Once the song was over, an older woman with short white hair came up to speak. Another lady came up with her, her dirty blonde hair in a low ponytail. There was a sunken look to her eyes.

"Hello everybody," said the white-haired woman. "I'm Maureen. And...thank you for coming to my granddaughter's funeral. She would've... She would've loved seeing all these people together." Maureen stopped talking, her voice choked with emotion. She wiped her eyes and sniffled, clearing her throat. "Anyway, um, I just wanted to say a few words about her.

"My granddaughter was a light in this world. She barely made it through her birth, and when I saw her for the first time, I immediately fell in love. She loved to help me around the house, and when she was old enough, she immediately began volunteer work at a food pantry and a hospital once a week. She comforted me when things became difficult—and she was such a kind soul. She would always help her siblings and play with them when her parents were busy."

She folded her quivering hands. "Once her parents divorced, I noticed a change in her. She was less cheerful, and she stopped volunteering for things. I was worried about her. I was going to call a friend whose parents also divorced when she was young, but I never got around to it. I was too late. When I...found her that night, I...I couldn't believe it. I just... I can't believe it." She paused for a moment, her body shuddering as the other woman gently rubbed her back. "But, today, I am thankful for the life she did get to live. May she be happy with God forever."

A few more people came up to the podium, but that was all Zira needed to hear to break down in sobs. She sank to the floor, and her father knelt beside her, draping his arm around her. He helped her up and escorted her away into the hall.

He found a bench for them to sit on and whispered consolingly, "Zira, shhh, it's okay."

She pulled away from her father's embrace. "Is it? I'm the one who provoked her granddaughter to commit suicide. Doesn't that make it my fault?!"

He said nothing, only staring sadly into his daughter's eyes.

Zira broke down again and fell into his arms. He rubbed her back, trying to soothe her. After a few moments of silence, he spoke.

"Zira, you're... You're a light too. You're *my* light. You always cheer me up when I'm sad or frustrated, and you always help me when I need it. I will always love you, regardless of whatever you did to that girl."

Zira froze at her father's words. *But I don't deserve your love.* She sat up and looked at him. "But... But I—"

He pressed a finger against her lips and shushed her. "No, don't say anything bad about yourself. I will always love you, *mi princesa*, no matter what. Okay?"

Zira collapsed back into his arms, unable to shake what he just called her. *I'm not a princess,* she thought as she squeezed her eyes shut. *I'm a villain.*

A Fresh Start

It was now Monday, and the rest of the week had passed by decently enough. The longer Zira followed her magic practice schedule, the buzzing energy inside of her became almost unnoticeable. It made her feel as though she were floating on a cloud.

As the teenager strode through the halls to her first class, she saw a girl with a long blonde ponytail sitting on the floor, papers and books scattered around her. She was frantically trying to gather them, but no one stopped to help her. They only walked on her papers and pretended she wasn't there.

A similar memory of a brown-haired girl flashed in Zira's mind. *Not this time.*

She ran down the crowded hall, dodging other students until she stumbled to a stop in front of the girl. Panting, she bent down to her level.

"Hi," Zira said, grabbing one of the student's crumpled papers. "Need some help?"

The girl looked up at her and smiled.

"If you don't mind," she said with a sheepish laugh. "I'm so clumsy. Just when I think I'm in the clear, something else happens. This time I walked right into someone when I wasn't paying attention."

"No worries. Happens to the best of us." She found it strange this girl wasn't afraid of her, but a potential possibility popped into Zira's mind. "Are you new here?"

She nodded while picking up more papers. "That's right. Today's my first day."

Zira's smile grew. *Finally,* she thought, *a fresh start.* "What's your name?"

"Brianna; what's yours?"

"Zira."

"Oh my gosh, that's so pretty!" she raved. "I love it."

Zira smiled sheepishly. "Thank you. Your name is pretty too."

"Thanks, but it's not one of my favorites." Brianna laughed.

They were almost done picking up all her items when trouble walked up to them in the form of a five-foot-two girl with hazel eyes and a bun of copper hair. Ivy.

"Hey, Zira," she said mockingly. "How's it on the floor with the rest of the bugs? Like this chick." She gestured to Brianna.

Brianna just sighed and resumed picking up papers, but Zira felt her blood boil and narrowed her eyes at her former friend.

"Get lost."

Ivy rolled her eyes. "Like you told Ember to get lost?"

"Ember did that to herself," Zira said as she looked away. "Where is she anyway?"

Ivy shrugged. "I don't know. I haven't talked to her since Friday."

Zira's brows furrowed. That was rather strange for Ember.

"And you're not concerned?"

"Not really. I'm currently more concerned with this blonde-haired bug." She shifted her gaze to Brianna. "Where'd you get that dress? The dumpster?"

Brianna didn't respond but stood and started violently putting things in her locker. Zira stood also, and as she handed Brianna the rest of her items, she saw tears in her eyes. Zira silently gasped and turned to face Ivy, who was smiling smugly.

"You've got a lot of nerve, Ivy Hartman."

"Like you didn't?"

Zira's internal fire wavered slightly. Ivy was right. Zira had been on the opposite side less than two weeks ago. Was she really any better than Ivy or the rest of her old friends? *No. I'm not better than them, but I changed. I'm heading in the right direction. They aren't.*

"Listen here, Hartman. You mess with her or anyone else in this school, you mess with me. Do you really wanna cross that bridge?"

"You know what? Maybe I do. I'm sick of you bossing us all around. It's time for a change." Her hands balled into fists.

"I did change. When will you?" Zira asked, her confidence beginning to shine through.

Brianna stood behind Zira and watched the action, an expression of uncertainty written on her face. "Zira, maybe you should step back and—"

"And do what? If I don't stand up to her, who will?"

Brianna didn't respond.

"No one," Ivy filled in. And then we'll win, just like we always did." She smiled mischievously.

Zira glared at her. "You'll never win. Not as long as I'm on the other side."

Anger twisted Ivy's face. "Stop acting like you're so entitled. Your reign will end, Zira Flores. I'll make sure of it."

"Oh, please, what are you gonna do?"

Ivy's arms started shaking. In one swift motion she lifted her left one back and angled her fist straight for the Witch's face.

Zira lit up her hands. "*Canoro lentaran.*" A light purple circle went out from her and traveled through the walls, leaving everyone unaware that they were moving slower than normal.

She looked at Ivy's fist coming straight for her, her eyes widening. The spell would cease in a few seconds. *What do I do?*

Zira did the first thing that popped into her mind. She copied Ivy's movements and punched her just as time went back into motion. Ivy went flying to the floor, yelping in pain.

"Aaah!" She held the left side of her face while everyone around them stared at her in shock. "What the hell, Zira?"

Zira froze. "I— You were about to punch me; I had to defend myself.... I'm sorry."

Brianna moved closer to her and placed a comforting hand on her shoulder, but she shrugged her off. "Not now."

The Witch looked around at the kids staring at her. Confusion and anger flooded her mind, racing through it like a highway. It almost felt as though she weren't in her own body anymore.

The other students whispered to each other. Nothing was audible, but Zira had the notion that they were saying the same things as the thoughts in her head. "*You're a monster.*" "*Why did you do that?*" "*You hurt someone again.*" "*Can't you just be good for once?*" "*What's wrong with you?*" "*Get yourself under control!*"

A student and teacher came rushing down the hall. The teacher looked at Ivy on the floor, and then at Zira.

"The principal's office, now," he ordered as he pointed down the hall.

"I'll go with you," Brianna whispered to Zira, then grabbed her backpack off the floor.

Zira weakly nodded, and the two girls began walking to the principal's office.

She looked at Brianna from the corner of her eye. *Why would someone I just met want to help a monster like me?*

After Zira gave the principal her account of what happened, someone knocked at the door.

"Come in," Mr. Baker said.

Ivy walked in with a few other kids trailing behind her. "We're here to give our account of what happened," she said with intonation as if it were a question.

"Ah, yes, Ivy. Come sit in this chair next to Zira, and the rest of you can wait on the bench outside. Someone will come get you when it's your turn to talk."

They all did as they were told.

"Okay, Ivy, tell me what happened from your point of view."

"Gladly," she slurred, giving Zira a smug look. "I was minding my own business, asking Zira here a question, and then she started picking a fight with me. I tried to remain calm, but she didn't. I noticed she was about to punch me, so I tried to defend myself, but it was too late. I was already on the floor with my face swelling." Once Ivy was finished, she grimaced and caressed her right cheek.

The principal cocked his head. "That's a very different story from Zira's."

"Well, of course it is; she's lying," Ivy said, her voice raised. "Just ask the other kids. I'll go get them." She pushed her chair back to stand, but the principal stopped her.

"Hold on; I didn't tell you to do that yet," he said. "But you are right. Both of you should go wait outside. Send the other three in."

They got up and left, and Ivy sent the other three in as she sat on the bench next to Zira with a large gap between them.

"So, how does it feel knowing you're about to get detention?"

Zira looked up at Ivy. "It doesn't feel like anything, because I don't know whose story Mr. Baker is going to believe." Her gaze dropped to her lap. *I should get detention, though.*

Ivy chuckled. "Oh, you will. I know you will."

"And how do you know this?"

Ivy looked at her perfectly manicured nails. "I may have done something to get those kids to lie for me."

Zira's eyes widened. "How could you?"

"Because I want revenge on you."

"Why?"

116

"Because you hurt Ember—and she's my *real* best friend. I haven't heard from her in days because of you! I bet it's because she's too upset to face anyone." Ivy's face scrunched up in pity.

"You haven't tried going to her house?"

"I don't know where she lives."

"Oh," Zira mumbled. "I always forget I'm the only one in our group she told."

Ivy eyes widened. "You know her address?"

"I've been to her house before, Ivy. Don't forget we were best friends before we even met you. She was my very best friend." Tears pricked her eyes, but she held them in. "And now she's gone. Because of me."

"A lot of things are gone because of you," Ivy said quietly.

"What do you mean?"

"Ember falls off the face of the earth, I get a swollen cheek, and our group separates 'temporarily.'" Ivy stared straight into Zira's eyes. "All because of *you.*"

It felt like the air left Zira's lungs. "I'm... I'm sorry. I know I can't say anything to make it better, but...I'm sorry, Ivy."

Ivy rolled her eyes. "Doesn't matter if you're sorry. That won't bring back our friends." She paused, and after a careful moment of consideration, she added, "But...you know what could? If you join our group again."

Zira's jaw nearly dropped. "You can't be serious, Ivy. I'm *never* intentionally being mean again. Why can't you guys understand that it hurts others?"

"Have it your way, Flores." Ivy stood up. "Be left with knowledge that you're the one who caused our perfect group to break up. I know the guilt will eat you alive." She started walking away. "It always did...."

As Ivy passed Zira, a chill went up her spine. What did Ivy mean by that?

"Hey, the principal said we have to wait here," Zira said feebly.

"I'm just going to the bathroom," Ivy said, waving a dismissing hand. "Chillax, idiot."

Zira closed her eyes and hid her face behind her hands. She was alone again. This was becoming too regular for her. She hated being alone, but she wouldn't be surprised if she was alone for the rest of her life. It's what she deserved.

But what about Haven?

Zira's eyes opened at the thought. She did have someone. But was she a constant friend or just an acquaintance who interacted with her every now and then? And where was she anyway?

It doesn't matter, Zira reminded herself. *I do have someone. Whether I see her tomorrow or in a week, we are friends. What kind, I don't know yet. But we'll figure that out later.*

The principal's door opened, stirring Zira from her thoughts. She looked up and saw his eyes scouring the halls.

"Where's Ivy?"

"She went to the bathroom, sir," Zira answered.

"Ah, okay. She should've told me that.... Anyway, once she gets back, you two need to come in."

Zira nodded, and he went back into his office.

Once Zira saw Ivy approaching, she stood and relayed the order.

Ivy nodded and opened the door. When they both entered, the students turned their heads.

"Ah, good. You're back," the principal said. "Okay, I've made my decision. According to what these bystanders told me, it seems Zira is innocent and only punched Ivy in self-defense. You four can get back to classes. Ivy, you will stay here so I can give you your punishment."

The biggest wave of relief came over Zira. It was short-lived, however, as guilt quickly filled her gut. *I punched someone. Shouldn't I get some kind of punishment?* She reminded herself that there wasn't anything she could do about it. The principal made his decision, and she needed to get back to her classes.

Zira grabbed her bag and followed the rest of the kids out of the principal's office. Two of them went down the hallway to their right, while Brianna stayed with her.

She playfully punched Zira's arm. "We did it! You didn't get in trouble."

"Yeah, that's...that's great." Zira trailed off. "Um, I have to get to class." She turned left and walked down the hallway, but Brianna followed her.

"What's the matter? I thought you'd be happy. You didn't do anything wrong. You were just defending yourself. And you only got into that situation because...you were standing up for me. I really appreciate that."

"Mhm," Zira responded.

Brianna grabbed her wrist. "Zira, please tell me what's wrong. I know something is bothering you. I've never seen anyone disappointed they didn't get in trouble."

Zira turned around, her eyes fixed on the floor. "I...I just... I *hurt* someone. Shouldn't I be punished for that?"

"No, because it was in self-defense. Ivy was about to hurt you out of her own free will. That's unjust because there was no need for it, but you only hurt her because you had to. What other

119

options were there? You could've taken the hit, but that doesn't seem right. It would have given Ivy something to gloat about, anyway."

Zira looked at Brianna. Maybe she was right: Maybe she hadn't hurt anyone unjustly. Either way, there was still a pit of guilt in her stomach.

"I don't know.... You're probably right, but I still feel bad about it."

Brianna smiled gently at her. "Hey, that's okay. I'm sure a lot of people who hurt others in self-defense feel guilty too. That's probably normal. But don't let that guilt eat you up. Ivy's face will get better. It's not something to worry about."

Zira gave her a weak smile. "Thanks. I really needed that."

"It's the least I could do after you stood up for me earlier. No one's...ever done that for me before. So, thank you."

"It's no big deal," Zira responded, shrugging.

"But it is to me. I used to get bullied a lot at my old schools, and none of the people I called my friends ever did that for me. You're special, Zira."

Zira blushed. The way Brianna was talking made her feel like she was genuinely a good person. "Thank you, Brianna. That means a lot." *Maybe I did do the right thing.*

"You're welcome." Brianna linked her left arm with Zira's right. "So, let's go to class. What do you have next?"

Zira smiled awkwardly. Her shoulders were scrunched up and there was an uncomfortable sensation in the arm that was linked with Brianna's.

"Um, math.... Can we not...?" She looked at their arms.

Brianna followed her gaze and quickly jumped back. "Oh, I'm sorry! I'm just a very affectionate person. I forget not everyone's like that...."

"It's okay, I promise," Zira reassured her. She looked at the clock on the wall. "We should really get to our classes, though. My math class isn't too far down this hall; what do you have next?"

"Spanish class. It's the same way…I think."

Zira laughed. "It's definitely not. *Sígueme.*" She turned in the opposite direction and motioned for Brianna to follow.

Brianna stood there with a blank expression on her face. "You speak Spanish?"

Zira nodded with a smile. "*Sí,* my father is Mexican."

Brianna smiled brightly. "That is so cool! Maybe you could give me some lessons," she added as they started walking down the hall.

"*Me encantaría.*"

Brianna simply stared at Zira, a puppy-esque look of mixed ignorance and pleading in her eyes.

Zira burst out laughing. "I said, 'I'd love to.' Man, you really need to work on that!"

"Hey, I'm trying!" Brianna responded defensively, smiling. "I've been busy moving for the last couple of months."

"I'm just kidding. I know not everyone gets into the languages they learn. I'm taking French and I love it, so I continue to brush up on it, but I know it's not for everyone."

"Yeah, my older sister took Latin and really got into it, but on the other hand, my mom took it and remembers nothing."

Zira laughed. "Well, my mom learned Spanish so she could better understand my dad. He already knew English because he learned it before he came here."

They kept talking until they arrived at Brianna's Spanish class. They said goodbye and planned to meet up at lunch.

A smiling Zira walked down the hall to her own class, a new feeling emerging. It was fuzzy and blissful, like she was in the middle of an amazing dream with plenty of time left before waking up.

I think I just made a friend. She allowed herself to embrace the new feeling and smiled even wider. *A real friend.*

Zira skipped the whole way to class.

Reunited

Later at lunch, Zira and Brianna sat down at an otherwise empty table in the back of the cafeteria.

"So, what do you like to do for fun?" Brianna asked as she took a bite of her salad.

Zira thought for a moment as she dug into her own salad. "Not much. I usually just hang out with friends at restaurants, stores, or the mall, but...I kind of don't have friends anymore. I do craft every now and then, though. And I love learning about different cultures and countries."

"No sports? No going to the park?"

Zira swallowed her food before answering. "Uh, not often. I'm not really an outdoorsy person."

Brianna froze, her fork stopping just before she could get it into her open mouth. "What? Okay, we've got to fix that. There's no such thing as an 'indoorsy' person. You're coming hiking with me and my family next Saturday. No objections!"

"Whoa, whoa, whoa," Zira said, surprised at her new friend's enthusiasm and persistence. "You didn't even ask if I was free."

Brianna shrugged, putting her empty fork down. "Eh, if you did have plans, you could've just said so. But since you didn't, I bet you don't." She smirked at Zira as she grabbed a red grape off her plate.

Zira stared into space for a moment, then gave into the truth. "No, I don't. You're right."

"There's no shame in that," Brianna added kindly. "I didn't have any plans with friends on the weekend for a long time."

"You're right. I'm glad you have the guts to admit that. Most of the people I know—er, used to know—would never admit something like that." She looked at her tray of food, her spirits depleting as she remembered her old friends.

After a few moments of silence, Zira heard Brianna clear her throat.

"Hey, so, are you open to hiking with me? It'll be fun; I promise." Brianna gave her an innocent smile.

"I'll have to check with my parents about it, but I hope I can come."

Brianna bounced with vigor and squealed. "Yay! I'm so excited. We're gonna have so much fun."

Zira laughed. "I hope so." She put her fork down. "I'm gonna hit the bathroom real quick; are you coming too?"

Brianna shook her head. "Nope."

Zira got up and left the cafeteria. When she reached the bathroom door and pushed it open, there was a familiar redheaded girl standing in front of the mirror, applying lip gloss.

When the redhead turned to look at who entered, she muttered, "Oh, it's you."

"Ember, where have you been? Ivy's been worried sick about you!" Zira couldn't restrain the panic in her voice. She quickly realized she was talking to someone who was no longer a friend and regained her composure. "Never mind. It's not my business." She started to go to a stall, but Ember stopped her.

"Wait, Zira. Can—can we talk? I just... I miss you." She looked up at her former best friend with desperation in her eyes.

Zira felt her mouth become dry and moved to stand parallel with Ember, a space between them. "Sure, we can talk. What is it?"

Ember put away her lip gloss and zipped up her makeup bag. "Zira, I'm so sorry for what I said to you the other day...about that girl."

"You really hurt my feelings, Ember."

"I know. It's just...I was upset you left us, but after thinking it over...you were right."

Zira's mouth gaped open a little. "Really?"

"Really. I realized we did do horrible things to people. So, I've decided to stop too." Ember gave Zira a small smile.

The Witch stood there, frozen in shock.

"So...are we friends again?" Ember asked, smiling.

Zira shook herself out of it. "Yeah. Yeah, I guess we are." She smiled back at Ember, and the two of them stood there for a few seconds, letting the reality of what had just happened sink in.

Eventually, Zira added, "And Ember, I'm really sorry about yelling at you that day. I know I hurt your feelings too."

"Don't worry about it," she replied with a wave of her hand. "So, do you wanna eat lunch together?"

"Oh, well, I'm already sitting with someone...but you can join us, though. I don't think she'll mind."

Ember grabbed her makeup bag. "Great! I'm gonna go put this back in my locker and grab my lunch bag. I'll meet you outside the cafeteria door."

Once Zira was done using the bathroom, she made her way back to the cafeteria, finding Ember standing outside of it like she said she would be. So far, so good. The girls entered, and Zira led the way to her table, which was right in front of them.

Brianna was eating her macaroni and cheese when she looked up to find an extra person at the table. "Who's this, Zira?"

"Brianna, meet Ember, my best friend."

Her face fell as Zira spoke the last words. "But...but you told me you didn't have any friends. Did you lie to me, Zira?"

Zira's face fell. "No, no, Brianna. When we met earlier, Ember and I weren't friends. We *just* made up in the bathroom. We had a big fight the other day and just now apologized to each other. I promise I would never lie to you." *Well, at least about that.*

Brianna blinked back the mistiness in her eyes and took a breath. "I'm sorry. I've just had bad experiences with friends in the past. I overreacted."

"No, you didn't. It's totally okay."

"Thank you. It's nice to meet you, Ember. I'm Brianna."

Ember shook Brianna's outstretched hand. "It's nice to meet you, Bree-on-uh."

They retracted their hands, and Brianna shook her head. "No, no, it's 'Bree-*ann*-uh.' There's a difference."

Ember nodded. "Sorry. I know so many people who don't care how their names are pronounced. I guess I've gotten used to it."

"No worries, but I only have one name. So, there's only one way to pronounce it." Brianna grinned.

"Oh, I completely understand," Zira added. "Whenever people read my name for the first time, they assume it's pronounced the same way as 'Kira' or like 'Z-eye-ruh.' I have to correct them every time."

"Hey, that's what we get for not being able to name ourselves."

"True that!"

Zira and Brianna fist-bumped from across the table.

Ember stared at them in bewilderment. "Okay.... Well, anyway, where are you from, Brianna?" She propped her chin on her fist.

"Arizona. We moved here two weeks ago. I've never been somewhere this cold!"

"Oh, is that why you're wearing a sundress?" Ember asked with a smile.

Brianna laughed. "Yep! We did not come here prepared. So, I wore one of my longer ones. And a jacket—because jackets make everything better. Especially this one."

"I'm more partial to cardigans," Zira said, touching her sweater. "They're comfier and look better with more of my clothes."

"Oh, I like cardigans too," Ember agreed. "So soft."

Brianna pushed away her empty bowl and grabbed the apple off her tray. "Hey, by the way, are either of you trying out for the musical? Auditions are this Thursday, right?"

Ember nodded. "Yep. I'm hoping to get the lead."

"Ooh, good luck! What about you, Zira? Are you trying out?"

Zira looked up as she took a bite of a carrot stick and swallowed it quickly. "No, I signed up to do props. I'm not sure if I'm made for the stage. It's a little too...in the public eye for me. What about you, Brianna?"

"Ooo, that sounds fun! I'm trying out for a role. I'm hoping to get a side part, but God will decide for me."

Zira and Ember both nodded. Zira continued to eat her carrot sticks, and Ember got her homemade lunch out. All three girls continued eating and talking for the rest of the lunch period.

And for the first time in a while, Zira felt truly happy.

Permanent Damage

The following Wednesday, Zira went to the drama club meeting after school. That's where she'd be meeting her fellow prop makers. The next day auditions were being held, and she was very excited to see if her friends would get their parts.

Why don't you try out? the back of her mind suggested. Zira swallowed. She had never done public activities at school because that would mean everyone would have to *watch her*—and if they could watch her, what if they saw her accidentally use her powers? Mistakes like that happened occasionally, especially if her emotions were strong. In her mind, it was too risky to even attempt. She knew she couldn't do it. And now, she did have a better hold on her magic, but she needed to learn how to completely control it first. But even then, Zira still wasn't sure she wanted to be in the public eye. Just the thought of it made her squirm. It gave her the inexplicable feeling that if people were watching her, they'd know everything about her. She shivered. It was too vulnerable.

Zira pushed the thoughts away and let her mind wander somewhere else. She ended up thinking about Haven.

She still hadn't seen her since the week before. She wished she knew what happened to her, but she had no information—no phone number and no last name. Zira was stuck.

There was one other thing she could do. She *could* try a tracking spell, but on second thought, she didn't want to. That felt like an invasion of Haven's privacy, and she wasn't about to break the trust of the first person who believed in her.

Zira opened the door to the musical meeting. She was met with about thirteen other people who were standing in the center of the room, chatting. They had moved the desks to one side of the room, and had a table set up with what Zira assumed was everyone's assignments in yellow filing folders labeled with the names of different departments on them. The props folder caught her eye, and she had to restrain herself from going to look at it. Zira hadn't even realized how excited she was to work on props until that moment. It felt great to be so happy about something that was going to help people. She never wanted the feeling to fade.

Zira walked over, put her backpack on a vacant desk, then turned to see if she saw any familiar faces. Her heart dropped to her stomach when she saw someone she *never* would have expected to see there. Across the room was a tall, tan boy with curly-black hair styled in a buzzcut on the back and sides. *Sundown?*

No, no, no. Please don't be doing props, please! Zira crossed her fingers. Then a thought popped into her mind. *What if I cast a spell so I could guarantee he won't be doing props?* Zira's heart

130

rate increased. *I mean...it's not the worst idea. That way I won't have to risk feeling guilty every time we meet up. I do know a semi-easy spell for this....* Her thoughts trailed off as she looked at the floor, but she quickly felt a twist in her gut. A girl with bright blue eyes filled her mind as it often had these past several weeks. *No! No, I can't do that. That would be wrong. I've hurt him enough. So what if I feel guilty around him? I deserve it for what I've done.*

Zira was standing there, absorbed in her thoughts when a woman with graying light brown hair walked into the room and started clapping.

"Attention, attention," she exclaimed to the group of children, putting her bag on the floor. She smiled brightly at them as they stopped talking and turned to face her. "Thank you all for signing up to help with this musical. It is very special to me, and I can't wait to work with each one of you."

Almost everyone in the room was smiling. Zira could feel the joyful energy radiating from the group, and her breath was taken away. She felt like she was on cloud nine as she looked at all the happy faces. And then her eyes landed on Sundown, causing her feelings to waver. She pushed away the anxiety and focused on the lady again.

"My name is Mrs. Willow, and I am the head of the drama department. Before we go over who goes where, I want to have a moment of silence for a special friend of mine. As you know, one of your fellow students passed away recently." Zira's heart dropped to her stomach. "She helped greatly on this musical. We wouldn't have this story without her. So, let's just take a moment."

Everyone remained silent, their eyes trained on the floor. Zira did her best not to cry, but tears welled up in her eyes nonetheless. *I'm doing this for you. And I won't let anything stop me.*

After a few moments, Mrs. Willow cleared her throat. "Okay, so this year, we sadly didn't get many volunteers, but I am grateful for the ones who are here." She got her clipboard out of her bag. "Let's see…. If you signed up for costumes, go to that end of the room." She pointed to their right. "If you signed up for props, move to this side of the room." Zira moved to where Mrs. Willow was pointing; three other kids joined her. One of which was Sundown. *Great.* And then she noticed his face was wet. *I'm so sorry, Sundown.* Immense regret and despair crashed down on her, and she had to hold back tears for the second time that meeting.

After Mrs. Willow directed the other people to where they were supposed to be, she counted heads and realized someone was missing. "Well, that's odd. Someone is missing from props. Do any of you—"

Before she could finish her question, a girl with deep umber skin and medium-length black braids frantically opened the door. "Sorry I'm late!"

Oh no, Zira thought when her brain registered who had walked in.

"It's quite all right, Ms. Raven. You may join the rest of the prop makers over there." The drama director gestured to the four kids on her right. Raven turned her head to them, locking eyes with Zira. Hurt covered her face.

This is just great.

Raven walked over to them and glared at Zira as she did.

This is not going to be as fun as I thought. Zira sighed, but then she straightened herself out. *No, I'm not gonna let this ruin the first good thing I decide to do.*

Mrs. Willow brought Raven up to speed, and then handed out the yellow folders to each group. She told them everything they'd be gathering or making was on the list, and that she was going to be closely observing their progress over the next few weeks to make sure it matched what she was looking for.

Raven opened the props folder and handed out the sheets. While they were all looking at their copies, she started reading the list.

"A small wicker basket, an icy blue scepter, a snowflake ornament...et cetera, et cetera. We can read the rest later." Raven closed the folder. "Okay, I think we should introduce ourselves, and then get to our game plan. I'll go first. I'm Raven. What about you?" She turned to Sundown.

"Shouldn't we share a bit more about ourselves so we're not total strangers to each other?" a redhead asked, her brows furrowed. "And maybe say why we're here? That feels kind of important."

Raven rolled her eyes. "Fine. I like experimenting with makeup, and my favorite subject is math. I signed up for props because I decided it sounded more fun than costumes. You go next."

"I'm Hazel, and this is my best friend, Violet."

The brunette linked to her arm gave them all a shy wave.

"I love sports and science," Hazel continued. "Violet here is Catholic, loves botany and outer space. We signed up for props because it seemed fun, and we knew the girl who helped write the musical. We felt like we wanted to contribute to her legacy...if that makes sense."

They all fell silent. Zira did her best to hold in her tears.

"Zira, it's your turn," Raven told her, anger laced in her voice.

She quickly shook herself out of it. "Hi, I'm Zira, and I like learning about different cultures and crafting. I signed up for props because I have experience with crafting, but mainly for...the girl who helped write the musical. So, um, yeah."

Raven turned to Sundown. "What about you, leather jacket?"

He eyed her. "Sundown. My name is Sundown. And I'm here because the girl who helped write this musical was my cousin. Some of you may have already known that." He glared at Zira as he said this. "But I wanted to help with it for her. As for hobbies, uh...I like basketball and board games."

They fell into silence again. Everyone glanced at each other for a moment before Raven continued talking.

"Anyway, I think we should also establish a leader. Someone who can report to Mrs. Willow on progress, and someone who can direct everyone else."

"Let me guess; you had *yourself* in mind?" Sundown asked, clearly annoyed.

"Well, yes, as a matter of fact." She looked at the others. "Why don't we have a vote?"

Zira nodded. "That sounds fair, but how about we give everyone a chance to say why they deserve to be leader first, and then we can vote?"

"Sure," Raven said unenthusiastically. "I deserve to be the leader because I know how to organize, and I always speak my mind." She turned to Sundown, as if to tell him to go next.

"I should be the leader because I won't let people get away with things." He eyed Zira again. "And because I can keep people under control. I have a younger sister."

Hazel nodded in understanding. "I should be the leader because I have a positive attitude." Her eyes drifted to Zira, who was watching her talk. She hesitated. "And...I won't yell at anyone for doing something wrong." She let out a nervous laugh.

Zira smiled at Hazel's caring nature; she could definitely use more of that in her life. "Violet, your turn—"

"I don't want to be the leader," she said, her voice soft. Zira was surprised to hear an Irish accent come from the small girl. "I'll just vote."

Everyone nodded, then turned to Zira.

She froze. "Um, I don't want to be the leader either. I'm just here to help."

Sundown scoffed. "Whatever."

Zira put an arm across her body. He had every right to be suspicious of her, and that's why it stung so badly. *Why did I have to hurt people?*

"Okay, now let's vote," Raven said. "Everyone gets to vote once. I'll say someone's name, and you just raise your hand." Everyone nodded in understanding. "Who votes for me?" Raven was the only one who raised her hand. "Oh, come on, people! I would make a great leader."

"This is fair and square, Raven," Sundown said. "Now, who votes for me?" He raised his hand, but no one else raised theirs. He looked away and put his arm back down.

No one started talking, so Zira decided to speak. "Who votes for Hazel?"

Both Violet and Zira raised their hands.

"What?" Hazel exclaimed, knowing that meant she was going to be the leader.

"Looks like you won, Hazel, fair and square," Violet said to her friend proudly, giving her a knowing look. "I love you more than I fear someone else."

Hazel looked into Violet's eyes. They stared at each other for a moment, seeming to silently communicate something.

After a moment, Hazel broke eye contact and sighed. "Are you sure about this?"

"You'll make a great leader, Hazel," Violet comforted, her voice low.

"She's right; you will," Zira said to her sweetly.

Hazel eyed Zira nervously and took a deep breath, forcing her shoulders to relax.

"Wait, but Hazel didn't vote," Sundown pointed out. "I mean, I guess you just vote for yourself now, so it doesn't matter." His shoulders slumped.

"Anyways..." Raven said, rolling her eyes. "Okay, Hazel, you're the leader. You'll be generally charge of us, and the one to report to Mrs. Willow and show her our progress."

"Got it. When do we start meeting to make the props?"

"Tomorrow, I think," Zira answered.

Hazel nodded. "Okay, I'll check with Mrs. Willow on that before we leave. If we do start tomorrow, make sure everyone looks around for some of the props we don't need to make, like the wicker basket and snowflake ornament."

Everyone nodded, and then they fell into awkward silence. Luckily, it didn't last too long because Mrs. Willow came to check on them.

"How's it going over here?"

"It's going well; thank you," Hazel answered her with a smile. "We're just about finished. One question, though: When do we start making props?"

"Tomorrow, after auditions."

Hazel nodded. Mrs. Willow took that as a cue to leave, so she went to stand in front of the table where all the assignments had been.

"Attention," she shouted at the lively group of tweens and teens. They all turned to look at her. "We are just about finished here. If you have any questions or concerns, please come see me before you leave. And thank you all again for volunteering. It really touches my heart you're willing to. See you tomorrow."

Everyone resumed chatting with their friends while getting ready to leave. Zira grabbed her backpack off the desk. When she turned around, Raven was standing there, facing her. Zira flinched.

"Geez, Raven, don't sneak up on me like that."

Raven narrowed her eyes at her. "I'll do what I want; thank you."

Zira's eyebrows knitted together in confusion.

The girl smirked and let out an unsettling laugh. "You think you're so good. But in reality, you're trash. Just a piece of dirt from the ground."

Zira's mouth gaped open, and she could feel a pit of fear forming in her chest. "I'm sorry for what I said to Ember. I just—"

"Shut up! I don't care how sorry you are. You ruined my life, Zira. After you yelled at Ember, she decided she needed to take a break from the group. The rest of us decided we shouldn't go on without her, so we separated too. Next thing I know, I find out Ember joined you!"

The gentle nature Zira once recognized in her friend had disappeared. Who was she standing in front of?

"And not only that, but my crush rejected me. I did what you suggested even after you left me. Once he read my note, he came up to me and said he just wanted to be friends, and he hoped it could stay that way. But I told him, 'No way.' If he didn't like me that way, I didn't like him at all anymore. You made me lose one of my best friends!"

"Ember didn't join me.' She decided I was right about not being mean and became my friend again. And I'm sorry about Mark...but he gave you a chance to remain friends and you didn't take it." Zira sighed. "I really am sorry. I didn't mean for your confession to go like that.... I was just trying to do the right thing." She tried to be as calm as possible while fighting the flood of tears behind her eyes.

"Well, maybe you should stop trying to do the right thing. At least then you won't cause any more damage." The hatred in

Raven's eyes pierced into Zira's soul. The Witch could easily see how much Raven wanted her words to get under her skin.

After a moment of intense staring, Raven shook her head and walked away, leaving the room.

Tears pricked Zira's eyes, but she blinked them back. She hesitantly walked out of the room. *It's my fault I ruined her life. Why did I have to be mean in the first place?* She walked down the school hallway, wiping her face.

What she didn't know was that a tan boy in a leather jacket overheard their confrontation...and that was the first time he ever had sympathy for the school bully.

The Right Thing

As Zira pushed open the school door and walked out, she was met with a familiar face.

"Oh, Brianna. What are you doing here?"

"I thought maybe you'd like to come over to my house after your meeting," the blonde gushed. "I could show you my room, and we could play games to get to know each other better! It'd be so much fun." She bounced up and down, barely able to restrain her excitement.

Zira smiled softly at Brianna's enthusiasm. "Maybe. I'll have to call my mom first to make sure it's okay." She pulled out her flip phone from the front pocket of her backpack.

"I'm not in a rush," Brianna said with a shrug.

Zira searched her contacts and clicked on "*Mami.*" She held the phone up to her ear and heard it ringing until it abruptly stopped, and an elegant female's voice filled her ear.

"*Hola, mija.* What do you need?"

"*Hola, Mami.* My friend Brianna just invited me to her house for a while; is it okay if I go?"

"Hmm, are you okay with finding your way home on your own?"

"Oh, of course! I walk pretty much everywhere anyway. And this is a safe town."

"That should be okay, then. I'll let Patrick know. Just be home by five-thirty."

Zira smiled brightly. "*¡Gracias, Mami!* See you later."

"And this is my room," Brianna said as they walked through the last door in the hallway.

Once Zira was fully in, she looked around. It was well decorated for someone who just moved in. Rows of pictures were taped on the left wall near a big window, there was a white desk in the far-right corner, and her bed was in the middle of the room.

Most noticeably, though, almost *everything* was pink. The walls were light pink, the carpet was magenta, there were baby pink streamers hanging from the ceiling, and her comforter and pillow cases were also light pink with a dark pink pattern.

And I thought I liked royal blue, Zira thought.

"Wow, everything is so...pink."

Brianna giggled. "Yep! It's my favorite color."

"Well, that was pretty obvious. Even your dress is pink!" Zira said, starting to wonder why Brianna wore a blue jacket. But she brushed it off.

"Not *all* my clothes are pink; I wear other colors too." Brianna added, playfully rolling her eyes. "But most of my clothes are pink."

"So, what are we gonna do?" Zira asked.

Brianna's smile widened. "Well, first, take off your bag and make yourself at home! You aren't a nanny here to evaluate me; you're my friend."

Zira laughed. "Okay." She took off her galaxy backpack and looked to her friend, silently asking where to put it.

"Over there's fine." She pointed to her white dresser on the other side of the big window, near the door.

Zira leaned her bag against it and turned back. "Now what?"

"Now, we have fun! We can play games or do silly quizzes— or—or anything. Whatever you want!"

Zira was taken aback by Brianna's enthusiasm, a smile escaping her lips. "*¡Vaya!* Umm... Oh, do you have any teen magazines? I love looking at those—at least the clean ones."

Brianna nodded. "Not exactly a magazine, but I have a teen book I got for my thirteenth birthday. Let me grab it. But you relax. Take off your shoes and get comfy!"

Zira did as she was instructed and took off her sparkly, black-heeled boots. She cautiously got on Brianna's pink bed and sat with her back to the footboard. She turned her head and looked at all the pictures on Brianna's wall. Most were polaroids. She saw lots of blonde girls and one blond man who she assumed was Brianna's dad, and she figured the oldest-looking blonde was her mom.

Wow, she has a lot of sisters. Well, if they are her sisters. Her mind traveled to Destiny, and a familiar ache filled her gut. Destiny hardly called or sent letters. Though Zira knew it was partially her fault for nagging her so much two years ago—leading to their fight—she still grew hot from anger. But she knew she couldn't give into it. Destiny had every right to live her own life. She knew she couldn't betray her only sister with anger, even if she felt Destiny had betrayed her.

Zira was pulled from her train of thought as Brianna walked back into the room with a white book.

She shut the door behind her and joined Zira on the bed, sitting across from her. "Found it!"

Zira forced a smile. *I am not letting my problems bring down what's supposed to be a good time with my new friend. I'll deal with it later.*

"Great!" She beamed.

Brianna opened the book. "Okay, do you want to take 'How much time do you put into your appearance?' or 'Am I *actually* ready for a boyfriend?'"

Zira cocked her head in thought. "Definitely the appearance one."

The teen girls' laughter filled the pink room.

"You didn't!" Zira exclaimed.

"But I did," Brianna said, trying to force herself to stop bouncing. "She didn't talk to me for a week."

Zira shook her head in disbelief. "Man, I can't believe you did that."

"What can I say? When you have crickets on hand and your sister is just sleeping on the couch, how can you *not* put one in her shirt?"

"Oh my gosh," Zira responded with a smile. She saw Brianna's side-table clock in her peripheral vision and drew in a sharp breath. "It's past six! I should've been home half an hour ago." She scrambled off Brianna's bed and quickly pulled a sparkly boot onto her foot.

"Oh, man, I should've checked the time," Brianna said. "I'm so sorry."

"It's totally cool," Zira said as she stood. "I just need to get home now." She grabbed her backpack and threw a strap over her shoulder. "This was a lot of fun, Brianna. See you tomorrow at school!"

"Yeah, this was great. We should do it again sometime soon."

Zira nodded with a smile. "A hundred percent. Okay, bye!" She rushed out of the room and down the hall.

"Bye!"

Zira found her way out of Brianna's house, then pulled her phone from her backpack. She flipped it open and saw five missed calls from her mother. Zira cringed and quickly called her back.

Her mom picked up after one ring. "Zira, why haven't you answered your phone?"

Zira cringed at her mother's loud voice. "Sorry, *Mami*. My phone was still off from school, and Brianna and I were so caught up in our fun that I totally lost track of time."

Her mother was silent for a moment "Okay, just get home safely. We'll talk about this later, okay?"

Zira nodded even though her mom couldn't see it. "Okay. *Adiós, Mami*."

"*Adiós, mija.*" She hung up.

Zira started walking down the side of the road and quickly realized she had no idea where she was. She pulled out her phone again and went to the GPS feature, typed in her address, and started following the path it set for her.

This could go horribly wrong, and then your mother will be even madder at you. Zira shivered at the thought. But she pushed her fear down and kept moving forward.

She made it home safely twenty minutes later. Her mom was waiting for her in the kitchen. "Hi, *Mami.* Sorry about..."

"We'll talk about it later, *Mija;* I'm just glad you're home safe." Estelle put her arms around Zira. "How did the journey home go?"

The teen hugged her back and they separated. "It was kind of fun. Being in an unfamiliar neighborhood was challenging, but walking places is my thing."

Estelle smiled softly at her daughter. "Well, that's good. Come on; let's go eat dinner."

They made their way to the dining room where Patrick and David were already seated, and the table was already set.

Zira sniffed the air. "Tamales." Her face lit up, and she sat down to dig in.

After helping clean up from dinner, Zira went to her room. A few minutes after starting her homework, someone knocked on the door. She knew who it was and did not want to let her in, but she knew she had to.

"Come in, *Mamá.*"

Her mom entered and sat on her daughter's bed. "*Ven aquí.*" She patted a spot on the bed.

Zira sighed and shamefully went to join her near the pillows. "Yes?"

"What happened earlier—not answering my calls while you were at Brianna's house—*cannot* happen again. I was worried, Zira. And I didn't even know where you were." Concern shone in Estelle's eyes.

"I'm sorry, *Mami.* I just forgot to turn my ringer back on. It was an accident."

"I know, and I understand that. But what if I had something important to tell you? What if Patrick had called you with an emergency? This isn't the first time it's happened either. You can't keep forgetting these things. It's not right."

"I know, *Mamá.* I'm trying." Zira looked down. Her mother's word choice made her think of what Raven said earlier. "*Maybe you should stop trying to do the right thing.*" Raven was wrong; she knew that. But was her mom right? Was Zira letting some of her responsibilities as a good person fade away?

"Sometimes it doesn't feel like you are trying, Zira. You really need to start doing your very best from now on...before something bad happens." Estelle reached forward and grabbed her daughter's hands.

A picture of a girl with bright blue eyes and pale skin appeared in Zira's mind. Tears welled up in her eyes, and it felt as though every emotion she was holding back burst through the now-open floodgates. "Well, it's not like I want any more bad things to happen! I *am* trying my best, Mom; can't you just accept that?" Zira yanked her hands from her mother's and turned to cry into a pillow.

Estelle gasped and put a hand on her daughter's back. "Zira, what's wrong? You never call me 'Mom' unless something's bothering you."

Zira looked at her mother. "I—I saw Raven at school today. She's on the props team. And after what happened with our old friends last week, she didn't have very nice things to say to me." More tears welled up in her eyes. "Why did I have to be mean in the first place, *Mami*? It caused nothing but pain!" She collapsed onto her mother, crying into her chest.

Estelle hugged her and rested her chin on Zira's head. "I don't know, *mija*. I don't know. Why do we do anything really? But you said you started bullying because you had been bullied and sort of learned how to speak up for yourself through that. Is that true?"

Zira nodded weakly.

"Well, you learned your lesson and stopped. Isn't that what matters? It's not good to dwell on the past. It just causes more pain. Trust me."

Zira put her chin on her mom's shoulder. "But things could've been so different if I hadn't become mean."

"That's true, but you were. You did what you did, and there's no changing that—but that won't stop you from doing better in the future. And who you are *now* matters, not who you were. It's best to just let the past go."

"That may take a while."

"There's no time limit," Estelle responded gently. "And I'll be with you every step of the way."

Zira took a deep breath and exhaled. Muscles that she didn't even know were tense relaxed.

Her mother always knew just what to say.

When Will I Learn?

The next day, Zira walked to school with a spring in her step. Magic practice had gone perfectly the night before. Zira managed to put a protective shield around her fold-up desk and was not able to break through it. After that, she snuck downstairs and made orange juice popsicles, freezing them with her magic. After all, a Witch must keep up her strength.

A few moments later, the large school building came into view, along with a red-headed and blonde girl at the doorway.

"Hey, guys!" Zira chirped.

"Hey, Zira," Brianna said with a smile. "You're in an awfully good mood."

"Well, I'm just excited to see my two friends kill it at auditions today. I bet you'll both get a part."

"I hope so," Brianna said nervously, biting her bottom lip. "I've never done anything like this before."

"Oh, please, Brianna—you'll be amazing," Ember said. "You're too fabulous to not believe in yourself. You need to have confidence, girl. Don't be afraid to shout, 'I am awesome!'"

Brianna laughed. "Thanks, Ember."

The three girls went into the building and walked down the hall.

"Do you mind if we go to my locker first?" Ember asked.

"No, that's fine," Brianna responded.

"Let's do it," Zira said.

Ember took the lead. "So, how did the meeting go yesterday, Zira?"

She cringed. "Pretty okay. Raven's doing props too, though, so that's just great."

"Oh, man, that can't be good. Raven always seemed...off to me. Did she blow up in your face?"

"Kind of...." Zira's eyes trailed to Brianna. Her friend's eyebrows were knitted together, and her face was scrunched up with confusion. Realization hit Zira: Brianna didn't know about her past...and she wanted to keep it that way. "But that's the past. Let's focus on the present."

"Who's Raven?" Brianna asked.

Ember scratched her head. "She's—"

"Just an ex-friend of ours," Zira cut her off.

"Oh, okay," Brianna responded, falling into silence.

They quickly arrived at Ember's locker, and she kneeled to open it.

While Ember swapped her books, Zira observed the tweens and teens around her. There were some chatting, others digging through their lockers, and others walking in groups or alone.

Zira smiled at them as they went about their daily routine. She felt a refreshing peace wash over her. Knowing she wasn't going to be contributing to their pain made her heart lighter and her happiness rise.

As she was soaking in the moment, two familiar faces appeared down the hallway and shattered her serenity. *Oh, no.*

"Guys, we have trouble coming our way."

Ember and Brianna looked up. Aurora and Sara were walking toward them with sly looks on their faces.

Ember stood, groaning. "Don't they have anything better to do?"

Before Zira could respond, Sara spoke. "Hey, what are you three doing?"

"Talking; why do you want to know?" Zira asked defensively.

"Because we just wanted to let you know," Aurora started, stepping toward her, "these 'friends' of yours will never stick around."

"Oh, really?" Ember said, taking a step toward the golden-haired girl. "Well, maybe you two are just stupid idiots who only feel threatened by Zira, and that's why you're taunting her."

Their old friends' smiles faded, and they looked at each other.

"Well, it doesn't matter what you think," Aurora riposted. "Zira likes ruining her relationships. She's done it to everyone she knows. Her best friend before she moved here, her brother, her friends—that's *us*, by the way—and eventually, it'll happen to you two."

Zira's face fell as Aurora listed her broken relationships. *She's right. I ruin every relationship I'm in.*

"You two need to get a life." Ember got between the Witch and the two bullies. "Zira didn't mean to ruin any of those things. And even if she did, I bet she regrets it now."

"Yeah," Brianna chimed in, crossing her arms with a nod. "I may not know what you're talking about, but I know enough about Zira to know she'd never intentionally hurt me. So, maybe you two should get lost."

Sara rolled her eyes. "Whatever, losers. We'll see you at auditions."

"You'll never get big roles, by the way," Aurora said. "Not with me and Sara trying out." She flung her hair as they turned away.

The three friends could hear them laughing and calling them nasty things as they walked down the hall.

Brianna rolled her eyes and turned her attention to a frozen Zira. "You okay?"

Zira blinked. "Yeah...I'm okay. Thanks for standing up for me, you guys."

"No problem," Ember said with a smile.

"But are you sure you're okay?" Brianna asked again, putting a hand on Zira's arm.

Zira moved away from her touch. "Yeah, I'm good."

"Just know what they said is crap, Zira," Ember added. "You never meant to hurt anyone."

Zira smiled. "Yeah...and you know what? I came here to have a good day, and I'm not gonna let them stop me."

"There ya go!" Brianna cheered.

After Ember closed her locker, they resumed walking down the hall.

"What were they talking about anyway?" Brianna asked, turning her head to Zira.

Ember was about to speak, but Zira answered first. "I don't want to talk about it."

Brianna nodded. "I get it. The past is hard to face."

Zira smiled gently at her, affection swelling in her chest. *Thank you for not pressing, Brianna. None of my old friends would have ever accepted that answer.*

The school day passed rather quickly, and there was still no sign of Haven. *Where did you go?* Zira kept mentally asking, wishing she were able to communicate telepathically. She missed her. When they first met, Zira was sure they were meant to be friends, but now she was beginning to doubt it.

Zira sighed and made her way to the theater to watch auditions. She knew Brianna and Ember were going to be amazing and she wanted to see them in action. She also couldn't wait to see who else was trying out.

She took a seat in the back to avoid being seen by the few people at the front, and just patiently waited for them to start.

About five minutes later, Mrs. Willow called the first person on stage. "Ember, please read the script, and then sing the song you were given."

Ember nodded and started.

"Why are you all so afraid? It's just the woods," she said mockingly, leaning to the side with a hand on her hip.

Zira's face scrunched up in uncertainty. The audition paper Zira saw had a description of the lead role: She was supposed to be a kind-hearted, fearless girl, not sarcastic and rude.

Ember finished acting, and Mrs. Willow told the pianist to start playing. Ember sucked in some air and waited for her cue.

"Ooohh, why is everyone afraid? Why doesn't anyone want to change? They say this forest is dangerous, but they've never even been here themselves...."

Zira cringed. Ember wasn't *that* bad, she tried to reason with herself...but she was loud and off-key, and her voice was a bit airy. Zira doubted Ember would get the lead role—or any major part, for that matter.

Ember finished and took a bow. She left the stage, and Mrs. Willow called on the next person.

Four people later, Brianna walked on stage.

"Woo!" Zira shouted. Everyone looked at her, and she shrank in her seat. "Sorry."

Their attention turned back to Brianna, who acted out the same scene as Ember. "Why are you all so afraid? It's just the woods." She rolled her eyes. "I'll be fine. I go into different woods all the time, and nothing ever happens."

Zira smiled at Brianna's performance. She didn't seem nervous, but she also wasn't overly confident. Maybe the characterization was a bit off, but it wasn't bad.

154

She finished the acting portion of the audition, and Mrs. Willow cued the pianist.

Brianna took a deep breath. "Ooohh, why is everyone afraid? Why doesn't anyone want to change? They say this forest is dangerous, but they've never even been here themselves...."

Zira closed her eyes and let herself feel the music. Brianna's voice was so soothing, and she could feel the tension inside her melt away. Her pitch was a bit high for the song, but it was nonetheless one of the best auditions she'd heard so far.

Brianna finished, took a bow, and exited the stage.

Zira sat through the next audition, her attention fully fixed on the actor until a boy in a leather jacket plopped into the seat next to her.

"Hey."

"Hey...." *What is Sundown doing? Doesn't he hate me?*

"So, are you excited for props? Raven's one of your friends, right?"

"Well, she was, but not anymore. I'm trying to become a better person. And none of my friends want to—except Ember." She eyed him, adrenaline building in her chest. "Why are you...um, here?"

"Since I'm doing props, I wanted to see who could possibly be in the musical to get some potential inspiration." He looked over at her.

She gave him a questioning look. "That's not what I—"

"Gotta go," he said abruptly and got up, speedily walking out of the theater.

Zira stared at the closing door for a few moments before looking back at the boy auditioning on stage, but her mind was elsewhere. *What was that about? Is he trying to get back at me for hurting his cousin? What if he's following me?*

Zira's heart pounded at the thought. She forced herself to take a breath and let it out. *No. I will not overreact. And if he is following me, I have powers. I can just secretly use them to get out of the situation.*

She left it at that and focused on auditions again, but the thought of constantly seeing Sundown for props meetings did not excite her.

Zira entered the classroom and found that everyone had already arrived for the props meeting. She put her backpack on an empty desk and sat down on the floor with the rest of them, making sure to stay as far away from Sundown as possible.

"Hello, everyone," Hazel said cheerfully. "Okay, so, what props did you find at home?"

Everyone placed their props in the middle of the circle, and Hazel pulled them to herself. She picked one up and exclaimed, "This is a perfect wicker basket! Who brought it?"

"I did," Zira said, shyly raising a hand.

Hazel looked up at her. "Nice work." She put the basket down and picked up a wooden spoon.

Once she was done looking at all the items they brought, she said, "Okay, good work today, everybody. Since we just crossed out nine items on the list, and it's still early in musical production, we don't really need to do anything else today. I'll let Mrs. Willow know what we have so far. See you tomorrow!" She stood up, followed by everyone else.

Zira grabbed her bag and left the room, finding Brianna and Ember waiting in the hallway for her.

"Hey, guys."

"Hey," Brianna said. "How was the meeting today?"

"Great. We have nine props already, so that's less work for us. How were your auditions?" Zira asked. "I mean, I was watching, but how did they feel?"

Ember stuck her head up with a proud smile. "I think I did pretty well. How do you think you did, Brianna?"

"I was so nervous. I'm not sure I'll get any parts." She averted her eyes.

"Brianna, you did amazing! I bet you'll get at least a side part, if not the lead." Zira's encouragement had a hint of desperation in its tone. She wanted more than anything for her friend to believe in herself.

"Thanks, Zira," Brianna said with a shy smile, her shoulders relaxing.

"How do you think I did, Zira?" Ember asked.

Zira grimaced. She did *not* want to tell her best friend what she truly thought about her audition, but she couldn't lie. That would be wrong.

"I thought you did...okay, Ember."

Ember's smile faded into a frown. "What do you mean 'okay'?"

"Just...you were a bit arrogant in your delivery. The lead role is supposed to be gentle and fearless, not mocking and rude. I think you used the wrong body language, and your voice sounded...a little airy when you sang. But you did your best, and that's what matters."

Ember's frown turned into a scowl. "What do you know about this stuff anyway? You're just a crafter."

"Ember! That's not nice," Brianna scolded.

Ember rolled her eyes. "Wasn't Zira mean to me just now?"

"I wasn't trying to be. You asked what I thought; that's what I thought. Also, I do know a lot about theater. My mom used to be in musicals and plays, and she taught me everything she knows."

Ember's face fell. "Oh yeah, I forgot. Well, you could've been at least a little sensitive. That was rude."

"I'm sorry," Zira said. *Ugh. When will I learn?*

"Whatever. Anyway, I'll see you guys tomorrow. I have to get home." Ember left them, walking down the hall.

"Bye." Zira waved to her friend.

Brianna turned to Zira. "What was that about?"

"Ember just...doesn't take criticism well. It's all right. She'll be over it by tomorrow."

"You know her better than I do," Brianna said, shrugging.

"Come on; let's go home. And you do know you don't have to wait for me after every props meeting, right?"

"I know, but I like to. It gives us more time to chat." Brianna gave Zira a friendly smile.

"It won't matter for long anyway—not once you start rehearsals."

Brianna sighed. "If I get the part."

"Stop that," Zira said firmly. "No self-doubt. You need to have confidence in yourself." She paused, then added in an afterthought, "But not so much that you start getting cocky."

"I don't think I have *any* confidence."

"You do. I saw it when you were on stage. You were in your element, dude. Just keep doing what you love." Zira nudged Brianna.

Her friend blushed, tucking a loose piece of hair behind her ear. "Thanks, Zira. That was...a really nice thing to say."

"You're welcome."

They pulled the school doors open and walked out to the already semi-dark world. "Well, this is where we split ways. Bye, Zira. And thanks for the pep talk; I really needed that."

Zira and Brianna smiled at each other for a few moments before Brianna said, "See you tomorrow," and began to walk away.

"See you tomorrow," Zira echoed.

A short time later, she entered her house and found Patrick chilling on the couch, watching TV. She took off her backpack and shoes and put them next to the door.

"Hey, *hermanito.*"

He looked at her. "Hey."

"Whatcha watching?" she asked, sitting down next to him.

"Something boring. There's nothing on." He laid back in defeat with a dramatic sigh.

Zira smiled, and then an idea entered her mind. "Wanna watch a movie?"

He popped up. "Really? You'd want to watch a movie with me?"

"Why not? I can do homework later. I have a light load today."

Patrick stood up with a bright smile on his face. He went right for the coffee table and started taking items off it to access their movie collection inside. "What are you waiting for? Come give me a hand!"

Zira laughed. "Okay."

Soon enough, they were enjoying a nice and quiet evening without their parents, alone in the house, commenting and joking about the movie, and sharing a good deal of laughter. Zira had a great time—which led her to wonder why she never hung out with her brother for almost two years straight.

Aisling: a vision or dream

The next day, Zira went back to school and found Brianna and Ember by her locker. Her face lit up with a smile. *I guess Ember got over what I said yesterday.*

Brianna turned her head to Zira. "Hey!"

"Hi, Zira," Ember said.

"Hey, guys." Zira waved. "So, Em, we good?"

"Yeah."

"So, Zira," Brianna said, "are you excited for our hike next Saturday? It's gonna be a blast."

Zira shrugged as she opened her locker and removed a book. "Uh, I'm not sure. Outside isn't really my scene, so we'll see how it goes."

Brianna shook her head. "Come on—it's gonna be so much fun! My family is going to love you!"

Zira gave Brianna an uncertain look, but a hint of a smile eased onto her face. "I guess we'll see."

"Hey, Ember, you can come too if you want." Brianna looked at the red-head.

"Sorry, I can't. My brother has this big concert thing." She scoffed and rolled her eyes.

The other two girls glanced at each other, and then back at Ember.

"Well, that should be fun, right?" Brianna asked hesitantly.

"No, it won't. He has been upstaging me since we were born. This is just another point to prove how *perfect* he is." She sighed. "It's fine. There's no getting out of it. You guys have fun, though."

"We will," Brianna exclaimed.

Zira closed her locker, and the three friends started walking down the hall. "So, your relationship with your brother hasn't improved since I last checked?"

"No way," Ember answered. "He's still a complete show-off and thinks he's *sooo* much better than everyone else." She made angry hand motions as she spoke.

"Right, don't know anyone else like that...." Brianna looked over at Zira, who lightly elbowed her in the side. "Ow!"

Zira shook her head and mouthed "stop." But Ember didn't notice any of this as she carried on ranting about her brother.

"He's just...errr! So annoying. I can't believe we're related."

"Just give it some time, Ember," Zira encouraged. "I'm sure you'll get along sooner or later."

"I doubt it." The red-head rolled her eyes. "But whatever. I have to get to class. See ya."

Ember sped away, leaving Brianna and Zira alone.

Brianna glanced at Zira. "Hey...do you...?"

"Do I what?"

Brianna's mouth formed a straight line as she looked away. "Never mind."

"You sure?" Zira asked as Brianna walked off toward a classroom.

"I'm sure. See you later!" Brianna waved.

"Bye." Zira waved back. *I wonder what that was about.*

After lunch, Zira was heading to her next class on the other side of the school. The hallways were mostly empty since she always left lunch early to be on time.

When Zira turned her first corner, she stumbled upon a scene that made her breath catch. Mal was standing in front of a girl with short brown hair.

Zira recognized the girl. It was Violet, one of the props team members. Her eyes were trained on the floor, and Mal had a mischievous smirk on her face. *Oh, not today, Mal.*

She marched up to them and tapped Mal on her back.

The black-haired girl turned to face her, and she immediately scowled. "What do you want?"

"I want you to leave her alone," Zira growled. "She didn't do anything to you."

"How do you know?" Mal said, taking a step forward. "She could've done something horrible to me and you're on the wrong side."

Zira scoffed. "I doubt that. Violet is one of the sweetest people I've ever met, and she basically never talks to anyone. So, odds are you're just being mean to her."

"And what are you going to do about it?"

Zira smiled slyly and made her right hand light up. "Just you wait."

Flordra garifiolte, Zira said in her mind. The new control she had over her magic made her stronger; she could say simple spells in her mind, and they would still work without the necessity of verbal incantation.

The words formed a purple square under Mal's feet and floated her away so quickly that Violet barely registered what happened.

Once Zira was sure she was far enough away, she let her magic fade from her hand and looked at Violet. "Are you okay? What did she say to you?"

"She was making fun of my accent and country," Violet answered with a sigh. "Thanks, Zira. I wasn't expecting that."

"Neither was I," a new voice said, stepping into the hallway.

"Sundown?" Zira said, already feeling the panic form in her chest. "What... What does that mean?"

"It means I believe you've reformed. I overheard Raven scolding you after the first theater meeting. It made me wonder if you had changed. So, I decided to talk to you, and you told me you were trying to change. I was still skeptical. But then I heard you talking to Brianna and Ember after the second props meeting. You were actually...sorry you hurt Ember. I was going to talk to you today, but I kept denying that I needed to. I was on my way to class when I overheard you defending someone. I knew I had to say something once you drove Mal away. And here we are, talking—and here you are, standing up against what you used to do. I'm sorry I was so cold to you before; I was just..." Sundown trailed off, putting a hand on the back of his neck.

"Hurt," Zira finished for him. "I get it. I hurt your cousin, and I'm so sorry. I wish I could take it all back." Tears filled her eyes, but she refused to let them fall.

"I could've helped her more too, but I didn't." He exhaled. "I'm sorry, Zira. I'm sorry I ever blamed you for my cousin's death. It wasn't your fault—at least not entirely." Sundown's eyes drifted to the floor, but Zira could still see a layer of mist threatening to break into droplets.

She walked up to him, allowing her tears to fall. "Sundown, you have every right to be angry at me for her death. I hurt her a lot, and I know I hurt you too. So, I'm sorry—for all of it." Zira wiped some tears off her face. "I just want to be better now."

Sundown looked at her. "Hey, you are doing better. You just stood up for Violet, and you don't even know her that well."

"But I've done other things I'm not proud of," Zira said wistfully.

"Then maybe we can help each other," he responded.

Zira looked up at him and saw him smiling warmly, causing her to return the gesture. "I like that idea."

They stared at each other for a few moments until Violet broke the silence. "Ahem.... Not to ruin this amazing moment, but we should really get to class."

"She's right," Zira agreed.

"Unfortunately, she is. But I'll see you Monday, right?" Sundown asked.

"Of course."

"Great. See you ladies." Sundown saluted them and turned around, walking down the hall to his right.

Violet and Zira looked at each other. The brunette cleared her throat and stepped forward. "Thanks again. I'm not sure what I would've done if you hadn't been here."

Zira gave her an uncertain smile. "You're welcome...but you seem like a strong person. I'm sure you would've thought of something."

"I doubt it, but thanks for the compliment. What class do you have next?"

"Art."

"Me too," Violet said with a smile, looking up. "Wanna walk together?"

Zira smiled back. "Sure."

Violet picked up her bag, and the two girls proceeded to walk down the hallway.

What Violet had said about herself nagged Zira. Finally, she asked, "Violet, why do you think you aren't strong?"

The brunette sighed. "Because I'm not. Ever since I moved here, I've made one friend. I'm too afraid to speak to anyone because I don't want them making fun of my accent."

Zira nodded. "Well, you were able to stand up for Hazel when you voted for her. So, I think you're stronger than you know."

"Thanks, Zira." She paused before continuing. "You know, there's a word in Irish: *aisling*. It means 'vision' or 'dream.' We both have dreams to be something more. I think we should promise each other not to give up on those dreams."

Zira raised her eyebrows. "Ash-ling?" She thought about it for a moment, excitement filling her chest. "Yeah, I think that's a good idea."

Violet smiled. "All right, here's the promise mantra my grandmother taught me. I'm going to say it first and then we'll both say it together. Ready?"

"Ready."

"'We both have dreams to be more than we are, so, let's promise to give it all our heart. This is our *aisling*.'"

Zira closed her eyes, thinking about all the good she wanted to do. She opened them. "All right, let's say it together."

"We both have dreams to be more than we are, so let's promise to give it all our heart. This is our *aisling*."

Zira felt like a weight had just lifted off her heart. She smiled. "Thanks, Violet. I think that just helped me more than I'll ever understand."

Violet grinned. "Glad I could help. Also, you say *aisling* perfectly. Hazel kept messing it up."

Zira laughed. "My French teacher says I have an ear for languages. Maybe it's because I'm already bilingual."

"You are?"

Zira burst out laughing. "No one ever thinks that when they meet me. *Si*, my father is Mexican. I grew up speaking English and Spanish."

Violet grinned again. "That's really cool. It's funny—I would never have guessed that we even had one thing in common. But it turns out we have a lot."

Zira smiled at her, and for a moment, it felt like all was right in the world. "I guess we do."

A Good Feeling

The following Monday, Zira was in the locker room, getting ready for gym class. She liked gym because it wasn't outside and she enjoyed exercise, but she also disliked it because she had to wear shorts and tennis shoes. Still, it could have been worse.

Zira walked into the large gymnasium, where the ceilings were high and the bleachers were folded against the walls. There were climbing ropes to her right with mats below, and the whole room was a basketball court. She stopped in front of the bleachers to her left and started stretching with the other students. The teacher observed them from across the room.

As Zira started arm stretches, a tall, tan boy with curly hair came to stand next to her. She glanced over and found Sundown looking at her.

"Hey," he greeted, copying her stretches.

She smiled. "Hey. I didn't know we had the same gym period."

"Well, until a few days ago, I thought you were a good-for-nothing jerk who only thought of herself. So, you know, we didn't really interact." He laughed.

She awkwardly laughed back. "Good point."

They continued stretching until the gym teacher came over. "Okay, people, today we're playing girls-versus-boys dodgeball. So, all girls to this side!"

"Good luck," Sundown said, waving at Zira.

"You too," she whispered as he started walking to the other side of the court.

The boys set up the balls. When they finished, Zira took a fighting position, something she did when she practiced magic.

Once everyone was in position, the teacher blew the whistle, and all chaos broke loose. Zira ran as quickly as she could to get a rubber ball, and she succeeded. She instantly aimed for the first blur of a person she saw and threw it.

"You're out, Sanchez!" the teacher announced.

Zira internally celebrated getting a boy out as she ran to grab another ball. She threw it at another blur but missed, then ran farther back to observe her surroundings.

"You're out, Brooks!" A girl with long blonde hair ran to the sidelines.

Zira took in what she saw: blurred rubber balls of blue, yellow, and red being thrown everywhere. Most of the boys missed, while the girls were a little distracted with dodging balls, so they didn't throw theirs often.

Zira wasn't sure how to win this one, but she wasn't about to give up. She decided on her plan: She would be sneaky, grab balls without anyone noticing, and throw them at the boys while they were busy throwing balls at the girls.

While she was surveying the field, two girls and one boy had been disqualified. That boy was Sundown. Zira let out a breath of relief. She wouldn't have to feel guilty since she couldn't hit him anymore.

She ran to the nearest ball and quickly locked on a target. Before she could throw it, however, a red blur was heading straight for her head. She instinctively dropped her ball and blocked her face. "You're out, Flores!" She cursed to herself and made her way to the sidelines, sitting next to Sundown.

"You did pretty well," Sundown said with a playful smile.

"Shut up," Zira responded, her face turning red from embarrassment. She did not take failing well—especially when other people were counting on her.

"Hey, you did your best, and that's all that matters." He put a comforting hand on her shoulder.

"Thanks, but um, no touching; I don't like it," she said as she picked up his hand and moved it off her shoulder. "And that's not because of you. That's a rule I have for everyone."

He shrugged. "All right. I'm cool with that."

The two continued watching the game in awkward silence. Zira could feel an invisible rope of tension that was connected to her and Sundown. She longed for that tension to go away instantly, but she knew it only would with time.

About twenty minutes passed, and the girls had won. Apparently, *aiming* paid off. Zira walked over and celebrated with her team. She saw Sundown giving her a thumbs up with an uncertain expression on his face. *I wonder what that's about.*

The teacher blew his whistle, snapping Zira out of her thoughts. "All right, everyone, we have half of class left. So, we're going to watch the losers try to do the rope challenge." He gestured behind him to the two ropes hanging securely from the ceiling. "Who wants to go first?"

All the boys remained silent.

"Oh, okay, none of you. Should've seen that one coming. How about you, Sanchez? You got out first. And then the next boy that got out, and so on to the last boy standing."

All the boys looked at each other and shrugged with a look that said, "Fair enough."

Everyone made their way to the ropes. All the girls took their place on the floor in front of the bleachers, giggling and whispering to each other that the boys would fail. Zira didn't laugh, however. She was going to cheer them on.

The first boy grabbed the rope and pushed off the ground. He wrapped his foot around the rope and put his soles together. He struggled a bit but slowly inched his way up. Zira didn't cheer him on because she had the feeling that verbally encouraging him would make him lose his focus.

Sanchez was about a quarter of the way up when his arms and legs gave out, and he slid down the rope, cringing in pain. Once he was safely on the floor, he took his hands off the rope and looked at them. Zira could see they were bright red.

"Okay, not bad, Sanchez. Take a seat. Stein, you're next."

Eddie Stein went to the rope and attempted the same exercise. He didn't make it as far as Sanchez, but it was progress for him, so the coach was proud.

Sundown was up next.

"You got this, Sundown! Woo!" Zira cheered.

Sundown smiled sheepishly at her, blushing. He took a deep breath and grabbed on the rope, pushing off with his left leg. He had a firm grip on it and started climbing his way up. He was in excellent shape, so he powered through it very quickly. His legs inched up as he climbed, using the same technique as the first boy. Once he reached the top, Zira resumed her cheering.

Sundown instinctively looked down at her. That was a mistake. He gripped the rope tightly and froze.

Zira's face twisted with confusion. "What is he doing...?"

"Come on, Qiu; get down here," the teacher yelled. "Is something wrong?"

Sundown didn't answer verbally. Zira could see him barely nod his head.

Ideas swam in her mind until she considered how he gripped the rope after he looked down. Realization hit her, and her whole body filled with fear. *Sundown's afraid of heights.*

Zira quickly stood and yelled up to him, "Hey, Sundown, it's okay. We've got you. Just make your way down." All the boys on his basketball team started whispering to each other, and then the girls. Zira realized she had just revealed Sundown's fear to everyone. *Oh, no.*

Eventually, Sundown nodded and started slowly inching down. The rope shook more than it normally did when he moved his arms.

He had about three quarters of the way left when he looked down again. He tried to grab the rope while his gaze was still fixed on the floor, but he missed. His head quickly spun back to the rope as his body went limp from not being able to keep himself sturdy with one hand.

Everyone gasped, and Zira started internally panicking, a familiar anxious energy coursing through her blood. "Sundown, grab the frickin' rope!"

He tried, but every time he reached for it, the hand that was already gripping the rope slid a little, which made him tremble more and the rope shake violently. "I can't do it."

"Yes, you can. I believe in you," she shouted to him through cupped hands.

"She's right. Grab the rope—please!" the coach yelled.

Sundown hand was slipping even more rapidly from sweat. Zira could see by his scrunched face how exhausted and scared he was.

"Come on, Sundown. It's okay. Just grab the rope," Zira repeated, the buzzing of her magic more noticeable than it had been in a while.

When he didn't grab it, the teacher lost it. "Come on, man; just grab the rope already!"

Before he could act on the screams of Zira or the teacher, his sweaty hand gave out, and he fell from twenty feet up.

"NO!" Zira yelled, the energy inside her spiking.

Sundown's scream filled the air. Most of the class instinctively looked away, except for two boys and the teacher who were running to catch him.

Zira's energy took over, and her instincts kicked in. She lit up her hands and put them in front of her, spreading out her legs and bending her knees. She whispered a spell to herself. *"Grana maukino."* She felt the energy leave her as a big, glowing outline of a circle formed around the crash pads. She needed to keep her magic activated to keep the spell alive.

No one noticed the partially glowing ground, and when Sundown reached the three guys, they all fell from impact. But it didn't hurt: Zira made sure of it. She let her magic fade to a dormant state and put her hands on her knees, panting. Her vision swayed and nausea overcame her. *It was worth it.*

The crowd opened their eyes to see Sundown and the rest of the people safe and mostly uninjured.

The coach scrambled off the ground and helped the others up. "Is everyone okay?"

They all panted, and Sundown nodded. "Yeah, we're okay."

When she felt strong enough, Zira rushed to him. "Sundown!" She put her arms around him, and he returned her embrace. Her physical touch rule was temporarily thrown out the window after seeing one of her only friends almost get badly injured. They separated. "Are you okay?"

"Yeah," he answered, then added quietly, "Thanks for your help." He scratched the back of his neck. "I owe you one."

Zira smiled at him; she could feel the rope of tension between them loosen a little. But before she could respond, the teacher butted in.

"What was that about, Qiu? You could've been seriously hurt."

Sundown looked at the ground. "I'm sorry.... I just...froze up. I've been afraid of heights for most of my life, but I didn't want anyone to know."

"But you've done this exercise before and have been fine," the teacher exclaimed, confused.

"Yeah, but...I never looked down before."

"Why did you look down this time?"

Sundown sighed. "I don't know. I just...did." He eyed Zira.

The teacher rubbed the bridge of his nose. "Look.... Next time, just..." Before he could get the right words out, the bell rang. "We'll talk later. But for now, everyone, get to your next class."

The students left, still whispering. Sundown's teammates surrounded him and bombarded him with questions. Zira wanted to help him, but they already entered the boys' locker room—and she had to get to her next class.

As she changed her clothes, she thought about what happened. *I...saved someone.* She was in complete disbelief as shock overcame every fiber of her body. *I can do good—and I can do good with my magic! I can't believe it.*

She left the girls' locker room with the biggest smile on her face. She had *never* felt this good about herself...and she liked it.

Apparently, practicing paid off.

Paper Dreams

Zira made her way to the cafeteria a little while later. She was still smiling, and her heart was still light, but there was also a fuzzy ball of anxiety in her stomach. She couldn't get Sundown off her mind. Was he okay? Did his friends handle his fear well? It was a lot to take in. She pushed it away for now, wanting to focus on her two friends.

After getting her lunch of breaded chicken, an apple, and a small salad, she made her way to the back, quickly finding Brianna sitting in their usual spot.

She sat down next to her. "Hey!"

"Hey," Brianna greeted back. "You seem happy."

Zira smiled brightly. "I am."

"Okay, I'll bite. What's up? Did Ember apologize?!"

"What?"

Brianna sighed. "I'm sorry. It just bugs me that she never apologized for hurting your feelings yesterday."

"It's fine, Brianna. That's just the way Ember is. She doesn't apologize unless it's something big. She doesn't even do *that* sometimes." As Zira momentarily reflected on past experiences, a weird feeling appeared in her gut, but she paid it now mind. "I promise you we're cool, though. I don't mind."

"I just... I don't know. I know some people don't apologize for their actions, but shouldn't they at least show some form of saying they're sorry?"

"Ember's form of that is being nice to me again," Zira explained. "Trust me: She wouldn't be talking to me if she wasn't sorry."

Brianna squinted in thought. "Whatever you say."

"Hey, guys!" Ember greeted as she arrived at their table.

"Hey," Zira and Brianna said simultaneously.

"So, how did classes go for you guys today?" Ember asked as she pulled out a sandwich from her lunch bag. "Science was extremely boring."

"Honestly," Zira started, "gym went a little...*unexpectedly* today, but it was okay in the end."

"Unexpectedly?" Brianna repeated.

"Well..." Zira debated if she should tell them what happened since Sundown seemed shy about his fear. She figured they would hear rumors later, though, so it was better for them to hear the true story. "A boy climbed one of the ropes, got really scared at the top, lost his grip while slowly inching down, and then fell from twenty feet in the air."

Both Brianna and Ember stopped eating and froze.

"What...happened to him?" Brianna asked, her eyes wide with shock.

"Oh. Two guys and the teacher caught him and cushioned his fall, so everyone was okay."

"Geez, you had me worried there for a minute, Zira." Brianna breathed out slowly, putting a hand on her chest.

"Yeah, way to freak us out." Ember rolled her eyes in a playful way.

Zira laughed. "I'm sorry, but it was so crazy! I can't believe he's okay."

"Yeah, that is a miracle. Thank God," Brianna said, starting to dig back into her food.

They all continued eating and talking until Zira finished. She got up to throw away her trash and return her tray.

On her way back to the table, Zira let her thoughts wander. As she zoned out, she stepped on something that made her foot slide out from underneath her. She landed on the floor with a thud, groaning as pain shot up her bottom and back.

Giggling came along with her groans, which made Zira sit up and look behind her. A black-haired girl and an auburn-haired girl were walking toward her, the latter holding a food tray. She scowled. Mal and Ivy.

"What do you two want?"

"Nothing," Ivy said, looking down at Zira.

"Except for this," Mal said, thrusting her tray forward and causing all her food to fly off and land on Zira.

The Witch's mouth gaped open, the warm food seeping into her clothes. This only made the girls laugh more.

"What was that for?" Zira asked in a frantic tone.

"For ruining our lives," Mal growled, throwing her arms to her sides. "We were the one who tripped you. Ivy put her tray on the ground when you weren't looking. How's that for some sweet revenge?"

The two girls fist-bumped.

Zira stared at them, her eyes filled with a new fire. The confidence she gained from saving Sundown came out in a different way. She was *angry* at her former friends.

"You look so ridiculous!" Ivy snickered.

"Yeah, you look like someone threw up on you!" Mal added.

As they continued making fun of her, Zira's fists shook with anger, and she glared at them venomously. She vaguely felt her magical energy appear in her hands and grab nearby food, flinging it telekinetically across the table and allowing it to make direct contact with Ivy and Mal.

They yelled in disgust and Zira snapped out of her anger, realizing what she had done.

"Where did this sludge come from?" Mal asked no one in particular, flinging mashed potatoes off her shirt.

"What's going on here?" a deep, masculine voice asked. All the students looked at the source of the sound and saw a tall man in a light orange dress shirt walking toward them.

"Nothing, sir; just some spills. We'll get it all cleaned up." Ivy smiled innocently at him as Mal moved to help Zira to her feet.

"Does everyone agree with her account?" he asked Zira and the other kids at the table.

The kids quickly nodded, but Zira hesitated to answer. *I just lost control and covered my old friends in food. If I rat them out, I should rat myself out. But I can't do that without exposing my powers....*

"Do you also agree it was just an accident?" the teacher asked Zira again, more sternly this time.

Zira shyly nodded her head. "Yes, sir."

The teacher nodded. "All right, then. We'll get a janitor to come clean it up. Accidents happen." He walked away.

"Who did this?" Ivy asked Mal quietly.

Mal eyed Zira. "It doesn't matter, Ivy. We got what we came for. Come on; let's go clean off this processed food." The raven-haired girl grabbed Ivy's arm, and they left the cafeteria.

Zira stood there in shame. *It's my fault.* She slowly looked around at all the kids staring at her. Tears filled her eyes, and she snapped.

"What are you looking at? Yeah, they defeated me. I'm no longer the queen bee. Who cares? Just..." Zira trailed off as she saw the fear in their eyes, and the image of a brown-haired girl popped into her head once again. "Just...just forget it."

She ran out of the cafeteria, ignoring Brianna's calls of concern, and made her way to the girls' bathroom on the other side of the school. After entering, she stared at herself in the mirror.

"Who are you?" she screamed at herself. "*Who are you?*" The witch stared at her reflection, the hot anger in her blood growing as her eyes flashed purple.

Zira's legs nearly gave out on her. She stumbled back and put her weight against one of the stall separators. She put her hands on her face and closed her eyes, letting the tears go. *What kind of monster am I?* She let out quiet sobs and sank to the floor, burying her face in her legs. *I was an idiot to think I was free earlier. I'll never be free. I lost control of my magic again and yelled at innocent tweens like I used to. I haven't changed at all. I'm failing my aisling.*

As Zira cried into her legs, the bathroom door swung open.

"Hey," a familiar gentle voice said. "Are you okay?"

Zira looked up to see Brianna staring down at her with concern in her eyes.

"I'm fine," she said, looking away.

"No, you're not," Brianna countered as she sat down next to her friend. "They hurt you, didn't they?"

"I don't want to talk about it," Zira said, fighting to keep her voice from quivering.

"Come on. I'm your friend." Brianna went to put her hand on Zira's shoulder, but quickly caught herself and put her arm back down.

Zira turned to face her. "Look, Brianna, they did hurt me. But...not in the way you think." She turned away from her friend again.

"In what way, then?"

Zira's lip formed into a straight line as she debated telling Brianna the truth about her past...but she decided against it. It was better that she didn't know.

"I just... It's complicated."

Brianna sighed, but then nodded. "Tell me when you're ready. There's no pressure."

A semblance of a smile eased onto Zira's face. *At least you can respect my boundaries. No one else ever did that except...my sister.* Zira's heart practically stopped as she made the connection. Brianna reminded her of Destiny. She popped up and tackled her friend with a hug.

Brianna's eyes widened, but she put her arms around Zira, nonetheless. "I thought you didn't like doing this."

Zira sighed. "Sometimes, it's worth it to make an exception." She pulled away. "But that's not becoming a regular thing between us, so don't even try."

Brianna laughed and stood up, then helped Zira to her feet as a red-head came into the bathroom.

"Hey, Zira," Ember said, "are you okay?"

Zira nodded. "I'm fine. Brianna helped me." She smiled at the blonde girl next to her, who returned the look.

"I would've come in here too, but Brianna asked me to give you guys some space," Ember explained, shrugging. "I didn't protest."

"It's cool, Ember. I wasn't even worried about that, but thank you both. I'm glad I can count on you guys."

"Aww, thanks," Ember said, beaming. "Come on, Brianna. We're gonna be late for our next class."

The two girls left Zira to clean herself off. As she was wiping the food off her shirt with a wet paper towel, she wondered how she got lucky enough to find three friends to call her own.

But there was still a lingering thought in her head. *Where are you, Haven?*

Justified Pain

Zira removed her key from her backpack and unlocked the front door. She walked into her dark house and flipped on the light. After taking off her bag, she opened the freezer and got out waffle cone-flavored ice cream, eating it straight from the container with a spoon. While everything may have externally appeared normal, her thoughts were raging inside like never before.

You're a mistake. You shouldn't be here. You haven't changed. You threw food on your old friends with uncontrolled magic. No one's safe unless you practice more.

Tears started pouring from her eyes. *I still can't control my magic. I punched a hole in a wall, burned my carpet, and dumped food on my old friends.* Zira drew in a heavy breath. *I thought practice was working. What am I doing wrong?* She assessed it in her head and quickly jumped to a conclusion. *I need to practice more. I skipped a few days ago to play video games with Patrick.*

"I can never skip again!" she announced boldly and scrambled to put away the ice cream.

She washed her hands, ran to grab her bag, and made her way to her room. After taking off her shoes and wiping her eyes, she thought about what spell to practice. *Maybe the ice one? I tried fire a while ago, so let's do the opposite of that.*

She set up the same table mechanism she had used before and took her place, not bothering to do a battle pose. After a deep breath, she put her hands over the table, and lit them up along with the table.

" *Whiari,*" she spoke.

In the center of the table, ice formed. Zira smiled and controlled its growth. She only wanted a medium circle to form.

Once she got what she wanted, she deactivated her magic and stared at her accomplishment in awe. Zira touched the table, an icy sharpness pierced her fingers. *Perfect.* She lifted her hands and put them back over the table, lighting them up again.

" *Whiari,*" she said again, making the ice spread. She wanted to freeze the whole table and then unfreeze it slowly.

Zira could feel the energy coursing through her arms and around the table. She could feel it getting stronger, causing fear to form in her chest. She ignored it, however, knowing the magic wouldn't learn how to control itself.

Once the ice reached the bottom of the table's legs, she attempted to pull the energy in her hands back into her core, but it fought her, allowing the ice to keep forming.

Panic overtook Zira as she realized she couldn't stop it. Her magic was too powerful, and she wasn't strong enough. She could feel every inch of her body being consumed by it.

Zira ignored her blurring vision and focused on the glowing table, which continued to gain more layers of ice. She let out a yelp as an electric pain shot through her. "Come on! Stop it!"

But her panic only made the ice form faster, and as her magic continued to course through her veins, it made her insides feel as if they were on fire. She let out small whimpers of pain.

Eventually, the table exploded, causing chunks of ice to fly everywhere as Zira collapsed from exhaustion and landed on her soft carpet. Her whole body felt sore, her eyes drooped, and her upper forearm stung like it had just been burned.

She did not lie on the floor for very long, but when she sat up, she saw a bloodstain on the carpet. *What?* Her face twisted with confusion and panic, but when she looked at her right arm, she saw a large gash with a good deal of blood pouring out. Now that she knew it was there, she fully noticed the stinging pain.

Panic seized her chest; she didn't know what she was going to do about this cut. She also wasn't sure what to do about the mess that her spell caused.... *Wait, where is the mess?* When Zira looked around her room, all the ice was gone. So was her retractable table, however, which meant she was going to have to explain that to her parents...but that wouldn't be too hard.

More lies, Zira thought to herself sadly.

She stood up and walked out of her room to the bathroom. She winced in pain as she removed her royal blue shirt to clean her fairly large cut. She considered taking off her white spaghetti-strapped undershirt too but decided against it. It didn't matter if it got wet. She deserved to feel uncomfortable anyway.

Zira leaned under the water tap and used her telekinesis to turn it on. As the cool, clear water washed away the blood coming from her gash, she reflected on what had happened. *I lost control...again. I'll never gain control over my magic, no matter how hard I try.* She didn't stop the tears from filling her eyes. *I hurt everyone I'm around—even myself. I really am a monster.*

Realization then slapped her across the face. *Wait—I hurt myself. I hurt someone who* deserves *to be hurt. I cause so much pain everywhere I go that it's about time I caused* myself *some.* More tears formed at the thought, the pressure behind her eyes increasing. But she didn't know why. She *deserved* this pain, so why should she be upset? She didn't have the right to be.

Once the blood stopped pouring from her wound, she turned the water off and grabbed an old towel from under the sink. She wet it and pressed it forcefully against her wound to stop the blood flow, causing her to grimace.

After a few minutes, she pulled the towel away from the area and surveyed the damage. The cut was nasty—and *deep*. Her mom would likely want her to go to urgent care tomorrow.

But what if I don't tell anyone? Zira's eyes widened at the thought, and she quickly forced her panic down. If she didn't tell anyone, it would probably take longer to heal. She could punish herself for being so mean to everyone. Zira felt a nagging feeling in her gut telling her not to do it, but it was high time she caused herself some pain.

Nodding, she promised herself she wouldn't tell anyone about the cut—at least not for now.

She grabbed some gauze pads, bandages, and medical tape from behind the mirror cabinet. After sticking the pads to the bandages, she wrapped them around her arm securely and used the tape to keep it in place. *There. Now when I wear long-sleeved shirts and sweaters, no one will notice.*

Zira cleaned up her mess, burying all the medical trash in the trash can, and then took her bloodstained shirt back to her room. She hung it up in her closet where no one would find it.

After putting on another shirt, Zira took out the orange potion from her shoe box. She sprinkled it on the bloodstained carpet and watched it disappear before her eyes.

After putting the potion away, Zira climbed into her bed and lay down. She yawned. *I guess a short nap wouldn't hurt,* she thought as she closed her eyes, letting the peace of sleep replace the heavy guilt inside of her.

Social Anxiety

The following Saturday, Zira was looking around in her closet, trying to figure out what to wear on the hike with Brianna and her family. She grabbed the only exercise skirt she had and tossed it on her bed along with some leggings. After that, she grabbed a white short-sleeved top and her blue-and-black sweater.

After putting everything on, she grabbed her black, heeled, below-the-knee boots and put them on. She loved the way the outfit looked, but she wasn't sure if Brianna or her family would approve. Either way, she didn't care. If she was going to hike, she was going to do it in style.

Zira had already packed her backpack the night before, so she grabbed it and went downstairs.

"Hey, *Mami*, I'm gonna call Brianna and see if they're almost here." She approached the breakfast bar and grabbed a buttered piece of toast off a plate.

"Okay, *mija*," her mom responded as she continued to spread peanut butter on a bagel. "Let me know so I can meet her parents."

Zira put her backpack down and pulled her phone out of the front pocket. She found Brianna's contact and selected it.

"Hello?"

Zira swallowed her bite of toast. "Hey, Brianna. You guys almost here?"

"Yep," Brianna responded cheerfully. "Should be there in about five minutes."

"Okay. See you soon." Zira hung up the phone and put it away, then turned to her mom. "They'll be here soon. I'm gonna go wait outside."

"I'll come with you," her mother said, putting down the butter knife and bagel.

The two of them went outside and stood on the tiny porch. Zira took a deep breath of the crisp autumn air, and a smile appeared on her face. Even if she didn't like outdoor activities, it did not mean she didn't like being outside every now and then. In fact, it was refreshing to spend a few minutes outside, especially in the fall. The air was crisp and cool, and it gave off a relaxing fragrance.

While Zira was lost in the moment, a white minivan pulled up to the curb of her yard.

"Zira, they're here," her mother said, tapping her on the shoulder.

The two of them walked to the curb as the back window rolled down.

"Hey!" Brianna greeted.

"Hey," Zira said back. "This is my mom. She wanted to meet your parents before we left."

"Well, here comes my dad," Brianna said as her father came into view, rounding the back of the car.

A tall man with short blond hair and light skin extended his hand toward Estelle. "Nice to meet you."

Estelle took it and smiled. "You too."

"Zira, I can take your bag and put it in the trunk," he offered.

She slid her backpack off her shoulder. "Thank you."

"No problem." He smiled and went around to open the trunk. "You can sit in the middle next to Brianna."

Zira nodded and turned to the car door, hesitant to touch the handle.

"It's automatic," Brianna explained as she pushed a button. The door slid open and revealed a very packed car. Every seat was filled except two: the middle seat in the back, and the middle one next to Brianna. Zira's eyes widened, and Brianna laughed.

"I know—there are a lot of us."

Zira smiled awkwardly. "I don't mind." She turned to her mom. "Bye, *Mami.*"

They hugged.

"Have fun," Estelle told her as they separated.

"I will," Zira responded sheepishly. *I hope.*

She climbed over Brianna and plopped down in the thin seat, squished between two girls. Brianna's dad closed the trunk, and Zira sat quietly as she listened to his and her mom's muffled voices talking behind the car. *Please don't embarrass me, Mamá.*

They finished up shortly and Estelle came back to the open van door. "All right, see you later, *mija*. Be sure to text me if you can. *Cuídate*, okay?"

"I will, *Mami*. Bye!" Zira waved.

"Bye," she said as she waved back, walking away from the van as the automatic door closed.

Once Zira watched her mom disappear through the front door, she attempted to buckle herself in. "Where's the seatbelt?"

Brianna revealed a small waist seat belt between them, which Zira took and clicked in on her other side.

When Zira looked up, she found a golden-blonde, light-skinned girl smiling at her. She blushed slightly. "Uh, hello?"

The girl laughed. "It's okay; I don't bite."

Zira sat up straight. Her heart was racing, and none of her muscles would relax. *Why, oh, why did I agree to come?*

Brianna's father hopped in the driver's seat again and pulled away from the house. Once they were barely ten feet away, someone kicked Zira's seat, and she jumped.

"Knock it off," Brianna said as she looked in the back at her snickering sisters.

The sister next to Zira leaned forward a bit, cocking her head. "You're so sensitive! You know what? I'm gonna call you 'Soft Serve'—like the ice cream."

Zira chuckled nervously and turned to Brianna with a pleading look.

"Faustina, stop it," Brianna said. "You're freaking her out."

"That's why she's Soft Serve."

Brianna rolled her eyes, but a smirk hid beneath her exasperated exterior. Zira's heart lightened at seeing the sisters

191

bickering. It reminded her that Brianna was comfortable with them, so there was no reason she shouldn't be.

"So, Zira," Brianna's father said, "what do you do for fun?"

Zira's mind immediately flashed to magic. But, of course, *he* couldn't know that. "Uh, crafts. And piano and singing—well, sometimes, anyway. I also like learning about different countries and cultures. It's cool to see another way of life."

He nodded. "That's."

They dropped back into an awkward silence until Brianna eventually spoke. "So, Zira, this is Faustina." She gestured to the golden-haired girl sitting on the other side of Zira. "And these two are Kitty and Raymond. We usually call her Rai, though. And you can either call my parents Mr. and Mrs. Decker or Mr. Sammy and Mrs. Regina."

"Hi." Zira waved to the two girls in the back, her eyebrows furrowing. "Oh yeah, you all have blonde hair."

Brianna giggled. "Yep. Our names also mean something. I'm named after my great aunt, Raymond is named after a saint, Kitty is named after my mom's childhood cat, and Faustina is also named after a saint."

"That's really cool. I'm not sure why my parents named me Zira, but I like it."

"I bet they had a good reason." Brianna smiled at her. "You should ask them."

"I will," Zira replied. "Although I do know why they gave me my middle name, which is Almira. It has origins in multiple languages, though my parents gave me it for the Arabic meaning, which is 'princess.'"

"Awww," Brianna and her family said simultaneously.

"How sweet," Regina added.

Zira smiled sheepishly, blushing. "Thanks. What about you, Brianna? What's your middle name?"

"Oh!" she exclaimed. "it's Ava."

Zira cocked her head to the side. "Why Ava?"

"After St. Ava, the patron saint of blindness," Brianna explained.

"Hey!" Faustina's face lit up. "You guys both have middle names that start with A."

Brianna looked at Zira. "I guess we do."

They exchanged warm smiles with each other.

After that, the passengers fell back into silence until Brianna's father spoke.

"So, Zira, what do your parents do for a living?"

"My dad's an accountant, and my mom's a doctor."

"That must be cool to have a doctor as a mom. Free appointments!" He laughed.

"Actually, that's incorrect," Zira told him matter-of-factly, "we still have to visit the doctors, and my brother and I have a different physician from our mom. If we get hurt, she'll check us over and then decide if we need to go to urgent care or the ER." Her left hand instinctively gripped her gashed arm. She wondered if her mom would *actually* take her to urgent care if she knew about it. Zira forced the guilt down and convinced herself she wouldn't. Even if she would, it didn't matter. *I deserve the lack of treatment.*

"Oh," Brianna's dad said, and then laughed. "Shows what I know. I'm a fisherman, so I'm not in the loop on this stuff."

"And he barely goes to the doctor." His wife gave him a slight glare.

"Oh, come on, Regina—it's not that big a deal," he responded. "I thought we moved past this."

"I tell you, not going to the doctor will come back to haunt you one day." She squinted at him.

Zira's eyes went wide, and she tried not to think about how that sentence applied to her.

Sammy glanced in the rearview mirror and made eye contact with Zira. "Anyways...Zira, how many siblings do you have?"

"Two," she answered. "An older sister and a younger brother."

"Names?"

"Destiny and Patrick. Destiny's off at college, though." Zira looked down and sighed.

"How long has she been gone?" Regina asked.

"Over two years...and she hasn't visited." Zira blinked back her tears. A feeling of desperation and pain filled her gut. She loved Destiny and missed her so much, but she couldn't help but feel betrayed.

"Oh," was all Brianna's dad had to say.

"Anyway," Regina said, breaking the awkward conversation, "Zira, have you ever been hiking?"

"Nope," Zira responded plainly, staring off into space. Her mind flashed to an image of Destiny and tears pricked her eyes. "Is there a CD we could listen to?"

"Yep," Regina answered. "We also have the radio. You pick since you're our guest."

"CD; I'd rather listen to whatever music you have than random people talking with a song in between," Zira answered in a partially annoyed tone.

Brianna's mom clicked on a few buttons, and then Christian music started playing. It wasn't too loud or too quiet—just right. Zira put her head back and listened to all the sisters singing along.

She could feel herself drifting to sleep until she heard someone moving behind her.

"Boo!" one of Brianna's sisters shouted in her ear.

Zira jumped forward and let out a shriek. She panted with her hand on her chest. "That wasn't funny."

Kitty snickered along with Rai. "It was pretty funny to me."

"Guys, knock it off," their mom said sternly. "That is not how we make new friends."

They continued to laugh under their breath, while Zira leaned back in her seat and forced her muscles to relax. They loosened up eventually, and she drifted off to sleep, the sound of Brianna's singing still in her ears.

The Hike

When Zira awoke, she felt someone shaking her and whispering her name. She fully opened her eyes to see that she was lying on Brianna's shoulder. Zira quickly sat up and wiped the slobber off her face. "Sorry, Brianna."

Her friend chuckled. "It's okay. I liked having you near me."

Zira blushed. *She likes being close to me? Why?* After a moment, the van door opened, snapping her out of her thoughts.

"Come on, you two slowpokes," Faustina said playfully. "Let's go."

Brianna and Zira got out of the car on her command and closed the door behind them.

Zira walked away from the car and started stretching. After a moment, Faustina came up and slapped her on the back. "You ready for your first hike today, Soft Serve?"

Zira moved away from her touch. "Uh, I guess so? I'm not really sure."

"Well, with hiking professionals like us, you'll do great," she encouraged, but then looked down. "Heels? In the forest?"

"Hey, if I'm going outside, I'm gonna look my best, okay?" Zira responded defensively.

Faustina laughed. "Okay, just please don't trip. We don't need you getting a sprained ankle."

"I'll be fine; I've been wearing heels since I was four. I watched *Charlie's Angels* when I was younger and copied them by wearing heels and running around the house playing spy."

"Hey, that's pretty cool. Wish I would've done something like that. I can wear heels, but only for so long. Then my feet and ankles start to hurt."

Zira shrugged. "They aren't for every girl—just the professionals." She smiled slyly at a gaping Faustina and walked to the trunk of the car.

Kitty laughed. "Aw, man, she got you!"

The sisters continued to joke around, sometimes making weird voices when they talked to each other, while Brianna stood by her dad and Zira.

Sammy handed both girls their backpacks, and Zira put hers on the ground as she got out her water bottle and phone.

After taking a sip of water, she flipped open her phone and texted her mom. *Made it safely. Going on the hike soon. Don't know if I'll have reception.*

Her mom texted back rather quickly. *Have fun! Don't worry about reception. Just don't get into trouble. :P*

Zira smiled. *I'm just going to pretend you didn't say that.*

After sending the text, her mom didn't respond, so Zira closed her phone and put it back in her bag.

197

"Ready to go, Zira?" Sammy asked.

She looked up at him. "Yep." She flung her backpack onto her shoulders and followed him as the rest gathered into a circle. She stood next to Brianna and Kitty.

"Let's start this hike with a prayer like we always do. Would you like to join us, Zira?"

Zira's eyes widened as everyone turned to look at her. "Uh...sure."

The family made prayer hands, and Zira copied them.

"Dear God," Sammy began, "protect us as we go on this hike. Make sure we have fun and embrace anything that wasn't in our plans today. And bless our special guest, Zira Flores, as it is her first time hiking, and we want her to remain safe and have a great time."

Zira blushed and cringed at the prayer directed specifically at her. *But I'm not Christian.*

"Zira, would you like to add anything?"

"Uhhh...no...if that's okay."

"No problem," he responded, then finished the prayer. "All of this we ask as we pray, Our Father, who art in heaven, hallowed be thy name. Thy kingdom come; thy will be done...."

Zira did her best to follow along, but she had never heard this prayer before in her life. "Heaven...daily bread...forgive...temptation...evil... amen."

They all made the sign of the cross with their right hands, going first to their foreheads, then to their chests, and then to their left and right shoulders. Zira just followed, the anxiety still buzzing inside her.

"All right, troops, let's move out!" Sammy announced, and they all started walking toward the trail.

Zira and Brianna stayed together in the back.

"What was that prayer?" Zira asked, a tinge of uncertainty in her tone.

"It's called the Our Father, a common Christian prayer," Brianna explained. "Why? Have you never heard it before?"

"Nope," Zira responded. "I felt...awkward back there. Like you were all in on this big secret, and I wasn't."

"I understand why you felt that way; you aren't Catholic. But you should know that God, the Creator of the universe, loves you just as much as He loves any of us."

An inexplicable warm sensation grew in her chest. "Really?"

"Really." Brianna smiled at her.

Zira had barely any idea who this "God" person was, but knowing he loved her made her feel sort of special.

Zira panted as she walked up the inclined dirt path.

"Come on, Soft Serve," Rai shouted down, smirking. "No giving up on us!"

"I'm...not," she breathed. "Just...tired." They had only been walking for twenty minutes, but to Zira, it felt like twenty hours.

"Okay, time for a break," Sammy announced as he moved off the trail to sit on a big rock. He took off his backpack and got out a pack of trail mix. "Anyone want some?"

"Yes, please," Rai said as she excitedly walked toward him.

Zira sluggishly moved to a rock and sat down, taking out her water bottle and peanut butter bar. While drinking her water, Brianna sat down next to her.

"So, you having fun?"

Zira wiped the excess water off her mouth. "Kind of."

"It'll get easier."

Zira looked at her friend like she had three heads. "No, it won't."

"Yes, it will," Brianna insisted, "and even if it doesn't, the view will be so worth it."

"I have my doubts," Zira said as she opened her peanut butter bar and took a bite. "I am glad I came, though. Even if I'm not having the best time."

Brianna nudged her. "You like us. Just admit it."

Zira smiled teasingly. "Maybe I won't."

Brianna rolled her eyes in mock exasperation.

Zira finished eating her bar and put the wrapper in her bag. "I'm gonna check for reception real quick."

Brianna nodded in response and stood. "I'll go get snacks from my dad."

"Sounds good." Zira took out her phone and flipped it open. She texted her mom, and to her surprise, it went through. Her mom texted back a moment later.

Mami: You have reception?

Zira: Yep.

Mami: Good! Now I can track you.

Zira: Mamá!

Mami: I'm just kidding. Well, unless you get lost. Then I can track you.

Zira: Yes, but I won't be getting lost with Brianna and her family helping me. I can't wait for you and Papi to get to know her parents better. I know you'll all get along.

Mami: I bet we will, mija. Okay, I'll let you go now. Have fun and keep me updated.

Zira laughed as she pressed her tiny buttons. *Okay, bye!*

Zira put her phone away, put on her backpack, and then stood. "Okay, I'm ready. Unless one of you isn't, of course; I just—"

"Relax, Soft Serve," Kitty said amiably. "We're almost ready. Thanks for letting us know you are, though."

Zira smiled at Kitty's gentle reply and sat back on the rock. She hoped the rest of the trip wouldn't be so steep, but her sense of reason doubted it.

A few moments passed before Rai approached her, sitting down on the rock next to her. "So, Brianna tells me you're studying French?"

Zira nodded. "Yep. I really like it."

Rai smiled brightly. "So do I! Most people in my class hate it, though."

"What? That's a crime. It's so...elegant."

"I know, right? I don't get it. What's your favorite word in French?"

Zira squinted as she thought. "Probably *étincelles*. It means 'sparkles.'"

"Ooh, that's a good one. I personally love *papillon*. Do you know what that means, or...?"

"Yep! It means 'Butterfly.' That's a good one too. Do you like butterflies or just the word in French?"

"I do like butterflies, actually," Rai answered. "My favorite is the holly blue."

Zira nodded. "I'm more of a crystal person, but bugs can be cool sometimes.... What's your opinion on spiders?"

Rai made a disgusted face. "I don't like them."

"It's true," Faustina shouted from afar. "You should see her when one gets in the house."

Rai glared at her older sister, and then looked back at Zira with an awkward smile.

"You're afraid of spiders?" Zira asked.

Rai nodded shyly. "Mhm. They're just so"—she shivered and made a gagging noise—"creepy. The way they crawl. Ugh. What do you think of them?"

"I think they're misunderstood creatures," Zira answered. "Most are harmless to humans, and actually help get rid of flies and mosquitoes."

"Huh. I didn't know that. But they're still creepy."

Zira chuckled. "Well, they can be to you. But I like them."

Rai smiled sweetly at Zira. "And you're allowed to like them, even if I don't get it."

Zira nodded enthusiastically. "Exactly! I don't understand why people can't get it through their heads that we're all different in small ways. I won't be afraid of what you're afraid of, and you may not like the same food as me, but that doesn't mean we can't get along."

"One hundred percent." Rai nodded with a proud smile on her face. "Hey, if you're not afraid of spiders, what are you afraid of, then?"

Zira's eyes widened. She felt like her breath had been abruptly sucked out of her lungs. *Myself,* her mind whispered, but she shook it off. *I can't tell her that.*

"You okay?" Rai asked, reaching out a hand.

Zira nodded. "Yeah, sorry. I just...don't like talking about my fears." She looked down.

"Talking about them doesn't make you feel better?" Rai asked, cocking her head.

Zira shrugged. "I don't know, but I doubt it."

"I know it makes me feel better," Rai said, "but maybe that's just me. I think you should at least try to talk about them with someone, though. It might help." She shrugged.

Zira looked into Rai's soft, kind blue eyes, and her breath escaped her. *She's trying to help me...but why?*

"I... I will. Maybe."

"Good." Rai smiled.

"All right, let's go," Brianna's dad called out.

Rai and Zira hopped off the rock and walked together to the rest of the group, where Brianna joined them.

Usually, Brianna's presence would make Zira feel more at ease, but not after that conversation with Rai.

"Talk about your fears," Zira repeated in her head. *Why? That won't take them away. It might just make them worse because then everyone I love will know I'm afraid of myself and they'll start fearing me too.* As she argued with her mind, she fought the tears threatening to pour out of her eyes.

Calm down. Don't make a scene. Just relax; you're okay. She took a deep breath and tried to silence her thoughts, but they still whispered the same thing over and over again:

They'd fear you if they knew.

"Come on," Faustina shouted down to Brianna and Zira. "You'll want to see this."

Brianna helped Zira climb the large rocks. The Witch cringed as her friend pulled her right arm; she could feel the stinging of her cut. But when they were finally on solid ground, Zira forgot about all of it. The most beautiful sight ever appeared before her eyes, and she couldn't help whispering, "Wow."

Brianna turned around and saw it too. "Whoa."

The sky was a purplish blue at the top which faded to pink, then to orange, and then to yellow clouds at the bottom. From their elevation, they could also see buildings and rows of trees in front of the colorful sky.

Zira felt like she was floating off the ground. The stinging in her legs became duller, and the only thing she could feel was pure bliss.

"I've never seen anything more beautiful in my life," Kitty said.

"Yeah, it's incredible, isn't it?" her dad asked. "I used to see some mind-blowing sunsets when I was younger. So, I did a bit of research and found this place."

"Wow," Rai said, latching onto his arm. "You spoil us, Dad."

Zira's eyes filled with tears. Tears of wonder and joy. She was speechless, and for some reason, she couldn't stop smiling.

As she looked at the sunset, she was reminded of how beautiful the world was—how humans were only a small part of the universe, which reminded her that she too was only a small part of the universe.

Zira exhaled, feeling her anxiety ease a bit. If she was such a small part of the universe, why should she fear herself?

She looked over at Brianna, who was smiling brightly, and wiped the tears out of her eyes as she stepped closer to her. "Thank you."

"For what?"

"For inviting me here. If you hadn't, I never would have seen this." She looked back at the sunset.

"It's amazing, isn't it?" Brianna asked.

"*You're* amazing," Zira responded.

Brianna's eyebrows shot up in surprise.

"I'm glad I met you." Zira added, looking at her again.

Brianna's face scrunched up with a smile, tears forming in her eyes. "I'm glad I met you too."

Zira looked back at the sunset, a new feeling swelling in her chest. It was a warm, fuzzy energy which connected her to Brianna. It made her smile. They had become closer on this trip, and there wasn't anything Zira wanted more.

A Dark Place

Zira yawned as she opened the front door. It had been a long day filled with so much uphill hiking, not to mention hiking downhill in the partial dark. That part wasn't so bad, though, since Zira liked the dark. Being able to see the moon so clearly made her heart soar. She felt connected to it somehow.

Her mom greeted her from the kitchen. "*Bienvenida a casa, mija*. How was the hike?"

Zira yawned again. "Tiring."

Her mom chuckled. "I can see that. Well, dinner will be ready soon. Then you can go to bed early if you want."

Zira immediately straightened up. "We'll see about that."

"I knew you would say that," her mom said with a wink.

Zira rolled her eyes with a playful smile. "Whatever, *Mami*. I'll be in my room. Call me when dinner's ready."

She dragged herself upstairs, took her backpack off, and gently lay on her bed, sighing. She was finally home. She really did enjoy hiking and spending time with Brianna and her family, but there was nothing like being home.

After a few moments, Zira got up and threw a different black skirt, another pair of leggings, and a dark green quarter-sleeved shirt onto her bed.

As she was putting her shirt on, she noticed that the bandages on her upper arm were *very* red. *Oh, no. I must have reopened the wound on the hike.*

She ran to the bathroom, her green shirt in hand, and locked the door behind her. Taking off the gauze wrap and pads, she was greeted with an open, actively bleeding gash. She put the dirty gauzes on the counter and ran her arm under cold water for a few minutes, then dried it with the same washcloth from before.

After that, she took more medical supplies from the mirror cabinet and stuck the gauze pads on the bandage wrap like last time, then wrapped it around her arm, cringing in pain as the pads pressed on her gash. She ignored it, however, and secured the bandage with medical tape. Once that was done, Zira wrapped the dirty gauzes in toilet paper and buried them in the trash.

Zira put on her dark green shirt and tucked it into her skirt. A moment later, she left the bathroom and belly-flopped onto her bed, wincing a little at the pain in her right arm. Then she snuggled into her mountain of pillows and took a deep, happy breath. Life was good, and despite all her problems, she was thankful to have a big bed, lots of pillows, and friends to call her own.

My friends, she thought, remembering Haven. *Where did she go? I wonder if I'll ever see her again.... I mean, I guess it's not like we were actually friends. She just said she'd be there for me.*

Maybe that just means talking on occasion. Zira could feel a heavy, cold feeling forming in her gut. She shoved it away. *No, I won't let this ruin my good mood. I still have Brianna, and Ember, and Sundown.* Zira sat up on her bed and thought about what she could do to distract herself.

Making a potion always lifts my spirits, she thought. A moment later, she ran to her closet.

Although Zira still felt like a failure at magic, she decided to keep her practice schedule. Practicing *was* helping; she could feel it. And this time around, she wouldn't skip for any reason.

Zira opened her closet and knelt on the floor, grabbing a pink shoebox and a journal whose hard cover featured a beautiful snowy scene with a big purple moon in the center, hiding behind a few thin tree branches. She closed the door, then placed the box and journal on her desk. She opened the former to reveal containers of random plants, spices, rocks, and gems. Potions were made with simple everyday ingredients, and most potions weren't that hard to make. Well, at least the ones Zira had done, anyway.

After grabbing some rubbing alcohol, a cup of water, and an empty cup from the bathroom, she sat down in her chair and cracked her knuckles.

It's time to get mixy. Zira smiled at the familiar saying, but Lynn's voice popping into her head made her waver. She took a deep breath and pushed the increasing pain away. *You're making this potion to feel better, remember?*

Zira grabbed the cup of water and poured some of it into the mixing cup. She did the same with the rubbing alcohol and then reached for a container of gems, but she stopped in her tracks. *Wait, what potion am I going to make?*

She let her arm fall to her desk and considered the question. "Let me see what I made last time." She grabbed the moon journal and opened it, flipping through the messy, scribbled-up pages until she found the first blank one. She carefully read the last filled-in page before it.

"Rosemary, one piece of cattail, a chip of topaz," etc., etc. Looks like I mainly used plants. Maybe this time I should try gems. Those always turn out really pretty.

It was decided. She pushed her journal to the side and opened a container of green gems. Taking the smallest one out of it, she dropped it into the mixing cup, put her right hand over the concoction, and let the energy buzzing inside of her make it glow.

"*Mecola,*" she spoke. This was the spell used to make ordinary things become *magical.*

The liquids in the cup spun around quickly, causing the green gem to dissolve and turning the clear substance light green.

Zira grabbed a pen and scribbled some notes into her journal. She opened another container and took four mint leaves out of it, dropping them into the cup, then put her hand back over the top and reactivated her magic.

"*Mecola,*" she said, and the potion puffed up smoke, making her jump.

The air now smelled strongly of mint. Zira scribbled more notes into her journal, then opened a container of purple gems, freezing when she saw them. She stared at them with wide eyes, unsure she wanted to add them. After all, she had never used them before. She knew, however, that the only way to discover more potions was to try new things—and Lynn had *always* encouraged her to try new things.

Zira took a deep breath. "Here goes nothing." She added two purple gems and reactivated her magic, putting her hand back over the cup. "*Mecola.*"

After she spoke incantation, a whirlpool began swirling in the center of the mixture, and the whole thing glowed a light purple. Zira's mouth gaped in awe.

The whirlpool increased its speed, and the glow brightened. Her eyebrows went up in surprise as she watched, not daring to interfere or else the potion wouldn't come to fruition.

Eventually, a burst of sparkly purple smoke puffed up into Zira's face. She closed her eyes and coughed, wiping the soot off her face. She looked at the ashy remains on her hand; it was as if a million sparkles were floating on her fingertips. Her heart fluttered in excitement. She looked into the cup and was met with a potion of glowing pastel lavender liquid.

While staring at the potion, Zira wrote down some more notes, then carefully took the cup in her hands, moving to sit on her carpet.

She put her hand in the cup and felt the potion. It was...soft? It felt rather like a blanket. *That's magic for you,* Zira thought. *It's weird.* She took her hand out and found that it was completely dry. *Strange.*

After staring at it for a few more moments, Zira decided it was time to put it on the floor. She slowly tipped the cup sideways, her hand shaking with anticipation and anxiety. The liquid slowly came out of the cup with the consistency of mucus. Once enough had fallen out, she tilted the cup upright, and a glob of potion fell onto the floor. There was now glowing purple matter on her carpet.

She sat there and stared at it for a while, but it didn't do anything. Usually after she made a liquid potion, it would quickly show her its purpose. This one was just a blob. Zira almost wondered if she had failed, but it couldn't have been. Failed potions don't glow. Then again, if it wasn't a failed potion, what kind of potion was it?

Zira sighed, scooping the globby potion off the floor and into her hands. Somehow, she managed to gather it all. *Well, that's strange.* She stood and stared at it. "What do you do?"

It did nothing in response. Zira sighed and dejectedly tossed it in the air, but instead of falling to the floor, it just floated there.

"What the...?" She advanced toward it, getting a closer look. Her heart rate picked up as she realized what this meant.

It was an anti-gravity potion.

Zira grinned and took the ball of glop in her hand. She ate it, which made her lips glow a light purple too. It disappeared in a flash, and suddenly, Zira felt icy tingles in her stomach and was ascending into the air, her hair floating all around her.

"I discovered an antigravity potion!" she cheered. She did a little dance in the air, but then her head hit the ceiling. "Ow."

She bounced off the ceiling and started floating toward her window seat. Her arms and legs flailed wildly as she tried to control her flight path.

"No, no, no!"

She stretched out her arms and caught herself on the window frame. She breathed a sigh of relief, then repositioned herself and used her feet to push herself off the window. She quickly realized she was headed straight for her canopy bed. The teenager instinctively activated her telekinesis and froze herself in the air, making her body glow her magic purple color.

She floated herself into a standing position on the ground, then let go of the telekinesis and began floating up again. This time, however, she was prepared. She caught herself with her hands and let the potion guide her body to be flesh against the ceiling. She looked around her room in this new angle. Everything looked the same but also different, as if all her furniture was still there but someone had rearranged it. *This is so cool.*

Once Zira was ready, she repositioned herself and pushed off with her feet, soaring to her window seat like a bird. She stopped herself with her hands and performed the same push-off move. She flew to her bed, angling herself correctly so that she went to the side, and then caught herself on one of the bedposts. She laughed.

"Ah, I missed this," she said dreamily, hugging herself close to the post. *Just having fun with potions like the good old days with...Lynn.* Her smile slowly faded.

Before she could decide where to go next, there was a knock at her door. "Zira, dinner's ready."

Oh, shoot.

"Okay, Mom, I'm coming."

There was a moment of silence.

"Zira, what are you doing in there?"

Her mind blanked, so she said the first thing she thought of.

"Wine!" she shouted. "*Mierda,*" she cursed under her breath, knowing her mother would not be happy about that answer.

"WHAT?" her mom shouted.

Zira knew she was coming in, so she quickly used her magic to lock the door. Her mom attempted to open it, but it wouldn't budge.

"Zira Almira Flores, we do not lock doors in this house. Let me in—NOW."

Zira cringed, anxiety forming in her stomach. She didn't answer, but used her telekinesis to float herself down so she could stand on the floor. She spoke the word that deactivated potions before they automatically ran out. "*Peiomasu.*"

She wasn't ready for all the weight added to her and fell to the ground.

"Zira!"

She quickly got up at her mother's yell, then activated her magic and made all her potion-making items glow. "*Ineldig.*" It all immediately became invisible to the non-magically trained eye.

Zira ran to her door and opened it. She was met with her mother's angry face.

"Zira, what were you doing in here that you had to lock the door for? You know that's against the rules!"

The teenager looked down. "I'm sorry, *Mami.* I just... I was... I'm sorry."

Her mom motioned for Zira to step aside, so she did. Estelle walked into the room. "I'm not leaving until you tell me what's going on. You said something about *wine?*"

Zira walked toward her mom. She focused on her breathing and tried to force her hands from fidgeting. "I swear I don't have any wine, *Mami*."

"Then why did you say that when I asked what you were doing?" Estelle's arms were crossed, and she had an eyebrow raised.

"Because...I didn't want to say what I was actually doing," Zira admitted. She had no idea where she was going with this, but she had to say something.

Her mother cocked her head, narrowing her eyes. "What were you doing, then?"

"I... I was..." She eyed her invisible magic items. *What do I say?* She looked back to her mom, a thought sprouting in her head. She went with it. "I was...making a surprise for you. I didn't want you to see it." *Lies.*

Estelle's face fell, and her arms soon followed. "Oh." She looked down, her cheeks turning a pale pink.

"*Mami*...?"

She looked back up. "I'm sorry, Zira. I shouldn't have freaked out like that. Thank you for telling me the truth. But please don't lock the door again. We trust each other in this house, which means we trust each other not to enter the room unless we give the knocker permission, or unless the knocker has reason to believe we're doing something we shouldn't be. But anyway, let's go eat *cena*."

Zira smiled through the guilt. "You're... You're welcome, *Mami*. And I know. I shouldn't have locked the door. I really am sorry."

"It's okay, *cariñita*. I know you didn't mean any harm. Just don't do it again, okay?"

Zira nodded, and they smiled at each other.

"Come on," Estelle said, extending a hand.

"Let me just put my stuff away properly." Zira walked to the other side of her bed. "I shoved everything under the bed before I let you in."

"Oh!" Estelle exclaimed. "Of course. Just come down when you're ready."

Her mom quickly rushed out and closed the door behind her.

Zira moved to the front of her desk, lighting up her hands and the invisible items.

"*Apairago*," she said, making them reappear. She sighed and started putting them away with a heavy feeling in her chest.

When will the lying end? she asked herself. *I know I promised Lynn to never tell anyone about my powers, but I'm so sick of lying to my parents. Now I have to make my mom a real gift to cover my lie!* She let out a loud, frustrated groan.

"How long will I do this for? All my freaking life? I don't think I have it in me...." Water filled her eyes, and she cried silent, heartbroken tears as she finished putting away her potion items.

After quickly writing down the potion's effects in her journal, she carried it and her shoe box back to her closet, putting it next to the one filled with her already made potions. She grabbed the latter and went back to her desk.

Zira took off the lid, grabbed an empty bottle, filled it with her anti-gravity potion, then corked the bottle and put it with the others.

After she put the box away, Zira took the rubbing alcohol and cups back to the bathroom. She put the rubbing alcohol back under the sink and started pouring the cup of water down the drain. As she did, she studied the water trickling out of the cup and going down a dark hole.

Zira felt like that water. She knew constantly lying to her family would lead to a dark place, and she couldn't help but wonder how many more lies she would tell before she reached that dark place.

The Space Between Us

Zira sat down at the dinner table with her brother and her dad on either side of her.

"*Hola, mija,*" her father said. "How was the hike today?"

Zira smiled. *At least I don't have to lie about this question.* "It was so much fun! I got to know Brianna better, and her sisters too. They're all so cool."

"Sounds like a blast. Was the hiking part fun too?"

"Eh, it could've been better, could've been worse—but the end was so worth it. *Mami,* did you show them the sunset picture I sent you?"

"*Sí,*" Estelle said while putting dressing on her salad. "They both loved it."

"It was the best. I also learned about...someone named God?" Zira said questioningly, unsure if that was correct.

"Oh," her mom said, looking up from her food. "Are they Christian?"

217

"Catholic," Zira corrected. "They prayed before we went on the hike. Brianna also told me God loves me; isn't that cool?"

"Sure," her dad said, shrugging.

"Come on, people—you can talk and eat," Estelle said, sounding flustered. "*La comida* will get cold!"

David laughed. "Okay, okay, relax, *mi reina*. The night is still young."

She took a deep breath. "I'm sorry, can we *please* start eating now?"

"*Sí*," he responded, giving his kids a playful look. "*Cavar en!*"

Both kids dug into their *tortas ahogadas*, a Mexican dish that looked like two pieces of bread with meat and onions in the middle, but made in the right household, it was so much more.

Zira tore a piece of bread off and ate it. The spicy flavor of the salsa made her mouth tingle, and she smiled, embracing the feeling. *Mexican food is the best.*

"So, Patrick, how was your day with *Papi*?" Estelle asked after taking a bite of her salad.

"It was amazing. We went to the movies, then the park, and then we played soccer. I hit *Papi* in the face. He was fine, so it was funny." Patrick giggled, and so did Zira.

Their mother sighed, but a faint smile was on her face. "Why do children find injuries so funny?" She shook her head.

"Because they are funny when everyone is okay," Zira declared, Patrick nodding in agreement. "Anyway, what movie did you guys see?"

"*The Incredibles.* I absolutely loved it. I hope it gets a sequel," Patrick answered, taking another bite of his food.

"Oooh, who was your favorite character?" Zira asked.

"Hmm, probably Dash. He was the little brother."

Zira smirked. "Was he annoying like you?"

Patrick narrowed his eyes at Zira. "I am *not* annoying."

"Are too."

Patrick growled quietly. Their parents looked at each other, unsure of where this was going. Patrick poked a piece of his hot food with his fork and threw it at Zira. It landed on her neck and hair.

"Ow!" Zira shrieked and flicked it away. She glared at Patrick. "Why did you do that?"

"You called me annoying!" he whined.

"Okay, that's enough," their father said sternly, and they both turned to him. Shame began to swell up inside of Zira.

"Patrick, you know you can't throw food at your sister," David continued. "Especially hot food."

"Yes, sir," he responded, looking down to the left.

"And Zira, you can't call him annoying," he told his daughter.

"It was a joke, *Papi.* I was going to tell him, but he threw the food at me first." She looked at Patrick. "Sorry."

"Oh," her dad said, his mouth gaped open a little. "All right then. Let's keep eating."

They continued eating, this time uneventfully. After dinner, they decided to watch a movie together.

Zira got cozy against her dad, and he put his arm around her. Patrick snuggled with their mom, who was on the other side of David.

As the movie started, Zira had a surreal feeling well up inside of her. She looked to the left at all the people she loved most.

How did I get so lucky with this family? She took in the moment. *I never want to leave.*

Zira's eyes fluttered open at the sound of her alarm. She reached over and turned it off. It was now Monday. *Yay,* she thought sarcastically. *Time for school.*

She slumped out of bed and made her way to the bathroom. After doing her morning routine and changing her gauzes, she went back to her room and put on leggings, a navy-blue skirt, and a dark purple quarter-sleeved shirt. She grabbed a black sweater and slipped on her sparkly-heeled black boots. She grabbed her backpack and headed downstairs, where her nose told her that omelets were being cooked.

"*Buenos días, mija,*" her mom greeted with a smile.

Zira yawned. "Good morning, *Mami.*"

She put her bag and sweater on the chair and then sat at the breakfast bar. Her mom placed an omelet with spinach poking out of the sides in front of her along with a fork and knife. The teenager grabbed the utensils and dug in.

A random thought came to Zira as she was eating. "*Mami,* how come you never make Mexican or Welsh-styled breakfast?"

"Because we're not only Mexican and Welsh; there are other countries in our family. Plus, we live in America. I don't want one heritage to overpower another for you kids. Oh, and it's also just easier to make an omelet for breakfast." Her mom shrugged, smiling.

Zira laughed. "Okay, that makes sense. I do love the Welsh and Mexican food you make, though."

"See? It's good to have a connection to both sides of your heritage—mine and your father's." Estelle smiled proudly.

Zira nodded. "*¡Sí!* And, uhhh...*y mae?*"

Estelle's smile widened. "Yep! You got it right."

Zira pumped her fist. "Yes! You need to teach me more Welsh, *Mami.*"

"I honestly don't know much. I had a really hard time learning it back in college. So, I dropped it. But now that I know a second language, I bet it'd be easier to learn. Maybe we can find some classes to take, or we can buy a student book and just learn that way." She shrugged.

"*Suena bien,*" Zira exclaimed.

She finished her meal and grabbed her bag and sweater, heading to the door. "*Adios, Mami. ¡Hasta luego!*"

As Zira stepped outside and made her way down the sidewalk, the cold air stung her skin, making her smile. A few minutes later, the wind picked up, burning her face and hands even more. *I wish I would've worn my heavy coat.*

Zira was greeted with warmth as she entered the school building, letting out a sigh of relief and heading to her locker.

Zira opened it and grabbed her science book. It was a little strange that Ember and Brianna weren't there, but she pushed away the bad feelings and started toward homeroom, which was conveniently in the same direction as Brianna's locker.

Her blonde friend wasn't there either. *Weird,* Zira thought. *Maybe she's just running late? It's not a big deal. I'll see her at lunch.*

Zira continued her walk to homeroom and ran into a familiar red-head. "Hey, Ember!"

"Zira, hi!" They fist bumped. "Have you seen Brianna?"

Zira shook her head. "No, I was going to ask you the same thing."

Ember put a hand on her chin and tapped her foot in thought. "That's weird. Maybe she's sick."

Zira nodded. "Maybe."

At lunchtime, Zira found Ember at their usual table, Brianna's presence still absent.

Panic shot through her, but she took a deep breath and walked over to the red-head.

"Did you find out where Brianna is?" she asked, sitting down.

"She's sick," Ember answered, taking a bite of her salad. "The teacher announced it in one of our shared classes."

"Oh, well, hopefully she feels better soon," Zira responded, relief flooding her. *Brianna's okay. And she didn't disappear.*

Ember nodded in agreement. "Are you gonna go get lunch?"

Zira nodded. She got a lunch tray and then headed toward the food, getting a fruit salad, a slice of pizza, and apple juice. She made her way back to the lunch table.

"So, how was your brother's concert?"

"Eh, the usual." Ember rolled her eyes.

"Sorry, Em, but I really think you're overreacting. Do your parents *actually* favor him over you?"

"Yes, they do! You've met my family; they're so full of themselves. Especially my brother."

"Right," Zira said hesitantly. "Um, don't you think that maybe...you would be happier if you tried to be nicer to your brother? That might help him be nicer to you too."

"I don't think anything could change him. He's a big bully to me." Ember crossed her arms and stuck up her chin. "You wouldn't get it; both your siblings are great."

"Yeah, but at least your brother's still around." Zira muttered, "Destiny barely calls, and she hasn't visited since she left." Anger rose inside of her.

"That's horrible of her," Ember fumed, rolling her eyes. "What a selfish witch with no respect for her family."

Zira flinched and looked at Ember. *Do I sound like that when I talk about Destiny? That's horrible.... Maybe I should say something else so Ember doesn't think of her as a greedy older sister.*

"Hey, I'm sure if she could, she would come visit. She's probably just busy with college and working out her money situation. Plus, I kind of pushed her too hard two years ago. I should go easier on her." She poked at her fruit with her fork.

"Yeah, maybe—or maybe you should be harder on her," Ember suggested darkly.

Zira looked up from her food with her eyebrows raised. "What?"

"Maybe you should give Destiny a hard time when she calls," Ember said in an almost enthusiastic tone. "That might make her feel guilty, and she'll come visit."

Zira's expression didn't change. "Ember, no. I'm not guilt-tripping my sister into coming home. She...hasn't really done anything wrong."

"But she's made you feel betrayed. She deserves to feel bad in return."

Zira continued to stare at her best friend in surprise. "Ember, I don't know what pills you took this morning, but they definitely weren't your allergy pills, because that is *not* happening. Okay?"

Ember glared at Zira. "Oh, come on. Don't act like you don't want to make her feel a little bad."

"Well, do I have that thought every now and again? Yes. But I know it's stupid, so I'm not going to do it."

"Your loss," Ember said with a shrug.

The rest of that lunch went by in silence, and all the while, the two best friends didn't realize how little they truly seemed to know about each other. Strange.

As Long As I Have Me

Zira left her last class of the day and headed for her locker. When she arrived there, a familiar face was standing in front of it, making her insides squirm.

"Hey, Z."

Zira rolled her eyes at the nickname. "You're not allowed to call me that anymore, Raven. Can you please move? I need to get to my locker."

Raven thought for a moment, then shook her head. "Nah, I think I like it right here. After all"—she sneered in a mocking tone— "we can have different likes and dislikes, right, Zira? You know, like...how *you* like ruining people's lives."

"I didn't ruin your lives when I decided to stop being mean. I ruined your lives when I recruited you guys to be in my posse."

"That was the best thing you ever did for us," Raven exclaimed, causing some students to turn their heads.

"It was not."

"Oh, please, Zira. Stop acting like you don't want to tell everyone what you think of them." Raven stepped closer to Zira.

"I don't, actually. So, please move." Zira body-slammed Raven out of the way and opened her locker.

Raven regained her footing and moved around Zira, leaning against a different locker. "I know you miss us. I know you miss what we used to do."

"And what did we used to do?" Zira asked, giving Raven an unamused expression.

"Tell everyone what they needed to hear! We just told them how to make themselves better, but some were weak to the truth—like that girl who killed herself." Raven's tone sounded much happier than it should have.

Zira stared at her ex-friend, the breath taken away from her. "Raven, do you even hear yourself? She wasn't weak to the truth. I'm the one who should've minded my own business and kept my opinions to myself!"

"Oh, come on. You were right about her. She never took any of our advice, and eventually, that caught up to her. You see, some people just—"

Zira slammed her locker shut. "No! I was wrong. I should never have said any of those awful things to her. Why can't you just leave me alone? I don't want to be reminded of my past. It was horrible."

Raven stared at her. "Are you saying we were horrible?"

Panic shot through Zira. "No, I never—"

"It's okay. I get it. We were horrible friends, right? The only thing we did was drag you down, and that's why you left us. But

226

I want you to remember one thing, Zira Flores." Raven slammed her hand into the lockers, causing Zira to flinch. "You're no longer the queen bee. This is our turf now. And we'll do whatever we like, including letting you know what *we* think of *you*."

"Bring it on." Zira narrowed her eyes. "Just know that whatever you say to people will have an impact on their lives. If you go around telling people your unsolicited opinions that hurt their feelings, they may never recover."

Raven laughed a little. "Well, we won't make the same mistake you did when you punched Ivy in the face."

Zira froze.

Raven's laugh turned into something of a cackle. "Feelin' bad, Flores? Well, you should. You've ruined a lot of lives within these walls."

Zira stood strong while Raven was looking at her, but once she walked away, Zira let go. She leaned against the lockers and cried into her hands. *It's all my fault. I don't deserve to be happy. I don't deserve anything good.*

Zira wiped her tears away and took a deep breath. The last thing she wanted was to go to the props meeting where Raven would be. She wanted to clear her head and think quietly for a while, and *then* think about going to the props meeting—but the girls' bathrooms would be crowded at this time. So, she decided to head for the one place she knew would be completely empty....

Zira entered her school's massive theater. She walked to the front and put her bag down, sitting in the seat next to it with a sigh.

Her mind swarmed with memories from her past. *I woke up with magic, burned my brother, caused a girl to commit suicide, destroyed a locker, punched one of my friends in the face, and now I'm trying to learn how to control my powers—but that's not going very well because when I was angry, I used it to dump food on Ivy and Mal!* Zira gasped, trying to still her pounding heart. *I'm scared of myself, and I can't control my powers. Not practicing magic was a terrible idea.* Tears welled up in her eyes, and she let them fall. *I wish I could just be perfect.*

She lifted her hands up and looked at them. *My powers make me more imperfect than anyone else will ever be, and I can't change that.* She let out a choked sob and scrunched up into a ball, crying into her knees while hugging her legs. *Why did I have to get these powers? Why? Why? Why?*

"They're a curse," she shouted, "and because of them, I will never be good enough!" She tried to stand, but she found herself plopping back in her seat, drained. "I'll never be good enough...." She sighed. *What do I do now?*

She looked up at the stage and saw a piano. Her heart froze. *Playing the piano used to make me feel better. I wonder if...*

She sluggishly walked behind the curtain and found the stairs, then ascended them. She walked onto the stage and straight to the piano as if it were calling her. She sat on the backless seat and opened the key-cover. An icy feeling filled her chest, and she took a deep breath, letting her fingers find their way across the keys.

228

Zira started playing the first song that came to mind. The lovely music filled her ears, making her heart lighten. A steady flow of bliss formed inside her and chased away the bad feelings, giving the Witch the sense that, even if for a moment, nothing was wrong anymore.

She sang loudly, her clear voice echoing throughout the theater and making more of her tension melt away.

Zira stopped playing the piano and took a deep breath, smiling as she did. *This feels...really good. I haven't played the piano in months. I forgot how much I enjoyed it.*

She took another moment to let herself truly embrace the happiness inside of her. She kept playing, her fingers flying gracefully over the keys as she continued to sing.

"This is the part when everything makes sense.

This is the part when everything comes to place.

This is the time when we can let down our defense

And just feel...the love around us."

Her fingers moved quicker as the rhythm picked up, and she closed her eyes to feel the music and let the rest of the heavy pit in her stomach melt away.

"There are people in this world that will love you,

And there are people in this world that will hate you too,

But none of that matters if you just stay true...to yourself!

Oh, whoa, oh!"

Zira continued to simultaneously hit the right keys and sing the right notes.

"It doesn't matter what happens as long as I'm still together,

And everything will be okay if I just dance in the weather.

It doesn't matter what will come to be..."

Zira stood up, pushing the piano seat back a little, and then let out the final high note.

"As long...as I...have...me!"

A chill went down her back as she opened her eyes and looked down at the keys, letting herself finish the instrumental.

Zira took her hands off the piano and sat back down, sighing happily. The tension she had from Raven was completely gone; it was replaced with the feeling that she was flying high above everything, similar to how she felt when she finished her hike with Brianna.

"That was amazing!"

Zira jumped and looked at where the voice came from. The drama director, Mrs. Willow, was walking down the aisle, clipboard in hand. Some kids were poking their heads in the room. Zira's anxiety returned as the realization that they had heard her sing hit her.

"I had no idea you could sing, Zira."

She stood up and quickly smoothed out her skirt, walking closer to the edge of the stage. "Um, well, I—I— My mother taught me, and I—I just came in here to—"

"And that piano playing." The drama director touched her lips with her fingers. "Mwah! Perfection. Where did you learn to play?"

"I've been taking piano classes for basically my whole life." Zira laughed nervously. "But, um—"

"And that song. I've never heard that song before. What's its name?" Mrs. Willow asked, her eyes shining behind her circular glasses.

"Oh, my mom wrote that when she was still in college. She did a lot of theater. I, um, just came in here to think. I'm sorry if I broke the rules. I didn't know—"

"Zira, my dear, you did nothing wrong! In fact, I'm very glad you came here. The girl we had pegged for the lead role in the musical dropped out due to unfortunate circumstances. So, we need a replacement. Would you like the role?"

Zira's eyes widened in surprise, and she took a small step back. "I didn't even audition, and you don't know if I can act."

"Well, let's do your audition right now. Show me what you can do—if you're willing."

Zira looked away. "I'm not sure...."

"Come on—do it," shouted one of the kids.

"Don't be a chicken!" another said.

Zira's breath caught. *I can't be known as a chicken. I'm supposed to be good, which means I have to face my fears so others will too.*

She looked back at Mrs. Willow, her brows furrowed in determination. "I'll do it."

"Wonderful!" The director took a paper off her clipboard and walked around the pit to hand it to Zira. "Just read the highlighted lines, dear, and I'll read the other character's part."

Zira read it over and then took a deep breath. "Okay, I'm ready."

She straightened herself out and took another deep breath.

"Why are you all so afraid? It's just a forest," Zira spoke softly but with the slightest annoyance in her voice, and she let one leg hold all her weight. "I'll be fine. I go into different forests all the time, and nothing ever happens."

"But what if the ice witch gets you?" Mrs. Willow said, her voice light and fear-filled.

"She won't; I'll be fine," Zira said with a smile, sticking her head up at the end. "It's not like she's even real."

"You'll be sorry," Mrs. Willow responded.

Zira started walking behind the curtains.

"No, I won't," she said in a singsong tone with a smile.

Mrs. Willow grinned widely. "Perfect! You're perfect, Zira."

Zira came out from behind the curtains, blood rushing to her cheeks. "You really think so?"

"No, I *know* so. I would be honored if you accepted my request for you to be in the play."

Zira smiled, but her insides felt like they were shaking. "I... I don't know...."

"Please? You'd be amazing! And I am not satisfied easily, my dear." Mrs. Willow smiled at her.

Zira looked down, and her face scrunched up with uncertainty. "What about props? I made a commitment to them."

"We'll be okay without you. You need to do this."

Zira looked up and saw Sundown nodding at her from the back of the theater. "Sundown? Are you serious?"

"Yes! So is she." He pointed behind him, and Zira saw a redhead walking in.

"Hazel?"

"Hi, Zira. I think you should do this. I mean...how often do you get the chance to be the lead in a school play? The props department will manage without you." She gave Zira a gentle smile and crossed her arms.

Zira felt something overcoming her, causing her heart to feel lighter and beat faster. Was that...excitement? *I guess I do want to do this.*

"Are you sure?" she asked one last time.

"Yes," Hazel shouted. "Please do this. If not for yourself, do it for her."

Zira's eyes widened and her heart leaped. *For her. The person I…. I guess doing this* would *be a great tribute to her.* She took a deep breath, excitement forming inside her. *It's the right thing. I can feel it.*

She smiled, her eyes misty. She looked up at all the anticipating faces and stopped on Mrs. Willow's. "Okay. I'll do it."

Mostly everyone cheered.

"Go Zira!" Sundown shouted.

Zira smiled and giggled. A new feeling sprouted inside of her as she looked at all the smiling faces. *I did this. I made them happy. I can do good, just like when I saved Sundown.* She looked at her friend again, and then jumped off the stage, sprinting to him. She tackled him in a hug.

Zira could feel him freeze, but he hugged her back a second later.

"Thank you," she whispered.

"For what?" he asked happily.

"For believing in me."

Zira felt him stiffen for a moment, but then he hugged her tighter and picked her up, spinning her around. He put her back down and they separated.

"I am so proud and happy for you, Zira."

Zira's face fell a little from surprise. "Thank you."

He laughed, and so did she.

Maybe I do deserve happiness.

Changing Is A Process

Rehearsals started up that Wednesday. Zira couldn't shake the anxiety about meeting her castmates and starring in a musical like her mother used to when she was younger. She wanted to make her proud and do her name justice.

Her mom's side of the family—the Howells—had a knack for performing. She was not about to let them down—or the girl she had already let down once before—not to mention the whole school was counting on her.

Maybe this wasn't such a good idea, Zira thought as she walked to school, doubt filling her, but then she shook her head. *No, I'm doing a good thing for her. That's what I want to do: be a good person.* She took a deep breath and continued her path, entering the warm school a few moments later.

As Zira walked down the hall, she saw kids glaring at her. Her face twisted in confusion, and fear filled her stomach. *Did I do something wrong?*

She ignored the feeling and made it to her locker. A few seconds after opening it, someone tapped her on the shoulder. When she turned around, her face lit up.

"Brianna!"

"I'm back, Zira," her friend exclaimed, and they both started jumping up and down.

"I'm so glad. I missed you."

"Awww, well, I missed you too," Brianna said affectionately.

Some of the kids passing by glared at Zira, causing Brianna's face to twist in confusion. "What's up with everyone?"

Zira shook her head, the fear returning. "No idea." She put some of her books in her locker and shut it. "Did they post the cast list yet?"

"Yes, but I'm just too nervous to look at it," she admitted with a sheepish smile.

Zira put a hand on her hip. "Come on. Let's go see if you got a part." She linked her arm with Brianna's and dragged her toward the bulletin board. Zira could feel a bit of unease flowing from the arm connected to Brianna, but she ignored it, knowing her friend wouldn't come with her unless she was forced.

They approached a crowd of people, waiting for an opening to sneak in. Once it presented itself, they dove for it. Zira looked at the list while Brianna covered her eyes.

"You got a part!" Zira exclaimed. "You're playing the lead's mom."

Brianna's arms flew down, and she glued her eyes to the list. "I DID? I can't believe it! Aaahhh!"

The kids around them covered their ears at Brianna's loud squeal. A few moments later, she spun around, facing Zira with wide eyes. "ZIRA. YOU GOT THE LEAD?"

"Yep. Surprise?" she said weakly, making jazz hands.

Brianna was about to say something, but a red-head shoving her way into the crowd interrupted her.

"Oh, hey, guys," Ember said. Before they could greet her back, she saw the cast list. "*What?*" She faced Zira. "*You* got the lead? You didn't even try out. What the heck happened?"

Zira laughed nervously. Her eyes looked everywhere but Ember's face, and she noticed that people were staring at them. "Can we move away from the crowd?"

Ember rolled her eyes. "Whatever. Come on." She grabbed her friends' wrists and dragged them down the hall to a quieter spot. "Explain, Flores."

Zira looked at the floor. "So, I didn't try out at auditions...but two days ago, I went to the theater before the props meeting to think. Then I started playing the piano and singing a song my mom wrote. The drama director heard me, and...offered me the part because the original lead dropped out." She forced the brightest smile she could manage.

"But—but you didn't go to auditions," Ember yelled, pointing at Zira. "You can't be picked."

"Well, technically, Mrs. Willow said they had to replace the original girl so she let me audition right then and there," Zira explained awkwardly, not knowing quite what to say. It felt like a cloud was covering her brain, making it hard to think. She was never good with friend confrontation, especially not with Ember.

"What?" Ember said, her tone drenched in contempt. "They didn't think I was right? I'm righter than anyone will ever be."

"Calm down, Ember," Brianna said gently. "Zira got the part fair and square, so you need to let it go. Sometimes we don't always get what we want, but that's okay, because God gives us what we—"

"Oh, save me your Christian bull-crap, Brianna," Ember spat, and Brianna's face shrank. "I don't care what your 'God' thinks of me. I *know* when I'm right."

"Ember, you can't say that to her. She's done nothing wrong." Zira put a protective arm in front of Brianna.

"Whatever." Ember rolled her eyes. "I'm going to class. See you later, 'friends.'" She stomped away, her arms straight at her sides.

Zira turned to Brianna, who was staring at the floor. "Are you okay?"

"Y—yeah. It's just...no one's ever said that to me before." She looked up at Zira; tears were filling her eyes. "Usually, it's about something specific the Catholic Church teaches, but she...she just insulted God. The One who created her. How could she...?"

Zira took Brianna into her arms, and her friend cried on her shoulder. "I'm sorry she said that to you. You don't deserve that."

"It's not your fault, Zira," Brianna said, her voice shaky. "I'm just sorry she got so angry at you. I can't believe your *best friend* would speak to you that way."

"It's okay. She's always had anger issues. We'll both get over our argument, but she *needs* to apologize for being so cruel to you. It's not right." Her tone was firm and unyielding. "And I won't be friends with her until she does."

Brianna stayed silent, and Zira kept hugging her, hoping it provided the comfort she needed.

Zira noticed people were staring at them as they walked by, but for once, she didn't care. The only person she cared about in that moment was Brianna.

Zira was on her way to her first rehearsal. She could feel the buzzing anxiety in her stomach, knowing she was going to meet her co-cast members for the first time—except for Brianna, that is, which provided some little relief.

Thinking about Brianna made Zira's mind wander to their argument with Ember earlier that day. After that conversation, Ember didn't sit with them at lunch or even say "hi" if they passed each other in the hall. It made Zira's blood boil, adding to her already present anxiety.

Why won't she just apologize for being a jerk to Brianna? I don't care whatever she said to me, but Brianna? She insulted her and her religion. Zira let out a frustrated groan. *What if this gets between the three of us? I can't lose Ember again...or the only real friend group I've been a part of.*

The teenager scowled, her fists balling up, but before her anger became too much to bear, an idea popped into her head. *What if you teach Ember a lesson?*

Zira stopped walking. *I could make Ember regret ever yelling at Brianna.* The Witch grinned mischievously. *I could embarrass her in front of the whole school. With my magic, it'd be easy. I could fill her locker with pudding or put a tarantula in there. That would show her.* She smiled in satisfaction, her anger melting away...but then a vague, familiar pit formed in her gut. It felt like when she found out her principal target of bullying died.

Zira's eyes widened. *No! I can't. I can't fall back into my old ways. I have to be better. I won't embarrass Ember. I'm sure we can figure something out. But right now, I need to go to rehearsal in a good mood.*

Zira shortly arrived at the theater door. She did her best to stifle her trembling and entered. Most of the cast were already there, including Brianna.

"Hey, Zira," she called out, waving.

Zira waved back. "Hi." She made her way onto the stage and stood next to her friend. "Has Mrs. Willow showed up yet?"

"Nope, we're still waiting for her," Brianna said. "Oh, and you can put your bag right over there." She pointed to a table covered in bags behind the curtains.

Zira walked over, put her galaxy backpack down, and then joined the rest of her castmates. She studied them: There was a short girl with bright purple hair, a boy with a medium build and ripped jeans, and a black girl with classic short dreadlocks. She smiled at them, excited to get to know these new people.

The small crowd was bustling with conversation, and with Zira lost in her excitement, no one noticed a lady walking in with a bullhorn.

"ATTENTION, PLEASE."

The kids covered their ears and crouched down a little, cringing from the loudness.

"Ow!" the boy in ripped jeans yelled in annoyance, his hands still covering his ears. "What was that for?"

"You all need to pay attention, and how do you get a bunch of tweens and teens to pay attention? You buy a bullhorn." She shrugged.

"All right, all right," she continued. "Everyone, please line up in order of height so I can get you all situated."

They did as she said, and Zira was put second to last on the end for shorter people. The only person who was shorter than her was the purple-haired girl, and Zira probably *was* shorter than her, but she was wearing heels. After all, that's why she wore heels. They made her taller, which helped her to feel fiercer and more confident. Being four-foot-eleven made her feel somewhat small, but she was nonetheless content with her height.

Mrs. Willow walked from shortest to tallest and checked off boxes on her clipboard. Once she stepped in front of the tallest boy, she stopped and turned around. "All right, you are the grandfather." She then pointed to the tallest girl near him and said, "You are a background townsperson."

She continued telling people their parts until she got to Zira.

Mrs. Willow beamed at the blonde-haired teen, a smile forming on her lips. "And you: You play the main character, Marigold. I know you'll bring honor to this school with your amazing talent. You all will." She looked at the other kids, taking in the moment.

"Okay, moving on." She looked at her clipboard and pointed to the purple-haired girl. "You play Marigold's friend, Cecilia."

The girl smiled.

"Okay, let's get this started! First, we'll gather in a circle and read our lines. I will pass out the scripts in a second. You all know who you're playing, so circle up according to the more prominent characters. Zira will sit down first, and then everyone can build around her."

Some of the kids glared at Zira, and she looked away. She knew why they hated her, and she didn't blame them.

Zira sat as instructed. Brianna sat on her left, and the boy who was playing Marigold's father sat on her right.

"Hi," Zira said.

"Hi," he returned, narrowing his eyes at her.

"What's your name again?" she asked.

"Carlos," he answered, tapping the R.

"Oh! You're Latino, aren't you?" Zira asked, her eyes lighting up in excitement.

"That's right—full Colombian blood under this thick skin," he said proudly as he hit his chest with a fist. "Why do you care?"

"Because I'm Latina too. Well, half Latina. My dad is Mexican. I can *rrroll* my *Rrrs* too," she said cheerfully. "I have a bit of an American accent because I've lived here my whole life, though. And my mom is mostly Welsh, so she doesn't have an accent like my dad. That might be the main reason."

He chuckled sarcastically. "Yeah, whatever."

"Is something wrong?" she asked, her face scrunched up in uncertainty.

"Yeah, you've been giving us Latinos a bad name with your behavior," he said angrily. "Or maybe not. You don't even look it. Maybe you're lying."

Zira's eyes glazed over, and she ignored his comment on her skin tone. "I'm sorry. Really, I am. I'm trying to be good now, though, and help people out. That's actually why I'm here." She gestured to the stage. "That's partly why I accepted Mrs. Willow's invitation to be the lead in this play: to give our school a good name." *And so I can make it up to...her.*

"Can you even sing?" he asked skeptically.

"Yes, actually. My mom used to do community theater. I loved it, so I copied her. She saw how I was taking interest and taught me how to sing, dance, and act."

"We'll see." He continued to glare at her. "And by the way, I still haven't forgiven you for the way you've treated me and my friends over the past two years. We'll never forget."

"Oh." She looked down sadly. "I didn't know I targeted you directly. I'm sorry."

"Well, you should be. Because of you, I almost shaved off my hair."

Zira's eyes went wide. "You did?"

"Yes, you called my hair stupid and said I'll always be ugly because of it. When I came home that day, I kept thinking about your insult and stared at myself in the mirror. I decided you were right and got out my dad's shaver. Luckily, my mom came home before I did anything drastic." He looked down to his right, his arms now crossed.

"I'm so sorry." Zira looked down again, fighting back tears. She took a deep breath and looked back at him. "Well, I'm glad you didn't shave it. I like your hair."

"You do?" he asked, grabbing one of his dark curls and looking at it.

"Yeah, it suits you." Zira crossed her arms and smiled as happily as she could.

He looked back at her and squinted. "Well, who cares what you say? My mom tells me other people's opinions don't matter. If you were truly good, that's what you would've said. You're still self-absorbed, and I still don't like you."

Zira sighed and averted her gaze. *Most people here will never see me as good. Why do I even bother?* But then her mind whispered, *because being good helped change Sundown's mind, maybe it will change a few others' too—and that's worth it.*

She smiled. *I can't wait to see Sundown tomorrow. Maybe he could come to my house after school, and we could get to know each other better. I don't practice magic tomorrow, so this is perfect! I'll have to ask him.*

After that rough conversation with Carlos, Zira felt happy knowing she had a friend to fall back on—a friend who had forgiven her for her past mistakes because she had decided to do good—and she owed it all to her little brother. *Thanks, Patrick.*

Mrs. Willow handed her a script, pulling her out of her thoughts, and the circle reading began.

Better

The next day, Zira looked around the cafeteria for Sundown with the intention of asking him about hanging out after school. She wanted to get to know him better and express how thankful she was that he had forgiven her for her past mistakes.

She also wanted to know what happened between him and his teammates after he fell from the climbing rope. Guilt and worry had constantly nagged at her that it was her fault: After all, she was the one who called up to him, exposing his fear to the school.

Finally, Zira spotted him in the lunch line.

"Aha," she exclaimed, speedily walking to him and tapping him on the shoulder. "Hi!"

His face lit up when he saw her. "Hey! What's up? Do you want to cut in front of me?" He squinted at her.

Zira stammered, "Uh— Um, no, I just—"

Sundown laughed. "I'm just kidding, but you can if you want." He stepped back a little and gestured in front of him.

Zira smiled sweetly and took the offer. They both grabbed a tray as the line moved forward.

"So, did you want something other than to cut the line?" Sundown asked.

"Well, actually, I wanted to ask you something," Zira said as she grabbed a salad.

"Oh, yeah? What is it?"

"Do you want to hang out tonight? You could come to my house, or if that's not your thing, we could go to a small restaurant. Or maybe we could—"

"Stop. I'd love to hang out tonight." He smiled. "Your house sounds great. I'll just have to tell my parents and leave on time so I won't be late for dinner."

"Oh, you may be able to stay for dinner—that is, if you like Welsh or Mexican food."

"Are you kidding? I love Mexican food! I'm half Hispanic, you know."

Zira's face lit up in surprise. "You are? I thought you were fully Asian."

He chuckled. "Nope. Half Filipino, half Spaniard. I guess my dad's genes were just stronger than my mom's."

They both laughed.

"So, can you speak *español?*" Zira asked.

Sundown shook his head. "No. My mom didn't speak it when I was growing up because my dad couldn't understand it, but I may ask her to teach me one day."

"You totally should," Zira exclaimed. "It's so fun being able to speak two languages. My mom learned Spanish when she and my dad were dating to better understand him, so both English *and* Spanish are my native languages. I don't have a Mexican accent like my dad, though."

"Eh, probably because of living in America. Either way, embrace who you are."

Zira smiled. "I like that."

"Thank you," Sundown said, grabbing a piece of pizza from the last section in the line. They both paid and turned to face the crowded cafeteria. "Shall we find a table, M'lady?"

"We shall. And...um, stuff."

They both chuckled and proceeded to walk to the table at which she usually sat with Brianna and Ember.

Ember, please come back to me. She was pulled from her thoughts as Brianna said hello to her.

"I see you have a good-looking friend with you," she added slyly.

"Yeah," she agreed, distracted as she kept thinking about Ember. After she sat across from her friend, she realized what she had agreed to. "What? No! Sundown and I are just friends, Brianna."

Sundown's eyes widened. "Wait, she was implying we *like* like each other?"

Zira nodded.

"Well, you *are* pretty."

Zira blushed. "Th—thanks. But...relationships aren't my thing. I still need to figure myself out." She looked down nervously, fidgeting with her hands.

Sundown laughed. "I was just kidding. I'm not looking for a relationship either. I called you pretty because you are pretty...but I meant that in a platonic way."

"Really?" Zira asked, a smile forming. "That's great to hear."

"Anyway, who's your friend here?" he asked.

"Oh, this is Brianna Decker."

"Nice to meet you...Sundown?" Brianna said questioningly as she shook his hand.

He chuckled. "Yep. Sundown is my real name. It's not very practical, but eh, who likes being practical? It's boring."

"Exactly," Brianna said triumphantly. "Finally, someone who gets it."

"I get it too," Zira said. "Do you think I like being practical?"

"Well, I figured not," Brianna responded, "considering those hiking heels." She snickered, then settled down. "But in what way do you get it?"

"Well, being involved in my parents' cultures, for starters. I grew up taking Mexican and Welsh food to school and had a lot of people looking at me weirdly." Zira's mind also flashed to making potions and practicing spells. "And, you know, other stuff."

"Yeah, that makes sense." Brianna took a bite of her mashed potatoes. "So, how did you two meet?"

"We both signed up to do props for the musical," Zira explained. "That's basically the whole story."

"Well, not entirely," Sundown chimed in, shooting Zira a strange look. "First, I didn't like her because she made fu—"

Zira cleared her throat to interrupt him. "Can I talk to you over there for a second?" She twisted to get off the bench and stood.

"Uhhh, sure?" Sundown answered and got up, letting Zira lead him to the corner of the café.

Brianna watched them, her eyebrows knitted together, but she shrugged it off and continued eating her food.

"Don't tell Brianna you didn't like me at first because I used to be the school bully," Zira said in the loudest whisper she could manage, gesticulating wildly.

"She doesn't know?" Sundown questioned, pushing down Zira's hands.

248

"No, of course not. She moved from Arizona and started here right after I decided to be a better person. I don't want her to know about my past. What if she leaves me?"

"Well, if she does, then good riddance. That would make her the problem, not you. You're not doing anything wrong anymore." Sundown shoved his hands into his jacket pockets. "I forgave you. And if..." He suddenly paused and swallowed. "And if *her* cousin can forgive you, she can too."

"I'm sorry," Zira whispered. "You don't know how sorry I really am."

"I have some idea; trust me," he responded, his eyes trailing to the floor. He finally looked back at Zira as he gathered his emotions. "But, like I said, if I can forgive you, so can she."

"I don't know, Sundown.... I'm not ready to face that yet. Can we talk about it later?"

Sundown sighed. "I guess so. But you're going to have to face it eventually."

"I know, but not now. I can't do it right now." Zira's mind flashed to Ember. "Can we just enjoy our lunch?"

Sundown smiled gently at her. "Sure."

They walked back to the lunch table, where Brianna lifted her head and asked, "What were you guys talking about?"

"Nothing important," Sundown told her before Zira could answer.

She shot him a grateful look, though guilt still twisted her gut. She pushed it away and added, "Besides, you two still need to get to know each other."

"And how do you suggest we do that?" Brianna asked.

"I'll ask you both a question, and you both answer," Zira explained. "That should spike some interesting conversation." She folded her arms, satisfied with her quick thinking.

"Let's do it. You ready, Bri?" Sundown asked his new friend.

She looked at him, determination written across her face. "As ready as I'll ever be."

They squinted at each other competitively, ready to see where this game would take them.

"First question," Zira announced. "If you were a pasta shape, what pasta shape would you be?"

"*What?*" they asked at the same time.

Sundown, Zira, and Brianna laughed as they walked to the school exit, the raised flower beds coming into sight on the other side of the glass doors.

"So, you killed her goldfish?" Sundown asked.

"Not intentionally," Brianna answered. "I didn't know goldfish couldn't have potato chips. They look like fish food."

"Yeah, really big fish food," Sundown said, opening the door for the girls. "How did no one stop you for weeks?"

"I wasn't allowed to have potato chips when I was younger because they're messy. So, I ate them when my oldest sister watched me because she didn't care. She would put some in a bowl for me and I would crumble half of them up and put them in the fish tank. I thought I was being nice." Brianna frowned. "Apparently, I wasn't."

Sundown laughed again, then looked to Zira as he let the door close. "Are we still going to your house?"

"Yep. Brianna, do you wanna come?"

"Sorry, I can't. I've got to get home. But have fun, you two!" She waved goodbye to them and walked to the sidewalk, then made a right and disappeared behind trees.

Zira and Sundown went left.

"So," Zira started.

"So," Sundown said back, looking at her playfully.

"What...happened with you and your team after you fell?" she asked hesitantly.

Sundown's eyebrows raised, and he looked down. "Oh."

"Only if you're okay with telling me, of course..." She drifted off, looking down also.

"I am," he told her, "It was okay. They were kind of hurt and mad I didn't tell them I had a fear, though. And...surprised. But they'll get over it. Besides, who isn't afraid of something?" He forced a bit of laughter.

"Definitely not me—" Zira quickly slapped her hand over her mouth after realizing what she had instinctively admitted. *Shoot. Now he's going to ask what I'm afraid of.*

Sundown gave her a weird look. "What...was that about?"

"Oh, um—uh," she stammered.

"Do you...not want me to know your fear?" he asked hesitantly.

"Yeah. Sorry. It's just... not easy."

"But you're trying, and that counts above everything else." He gave her an affirming smile.

She returned the look. "Thanks."

"No problem."

It didn't take them long to arrive at Zira's house. It was two-story with deep green shutters and a wide driveway in front of the garage. Zira used her key to get in and turned on the lights.

"So, what do you wanna do first?" Zira took off her backpack and put it by the door. "I could give you a house tour."

Sundown brightened up at the suggestion. "Sure! Sounds like fun. Where should I put my bag...?" He gestured to the backpack he was removing.

"Oh, here." She pointed to where she put hers.

He put it down, then faced her. "So, where do we start?"

Zira led him to the door by the refrigerator. "Right here." She opened the door and turned on the light. "This is my dad's office. He sometimes works from home so, uh, yeah." There was a couch, a large sectional desk, and a few bookshelves.

"Nice."

Zira led him out to the kitchen, which was only a few steps away. "This is the kitchen."

He looked around and took in the sight, nodding.

She led him to the cove on the other side of the kitchen. "Here's the dining room, where we eat our dinner."

"Dinner's always good."

"And this," she said as she led him into a nearby room, "is the living room! With our many seats."

Sundown touched the couch. "So soft."

"I know, right? I love our couch too, but there is more to see."

"I know," Sundown responded, rubbing his hands on the couch as many times as he could. "Okay, let's go."

She led him to the hallway next to the stairs and pointed to the first door on the left-hand side. "That's the basement. I'll show you down there later." She pointed to the next door on the left. "That's the bathroom." She gestured to the only door on the right. "That's the cupboard." And finally, to the door at the end of the hall. "And that's my parents' bedroom. I can't show you in there." She laughed nervously, and they both left the hallway.

She turned to the stairs. "And these are the stairs that lead to the second floor."

"Oh, really?" he said, smirking. "'Cause I thought they led to China."

Zira rolled her eyes. "Come on."

They went up the stairs, arriving at another hallway with a few doors. Zira immediately led him to her room's door. Before they went inside, however, she told him what the other three doors were for.

"That's Patrick's room," she said, pointing to the door closest to the stairs, then at the next door on that side, "and that's the bathroom." Finally, she pointed to the last door at the end of the hallway, which was in the middle wall. "And that leads to the attic, which is not finished, so we aren't allowed in."

Sundown nodded. "Right."

Zira turned back to her door, grabbed the knob, and opened it. "And this is my room—the best room, if I do say so myself."

"Oh, wow, you've really personalized it!" He gaped as they walked in. "It's so big, too."

Zira sat on her bed. "Yeah, I used to share it with my sister, Destiny, but she left for college two years ago."

"Oh, well, at least you get more space."

"Thanks, but I'd rather have my sister," she said sadly.

There was an awkward silence for a few moments, causing Zira to feel the rope of tension connecting to them again, but she pushed it away and perked up.

"Anyway, that's enough about me. What's your family like?"

Sundown sat opposite Zira on her bed. "The average American family, I guess. I have a younger sister, but that's all for siblings. We get along pretty well, but it can be annoying when I have to babysit her multiple times a week. My parents are not happy when I complain about that. But yeah, that's kind of it. I get along with my parents as well as most teenagers do. So, there's not much to tell there."

"Yeah, my sister and I used to be really close. But when she left for college, we just kind of…lost touch. She calls every now and then, and it's nice, but it's not the same as it used to be…especially since our fight."

"Oh, I'm sorry." There was awkward silence once again, but then Sundown lit up. "Hey, do you have any games we could play?"

Zira perked up. "Yeah, we have lots! Twister, Clue, checkers, chess, and more. What are you in the mood for?"

Sundown thought for a moment. "Do you have any video games?"

"Yep. We have the old NES. There's a, um…hunting game on that, if you're interested…." She looked at him expectantly.

He grinned. "That sounds great. Let's go!"

They left Zira's room and descended the stairs to the basement. Zira turned on all the lights and watched as Sundown's eyes widened in awe once he could see the large, open area.

"Whoa," he breathed. "This place is huge."

"I know, right?"

They were currently in the main basement area, which had cream-colored carpet, a medium-sized TV on a black stand, and plenty of beanbags.

Zira sat on a beanbag that was in the middle of the room. "It was already finished when we moved in. All we had to do was buy some stuff and turn it into a fun hangout space!"

"Well, this is pretty cool," he said, taking a seat in the beanbag next to Zira. "Are we gonna set up the game?"

"Yep." Zira scrambled off her beanbag and went to turn on the TV. She switched the source, changed the game in the NES, and then pulled out two orange guns from a drawer on the stand. She plugged them both in and then handed Sundown one. She turned on the NES, then the game loaded up, and the two friends got in position.

"You ready, Qiu?" Zira asked with a smirk.

"I was born ready, Flores."

She rolled her eyes, and they focused their attention on the screen. After picking a level and difficulty, the game started, and ducks began to appear on the screen.

They both shot at them, repeatedly pulling the triggers on their fake guns. Sundown got some ducks and Zira got some ducks, but they were both feeling something much more important in that moment: sheer, unbridled joy.

As they hunted together, countless thoughts ran through Zira's head. *Am I really playing a game with Sundown? I can't believe we're* actually *friends after everything that's happened. Are we truly friends?* She pushed the negative thoughts away. *No, we're real friends, and we* are *playing a game together. It's just...unreal.* Her breath was taken away from her. *I never thought I'd be playing a game with her cousin. We've come so far.* She smiled, tears threatening to fill her eyes, but she held them in and focused on the game.

After a few minutes, they both started missing more frequently. The ducks would appear and fly away too quickly, causing them to shoot late.

Through all that, though, they both finished with over one thousand points, Zira's being four hundred higher.

Her arms went up in victory. "Yes!"

"Hey, no fair. This is your game." Sundown jokingly turned his back on her and crossed his arms.

"No excuses, Sundown," Zira said teasingly. "I beat you fair and square. I will admit, though, you did better than I thought you would."

He turned around to face her. "Really?"

Zira nodded. "You wanna go again?"

"Sure; why not? Maybe I'll beat you this time."

"In your dreams, Qiu." She picked a different level, and the game started. Zira quickly shot the first duck.

Later that evening, they went to Zira's room and asked each other random questions. It did exactly what Zira had hoped: It sparked up conversation and allowed them to get to know each other better.

"You really don't like bats?" Zira asked, lying upside down on her bed and looking at him.

He shivered. "Nope. They're creepy and probably full of diseases."

Zira shrugged. "They can carry diseases, but regardless, I think they're cool. They only come out at night, they can fly, and they're usually a dark color. They're practically my spirit animal."

"To each their own, I guess. Why do you like black so much anyway? You don't strike me as a goth girl." He took a sip of soda.

"That's because I'm not. Liking black doesn't make you goth, you know." She narrowed her eyes at him playfully.

"I know, but most people I know who like black aren't as...cheery, I guess. It's just interesting to me." He shrugged.

"Well, I like black because it goes with everything, it stands out during the day, and at night you blend in with everything like a chameleon. I just like it. I don't know what else to tell you." She sat up and turned to face him.

"I guess people just like what they like."

"Yeah, I guess."

There was awkward silence for a few moments, that small rope of tension forming again.

Sundown broke it. "It's, um, your turn to ask me something."

"All right." Zira tried to think of something, but the atmosphere of the room had inexplicably changed. She studied Sundown; his eyes were downcast, and he was picking at his fingers.

"Zira," Sundown said, finally looking up, "ask me something."

Her eyebrows rose slightly. "Um, okay.... When's your birthday?"

"My birthday? December 1st. Why do you ask? That's not the usual question you ask during this type of game."

"Just wondering." More awkward silence ensued.

I should say something....

"Sundown, it's your turn to ask me something," Zira said.

"Hey, I'm thinking, okay?! It's not all about you, Zira!" He lunged forward as he spoke.

She stared at him with wide eyes, tears forming in them. "Okay.... I'm—I'm sorry I rushed you."

Sundown rubbed his face, taking a few deep, heaving breaths. "No, I'm sorry. It's just...I got distracted by something we were talking about. And it reminded me of something I've been wanting to ask you."

Zira sat up straighter. "Well, go ahead."

Sundown took a deep breath. "Why did you target my cousin in the first place?"

Zira felt the breath leave her lungs. "Oh...I...I just kind of did. I'm not sure what you want me to tell you."

"I want you to tell me the truth, Zira," Sundown responded firmly. "I know you didn't just randomly pick your main victims. There was something about her you targeted *specifically*. And...I feel like I have the right to know."

"And you do, it's just..."

"Just what?" Sundown asked, standing.

Zira scooted back on her bed so Sundown could sit in front of her.

"I..." She trailed off, looking away as tears filled her eyes again.

"You can tell me. Whatever it is, I can take it." Sundown's voice broke slightly, but his tone remained resolute.

Zira looked up at him and saw that his eyes were also filled with tears. The pressure behind her eyes built and the tears spilled, running down her face. *He needs to know what happened,* her mind whispered, and she knew her inner voice was right.

She took a deep breath. "Sundown, I targeted your cousin because...because she was shy, unconfident, lonely, and seemed afraid even when I just said hi to her. I guess— I guess I saw my former self in her. I saw the scared pushover I used to be, so I thought that if bullying made me gain confidence and friends, maybe it would do that for her too." She hesitantly looked up at her friend. Tears streamed down his face, and he remained silent as he looked at Zira's comforter.

"I don't know why I thought it worked like that. I just did. It was a twisted, messed-up way of thinking, and I have regretted everything I said to her since the day I found out she died. There is no excuse for what I did to her—or anyone else. But I really am sorry." Zira sniffled. "And I understand if you don't want to be my friend anymore. I don't deserve friends. Especially not one as good as you." Zira scrunched her knees up to her face and cried into them, waiting for him to leave and never come back.

"I ignored her for so long," Sundown said after a long moment of silence, making Zira look up. "She tried so hard to be my friend. When we started middle school, I refused to associate myself with her. I was embarrassed. I thought everyone would make fun of me if my autistic cousin followed me around everywhere, but all she wanted was a friend—someone she could count on to be there. I wasn't that person. No matter how hard she tried, I just didn't care." He paused, letting the deafening silence fill their ears for a moment. "I didn't care until it was too late. About a year ago, I noticed how depressed she seemed to be. I started worrying about her. I tried to help her and spend time with her, and I invited her over to hang out. But...she rejected it. She didn't want my help. And now she's gone."

They sat there in the silence of their grief for what felt like hours. Eventually, Zira spoke.

"I'm sorry for what I did to you and your family. I wish I could take it all back, but I can't."

Sundown wiped his face. "Neither of us can. I guess we just have to do better."

Zira exhaled. "I guess so."

He looked at her. "I'm sorry I treated you the way you treated her. You didn't deserve that. No one does." Sundown sniffled, more tears falling from his eyes.

"It's okay," Zira managed to choke out. *I do deserve it.*

They sat in silence for a while, only breaking it when Sundown had to leave.

"I'm sorry our hangout had to end on such a sad note," he said, standing in front of Zira.

Zira sniffled and wiped her nose. "It's okay. I understand."

"I wish the hurt would just magically go away after talking about it," Sundown admitted, "but it doesn't. I don't think it ever will."

"I'm sorry."

"Stop apologizing. It's not entirely your fault. I share some of the blame too." He took a shuddering breath. "But I'll see you tomorrow. Have a good night."

Zira looked up as he opened the door. "You too."

He looked back at her, then closed the door behind him.

A New Love

The next day was the last day of school for the week, and it was also the second rehearsal. Zira was more nervous than excited about it, though. She didn't want to face more hatred toward her, even if she felt she deserved it. However, she was going to power through the rehearsals for the co-writer's sake and the school's sake. She *needed* to do this to prove she was truly good inside, even if the only person to whom she proved it was herself.

As she walked down the hallway, she bumped into someone, and a book fell to the floor.

"Oh, sorry," Zira said, reaching down to grab it, but the other person stepped on it, making Zira flinch back. She looked up and saw a girl with bright red hair and teal eyes staring down at her.

"Hi, Zira."

Zira gulped. "Hi, Ember."

"So, I don't see Brianna with you." She sounded annoyed, and her arms were crossed.

Zira stood. "Uh, yeah. I haven't seen her yet, but I'll probably see her at lunch. Why do you care anyway?"

"Because I may have something I want to say to her." She pressed her lips together and looked away.

Zira's mouth formed an "O" in surprise. "Are you...going to apologize to her?"

"Maybe," Ember said reluctantly. "I haven't decided yet."

Zira nodded slowly. "Okay, well, that's a start. Are you still mad at me, or...?"

Ember sighed and uncrossed her arms. "No. It's all in the past."

Zira smiled. "Great. Well, I guess I'll see you at lunch, then." She started walking past her but then stopped and retraced her steps. "We may have another person joining us for lunch. His name is Sundown. I met him at props."

Ember smiled, but a strange feeling appeared inside of Zira.

"Awesome," Ember said. "I'm so glad we have another person in our group."

Zira let the feeling go and smiled back. "Great. See ya then! Glad we could work this out."

Zira put her lunch tray on the table where her three friends were already seated.

"Hey, guys," she said, sitting next to Sundown. "You got any weekend plans?"

"Not this time," Brianna said, putting her fork down. She rested her head on her hand. "What about you?"

"Nope. What about you two?"

"Well," Sundown started, "I have a game at an opposing school tomorrow. I'd invite you guys, but it's forty-five minutes away and that's quite a drive."

"What time is it?" Brianna asked, sitting up straight.

"Ten forty-five. Why?" Sundown asked.

"Because my parents may let me go if one of my older sisters comes with me." She looked at Zira. "And maybe a friend."

Zira smiled. "My parents would probably be okay with that. You in, Ember?"

"No, I have plans with my family." She rolled her eyes. "But you guys have fun."

"Well, if it works out, that'll be great," Sundown said eagerly, pumping his fist in the air.

"But what about after the game?" Zira pointed out. "It'll still be early."

"We could go over to one of our houses?" Brianna suggested.

"I can't," Sundown said, taking a sip of his drink. "After the game, I have to go to Mutual."

Zira and Brianna stared at him dumbfoundedly, and Ember was too busy eating her food to notice he said anything of importance.

"Oh, it's what my youth group is called," he explained quickly. "People not knowing what that is gets kind of old. I wish there was a way to educate people on different religions, but schools probably wouldn't do a very good job at that." He chuckled nervously.

"That could be nice," Zira said. "My family isn't religious, and I've never had super religious friends, so I don't know about this stuff."

"Yeah," Brianna agreed. "I never learned stuff about other religions. But I know how you feel; that's how I feel when people don't know Catholic terms."

"I assume Catholic is your religion?" Sundown asked hesitantly.

Brianna blinked at him. "I am a Roman Catholic. Roman Catholicism is a Christian religion." Her face twisted into something akin to a glare, but it wasn't quite that. "And you complain about people not knowing what your youth group is called?"

He sighed. "Okay, I guess I'm not good at it either. Maybe we can teach each other?" A soft smile played on his lips.

Brianna beamed back. "I'd like that. But what is your religion anyway? You haven't said."

"Oh, I'm a Jesus Christ of Latter-day Saints. Or in other words, Mormon. But we're not supposed to be called that, though that's what we're more commonly known as."

"Oh, I've met a few Latter-day Saints! They've all been really outgoing and welcoming. I admire them a lot."

"Yep! We're a pretty friendly bunch. Hey Ember, do you have a religion?" Sundown asked.

Ember looked up at Sundown, her mouth full of salad. She quickly swallowed and answered his question. "Well, technically my family is Christian, but I don't associate with that stuff. It kind of feels like they want to stop you from having fun."

"That's not true!" Brianna and Sundown said simultaneously, almost jumping out of their seats. They looked at each other and smiled.

"You first," Sundown said.

"No, no, you."

"Okay," he said with a chuckle. "Religions—well, my religion, anyway—don't prevent you from having fun; they help you realize what true fun is. Following God brings you happiness. As long as you're on His side, nothing can stop you."

Brianna nodded. "Exactly. I didn't realize how similar our religions were. That's really cool."

"It is," Sundown said, amazed.

"Well, I don't know about that," Ember said skeptically. "How do we even know God exists? I mean, it's not like anyone's seen him before." She rolled her eyes.

Brianna stared at Ember, flabbergasted. "You're kidding, right? There are many people who have seen Him. God literally became human to save us from our sins by dying on the cross. How do you not know about this?"

Ember, Brianna, and Sundown continued to have a religious debate for the rest of lunch while Zira just watched and listened, learning as much as she could. Whenever they mentioned God, her heart leapt a little.

I don't exactly know who you are, God. But you seem...kind of cool.

Focus On The Positive

Zira closed the front door behind her and walked down the steps. Brianna and Faustina were already waiting for her in their navy-blue five-passenger Hyundai.

"Hi, Zira," Brianna greeted as Zira entered the back.

"Hi!" she replied. "You ready for the game?"

"Oh, yeah," Brianna said. "Seeing Sundown kick butt playing basketball is going to be a blast."

"No doubt. I've never been to a basketball game before, but I'm excited to experience it."

"You're gonna be a nervous wreck there, Soft Serve," Faustina said, pulling away from Zira's house. "Everyone is going to be screaming and cheering and maybe even throwing food."

"Stop it, Faustina; you know that's not true," Brianna said, giving her sister a glare.

She shrugged. "That's how it was for me in high school."

"Well, we aren't in high school. This is a middle school game. It'll probably be more chill." Brianna crossed her arms and stuck her nose up.

"Maybe, but from what I remember, going to a different school for a game was always risky because you were against the majority. I don't know; maybe things have changed in the last six years since I've been in middle school."

"Well, anyway, it'll be fun—and we can take the competition, right, Zira?" Brianna asked Zira, turning in her seat to face her.

She's wearing that blue jacket again. Why does she always wear that thing?

Zira pushed away the thought and cleared her throat. "Sure."

"Don't be so scared, Soft Serve. It'll be fine." Faustina paused, then added, "Maybe."

"Faustina!" Brianna scolded, causing her sister to laugh. They soon began bickering.

Zira zoned out, thinking about the game. She hoped that it wouldn't be too loud and that she wouldn't experience any confrontation. If it did, she might lose control of her magic again, and this time, there was a high change of someone noticing.

No. That won't happen. I've had a better hold on it since I started practicing. I can and will control it.

The rest of the car ride was filled with music and talking. Faustina kept making comments Brianna didn't like, thus starting various arguments. Eventually, they arrived at the school for the basketball game about fifteen minutes early.

After making their way inside and grabbing snacks, they walked to the bleachers while Zira quickly fled the scene to use the bathroom. But news flash— Zira had never been to this school before, so she needed to ask where it was.

She approached a rather tan man and tapped him on the back. He turned to face her.

"Excuse me, but where is the bathroom?" she asked.

His eyebrows knitted in confusion. "I no speak Inglés."

Zira's eyebrows shot up. *He speaks Spanish. My time has come.*

"*Disculpe, ¿dónde está el baño?*" she repeated.

"Ah," the man exclaimed, his lips forming into a smile. "*Justo al final del pasillo a la derecha.*" He pointed behind Zira.

She nodded. "*¡Gracias!*" She turned and walked down the hall, keeping an eye on the right wall for the ladies' restroom.

That's so cool! I finally got to use Spanish in public with someone who I'm not related to. She jumped and did a little dance of excitement while squealing. "I love being Mexican!"

After a little more walking, she found the bathroom and went inside.

Zira returned to her seat just before the game started, eagerly explaining to Faustina and Brianna how her bilingualism came in handy, but once the players started walking onto the court, a staff member asked her to quiet down. She happily did so. After all, she was here to watch her friend kick butt at basketball.

The referee blew the whistle and dropped the ball. A player on Sundown's team—the Owls—took hold of it first and dribbled it to the opponents' basket. He passed it to a teammate, who then passed it to another teammate. Standing in place, the player who held the ball dribbled it and eventually took a shot. He made it! He pumped his fist in victory, knowing he landed three points for Crystal Sky Middle School.

And so the game began.

It was now twelve-thirty—halftime and lunch time. Faustina and Brianna went to use the bathroom and get hot dogs for the three of them while Zira stayed behind and watched the teams on the sidelines.

After spotting Sundown, who was drinking water near the end of the team's bench, she realized nothing was stopping her from going to see him. She stood and walked down the bleachers, then tapped him on the shoulder.

He started choking on his water, and she hit him on the back a few times.

"You okay? You good?"

He cleared his throat and put down his water before standing up straight. "Yeah, I'm good. But hey, you're here! I'm so happy you're here!" He instinctively hugged her.

Zira's body tensed. His arm was pressing on her gash, sending a jolt of pain down her arm.

He quickly realized what he had done and pulled away. "Sorry."

"It's okay," Zira said, gently putting a hand over the gash. "So, how's the game going? I see you guys are winning."

"Yeah, we are, but we could be doing better. If I hadn't missed that one shot, we'd be up by five, and if Danielle would have blocked that one guy from shooting, we'd be up by seven." He shook his head in disapproval.

"But at least you're winning," Zira countered cheerfully. "I know you can win this thing, Sundown. Just believe in yourself and in your team. Don't focus on the negative; focus on the positive." *Maybe you should listen to your own advice, Zira.* She immediately felt uncomfortable and defensively crossed her arms.

Sundown smiled. "Good advice. I needed that."

Zira opened her mouth to say something else, but the referee blew his whistle, signaling the end of halftime.

Sundown used his thumb to point to the court. "I've gotta go."

"Good luck out there." Zira waved to him as she walked up the bleachers and sat, still waiting for Brianna and Faustina to return.

The opposing team took hold of the ball and quickly dribbled to their net. The player shot but missed, so now Danielle—a tall blonde girl—had the ball. She dribbled down the court and passed it to Sundown, who caught the ball and shot it. It went in without any flaws. Once it came out of the net, the other team quickly retrieved it and dribbled down the court.

Zira watched with intense interest until Brianna and Faustina came up with their food.

"Here's your hot dog," Brianna said as she handed Zira her food and sat beside her. "What did we miss?"

"Sundown scored; they're now up by five points. The second half only just started, though, so it's anyone's game."

The game continued with many thrilling ups and disappointing downs, but at last, Crystal Sky prevailed and won by four points. The team celebrated, and while they were screaming happily, Brianna and Zira ran down the bleachers to congratulate their friend.

"You guys did it," Brianna exclaimed as she jumped on Sundown's back, which caught him off guard, but he quickly recomposed himself and grabbed her legs to support her.

He laughed. "We did. Thank you so much for coming, guys. It really means a lot."

"Of course," Zira said. "You're our friend, and friends are there for each other." *Except Haven,* her mind persisted. *She may not be an actual friend, though—just an acquaintance.* Zira shook off the thought and smiled, focusing again on the present.

"Well, thank you." Sundown looked back at Brianna. "Both of you."

"There's no escaping us, Sunny-boy," Brianna said with a proud grin, leaning her face against his. "You're stuck with us for life."

"I hope so," Sundown said heartily.

"So, what are you two going to do now?" Sundown asked as Brianna hopped off his back and stood in front of him.

"Well, Zira here invited my whole family over for dinner," Brianna said.

"Oh, sounds fun. Have a great time, girls—and thanks again for coming. I do have to go now, though." He gestured to his celebratory but impatient team. "See you Monday?"

"See you Monday," Zira said.

"See you Monday!" Brianna echoed.

"Bye!" Sundown said quickly as he turned away and joined his team.

Brianna smiled at Zira. "Come on. Let's go."

They walked back to Faustina, and the three of them went to the car in high spirits.

Just Let Yourself Feel

"Are they here yet?!" Zira asked, running from the steps. She went too fast and slipped on the carpet, falling on her face. "Ow."

"Oh!" Estelle rushed from the kitchen and helped her daughter to her feet. "Zira, honey, calm down. They're just people."

"They are not just people. They are some of the best people I've ever met. I hope you and *Papi* get along with them." Zira fidgeted with her hands.

"It'll be fine, *mija*," her dad comforted, putting his hands on Zira's shoulders as he came to stand behind her. "I'm sure we'll all get along."

"I hope so," she replied, staring anxiously at the front door. *Come on, Brianna. Show up already.*

As if on cue, she heard muffled voices approaching the door, and then the doorbell rang. Zira jumped even though she was expecting it.

"They're here. Everybody, shut up!"

"Zira, mind your mouth," Estelle scolded. "Don't speak that way in front of the guests." She returned to the kitchen to finish making dinner.

Zira rolled her eyes as she pulled away from her dad and answered the door. "Brianna?"

"We're here!" Brianna exclaimed, joyously throwing up her arms.

Zira laughed. "I can see that. *¡Entra, entra!*" She wiped her sweaty palms on her silky brown skirt, realizing she accidentally switched into Spanish. This was a common occurrence when nervous.

"Huh?" Kitty asked as she walked in. "What did she just say?"

Zira fidgeted with her hands and let out a nervous chuckle. "Oh, I said, 'Come in.' Just...in Spanish."

Brianna's brows were furrowed in concern; she could clearly see the stress her friend was experiencing. "Zira, calm down. We're just here to have fun."

"*Sí, sí, claro.* Let me just go get Patrick, and then we'll start introductions." Zira began walking backward to the stairs, keeping her eyes fixed on Brianna's family, when Patrick spoke from behind her.

"I'm here, Zira."

She shrieked and hit the floor. It took her a moment to recover before standing, fixing her skirt, and turning to face Patrick. *"¡No me asustes así!"*

"*Lo siento,*" he responded in a low voice, his eyebrows knitted together.

275

"You could've given me a heart attack." Zira faced Brianna's family again and took a deep breath to steady her frenzied nerves.

"Relax, Soft Serve," Faustina said as she made her way to the front of the group. "It's only us."

"I'm perfectly relaxed," Zira said despite standing as straight as a plank.

"No, you're not," Zira's father said, looking at her. "*Cálmate, Zira. Son tus amigas.*" He returned the soft smile his daughter was now giving him and turned to Brianna's father as he held out his hand. "David Flores."

He accepted the gesture and shook David's hand. "Samuel Decker. You can call me Sammy. By the way, I noticed you speaking Spanish; where are you from?"

"The great country of *México*," David answered proudly. "I moved here a while back to go to college, which is where I met my beautiful wife, Estelle." He gestured to her as she continued making dinner in the kitchen.

She smiled at them. "Hello!"

They waved.

"I learned English before I came here," David continued, "and after my wife and I got engaged, she surprised me by saying she had been taking Spanish classes behind my back. So, we are a very bilingual family."

Sammy nodded. "That's neat. We're mostly European, but my wife was born in Australia."

"Regina Decker." She stepped forward and shook David's hand.

"*Mucho gusto,*" David said. After seeing Regina's confused expression, he added, "Uh, 'Nice to meet you.'"

She burst into laughter. "I'm just teasing. I know some basic Spanish. But anyway, these are our daughters." She gestured to the four blonde teens near her. "Our oldest is Faustina, then Kitty, then Rai, and then Brianna, who is already friends with your daughter. Otherwise, what are we doing here?"

David nodded and greeted them all. "Well, you already know Zira, but this is our son Patrick."

"Nice to meet you, Patrick," Regina said. "You look so much like your father. You have the same skin color."

"It's a Latino thing." David chuckled. "Well, at least for some. I did know quite a few light-skinned Latinos when I lived in Mexico."

"Looks don't matter," Sammy said.

"What you are does," Regina finished with a smile. "I'm Australian, but we moved to the U.S. when I was young, so I don't have an Australian accent. Sometimes people don't believe me when I tell them where I'm from." There was a glint of sadness in her eyes. "But I'm glad you do."

"I'm glad Brianna believed Zira when she told her she was half Mexican," David replied. "Some people don't believe her— or our other daughter Destiny—just because they're light-skinned and got all the recessive genes, I guess."

"Of course," Regina said. "We know how it can be from experience." She looked into David's eyes with a smile.

David met her and Sammy's gaze as he returned the smile, and the three parents had a moment of understanding.

"Well, anyway, come on in. Let's sit in the living room." He walked around the chair and down the dip in the floor to take a seat on the couch; the two adults and Patrick followed.

"Hey, I'm gonna go show the girls my room," Zira said, pointing at the stairs.

"Okay," her father replied. "Have fun."

Zira smiled, then ran to the stairs. "Come on!"

The Decker sisters followed as Zira led them down the hall to her room.

"Welcome to my place of residence," she said loudly with a flourish.

"Oh, wow," Kitty exclaimed as she walked in after her sisters. "It's beautiful!"

Zira smiled. "I know."

"You have such a big bed," Rai said as she belly-flopped onto it. "And your comforter is so soft!"

Zira giggled lightly. "I knew that too."

Faustina stood near Zira's desk, looking at the pictures on the wall above it. "Who's this?" She pointed at a photograph of a brunette, whose arm was wrapped around Zira.

The Witch walked over, and her eyes fell when she saw the picture. "Oh. That's my sister Destiny."

"I forgot you had a sister," Faustina said thoughtfully, dropping her hand.

Zira looked at Faustina with visible confusion. "My dad literally just said he has another daughter."

"Oh, sorry," Faustina replied. "I...kind of zone out when adults talk. Anyway, um, where is Destiny?"

"College in Idaho. I haven't seen her for over two years." Zira exhaled. "She never visits, and she doesn't call much...but it's fine. She's probably just busy with college stuff."

"She doesn't even come back in the summer?" Rai asked, sitting up on Zira's bed.

I guess they all forgot what I told them last Saturday.

"Nope. She claims, 'it's too far' and 'it's easier to stay in Idaho,' but it still hurts...." Her eyes trailed to the floor, and she fought the tears trying to fill her eyes.

"I'm sorry," Kitty said, approaching her. "I couldn't imagine how hard that is. If Faustina ever did that to us, I'm not sure what I would do."

"It's okay. Really, it is. Plus, it was nice the last time Destiny and I talked. So, you don't need to worry."

"Are you sure?" Brianna finally spoke up. "Because every time you mention her, you get all sad. You said it's okay and you still talk sometimes, but I don't really think it's that simple. I think it means you're trying to convince yourself it's okay."

Zira stared at Brianna in shock and confusion. *How does she see right through me?*

"I... I didn't even realize..." More tears filled her eyes, easily winning the battle of wills. "But I think you're right. I think I am trying to convince myself it's okay—that I'm okay with her being gone—when I'm not."

Brianna looked at her friend, her eyebrows drawn in sympathy. There was a desperation in her eyes, as if she wished she could magically make everything better.

Zira wiped her tears.

"I'm sorry," she said, her voice breaking and her clogged nose deepening her pitch. "I just... I..."

Brianna walked forward and placed her hands on Zira's shoulders. "You have nothing to be sorry for, Zira. You just miss your sister; there's nothing wrong with that."

Zira looked into Brianna's blue eyes, not shying away from her touch. It didn't make her feel uncomfortable this time. *She's right...but then why do I feel guilty?*

"But— But I just—"

"No," Brianna interrupted. "No excuses. You need to let yourself feel what you're feeling."

No one said anything for a moment. Brianna and Zira simply stared into each other's eyes for a long time before Zira broke the silence by crying harder. She slowly put her arms around Brianna and cried onto her shoulder.

Her friend hugged her back and whispered, "It's okay, Zira. Just let yourself feel."

The three other sisters stared at them but eventually went over to join in the hug.

Not all moments with friends needed to be happy, Zira realized, and this was the second time she learned that.

What's Best For Me

"So, girls, how's the musical coming along?" Brianna's dad asked, taking a bite of his chicken mole. It was a Mexican meal consisting of a piece of meat covered in a spicy, deep brown sauce and a side of tangy yellow rice, and he enjoyed every bit of it.

"Oh, fine," Brianna said, then looked at Zira, who was seated beside her at the table.

"It's going...well," Zira said. It wasn't a lie—it was objectively going rather well, considering the school bully was the lead—but it certainly contained an element of deception: It wasn't going well for Zira, though she certainly wasn't about to tell that to everyone. "Not much has happened since rehearsals only started three days ago, but it seems to being going all right."

"That's good," David said with a breath of relief. "Considering what happened with that girl, I was worried everyone would be on edge."

His wife kicked him under the table.

"Ow! What was that for, Estelle?" David looked at her, she nodded toward Zira. He glanced over at his daughter and saw that she was now spaced out, a horrified expression written on her face. "Oh."

Sammy cleared his throat. "What happened?"

"Oh, uh..." David struggled for words. Zira could tell he didn't want to make her uncomfortable, but she knew her father's reasoning, and she understood that Sammy had a right to know what happened at his daughter's school. "A girl...committed suicide."

The Deckers all froze, their eyes widening.

"What?" Brianna exclaimed. "When did that happen?"

"The end of October," David answered. "Right before you guys moved here."

"Oh." Brianna's posture relaxed. "Why weren't we told?"

"I guess since you showed up after they announced it, they didn't feel a need to." David shrugged, picking up his drink.

"Yeah.... But Zira, why did you mention it?" Brianna asked.

Zira swallowed dryly, doing her best not to break down in tears. "I'm sorry. But I... I couldn't."

Brianna's eyes widened, realizing she made Zira feel uncomfortable. "Sorry."

"It's okay." Zira felt a surge of relief. Brianna was so respectful of her boundaries. It was so refreshing to be around someone like that.

Regina cleared her throat. "Anyway...so, what, uh— What do you guys do for fun?"

"We like going to different museums all around the state and going to historical landmarks," David answered, happy to move on from the previous subject. "Libraries are a favorite spot of

Zira's, and we like trying new restaurants whenever we eat out. What do you guys do?"

"We like outdoorsy stuff. Hiking, camping, the beach. You guys should come sometime."

"I did like camping when I was younger," Estelle said airily. She stared ahead with a faraway look, but the glossiness soon left her eyes. "I mean, being outside is generally a healthy thing, but now I only think of all the diseases you can get when you're in nature for an extended period of time. Got an open wound? You're at risk for an infection."

Zira froze, touching her right arm above her gash. Her thoughts were interrupted when Faustina spoke.

"Why would you say that when we're eating dinner?"

Estelle blushed. "Sorry."

Everyone resumed eating for a moment, and then Brianna asked somewhat awkwardly, "So, what games do you guys like to play?"

Patrick perked up quickly. "Clue, Life, Monopoly—lots of board games. And we have an NES downstairs."

"What about charades?" Kitty asked brightly, her short hair swaying as she looked up. "We play charades all the time."

"We aren't really into that game," David replied, shoving a fork full of food into his mouth.

Rai stared at him in amazement. "What? Why not?"

Estelle cleared her throat. "We just...haven't played that game since..." She trailed off and looked at her daughter, who was staring at her half-eaten chicken mole.

Zira threw her fork onto her plate, causing everyone to flinch at the loud clanging noise. "We haven't played that game since Destiny left for college. You know, just because I'm not happy she's gone doesn't mean you can't mention her like she's a normal person while I'm around." She glared at her mom, and her parents glanced at each other.

"Well, all right," David said. "Why don't we play charades after dinner, then?"

"Fine with me," Zira said, her teeth clenched in anger.

"All right, then," Regina said as she nervously clasped her hands. "Sounds good."

No one said anything for a while.

After Estelle found the charades cards, both families gathered in the living room in front of a table labeled with various sticky notes for everyone's card piles. They decided that Patrick would go first since he was the youngest, and that whichever player got five guesses first would win.

Patrick picked the top card off the deck and nodded. He put it down and positioned himself in a fighting stance, then threw air-punches and pretended to block someone else's hits. It was obvious what he was trying to mimic. Zira rolled her eyes.

"Boxing," Kitty shouted before anyone else could.

"Correct!" Patrick pointed at her, then placed the card behind her sticky note as he sat next to Zira. She gave him a slight glare, and he scooted away from her, pursing his lips.

Kitty pumped her fists before standing. She picked up the next card, read it, and put it down, then proceeded to lay on the floor and start...wiggling?

Everyone looked confused, waiting to see what would happen next, but Kitty kept wiggling.

She's a worm. It's so obvious.

Eventually, Rai guessed what Zira was already thinking. "A worm?"

"Yep," Kitty exclaimed.

Shocker. Zira rolled her eyes again. *Idiots.*

It was Rai's turn next. After putting down her card, she began to run in place, periodically looking over her shoulder with wide eyes.

"Being chased?" Regina asked.

Rai kept going, then turned and pretended to stack something.

"A builder?" Faustina guessed. "Or maybe a construction worker?"

Rai continued, turning to face them and once again pretending to stack something. Everyone stared on in confusion until she started to blow furiously into the air three times.

"The three little pigs," her mother said triumphantly.

"You got it!" Rai jumped around in excitement, her medium-length hair bouncing with her. She put the card in her mom's pile.

Regina stood, read the next one, rubbed her hands together in preparation, and then put her right hand out and mimed what looked like cooking in a pan.

"Cooking?" Estelle asked.

Regina ignored her and kept going. She pretended to flip something in the pan.

"Making pancakes," David exclaimed.

"Yes—yes!" Regina placed the card behind his sticky note on the coffee table and sat back on the couch.

David got up and picked a new card. He read it with a confused face, then put it on the table. He took a deep breath and started, putting out one hand in a fist as if he were gripping something. He spun his hand in a circular motion and quickly thrusted it down, then repeated that sequence a few times.

Zira sighed. *He's a witch. What a pathetic imitation. I am so not guessing this one.*

No one else could figure it out, however.

"A thing...you spin?" Regina guessed hesitantly.

"Really, Mom?" Kitty asked.

"Well, *you* try to guess!"

"Fine." Kitty narrowed her eyes, focusing. "I think he's a...baker?"

"What?" nearly everyone asked in unison.

"Hey, this isn't an easy one," Kitty defended.

Yes, it is, Zira returned internally, annoyed.

She looked around at the other players in the room and saw their faces twisted in confusion. She sighed. *Guess I'm taking this one.*

"A witch," Zira said, an unamused expression on her face. "You're a witch."

"Finally, someone got it!" David placed his card in Zira's pile. "Am I really that bad at this game?" He resumed his seat beside his wife.

"Well, no," Sammy answered, "but you could've pretended to brew a cauldron or something."

Zira glared at him while picking up her card.

"Or you could've pretended to read a spell book," Rai suggested, "or maybe fly on a broomstick."

"Or looked evil," Faustina added. "Or hunched over like the—"

"Witches do not do those things," Zira furiously interrupted before she could stop herself.

Everyone stared at her with wide eyes.

"How do you know?" Rai asked, raising an eyebrow.

Zira slapped a hand over her mouth, an uncomfortable sensation of awkwardness crawled up her spine. "Because...the most recent book I got from the library is about the history of Witches and Warlocks. Only the rich had cauldrons, and even fewer flew on broomsticks."

"Well, *cariña*, that book is probably fictional," Estelle said. "And since when did you get so interested in Witches?"

"Since I read a fantasy book about them. I wanted to know more about real Witches, so I found a book on the subject." Zira crossed her arms and stuck up her nose. There wasn't so much as a hint of guilt forming inside her from lying. This Witch misinformation would not be ignored.

"Well, isn't that kind of dangerous?" Rai questioned. "Witchcraft can lead to possession. There have been many accounts of it in the Catholic church."

"It's not witchcraft," Zira yelled, clenching her fists as the energy in her veins spiked. She would admit it to no one, but ever since her mom hesitated to mention Destiny at the table, she had noticed an inexplicable rage sloshing around inside her. Maybe she was angry with Destiny for leaving, or maybe she was angry with her parents for sheltering her from that difficult subject. Either way, the fury flowing through her body wasn't going away anytime soon.

Brianna reached out a hand, slowly moving towards Zira. "Hey, calm down. It's just—"

"NO! I will NOT calm down," she shouted, making Brianna flinch and avert her gaze. "I'm sick of people ignoring me." She looked at her parents. "Especially you two. You've treated me differently ever since Destiny left."

"Zira, I don't like your tone," her mom said sternly, standing. "I think you need to—"

"No, I don't need to do *anything*. You don't always know what's best for me, Mom." Zira felt the energy building, but instead of fearing it, she embraced it, the flow increasing.

"You don't always know what's best for yourself either," Estelle told her with rising anger, staring her fixedly in the eyes.

Zira's eyes welled up with tears, and she could feel the energy inside lighting up her palms. "Don't you think I know that? Because I was insecure, I decided to take it out on other kids! I ended up killing that girl because of what I did!"

The lights flickered with the Witch's thundering voice. She felt part of her magic energy leave her along with the fire for this fight.

Everyone stared at Zira in shock, their eyes wide and their bodies frozen. It was as if they didn't notice the lights.

Zira stared back, fear consuming her mind and soul. *I lost it again.* She looked at the floor and let out a cry, trying to cover her mouth with her hand.

"Zira..." Estelle stepped toward her daughter, her arm outstretched.

The Witch turned her back to her mom.

"I'm sorry," she choked out, then ran upstairs to her room, slamming the door shut. She collapsed on her bed and sobbed into her pillow.

I am a monster.

The Distance Grows

Zira awoke to a knock on her door.

"Zira, are you okay?" came her mom's voice. "Can I come in?"

"No," she responded weakly, but it was so quiet that her mom didn't hear her.

"I'm coming in." Estelle opened the door and saw her daughter's red, puffy face. "Oh, *mija*...." She walked to the bed and knelt in front of her.

The teenager avoided eye contact.

"*Lo siento, hijita.* I didn't know why you were so upset. I would've handled it differently if I did."

Zira's eyes brimmed over with tears. "*Lo sé, Mami,* but I'm the one who should be sorry. I overreacted to the witch stuff, and then I—then I mentioned how I killed that girl. In front of Brianna. I never wanted her to know...the monster I was." *The monster I am.* Zira pushed the thought away. *Not in front of Mami.*

290

"You are not a monster, *mi amor.* You made a mistake. We all make mistakes, and if Brianna can't accept that, then she's not a real friend."

"But I took out all my aggression on others," Zira said, frustrated with herself. "I yelled at that girl because I slipped on a stupid book. I wish I had died when I slipped. Then she would still be here."

"Zira!" her mother exclaimed. "How could you say such a thing? Your classmate's death was a horrible thing. She took her life before it ran out on its own... she wasn't meant to die. But neither were you. There's a reason you're here. And I am so glad you are...but I don't like this kind of talk. Are you sure you're not...?"

"Not what?" Zira asked, repositioning to sit up.

"Not suicidal?" her mother asked, holding back tears.

Zira flinched at the word. "*Mami,* I am not suicidal. I would never try to kill myself." *Even if I should.*

Estelle still looked uneasy. "But...you've been so different these last couple of weeks. Not even just these weeks—you've been different ever since Destiny left. I understand that was a hard change, but now...now you've grown so distant. You keep having breakdowns. I think therapy might be good for you."

Zira's breathing quickened. "No, no therapy." She shook her head in a rapid motion. *Not another person to lie to. Not another person to hurt.*

"But I really think it'd be good for you, *mijita.* You're so...fragile, and I don't mean that in a bad way. I just mean maybe you could be—"

"Perfect?" Zira asked, desire filling her chest.

"No. *Happy*," her mother corrected, looking into her daughter's blue eyes. "No one can be perfect, Zira."

She sighed. *I know, but I wish I could be.* "I still don't want to do therapy, *Mamá*."

"Zira, we have to do something. I can't stand seeing you suffer like this. I'll give you till this Saturday to think about it, but in the end, *Papi* and I will do what we think is best."

Zira looked down. "You're not letting me choose. I don't even have a say."

"Zira, look at me." Estelle placed her hands on her daughter's cheeks, tilting her face up. "Sometimes, you need other people to help realize things, and sometimes, other people know what's better for you. I know you already know this, but I think the reason you don't want to do therapy is because you're afraid. And we can't listen to fear."

Well, duh. I'm afraid to expose my secrets to some random person, but mostly, I don't want another person to lie to.

"I know, *Mami*, but I really don't want to do therapy."

Estelle retracted her hands. "Fine. For now, your wish is granted. But *Papi* and I will talk it over, okay?"

Zira nodded. "Okay."

"I love you, *mija*," Estelle said softly as she stood.

" *Te quiero, Mami*," Zira replied, looking down at her bed.

Estelle leaned over to kiss Zira on the head, then started walking to the door. "Get a good night's rest."

"I will."

"Good night," Estelle said and left the room.

Zira stared down at her comforter. *I guess I'll just have to get used to lying my whole life.* She got out of her bed and checked her phone for messages, finding none from Brianna. *Great. Now she isn't talking to me.*

Zira changed her clothes, proceeding to the bathroom. While brushing her teeth, she realized she hadn't been able to practice magic after the Deckers left.

I already lost control, and that was with keeping the schedule. Should I stay up? That thought sent an uncomfortable feeling down her spine. *No, I'll just practice double tomorrow. I can't go behind my parents' backs and deny curfew. I feel bad enough as it is.*

She finished in the bathroom, quickly changing her gauzes before leaving. She snuggled into her bed, already feeling the pull of unconsciousness.

I wish I could just sleep away all my problems.

Moonlight

The following night, Zira lay awake, staring up at the top of her canopy bed.

Monster, her mind raged. *Killer. She'll never forgive you. You don't deserve her. What if you end up killing her? She hates you now.*

Tear after tear fell from Zira's eyes as fear coursed through every inch of her body like electricity. It felt prickly and hot, like her insides were on fire.

Why did I have to become mean? she asked herself. *Then Brianna would be talking to me, and Patrick wouldn't feel left out, and that girl would still be alive!* She squeezed her eyes shut and turned onto her side, hugging her comforter close. She went into the fetal position and let her body tremble uncontrollably.

My fault, my fault, my fault, her mind whispered incessantly. The phrase engraved into her very being. *Evil...evil...evil....*

Zira had enough. She ripped the covers off her and jumped out of bed, pacing around her room. She could feel the energy and anger flowing through her, wanting to break free.

"Why did I have to be mean?" she said aloud, raking her hands through her hair. "Why did I have to yell at that girl? Why did I have to get so angry last night?" She let the tears fall once again, not knowing when they would stop. "I don't know. I don't know. I *don't know*!"

Zira stopped pacing and let herself feel her emotions. Fear. Anger. Sadness. Grief. Guilt. None of the thoughts racing through her mind helped her. She had to let it out.

A frustrated yell echoed inside her skull and reverberated in her room. She violently flung her hands out and let a little bit of the energy inside her go. The Witch opened her window, letting in the cold November air.

She rushed to her window seat and kneeled on it as she looked out at the cloudless, dark blue sky. The moon was bright and full, casting its silver rays on the world below. Zira stared at it, awe and fear developing inside her as the tears slowed down and the trembling decreased.

So breathtaking...but no one appreciates you. No one says, 'aw, man, it's a moonless night' like they do when the sun is clouded. The sun is hot and causes so many problems, but you...you are cool and light a path for us. I wish I could be like you. I wish I could light a path for people and help them, instead of being like the cruel, hot sun, who causes pain and burning wherever she goes. Why can't I be as bright as the moonlight?

Zira stared at the moon and stars for a while longer. At last, she sighed and closed her window. The tears had stopped flowing, and her racing thoughts were slowing down. The moon always made her feel better.

Why can't I do that for people?

When Zira awoke the following Monday, she quickly checked her phone for new messages, sighing when she saw that it was empty.

Although she hadn't messaged Brianna, she hoped Brianna would message her. Zira had been waiting for Brianna's reply about what happened on Saturday, but there was still nothing.

She probably hates me now. Who would want to be friends with a killer, anyway? She put her phone back on her side table and got out of bed. *Is there any point in doing good anymore? Brianna will probably leave me. Haven disappeared. Why even bother?*

But the image of a freckled face with blue eyes and brown hair appeared in her mind, causing the air to leave her lungs.

No. I can't stop doing good, no matter what. I don't want to be the cause of something so horrible ever again.

After getting ready for school, she went downstairs and found her dad sitting at the breakfast bar, her mom making breakfast on the other side.

"*Hola, princesa,*" her dad greeted with a smile. "*¿Cómo dormiste?*"

"*Bien, supongo.*" Zira sat down near her dad, a stool in between them. "I couldn't fall asleep last night because I kept thinking about everything and how Brianna's been ignoring me. Why did I have to freak out and yell my biggest secret?" The teenager groaned. "She was never supposed to know." She put her arms on the counter and rested her head on them, sighing.

"Well, if Brianna doesn't want to be your friend, that's on her," Estelle said, putting a plate of eggs and pancakes in front of Zira. "We talked about this the other night."

"I know we did, but knowing she's wrong to leave me doesn't make me feel any better. She probably doesn't even believe I'm trying to change." Zira squeezed her eyes shut and put her hands on her head, trying to will the past Saturday night out of existence.

"I know, *mija*," David said, placing a comforting hand on his daughter's shoulder, "but Brianna and her sisters seem like smart young women. I bet they'll forget about it and move on."

Zira picked up her fork and started tearing into her eggs. "I doubt it, but I'll find out today anyway. Hopefully Brianna will sit at our usual spot at lunch."

David took his hand off Zira. "Well, good luck. I'm proud of you for confronting your problems."

"*Gracias, Papi*, but I'm nothing to be proud of. I *killed* someone. I should just be locked away in jail for the rest of my life." She leaned her head on her left hand while using the other to poke at her food.

David and Estelle shared an awestruck look.

"You did not kill someone, Zira," Estelle said firmly. "You yelled at her. Those are two entirely different things."

Zira shook her head imperceptibly, knowing her parents would never see it the way she did. "Whatever you say, *Mamá*."

David and Estelle looked at each other again, worry etched into their expressions.

New Peaces

Zira's gut was filled with dread as she entered the familiar glass doors of Crystal Sky. She didn't want to be at school. Most kids didn't, but her desire for truancy was much more specific. She couldn't stop thinking of all the memories she had from that school—the bad memories. The times she picked on kids for their weight or clothes or for being bad at their hobbies. The times she would yell at others when they picked on her. All the times she scared or intimidated others. And worst of all, the time she yelled at a depressed girl because *she* slipped on a book. All she did was slip, and that caused her to have a temper-tantrum which resulted in disaster.

Zira shook away the nightmares of reality and continued walking to her locker. When she grabbed her necessary items and closed it, a familiar person was standing behind it.

"Brianna," Zira breathed in shock.

"Hey," she said. "We need to talk."

Zira slowly nodded. "Okay."

Brianna began to walk away, and Zira followed. Their path ended at the biggest stall in the girls' bathroom. Brianna locked the door behind her and faced her friend. "Zira, what happened on Saturday?"

Zira stared intently into Brianna's light blue eyes. "Well, I got mad at everyone for spreading misinformation about Witches, and then I yelled that I killed someone."

"Why were you so mad about the witch thing anyway?"

"Because earlier at dinner, my parents hesitated to mention Destiny's name—and after realizing I still wasn't okay with Destiny being gone, I got mad at them for censoring her name. They've done that ever since she left, and I was sick of them acting like I couldn't take the reminder of her absence. Maybe if they hadn't censored it from me all these years, I would be okay that she was gone." Zira crossed her arms. "And when people started spreading Witch misinformation, I couldn't take it anymore, and I snapped. I'm sorry."

"I forgive you," Brianna said softly.

"You do?" Zira looked at her friend in amazement.

"I do," Brianna said, "but what I'm confused about—and a little mad about—is why you didn't tell me about the girl, S—"

"No," Zira exclaimed, jutting out her hands to stop Brianna, who stared in surprise. "S-sorry. I just don't like hearing her name."

Brianna's eyes softened. "Of course. I won't say it."

"Thank you," Zira said as relief washed over her.

"Anyway," Brianna continued, "I want to know why you didn't tell me about her death—and why you didn't tell me you had something to do with it."

Zira put an arm across her body and squeezed her eyes shut.

"Come on, Zira; I just want to know. Please. Some of my old friendships were ruined because of secrets. I don't want that to happen to us."

She looked up at Brianna's pleading eyes. After a moment, she answered, "Okay. I didn't tell you because I was afraid. I was afraid you'd leave me—afraid you'd hate me. You see, I used to rule this school. I used to be the number one bully here, and because of it...that girl is dead."

Brianna's face twisted in concern. "Zira, I would never hate you. And even though you used to be...um..."

"A jerk?" Zira asked abruptly.

Brianna nodded. "Yeah, a jerk—it doesn't matter to me. You're clearly not like that anymore. You stood up to Ivy for me, and that's proof enough."

Zira stared blankly at her friend's kind smile until she smiled too, tears filling her eyes. "Thank you."

Brianna moved closer to Zira. "Of course."

Zira let the tears fall freely, feeling as if a weight had been lifted off her shoulders.

"Is something wrong?" Brianna asked, cautiously reaching out a hand.

Zira sniffled and wiped her eyes. "No. I'm just so happy you forgave me."

"Aw, Zira..." Brianna said no more and took her into a hug.

Zira didn't fight it, but instead returned the embrace. "Will your sisters forgive me too?"

"Trust me: They already have. We Catholics are a 'forgiving however many chances you need as long as you're sorry' kind of bunch."

Zira smiled and breathed a long exhale. She had found new peace within these walls.

After school, Zira and Brianna headed to rehearsal, both in great spirits. Zira's secret was off her chest, and she could tell that Brianna felt peaceful knowing the cause of Zira's unease. It made them closer and their friendship stronger.

Once they arrived, they made their way to the front of the seats where the other students were already gathered. They put their bags on two of the theater chairs and stood there, waiting for Mrs. Willow. Once she arrived, everyone quieted down in fear of her bullhorn, but that plan failed.

"Attention, attention," she shouted through her bullhorn.

The kids groaned.

"Why use that thing when we were already quiet?" a tall boy asked.

"Because it's good to keep you kids on your toes," she answered with a smirk, putting down her items and whipping out her clipboard. "Today, we're going to complete the same tasks as last week, but we're going to use a few props while we do it. Brianna?"

"Yes, Mrs. Willow?" she asked, standing up straight.

"Could you come help me with the props?"

"Of course," Brianna replied happily.

"Thank you, dearie. We'll be back very quickly, so just talk amongst yourselves." Mrs. Willow and Brianna walked to the exit and out of the theater.

Once they were gone, everyone started chatting. Zira didn't feel comfortable trying to join a conversation since no one there seemed to like her, so she took a seat and listened to the noise until a group of boys approached her. She looked up at them nervously.

"Hi," said the boy in front with a mischievous look on his face.

"Hi," Zira hesitantly replied. "Do you want something?"

"Not much...." He trailed off for dramatic effect as he knelt to Zira's height and stuck his face in front of hers. "We just want you to pay for everything you've ever done to us."

Zira's eyes widened, and she put up a wall to block the tears. "What did I do to you?"

The other two boys rolled their eyes while the one in front laughed sarcastically.

"Like you don't know," he whispered loudly. "I ended up in the hospital because of you."

The tears penetrated Zira's wall. "How— How did I put you in the hospital?"

"You told me in seventh grade my skateboard tricks were horrible, and I'd never be good enough. You did that every morning for over a month, and I couldn't take it anymore. I was determined to get your approval. So, I practiced the most advanced trick I could find on the internet on my hilly driveway. You know what happened after that?"

Zira's face was scrunched up to prevent the tears from spilling. "No."

"I made a wrong move and slammed my head on the driveway. I wasn't wearing a helmet, so I got a concussion and went to the hospital." Zira could hear the hatred bleeding through his voice. "Because. Of. *You.*"

He backed away from her and stood up straight again.

Zira wiped the tears from her eyes. "I'm sorry."

He scoffed. "Yeah, like 'sorry' will make up for the expensive hospital bill my mom couldn't afford. Like 'sorry' would make up for the way you teased my friends for their bad grades and weight. And 'sorry' *definitely* won't bring that girl back from the dead."

Zira's breath left her lungs. "Wha— What?"

The boy chuckled. "Did you think word wouldn't get around? Everyone in this school knows you killed that girl. I guess it's time to face the music, Zira, y*ou're* the one being humiliated now. How's that for a change?"

Zira put her hands on her cheeks and began to hyperventilate. "I'm— I'm sorry. I don't know what I'm supposed to do to make it up to you."

The boy's face became cynically thoughtful. "Hmm. Well, maybe *you* should be put in the hospital?" He cracked his knuckles.

Zira couldn't think straight. Her vision was blurry, and her head was spinning. She could barely feel air entering her lungs. "No.... No...."

"'No'? You're going to say 'no' to getting what you deserve? A fraction of the pain you caused us?" He scowled at her. "It's not like I can hurt you here and now anyway. Mrs. Willow will be back in less than ten minutes. But know this, Zira Flores: You're a cruel, heartless killer. I think *you* should've killed yourself, not that poor girl." He backed away from her, cursing at her as he did. He and his gang finally walked away, leaving her frozen in regret and anguish.

Zira couldn't take it anymore. She grabbed her backpack and ran to the back of the stage, then through a door and a long hallway. She took a right at the end of it and sprinted to the exit. She ran down the ramp and to a tree that was by the woods, decently away from the sports fields. She positioned herself behind it so no one would see her if they came out of the theater door. Zira put her bag beside her, curled up her legs, and cried into them.

She knew everything that boy said was true. *She* should've been in the hospital, not him. *She* should've gotten the public humiliation and shame, not everyone else. And *she* should be dead, not the girl.

"AH!" Zira screamed with full force into the evening air.

"I hate myself," she whispered, then broke down again.

During this moment, a girl with short brown hair made her way to the soccer field. She dropped her ball and backed up, getting ready to hit it as hard as she could, but Zira's cries arrested her attention and made her freeze. She looked over at the woods and listened carefully. There came another sob, and then another. She abandoned her soccer ball and walked over to the trees. Zira was too absorbed in her sorrow to notice the girl peering around the trunk, staring blankly at her.

"Zira?"

The Witch jumped and quickly looked up. Even in the low light, she recognized that face. She would never forget that face.

"Haven?"

"Hi, Zira." She gave her a sheepish smile which quickly faded. "Is something wrong?"

Zira hesitated. "Yes, something is wrong." She sniffled. "It feels like everything is wrong some days."

Haven sat down beside her. "Want to tell me?"

"Maybe...but first, I want to know what we are. Are we friends? Acquaintances? People who pop in each other's life every once in a while? What, Haven? What?" Zira wiped the tears off her face as she spoke. "Because you told me you'd be there for me, and then you just disappeared."

Haven sighed. "I'm sorry I disappeared, Zira. I had some...stuff to take care of. But it's over now, and I won't go anywhere again. We are friends, okay? Trust me."

"But I trusted you last time. If we were really friends then, why did you disappear without telling me? Where did you go?" Zira questioned, her volume rising.

"It was just some...private matters, okay?"

"No, it's not okay. I trusted you. You told me you'd never leave me, and what did you do right after that? You left me. So, how can I trust you to not leave me again?" Zira turned away from her.

Haven looked down sadly. After a few moments, she answered, "Zira, I...I used to be just like you. I was a huge bully in elementary school and at my old middle school. The reason...I was like that was because my mom died from cancer. One day, someone made fun of her old bandana that I was wearing, and then they started to make fun of my mom. I got so angry that day...." Haven took a moment to process her emotions.

"The next day," she continued slowly, "I brought a knife with me to school and...I attacked him."

Zira now fully faced Haven, listening intently to her story.

"His mom was so mad that... she pressed charges against me. I went to juvie." Haven looked at Zira, whose eyes were wide and mesmerized with shock.

Haven took a breath and continued, "I was in juvie for a few months. I learned my lesson there. Once I got out, my dad thought it would be best to switch schools, so I came here. There were some legal issues with me getting out, though, so I was taken out of school to go to court, which was hours away from here. Luckily, we won, and now I'm back." She gave Zira a small smile. "So...was that answer good enough for you?"

Zira's mouth was agape. She felt a numb emptiness, but her mind was simultaneously overflowing. "I... I'm sorry. I had no idea that's where you were. I just couldn't figure out where you'd gone, and when you didn't show up, I wasn't sure what to think. And now here you are, and I have to be a rude jerk to you even though you're probably the only person who actually understands what I've been through, and I probably don't deserve you—"

"Whoa, whoa, whoa, Zira, calm down. It's okay. I'm not mad. You had every right to be angry at me. I just disappeared off the face of the earth. I would've been mad too."

Zira wiped her puffy eyes.

"Seriously?" she asked, her voice congested and stuffy.

"Yes, seriously. And look, we both probably don't deserve anyone. But you know what?"

"What?"

"Life was gracious enough to give us a second chance, and that's important to remember. Not everyone gets one. So, let's take this chance together, and be better for it." She stood up and offered Zira her hand with a soft smile.

Zira looked into Haven's deep brown eyes. They were full of sincerity and kindness, but something else was there: a glint of sadness. *Probably because of losing her mother.* Zira felt a pang of empathy. She had also lost her sister, but she knew it was different.

Zira took a moment to recuperate before accepting Haven's hand. Then the brunette pulled her up and they smiled at each other.

Haven let out a breath. "All right, enough of this heartfelt emotions crap. You need to get back to rehearsal."

Zira laughed. "Let me just grab my bag." She retracted her hand and bent over, grabbing her backpack, then walked with Haven to the theater.

And during that walk, both friends felt as though they had found a piece of them that had been missing their entire lives.

Strange Humor

The next day, Zira, Brianna, Ember, Sundown, and Haven had lunch together at school. It was the fullest their table had ever been.

"So, Haven, what do you like doing for fun?" Sundown asked, taking a bite of his grilled cheese.

Haven wiped her mouth. "Oh, well, I play soccer, I read, I like hiking—"

She was cut off by Brianna's enthusiastic shriek. "You like hiking? My family and I love hiking. You should come with us sometime."

Haven had an uncertain look on her face. "Uh, maybe." She chuckled nervously. "I also just like sports in general. There's not much else except..."

"Except?" Sundown repeated.

"Sewing," Haven answered, her face turning red.

Ember burst out laughing. "You like sewing? But you look like a tomboy."

"Well, just because I 'look' like a tomboy doesn't mean I am one hundred percent a tomboy. I've also been told I don't look Polynesian, but I am."

"Oh really?" Brianna asked, making an "O" with her mouth.

"'Ae, one-hundred percent," Haven replied, proudly putting a fist against her chest. "I'm half Native Hawaiian, and half Māori. My dad's from New Zealand."

"That's so cool," Brianna said with a grin. "My ancestors were Australian, so we might be closely connected."

"That's, uh... That's pretty cool." Haven took a sip of her drink and avoided eye contact with Brianna, who didn't reply.

Zira broke the awkward silence. "I'm half Mexican, and I bet you didn't know that."

"I keep forgetting," Ember said with a chuckle. "You just don't look like it. I guess all your mom's genes overpowered your dad's."

Zira chuckled back. "Yeah, maybe."

"It's like the Mexican genes didn't like you."

Zira didn't know why, but that joke stung.

"I'm still Mexican, though," she said defensively. "And there are plenty of light-skinned Latinas."

"Yeah, but you can't deny that you look white," Ember riposted.

"I mean, that's true, but I *am* half Mexican. It doesn't matter what you look like; it matters what you are," Zira added firmly, her voice rising slightly.

"Whatever you say, Z." Ember shrugged.

Zira looked down. *But it's true.*

Her thoughts were interrupted when Sundown started talking. "Well, I'm half Spaniard and half Filipino. Which do you guys think I look more like?"

"Filipino," the four girls said in unison, not even bothering to take a new look at him.

"Yeah, that's what I thought." He looked at Ember. "Hey, Ember, do you know your ethnicity?"

"Nope," she answered distantly, looking down at her lap.

The other four shared a look.

"Ember, what are you doing?" Zira asked, perturbed.

"Give me one sec, Zira."

Zira's face twisted in confusion. She ducked her head below the table and saw a phone in Ember's hands.

"Hey, Ember, you could've told us you wanted to text someone. No need to keep it a secret."

"Oh." Ember looked up. "I always do this at dinner. Guess it's a bad habit."

"So, do you want to talk or not really?"

"Let me just send this one real quick." They waited until Ember put down her phone and looked at them. "So, what's up?"

"I asked if you know your ethnicity," Sundown answered.

"Oh, no, I don't, but I don't really care about that stuff. I grew up here in America; who needs anywhere else?"

"Well, I like Mexico," Zira said.

"And the Philippines is a pretty cool place," Sundown added.

"My grandparents live in New Zealand, so of course I visit them," Haven said, "and I really like it over there."

Ember shrugged. "Eh."

"All right, so what are you interested in, then?" Sundown asked, taking another bite of his hamburger.

"I like fashion."

"What about reading?" Haven asked. "You've got to like reading."

"No, not really," Ember replied, picking up her phone. "I prefer movies."

"Well, what movies are you into?" Brianna asked.

"I really like action and adventure movies," Ember answered, pressing some buttons. "*Jurassic Park* is one of my favorites."

"Ember, if you don't want to talk right now, that's okay," Zira said, "but I'd appreciate it if you'd pick one: the phone or talking." A strange feeling filled her gut. It felt somewhat like hurt, but that didn't make any sense; Ember did nothing wrong.

Ember looked up at Zira. "Who are you? My mom? My brother?" She lifted an eyebrow.

Zira froze. "But you always go on about how annoying your brother is...and how bossy your parents are. I wasn't trying to be annoying or bossy, Ember. I'm sorry."

The red-head burst into laughter. "I'm kidding, Zira—geez. Take a chill pill. Anyway, back to movies." She put her phone away. "Other than *Jurassic Park*, I enjoy *Spider-Man* and most other superhero movies. What about you guys?"

Everyone stared at her blankly, and she knitted her eyebrows in confusion. "Why are you guys looking at me like that?"

"Because you just hurt Zira's feelings with that brother joke," Brianna said.

"And then you didn't even acknowledge you hurt her," Sundown continued.

"That's not cool at all, Ember," Haven finished. "Apologize to her."

"What? Why? She doesn't care. She never has." The redhead turned to her. "Right, Zira?"

Zira nodded her head, but her eyes were fixed on the table. "Yeah...I don't care. It's fine, guys."

"Are you sure, Zira?" Sundown pressed, concern shining in his brown eyes. "You seem tense."

Zira relaxed her shoulders and looked at him. "I'm totally fine." She forced a smile.

Everyone remained quiet. Sundown nudged Zira and stood, nodding his head toward the exit. She got the message and stood also, then followed Sundown to the corner of the room. Brianna joined them.

"What's up?" Zira asked Sundown, facing both of her friends.

"Did Ember hurt your feelings?" Sundown asked, making eye contact.

Zira's eyebrows went up a little and she looked at the floor. "No."

"You're lying," Brianna said. "You always look away when you're uncomfortable. I knew it: You're letting her get away with hurting your feelings."

Zira looked at her friends; the concern in their eyes weakened her will to fight the truth, and she let herself feel the sting in her heart. "You're right, guys. She did hurt my feelings—

twice, actually. But I know she doesn't mean anything by them, so why does it matter?"

"Because they make you uncomfortable," Brianna said, "and she needs to know that so she doesn't make you feel uncomfortable again." She paused, then added, "I know you don't want to cause conflict, but if you don't point it out, things will just get worse. Open communication is the best policy in keeping a healthy relationship."

"Wow, I couldn't have put it better myself," Sundown said, eyeing Brianna. "It's almost like you've been in a similar situation before."

"Yeah, almost.... Anyway, go on, Zira. Tell Ember how you really feel."

"You're right," Zira said, nodding. "Come on."

They all walked back to the table and retook their seats.

"What was that about?" Ember asked before any of them could say a word.

Zira looked straight into Ember's blue-green eyes. "They were right. You did hurt my feelings with those jokes."

Ember looked somewhat stunned. "But you never cared about those jokes before. You know, the ones where we teased each other about being a bad person."

"Well, that was when we were mean. But...now they hurt." Zira looked at her friend with desperate eyes. "Please don't use them anymore."

Ember shrugged. "All right. Whatever you say."

Zira let out a breath of relief. "Thank you. Now we can all move on."

"But she didn't apologize," Haven stated, looking fiercely at Ember.

Zira shrugged. "That's just the Ember way. And technically, she didn't do anything wrong. Hurting my feelings was an accident."

"Yeah, Haven, it's okay," Ember said, placing a hand on Haven's arm. "You can stop acting all tough."

Haven tensed at her touch and shook her hand off. "Okay, firstly, please don't touch me. Secondly, I'm keeping an eye on you." She pointed at her eyes with two fingers, and then at Ember.

Ember scoffed. "That's not very friendly, Haven."

"She's right," Zira told Haven. "Knock it off."

Haven groaned. "Fine."

The following day, Zira found four familiar faces by her locker. A bright smile covered her face as she approached them.

"Hey, guys!"

"Hey," Ember greeted. "Oh my gosh, I love your outfit, Z. Red looks amazing on you."

Zira looked down at her dark-red shirt. "You think so?"

"Hmmm," Haven said, framing Zira's face with her fingers to get a better look at her. "I would say her skin tone is definitely on the cooler side, but it doesn't look bad on her."

"You're kidding, right? Red is perfect for her," Ember said firmly. "It shows power and strength."

Zira cringed at the word "power." *You have no idea what you're saying, Ember.*

"Yeah, but it's a loud color and Zira's not a very loud person," Haven rebutted. "I think cooler tones would complement her better."

"But add too many cool tones and it'll wash out her face! No, she needs reds, yellows, and purples." Ember made a chef's kiss gesture. "Perfect."

"But what if she doesn't like those colors?" Haven retorted, scowling slightly.

"And what if I don't like—"

"Woah, ladies, why don't we let Zira dress the way she wants to?" Sundown interrupted. "Zira, what's your favorite color to wear?"

"Blue," Zira answered happily, turning to open her locker. "Royal blue."

"She has spoken, girls," Sundown said with prayer hands and a slight bow, causing Zira and Brianna to chuckle. "Zira likes to wear *royal blue* the most."

"I could whack you over the head right now," Haven said with a deadpan expression. "You know that, right, Sundown?"

"Oh, yes, I do know that, Haven, but," he said contentedly, putting his arm around her, "I know you won't, because you're really a softy deep down."

Haven lifted her eyebrows, her face still unamused. "Get your arm off me, Sun-Boy."

Sundown swiftly did as he was told, pursing his lips. "Sorry."

Haven smirked.

"Anyway," Brianna said, clapping her hands. "Did you hear, Ember? Our Spanish teacher is sick, so class is canceled today."

Ember's face broke into a smile. "That's great!"

They all stared at her.

"What do you mean by that?" Zira asked.

"I mean, I hate Spanish, so I'm glad class is canceled," Ember explained.

"But it was only canceled because our teacher got sick," Brianna said. "Doesn't that make you less glad?" Her face twisted slightly in confusion.

"Eh, not really. I hate school, so I don't particularly care about the reason I have less of it. Besides, she probably just has a cold or something. She'll be better in a few days."

The four friends exchanged looks.

"I guess," Zira said as she closed her locker. "But you know, learning a new language isn't so bad. I can help you study if you want."

Ember waved her hand in dismissal. "Nah, I don't want help. My parents need to know I'm smart enough on my own for another language."

"There's no shame in needing help, Ember," Sundown said gently. "I needed help learning math last year."

"Yeah, but you don't have parents like mine," Ember told him bitterly. "Forget it. I don't want to talk about them right now. Zira, are you still taking French?"

"Yep! I love it. *Je l'adore.*"

"Wow, I wish I could get into languages like you. You're already bilingual; how many more languages do you need to learn?"

"All of them," Zira answered happily. "I plan on finishing up French and convincing my parents to take me to Paris. I really want to talk to native French speakers and see how good I am."

"Wow, what a show-off," Ember said with a laugh, rolling her eyes.

"Excuse me?" Zira asked, her smile fading.

"I just mean that it's a little braggy to want to go to a different country just to speak their language because you learned it. Are you trying to prove something to yourself?"

Zira looked at her best friend in confusion. "Um, no, it's not braggy, and I'm not trying to prove something to myself. Where did you get that from?"

"All I'm saying is that you're kind of attention seeking." Ember put a hand on Zira's upper arm. "But that's okay. You don't need to be like that. We love you for you."

Zira looked at Ember's hand on her arm, feeling tension emitting from that spot. *Ember's touch didn't bother me when she first reformed, so why does it now?*

"I'm not trying to get attention, Ember." *Seriously, that's the last thing I want.* "And stop touching me. You know I don't like that." She shrugged her off.

Ember laughed. "I'm just kidding, Zira. I know you don't like attention. Geez, take a joke."

The other three stared at her in confusion, but Zira stared at her with hurt.

"Ember, I just told you yesterday I don't like the kind of jokes that make me sound like a bad person, and you *know* I don't like physical touch. Why would you do those things?"

Ember snickered. "The arm touch was part of the joke. Chillax."

"Okay...but what about me not liking those jokes?" Zira asked again, deadpan.

Ember shrugged. "I just forgot. You only told me yesterday. I have a bad memory." She looked at her watch. "Oh, no, I'm gonna be late for class. Gotta go, peeps." She made a peace sign and rushed off.

The four friends watched her leave.

"Well, that was weird," Brianna stated.

"What gave it away, Brianna?" Haven asked sarcastically.

"What's that supposed to mean?" Anger was present in Brianna's tone.

Haven put her hands up. "Nothing, nothing. Just that you don't have to state the obvious, Blondie."

Brianna growled at the brunette. "You know what—?"

Sundown stepped between them. "All right, all right, calm down, you guys. Zira, did you think that was weird?"

Zira's face was twisted in confusion. She opened her mouth to say something, but then closed it and shook her head. "No, Ember's done stuff like this before. It's fine."

"Are you sure?" he asked, raising an eyebrow.

"Yeah, it's fine. No big deal." Zira forced a smile, ignoring the pit in her stomach. *It doesn't feel fine,* her mind whispered. *But it is,* she told herself forcefully.

Sundown gave her an uncertain look but moved on. "All right, cool. We should get to class."

"Agreed." Zira nodded, and then an idea hit her. "Hey, do you guys want to come over after school? I figure it would be nice to spend actual time together as a group instead of just at lunch or in between classes."

"I'll ask my mom, but I'll probably be able to," Brianna said. "Ember would be coming too, right?"

"Yep. I mean, I'll invite her, but there's no guarantee she'll come."

The other three shared an uncertain look.

"Okay, sounds good," Sundown said after a moment of silence. "I'll ask my parents."

"Same," Haven added.

"Sounds like a tentative plan," Zira said enthusiastically. "See you guys later!" She waved as she started walking to homeroom.

You know, you have magic practice tonight. You can't skip again, what if you hurt someone because of it? Or expose yourself? You're not upholding your promise—your aisling.

Zira squirmed a little and hugged her science book over her chest. *I am not breaking my* aisling. *I will practice double tomorrow night. This is important, and I already invited them over.*

But that didn't make the thoughts go away, or the new guilt sprouting in her stomach.

Us Against The World

Later that night at around five-thirty, Zira was waiting for her three friends to arrive. Ember was unable to come. She said she had "a family thing," which didn't surprise Zira. The Johnsons always had something going on.

Regardless, she could feel herself bubbling with excitement and a tinge of nervousness. They hadn't hung out as a group outside of school yet. *I hope this goes well....*

About five minutes later, the doorbell rang. Zira jumped off the kitchen stool and rushed to answer it. When she opened the door, she found all three friends standing on her porch.

"Hey," Haven said coolly, leaning against the side of her house.

"*Hola*— I mean, hi, guys! *Bienvenidos.*" Zira sighed and shook her head. She was back in nervous Spanish mode.

"Hi, Mrs. Flores," Brianna said to Zira's mother, who was setting up a plate of snacks in the kitchen.

"Hello, Brianna," Estelle responded with a bright smile. "It's nice to see you again."

"You too."

"So, this is where you live," Haven said, looking around as they entered. "It's nice. I like it."

Zira giggled nervously. "*Gracias. Me encanta mi casa.*" She facepalmed after realizing that the wrong language came out.

"What did you say?" Sundown asked.

"I said, 'Thank you. I love my home.' Gosh, I really need to stop slipping into Spanish mode whenever I'm excited." She chuckled awkwardly.

"She did it when my family came over last Saturday," Brianna said to Sundown. Turning to Zira, she added, "It's not that bad. Other than the fact no one can understand you...but I'm willing to overlook that if you like speaking Spanish." She smiled.

Zira smiled back, a bad idea forming in her brain. "Well, in that case, *¡bienvenidos, hijos de puta!*"

"Zira!" Estelle scolded from the kitchen.

Zira just giggled, smiling at her mom while her friends looked at each other in confusion.

"What did she say?" Sundown asked, a little panic in his voice.

"Trust me; you do not want to know," Estelle answered, fighting a smile. "All right, let's move on from that and focus on these snacks." Estelle lifted a big tray of various food onto the breakfast bar. There were vegetables, pigs in a blanket, some fried oval things, and a lot of meat and cheese. Zira's friends' eyes widened in awe as they all darted over to chow down.

"Aw, man," Haven said in adoration after she took a bite of a pig in a blanket. "Thanks, Mrs. Flores!"

"Anytime. Now, I have some work to do, so I'm going to my bedroom. If you guys need anything, just yell."

"Okay, we will, *Mamí*!" Zira said as she left and disappeared in the hallway.

After Zira heard her door shut, she turned to her friends. "Okay, who's ready for the best night ever?"

"Uh, I am—duh," Haven mumbled with a mouth full of food.

Brianna glared at her. "Haven, wait to talk until after you've swallowed your food."

"Oh, what? You think this is disgusting?" Haven asked in an annoyed tone. "Well, have some more." She proceeded to open her mouth wide and get in Brianna's face.

She squeaked a little and tried to push Haven away. "Stop it! That's gross."

"Haven, what are you doing?" Zira scolded authoritatively.

Haven retreated and swallowed her food. "She started it. I was just minding my own business, and she had to get all on my case about my manners."

"Yeah, because it's bad manners to talk with your mouth full," Brianna said, narrowing her eyes at her.

Haven scoffed and rolled her eyes. "Who are you? My dad?"

"No, but I wish I were, because then maybe you would—"

"Stop!" Sundown shouted. "There's no reason to fight. Haven can talk with her mouth full if no one cares, but since Brianna does care, you can't do it, okay?"

"Yeah, whatever," Haven agreed in a whiny tone.

"And Brianna," Sundown said, using a tone he likely used with his younger sister. "you could've respectfully told her you didn't like her talking with her mouth full, okay?"

"Yeah, all right," Brianna said begrudgingly.

"Good," Zira said. "Now apologize to each other."

"What?" they asked in unison.

"You heard me."

"Fine." Brianna turned to Haven. "I'm sorry."

"I'm sorry too," Haven replied, avoiding eye contact.

Zira thought she saw a hint of sadness in Haven's eyes. Something like longing? Grief? But what would she be grieving? The teenager decided not to worry about it.

"Good," Zira repeated definitively. "Now, finish your snacks, and then we can go up to my room."

"To do what?" Brianna asked, grabbing a fried thing, which were apparently fried jalapeño poppers.

Zira just smirked. "You'll see."

"Okay, okay, truth or dare, Zira?" Brianna asked through her laughter.

Zira thought for a moment. "Truth."

"What do you think of Ember?" Haven asked before the other two could even get a breath out.

Zira froze. "What?"

"What do you think of Ember Johnson, your best friend?" she repeated slowly.

"I know who you're talking about, Haven."

"Then answer the truth."

"Yeah," Brianna chimed in. "We agreed to answer anything, and that includes this."

Sundown nodded in agreement.

Zira looked around at her friends. "Why do you want to know that?"

"We'll explain after you answer," Haven said.

Zira looked at Brianna, who nodded, causing Zira to sigh as she restrained herself from rolling her eyes.

"All right, um...I think she's pretty cool. I mean, she's been my best friend for almost two years now, so you know. I think she has a good heart, but sometimes it's just...misguided. Like, a little while ago, she asked me if I wanted to get back at my sister for abandoning me. What is up with that?"

The three others shared a look.

"That's pretty weird, Zira," Sundown said.

"I know, right? But besides that, she's a nice person overall. I do think she overreacts sometimes, and I can't believe she made the type of joke I specifically told her to not make— Wait, when did this become me just rambling about Ember?"

Haven looked at Sundown as she spoke. "Since... Since the three of us had a talk about her."

Zira's eyebrows shot up. "Since you guys what?"

"Look, Zira," Sundown said with a sigh, "after you left to go to homeroom this morning, we started talking about what Ember did. She made the type of joke you weren't comfortable with *a day after* you told her you didn't like those jokes anymore. That's not okay."

Zira sat up straighter. "She just forgot."

"I know that's what she said," Haven added, "but I think she can't let go of her old habits. I mean, I heard about what she said to you and Brianna after you got the lead in the musical. It's not cool."

"And you just admitted she tried to get you to take revenge against your sister for unintentionally hurting you," Brianna said softly. "That doesn't sound good. It sounds to me like she's a bad influence."

Zira looked between her friends. "I can't believe this. You really think Ember is no good?"

"I don't know, Zira," Haven answered. "I'm just trusting my instincts, and my instincts say she's bad news. Like she's...hiding something."

Brianna and Sundown nodded in agreement.

"We feel the same way," Sundown said, staring straight into Zira's deep blue eyes.

The Witch sat there and took it all in, waiting a few seconds before responding.

"So, what do you think I should do about it? Should I leave her?"

Sundown put his hands out. "Now, we didn't say that."

"We think you should talk to her," Haven said, "and ask for the truth."

"Yeah, tell her how you're feeling and see what she says," Brianna finished for the group, giving Zira a comforting smile.

Zira thought for a moment. "I will admit she has been kind of different the last couple of weeks. In some ways, I feel like I barely know her now, but I'm not sure I can believe she's lying to me. I mean, she's never done that."

"Are you sure?" Haven asked. "You guys used to be hardcore mean. There's a chance she's being mean to you too."

Zira bit her lip as she thought. "I'm not sure, guys. I'll think about what you told me, but I can't promise I'll talk to her."

"It's okay; take your time," Sundown encouraged. "Just let us know what you decide."

A thought hit Zira. "Is there a reason you guys aren't telling her how you feel?"

"Because...honestly, we're only hanging out with her for your sake," Sundown admitted, rubbing his neck.

"Seriously?" Zira asked, her eyebrows shooting up.

"Well, that, and she won't listen to us," Haven pointed out. "The only person she listens to is you."

"Yeah, whenever we try to talk to her, it's like we don't exist." Brianna sighed sadly.

Zira remained silent, fidgeting with her hands as uncertainty filled her chest.

"Hey, again, it's no rush," Sundown added. "Just tell us what you decide to do, and we'll help you."

Brianna nodded. "Yeah, I mean, I know this is a tricky situation."

"Well, I still don't trust her," Haven said, crossing her arms. The other three gave her a disapproving look, which caused her to add, "But it's okay if you still end up being her friend."

"Yeah, we're here *for* you, Zira," Sundown said affectionately, "not to be against you."

Zira smiled. "Thanks, guys. It means a lot that you care this much."

Brianna perked up. "Of course we do! We're your friends."

"Yeah, it's us against the world forever, Zira, regardless of what happens," Haven said, her forehead creased in determination. "Even if the whole world hated you, we'd still be at your side."

Brianna and Sundown nodded in agreement, and Zira smiled softly at all of them.

"Thank you, guys. That means so much."

After some hesitation, she opened her arms. "Come on; group hug."

The other three shared looks of surprise.

"Seriously?" Haven asked.

Zira nodded. "Seriously. But don't get used to it!"

They all laughed, and then tackled her in a hug.

Buzzing Guilt

The following day was Wednesday, and Zira woke up thinking about what her friends had said the previous night. She tried to shake it off when she went to brush her teeth, but their words kept cycling through her mind.

As Zira removed her old bandages, she noticed a dull pain in her upper arm. She studied her gash and noticed that it was swollen. She sighed. *Whatever. I don't even care anymore.*

A few moments later, she went downstairs and found her mom in the kitchen, making waffles.

"*Hola, Mami,*" Zira greeted as she put her bag on the living room chair.

"*Hola, cariña,*" her mom returned, taking a bite of her waffle. "How did you sleep?"

Zira shrugged, walking over to the breakfast bar. "Okay, I guess. It wasn't too bad. I just keep thinking about what my friends said about Ember. Do you really think they're right?"

Estelle placed a plate of waffles in front of her. "I can't say for sure, Z. All I know is if they think something's off, it's worth looking into."

"Yeah, you're right. I'm just scared of what the outcome could be."

"I know. I would be too. Sometimes, though, it's for the best when we cut people out of our lives. There's not much we can do about it except move on." Estelle paused. "You know, it could be that Ember is a little confused right now. Maybe if you talked to her, it would help patch things up. You never know."

I'm not sure. Zira cut into her waffle. "We'll see."

After classes and before rehearsal, Zira found Ember standing by her locker.

"Oh, hey," she said with a smile, but there was an empty feeling in her gut. Had it been there before?

"Hey, Z," Ember replied. "So, wanna know something amazing?"

"What?" Zira asked as she opened her locker.

"I got us tickets to see our favorite band this weekend!" She shoved two tickets in Zira's face.

Zira squealed and grabbed them. "How did you get these?"

"My uncle works at the venue. He was able to get them for me! So, what do you say? Will you go with me?"

Zira looked up from the tickets. "Uh, duh. Well, I'll have to ask my parents first, but they'll probably say yes." She grinned, but when she looked back down at the tickets, she noticed the location. "Uh, Em, this place is almost *four hours* away. And the concert starts at seven. I'll never be allowed to go to this on a school night." She handed them back to Ember.

"I had a feeling you would say that. Don't worry about it: My uncle said he would take us, rent a hotel room, and drive us to school on time the next morning. So, it'll all work out!"

Zira didn't need long to think about it. "No, my parents would never go for it."

"Okay, time for Plan C. You tell your parents you're sleeping over at my house on Sunday, and that you'll go to school with me. They'll never know where you've been."

Zira's eyebrows rose in shock at her suggestion. "You mean *lie* to my parents—go behind their backs and sneak out of the county?"

"Yes!" Ember said with a giggle. "How fun is that? Getting a taste of freedom."

"Ember, that's *wrong*," Zira said, her eyebrows knitting together. "I can't do that."

The red-head's smile faded. "It's not wrong. It's proving to your parents that you can do fun things and still be responsible. When you tell them you snuck away, they'll be so impressed you managed to get to school on time and respect you even more."

Zira looked at her in horror. "Ember, what has gotten into you? If my parents found out I even left the *neighborhood* without their permission, I'd be in so much trouble."

"Oh, come on; your parents spoil you. You'll totally get off the hook when you tell them what you did, just like when you told them about the bullying thing."

"That was different, Ember," Zira explained defensively, holding back tears. "They knew I had learned my lesson and saw that I was torn up about what I had done." *Why would she even mention that?*

Ember sighed. "Whatever, Z. If you can't go, that's okay. I'll just figure something else out."

"That would be best."

"All right, well, I'm gonna go. I know you have rehearsal. See ya later." She waved and turned, walking down the hallway.

Zira stood there in silence, thinking about Ember's suggestion. *That was a horrible plan. Then again, this is Ember. It definitely wasn't the worst plan she's come up with. But that was back when we were mean; we're good now, and we can't just go sneaking behind our parents' backs and lying to them.* Her friends' words from the night before filled her head. *"Tell her how you're feeling and see what she says."*

Zira looked up and saw that the redhead was still within view. "Hey, Ember."

"Yeah?" she said, turning around.

Zira didn't know what to say. *I have to tell her what I'm feeling. Lying and sneaking is wrong.* She opened her mouth to talk, but then another thought hit her, and she froze. *You sneak around and do Witchery without your parents knowing, and when they ask, you lie to them. You're just as bad as her, if not worse.*

"Hey, you still there?" Ember asked, her tone laced with confusion.

Zira shook herself out of it. "Yeah, I'm still here."

"Everything okay?"

"Yeah, everything's great. I just wanted to say I like your shoes."

Ember looked down at her black velvet flats. They were plain with no embellishments. She looked back up at her friend. "Thanks...?"

"You know, I like them for you," Zira explained, shrugging.

Ember nodded and smiled. "Yeah, they do look great on me." She turned back around and walked away.

Zira pondered what had just happened. *I don't need to tell her what I think of her because I'm no better than she is. I've done even worse things than her. No one's perfect—that's what Brianna told me the Bible says.... But she also told me it says we should move on from our mistakes and start a new life.... Which is what I'm doing...sorta. Ember will never be able to change if she doesn't know she needs to. But then again, does she need to?*

Zira thought about it all for a second: her relationship with Ember, Ember's behavior, and the Bible passage. Then she decided to do something she had never done before.

"God," she started out, looking up at the ceiling, "please help me figure out my relationship with Ember, and what I should do about my Witch powers and my parents. I can't figure it out on my own. I need your help. Amen." A sense of peace overcame her, and she took a deep breath, smiling.

After closing her locker, she headed for rehearsal, though there was still something nagging at her. *I think I know what that is now.*

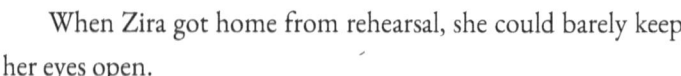

When Zira got home from rehearsal, she could barely keep her eyes open.

"I think I'm gonna go take a nap if that's okay," she told her mother.

"Of course, *mija*. I'll wake you for dinner. We're having cawl."

"Yum," Zira responded. Cawl—a stew with meat and vegetables in it—was a family favorite at the Flores house. It was associated with Wales, where her mother's grandparents were from, which added a rich heritage to the dish.

Zira went upstairs and got comfortable on her bed. She felt so peaceful and relaxed, at least until a thought hit her. *Shouldn't you be practicing magic? You said you would practice double today.* She squirmed, now feeling uncomfortable. *I will later. I'm too tired to do anything except sleep,* she tried to convince herself, but the thoughts still rained down.

She was eventually able to go to sleep, but not without a gaping hole of guilt forming in her stomach.

After dinner, Zira went to her room to complete her schoolwork. She knew she needed to practice magic, but her parents would not be happy if her grades started slipping. If she had time, she tried to reason with herself that she would practice before bed, but she doubted it.

While she was stumped on a math equation, a sudden pain ran through her upper right arm. She grimaced, but she ignored it and tried to focus on math.

After twenty minutes of accomplishing nothing, she took off her sweater and realized the pain was coming from the area near her gash. *Oh, no.*

Zira lightly touched her bandages and winced in pain. "Well, that's not going to work." She debated whether she should take off her gauze and see if there was any more swelling, but she decided against it. She needed to get her homework done and practice magic if she could. Her pain didn't matter anyway.

She finished her homework and saw that it was an hour till bedtime. *I might have time for one spell.... I hope no one hears me, though. It's a bit late to be making a ruckus.*

Zira was about to set everything up when someone knocked on the door.

"Who is it?"

"It's Patrick," a young voice answered.

"Come in."

He entered the room and stood by her bed. "Hey, Z, do you wanna play cards?"

"I would, but..." She trailed off, not knowing what she could say to her brother without lying.

"But...?" he said, making a hand motion for her to continue.

"But..." Nothing else came out. Guilt and anxiety battled for dominance inside her stomach.

"Do you have homework?" Patrick asked.

"No, I finished that," she answered, biting her lip.

"Well, then, why can't you play cards with me?" he asked, a desperate look in his eyes. "You said things were gonna be different...."

Zira's eyes widened, and tears threatened to fill them. She put her hands out. "No, no, no. Things *are* going to be different. I'd love to play cards with you."

He pumped his fist. "Yes! Let's go." He grabbed her hand and dragged her out of the room.

Zira winced as he pulled her right arm, but she pushed down her pain, making sure to not expose herself.

As they played, the pit of guilt in Zira's stomach grew, and so did the buzzing of her magic. *I should be practicing right now...but I couldn't just ignore Patrick like I had done for so long.* She sighed. *Decisions are tough.*

Once they were done, the hour of bedtime had struck. Patrick returned to his room, and Zira crawled into her bed, the buzzing energy inside becoming more noticeable due to the lack of distraction. It felt as though her entire soul were filled with guilt. She *needed* to get herself under control.

The following evening, Zira and Brianna went to rehearsal, where Mrs. Willow had an announcement.

"Great news, everyone. Before rehearsal tomorrow, we're going to have you try on some of the costumes here at the school to see what fits or what needs modifications. They will also be taking your measurements and clothes sizes in case we need something new. How exciting is that?"

Everyone cheered.

"So, tomorrow's rehearsal might run a little late. Please tell your parents, and if you can't stay late, that's fine. Just let me know!" After everyone nodded, she clasped her hands and said, "Okay, let's get today's rehearsal started!"

Zira was fairly distracted during rehearsal. Between the guilt that gripped her and the buzzing inside getting louder, she couldn't focus for the life of her. She promised herself she would practice magic as soon as she got home, but then...

"Hey, Zira," Haven asked after rehearsals, meeting Zira outside the school, "do you...want to come over to my house? My dad isn't home, so I figured it'd be a good time for you to come over."

She wanted to say no, but the hopeful look in Haven's eyes knocked away that option. *She's been through so much; who am I to say no?*

"Sure. Let me just call my parents."

Even as Zira stayed at Haven's house for two hours, laughed, sympathized, and began to understand Haven's missing pieces, she still felt guilty for not rejecting the invitation.

After she got home, she planned to practice magic after dinner, but she had a huge load of homework, and then the rest of her family wanted to watch a movie. So, she did that instead, then went to bed.

What happened to practicing magic? You're not fulfilling your aisling, Zira's mind said as she drifted off to sleep, the buzzing of her magic becoming more profound along with the guilt.

Trouble

The next morning, Zira was immediately greeted with a sharp pain in her right arm. *Oh, whatever. I don't have time for this. I need to practice magic when I get home. It has been way too long. First school and then rehearsal—those are part of my* aisling *too.*

As Zira walked around school, she could feel a familiar gripping uneasiness in her gut. She kept looking over her shoulder and jumping at the slightest sound, which made it difficult to focus in class. She barely even noticed that Ember didn't sit with them at lunch.

What's bothering me? she asked herself, trying to dig deeply and gauge her emotions, but all she could recognize was anxiety and guilt. And the buzzing of her magic. It was now more noticeable than it had been in weeks. *It must be because I haven't been practicing.*

At rehearsals, Zira was the first student to give her clothing size and be measured. She was excused and headed to the theater.

Although she knew she wouldn't be alone for long, the thought of quietude comforted her as if she could already feel the peace.

When she opened the door, she found Ember standing on the stage, singing her heart out.

"Ember, what are you doing?" Zira asked once she was close enough for her to hear.

Her friend looked down with a beam. "Just practicing my awesome singing and waiting for you to get back. I knew you'd get lonely in here by yourself."

"What are you talking about? More kids will come in here soon," Zira said as she made her way onto the stage, stopping a fair distance from Ember.

"No, they won't. I overheard people talking at lunch—you know, since I sat at a different table—and a lot of theater kids were talking about waiting for everyone to finish so they wouldn't be stuck in here with you." The red-head sat, a glint of something in her eye that Zira couldn't place.

Zira's mouth gaped open. "What? Why?"

"Because they're sick of you. They hate that you're the lead. Honestly, they want nothing to do with you." Ember let out a short laugh. "It's kind of funny."

"How is it funny? I'm hated by everyone! They never learned that I changed." Zira's eyes welled up with tears.

Ember shrugged. "Yeah, well, I guess that's what happens when you try to reform. No one believes you. So...what's even the point?"

"What are you talking about? No one has done this to *you* since you reformed. That's proof people may trust me one day."

"Well, I have had some people try and tell me off. But most go away after I tell them what's really going on."

"And what's 'really going on?'"

"That I never reformed," she said with a small smile.

Zira's eyes widened, her magical energy spiking. "What?"

"I never reformed, Zira. I was pretending for you so you'd come back to leading this school after you found out people would never treat you differently." She smiled mischievously.

"What? Ember, that's sick! I thought you were trying to be my friend...."

The red-head stood, her fists balling "Don't you see? I *was* being your friend. I was trying to show you who you really are: the most powerful person in this school."

More tears filled Zira's eyes. "I don't want to be the most powerful person in this school. Even if people still see me that way, at least they're not afraid of me anymore. I've had multiple people tell me how much they hate me, and that's proof they may accept me one day."

Ember smirked. "And you know why they told you off?"

"Why?" Zira asked through clenched teeth.

"Because you were being nice to them. If you had yelled at them and told them to back off, they would've listened to you, Z. Don't you get it?"

"No, I don't get it!" Zira yelled back.

"I'm the one who told people you caused that girl to commit suicide," Ember said, revealing the darkest truth with the most innocent smile on her face.

Zira felt as though a knife went through her heart.

"Wha...what?" she stammered, the tears now falling freely. She took a step back.

"I did it to show you the only way people respect you is when you yell at them and assert your dominance," Ember exclaimed. "To show you you're meant to be the queen bee of this school. Now everything can go back to the way it used to be. You, me, and our old friends. We'll once again rule this school."

Zira put her hands in front of her and shook her head in disbelief. "Ember, there's *no* way I'm going back to being mean!"

Ember's confident posture dropped slightly. "What? Why?"

"Because I HATE IT!" Zira felt the buzzing energy spike in her core, and her unfiltered rage made Ember flinch. "The moment I heard that girl died, I questioned everything I ever did in this school. I don't want people to cower in fear at my words; I want people to like me. I want them to see I've changed and that I can be better. Why would you do any of this?"

Ember scowled at Zira, baring her teeth as if she were a tigress. "Because I liked it when people were afraid of me. Now they look at me like I'm just like everybody else. Well, I'm not. I'm better than them, and they need to *know* it!"

Adrenaline and energy coursed through Zira's veins, all emotions swarming furiously in her mind. "Ember, we are *not* better than anybody else! We're just normal people like them, and they don't need to give us anything. Why would you think you're better than them?"

"Because my parents have favored my twin brother over me my entire life. And then one day, I realized it's because they *knew* I was too good, so they never let me show my true potential. Out of FEAR!"

"My friends were right," Zira said, closing her eyes and clenching her fists. The adrenaline and energy coursing through her veins grew stronger, and she embraced it.

"Right about what?" Ember asked mockingly.

Zira opened her eyes and met her old friend's gaze head-on. "That you're a bad influence who's too self-absorbed to see when you're hurting people."

Ember gave her a disgusted look. "Oh, please, they don't know anything. Two of them believe in God, and they're always, like, 'Oh, I know everything because I follow God. I'm so special and smart. Blah, blah, blah—'"

"Shut up," Zira said, her arms and fists now shaking.

"What did you just say to me?"

"I said, SHUT UP!" Zira arms shot in front of her body, making an X-shaped motion. As the Witch thrust her arms down, she released her clenched and glowing fists. Magic exploded from her hands and made a purple dome spread out from her. When it hit Ember, both girls' visions went black, and they fell to the ground.

Back Into The Dark

Zira awoke, dazed. She groaned as she pushed herself up and rubbed her tired eyes. Once her vision cleared and she could see what lay before her, her heart dropped. She quickly got up and ran to the motionless red-head.

She put a hand on Ember's neck, still able to feel her beating pulse. A wave of relief washed over Zira, and then she grabbed her ex-friend's limp arm, shaking it.

"Ember?" she asked, panicked. "Ember, wake up!"

The girl lay still.

Zira violently shook her whole body. "Ember!"

Nothing happened.

It felt like Zira couldn't breathe. She stood, her vision blotching and the theater swaying before her eyes as she stared at her motionless friend.

"No.... I did this.... it's my fault...." Tears poured out of her eyes, and she put her hands on her face as she began to hyperventilate. "What am I gonna do? She's hurt because of me.

343

I can't stay here.... Everyone will be afraid of me, and I'll have no place to go. My own parents won't even want me!" She took shallow breaths, her heart racing a million miles a minute.

An idea hit her, and she stabilized slightly. "I have to...run. I have to run from everyone. They'll be safe if I'm gone."

She took one last look at Ember, then ran for the back door that led to the fields. She rushed down the ramp and ran to the sidewalk, sprinting down it in the dim light. She arrived at her house shortly and attempted to open the front door, but it was locked.

Zira touched her forehead against it in defeat, but then a thought entered her mind. She rushed to the small garden next to their front door and started looking around, then found a smooth rock and pulled it up. There was an empty pill bottle glued to it by the cap, which she unscrewed. A shining key fell onto the grass.

Throwing the rock and pill bottle into the garden and grabbing the key, she rushed back to the door, unlocked it, and burst into the dark house. Her heart was racing, her lungs were out of breath, and tears were trying to fight their way out of her eyes, but the Witch remained undaunted in her task.

Zira ran upstairs to her room, threw the key onto her bed, and darted to the closet. She grabbed a dark purple backpack from the top shelf and started shoving clothes into it. Once it was full, she zipped it up and swung it onto her back, then ran to her desk. Finding a notebook and pencil, she rapidly wrote a short note to leave for her family. They deserved to know what happened, but she didn't deserve to be found.

Zira ripped it out and ran back downstairs, leaving it on the breakfast bar. After shoving a few more supplies into her backpack, she burst out into the dark night and ran down the steps, making her way back onto the sidewalk. She stopped abruptly, however, when she realized she didn't know where to go. She couldn't walk forever, or else she would never make it anywhere.

An idea suddenly burned in her mind. She activated her magic, making her hands glow brightly in the dark.

"*Teleprasportio,*" she said, thinking of a forest. She disappeared in a puff of purple smoke and sparkles and reappeared, surrounded by big trees.

Falling to her knees, she gasped for air, able to feel the weakness in her body. *Stupid, energy-draining spell.*

After catching her breath, Zira stood and turned around, freezing at what she saw. She was on a mountain somewhere near her town and had a perfect view of all the buildings, the streets...everything.

While staring at the yellow city lights, more tears filled Zira's eyes. This was her goodbye to it all. She would never see any of it ever again. She fought her sadness and closed her eyes, turning away from the town.

There was no looking back.

She's Gone

At Crystal Sky Middle School, all the cast members were coming back to the theater after completing the costume requirements, but no one had yet noticed that someone was lying on the stage.

The boy in front of the group saw the motionless body first. "Ember?"

She didn't respond.

"Ember!" he called out as he climbed onto the stage and ran to her. He knelt beside her and carefully moved her onto her back. He saw the blood stain on her shirt and quickly pointed to the kid running up to them. "You—call 911!"

Brianna, who was now on the other side of Ember, put a hand on her neck to check for a pulse; there was one. She let out a breath of relief.

A moment later, Mrs. Willow entered. "What's going on here?"

The purple-haired girl spoke up. "Someone's seriously hurt, so we called 911."

Mrs. Willow gasped, and a hand flew to her chest. "Oh my. Who is it? Zira was the only one in here...." She rushed onto the stage.

"It's not Zira," the boy said as Mrs. Willow knelt beside him. "It's Ember. She's in my math class."

Her eyes widened as she stared down at the motionless girl. "What happened? And where is Zira?"

Everyone looked at each other.

"I bet Zira hurt her," said the boy next to Ember.

Brianna's mouth gaped open, and her eyebrows creased in annoyance. "There's no way Zira did this."

"Well, then, who else did? It was either her fault or somehow Ember hurt herself, but I doubt that."

Brianna scowled at him as she stood. "I'm going to find Zira. I bet she's in the bathroom."

When she got to the front row of seats, she noticed Zira's galaxy backpack was still on one of them. "See, Zira's bag is still here. She's definitely in the bathroom."

"All right, all right," Mrs. Willow snapped as she clapped her hands. "No one's responsible for anything right now. Someone has been hurt on my watch, so it's my job to take responsibility. Everyone off the stage! The paramedics will need space to help Ember. You may stay until they show up, but when they do, everyone, please clear out of the theater. Evie and Steve, go tell the other crew members everything has been canceled until further notice. I will stay with Ember."

The students did as they were instructed and started gathering their belongings. Brianna grabbed her and Zira's bags and began her journey to find her missing friend, but after checking the closest bathroom, Zira wasn't there.

Brianna felt her heart rate increase, but she pushed away the ball of fear forming in her gut. *Maybe she's in the other girls' bathroom.* A quick check, however, proved otherwise.

The ball of fear grew. "Okay, don't freak out. Maybe... Maybe she went to see Sundown."

She entered the props room, but Zira wasn't there either.

Sundown looked at Brianna, his face twisted in concern as he approached her. "Brianna, what's wrong?"

"I can't find Zira," she answered. "She wasn't in the theater, but Ember was—and she's hurt, Sundown, really hurt." Tears filled Brianna's eyes. "What do we do? What if Zira accidentally hurt her? What if—?"

Sundown grabbed her shoulders. "Brianna, calm down. If Zira really did run in fear because she hurt Ember, she probably just went home."

Brianna wiped away her tears. "You sure?"

"I'm sure," he said, giving her a reassuring smile. "Since everything is canceled, let's go to her house and see."

Brianna nodded. "Okay, yeah. Let's go."

When they arrived at Zira's house, they noticed that all the lights were off and that the cars were gone. They rang the doorbell nonetheless, but no one answered.

"Why isn't she answering?" Brianna asked, panicking. "I don't think anyone is here. If Zira isn't here, where is she? She could be—"

"Bri, calm down. If she's upset, she might be ignoring us." Sundown turned the doorknob, and to his surprise, it was unlocked.

"Zira?" he called as he went in, Brianna following behind. "Are you okay?"

Brianna put their bags by the door. "Zira? I have your bag."

"What's this?" Sundown asked, picking up a piece of paper off the breakfast bar. His eyes widened as he read it, making Brianna's anxiety increase.

"What is it?" She whimpered as she walked up to him.

"She's... she's gone."

"What?" Brianna exclaimed, panic shooting through her.

"This...this is her goodbye note...." He slowly handed it to her.

Querida Familia,

I've left. I can't stay somewhere I don't belong. All I do is hurt everyone I'm around, and I'm sick of being the cause for people's pain. So, I'm going somewhere I can't hurt anybody.

Don't come looking for me. I deserve to be where I am.

Adiós...para siempre.

Zira Almira Flores, your former daughter and sister.

Brianna felt like she couldn't breathe. *Zira left? Why? Did she really hurt Ember? There's no way it was on purpose. If it was an accident, though, why did she run so far away? What had happened?*

A sob escaped Brianna's lips.

"Bri...?"

"She's gone!" Brianna wailed and looked up at Sundown. "She's gone, Sundown! My best friend is gone! And I may never see her again." She put her face in her hands and cried.

Sundown stared at her for a few seconds. Then he snapped out of his daze and put his hands on his friend's shoulders. "Brianna. Brianna, look at me."

She did as she was told, her face red and puffy.

"She's not gone. We can't give up hope. We'll find her. She's out there somewhere, okay?"

She stared at him with blank disbelief as she panted.

"Come on, Brianna. I know you're strong. You lost all your friends back in Arizona before you moved, didn't you?"

Her eyes widened. "How— How did you know that?"

"Because you've said some stuff that implied it. They weren't there for you when you needed them to be, though, were they?"

Brianna shook her head. "No, they weren't."

"Well don't be like them. Zira needs you right now, and you need to be there for her, no matter what it takes." Sundown stared intensely at her, and she returned his gaze as her breathing slowly evened out. "Okay?"

Brianna nodded her head with a blank expression. "Y-yes. Okay."

"Good," Sundown said, letting out a breath of relief and allowing his head to go limp, "because I was scared that wouldn't work." He removed his hands from her shoulders.

Brianna gave him a questioning look. "Oh, come on. You have way too much confidence for that."

"No, I don't. You really don't know half of it."

"But I'd like to," Brianna said longingly, giving him the best smile she could muster.

Sundown looked at her in surprise, a small smile forming on his lips as well.

After a moment, she shook her head. "But not now. We have a friend to find."

Sundown nodded in determination. "Yes, we do."

David Flores' phone rang, and he picked it up, using his shoulder to press it to his ear. "*Hola, mi vida.*"

"David, I just got some very bad news from Regina Decker," Estelle said, talking so quickly he could barely understand her.

David froze and stopped typing. "What happened?"

"Well, Brianna and Sundown got dismissed from musical preparations early, but they couldn't find Zira—only her bag. They got worried and went to our house only to find the door unlocked and a note on the breakfast bar."

David stood. He didn't know where she was going with this, but he had a bad feeling in his gut. "What was the note?"

"It was..." Estelle trailed off, her voice breaking. She sniffled a few times, and then continued. "It was Zira's goodbye note."

"What?"

"Zira ran away from home," Estelle said, her voice breaking again. David could hear her crying. "I left work already; you need to get out of work and start looking too. I've called the police, and I'm going to call others to help too. You go get Patrick."

David slowly nodded his head. "Okay, will do, *mi reina. Adiós.*"

"*Adiós.*" Estelle hung up.

Tears pooled into David's eyes. His daughter ran away? What was he doing wrong? His mind flashed to the future, to Zira's graduation, to her wedding. Would she even have a wedding anymore? He couldn't imagine not escorting his princess down the aisle. It all felt so wrong.

The tears escaped his eyes and streamed down his face. David grabbed the chain around his neck and pulled out the locket from under his shirt, grasping it tightly. "Oh, Zira. *Por favor vuelve a casa, princesa.*"

Reminiscent

Faustina, Brianna, and Sundown arrived at Haven's place about ten minutes after they left the Deckers' house.

"We'll go in; you stay here," Brianna told her older sister.

Faustina nodded. "Okay."

Sundown and Brianna exited the car and walked to the apartment complex that Haven called home. They headed to the stairs on the side of the wall, rushing up them as quickly as possible. After walking down a hallway, they reached the correct door: B2.

Brianna took a deep breath, then knocked.

No one answered. Brianna felt an inexplicable emotion exploding inside her, and she pounded on the door. "Haven!"

Sundown pulled her away. "Calm down. Maybe no one's home."

That theory was quickly debunked when a short brunette opened the door, yawning.

"Oh, Brianna, Sundown, what are you guys doing here?" she asked, slumped against the door frame.

Sundown cleared his throat. "We're here to—"

"Are you okay?" Brianna cut him off, addressing Haven.

"Yeah," she answered. "What made you think otherwise?"

"You just look out of it," Brianna responded.

"I was sleeping." Haven shrugged. "I have sleeping issues, okay? I often take naps after I do my homework. What's it to you?"

"Oh, sorry."

"Why are you guys here again?" Haven asked, losing her patience.

"Zira ran away," Sundown blurted out. "We came to see if you wanted to help look for her."

Brianna couldn't fully read Haven's expression. There was no doubt that she was no longer annoyed, but she didn't look surprised either.

"Let me grab my coat and leave a note for my dad."

"Okay," Sundown said as she rushed away.

"Hurry!" Brianna called out.

A few moments later, Haven came out of the hallway with her coat on, and she held a piece of paper which she proceeded to put on the fridge.

"Where do you think she could've gone?" Haven asked as she returned to the door and sat to put on her tennis shoes.

"We're not sure," Sundown admitted, "but it can't be far. She's only thirteen."

"What if she got on a bus?" Brianna asked. "She could be halfway to Virginia by now."

"That's ridiculous," Haven said as she finished tying her shoelaces. "If I know one thing, it's that kids who run away don't *really* want to run away. You should know this, Brianna." She stood and gave her friend a "duh" expression.

"What's your problem with me?" Brianna asked, scowling.

Haven's face fell. "What?"

"What's your problem with me? Because ever since we met, you've treated me coldly, and I want to know why." Brianna crossed her arms.

Sundown tried unsuccessfully to butt in. "Girls, I—"

"I have no problems with you, Brianna," Haven said flatly. "That's just my personality. Do you see me being all friendly to Sundown here?" She gestured to him.

"No," Brianna said, "but you attack me for no reason, and you seem annoyed with me all the time. Why? Because it's really getting on my nerves, and I don't want to go searching for Zira if you're just going to get at me the whole time."

"Oh, your nerves," Haven shot back. "Do you ever think of someone besides yourself?"

Brianna made a squeaky, irritated noise. "Of course I do! I think of everyone around me, which is more than you can say for yourself."

"I think of others. When my mom was sick, I helped take care of her every single day—"

"Your mom was sick?" Brianna's anger suddenly depleted, concern replacing it.

"Yes. She had lymphoma." Haven's tone was icy and bitter, and she still breathed heavily from the argument.

"Oh my gosh," Brianna said, cooling down. "Is she okay?"

Haven froze, hesitating. "No.... She died when I was nine."

Brianna felt tears prick her eyes. "I'm so sorry, Haven. I had no idea."

Haven looked into Brianna's light blue eyes, her face scrunching up. "No, no, I'm the one who should be sorry. You're only sweet and kind, and a genuinely good person. I'm the one who's been treating you unfairly."

"But why?" Brianna asked, desperate to know the truth.

Haven looked down. "Because...you remind me of her."

"Of your mom?" Brianna asked, raising her eyebrows.

Haven nodded. "Mhm. She... She was always so cheerful and positive. When she got sick, I knew she was in pain, but she somehow managed to become even more cheerful. You're the same way: You're cheery and happy, and...and you do so many things that remind me of her." She looked back into Brianna's eyes, tears filling her own. "And...that's not the easiest thing to be around. But it's worth it, and I still want to be friends, but let's do it the right way this time."

Brianna smiled through her tears. "I would love that."

Haven let out a soft laugh, and they hugged.

"I'm sorry too," Brianna said with a sniffle as she pulled out. "Your being annoyed with me made me treat you unfairly too."

"Aww, now that's what we like to see," Sundown said with a dreamy smile. "But we've got to get a move on, because we have another friend to find."

"Right," Haven said, then she put her right arm in the air, making a charging motion. "To whosever car we're taking!"

"To the car!"

Brianna and Sundown copied her motion.

Haven locked the door to her apartment, and they walked down the stairs, both girls unable to stop smiling at each other the whole way to the car.

Still Here

Zira had gone as far as she could. Her legs felt as if they had twenty bricks taped to them, and she collapsed onto the ground in front of a small cave, her backpack dragging in the dirt. She lay there and took deep, long breaths.

Once her heart slowed down, she sat up and unzipped her bag. She pulled out a bottle of water and took a couple sips, then put it away and surveyed her surroundings. The teen could still see her town, but it was more eastward now. As far as she could tell, the only thing around her for miles were trees; some were dead, others alive with fall colors on them, and others with leaves of pine. This would be her resting spot for the night.

She gathered some wood and made a firepit with a circle of stones. Before using her magic to start a fire, she took a few more breaths. She felt *awful.* Her eyes drooped, every muscle felt sore, her skin felt like ice, and the cut on her arm was burning worse than it ever had. But other than that, everything was just peachy.

After taking a moment to rest, she stretched out her hands and focused the energy throughout her body into her palms. They glowed a deep lavender, swirling with silver and white sparkles. She used the same energy to light up the woodpile.

"*Fuhian.*" As she cast the spell, a bright yellow and orange fire burst to life, warming the air around it. Zira embraced the hot feeling on her skin and let some relief wash over her.

Despite the warmth of the fire, she was still shivering uncontrollably. Apparently, forgetting her coat had consequences. It didn't matter, though. She didn't deserve the comfort of a warm coat.

While sitting there, Zira let her mind wander to a dark place. *You're a monster. You failed your aisling. It's a good thing you ran away; everyone's better off without you. No matter how much good you do, it will never make up for killing that girl. Why don't you kill yourself?"*She flinched at the last thought.

Kill herself? That would be wrong. If her family found her dead, they'd be devastated. No, she wouldn't kill herself—just distance herself. If she wasn't around them, what harm could she do? It felt like the only choice she had.

Zira stared at the fire to focus on something other than her thoughts. A gray bird with a white pattern landed near her. It had a green head and orange feet, and it peered curiously up at the Witch.

Zira cocked her head. "Why are you here? No one should be near me."

The bird cooed and flew-hopped toward her, looking up at the Witch with interest. It cooed again.

Zira stared into its blue eyes. It was almost as if it were trying to tell her something.

"What?" she whispered.

It ruffled its feathers and cooed again. Zira felt a smile tug at her lips, but her thoughts ruined the moment. *You'll probably hurt him too. You're not safe to be around anyone.*

Zira clenched her hands into shaking fists, and tears filled her eyes once again. The bird seemed to chirp in question.

"Get out of here, you stupid, dumb bird! I'm dangerous. Don't you see? I'll hurt you too. Just get away from me!"

The bird chirped once more, and then took flight.

Zira sighed, letting her dark thoughts back in. *No matter what you do, you'll always be a Witch.* She froze. That was true. No matter how far she'd go, she'd always have her powers. They were the reason she was in this mess. If she had never gotten them, nothing bad would have ever happened.

"AAAH!" she screamed into the night, standing as she did. "God, if you put me on this earth for a reason, what was your reason? Tell me! Why am I here? Why do I exist? Why do I have powers? I wish you would've never made me!" She fell to her knees and sat on them, breaking down in sobs. Then she looked back up at the starry sky. "Help me, God! Help me forget myself!"

After a moment, Zira looked down at her hands and activated her magic. The purple was so beautiful, but what it did was so *deadly*. She scowled at her powers. "I hate you."

Almost as if it were listening to her, the purple energy faded, and Zira was left petrified. She felt no energy coursing through her anymore. What was happening? Why did she feel so empty and helpless? Did her soul just...disappear? No, she was still alive—but did her magic finally leave her?

Someone tapped her on the back. Zira shrieked and turned around, fists raised in defense, but her breath caught when she realized that the person who tapped her ... was her. Only not her. It was a purple outline of herself. It had her hair, her clothes, and her face, but she was transparent. It looked just like her magic, sparkles and all.

"Hello, little one," the purple figure greeted.

Zira slowly put her hands down. "Hello?"

"Nice night, isn't it?" The sparkly outline looked around, smiling.

"I guess," Zira said. "Who are you?"

"I'm you." Her smile grew larger as she sat across from Zira. "Well, the magical side of you."

"So...you're what gives me my powers?" Zira asked, not following.

"Kind of, but not really. You see, the magic world is vast and intricate. There are many different types of magic, ranging from simple to almost impossible. Witchery is on the more complicated side."

"Tell me about it." Zira rolled her eyes.

"You don't like being a Witch?" Magic-Zira asked in surprise.

"Well, no. I used to, but all my magic does is hurt people. I killed a girl because of those powers. I would give them up if I could."

Magic-Zira's eyes widened. "No, you never want to say that."

"Say what? That I would give up my powers?"

"Most Witches say that at first," she told her other half, a small smile on her lips, "but after a while, they learn to love their powers. It makes them...unbreakable in a way."

"Well, I am breakable," Zira said, looking at the ground.

"No, you're unbreakable," Magic-Zira snapped.

"No, I told you, I'm breakable. I'm the most fragile person I've ever met," Zira shouted back. "I think I would know. I'm the one who can't handle anything in my own life."

Magic-Zira sighed. "The view you have of yourself is important, but you'll see your worth in time."

Zira suddenly felt herself fill with rage. "No, I won't! Don't you understand? I'm a monster. I'd never be unbreakable, even if I had all the powers in the universe!"

"Zira, please—"

"I hate people telling me they know me. No one really knows me except ME." she screamed, lunging forward to tackle the magical side of her, but it didn't work. The purple and sparkles vanished, and she felt the energy inside her return, a feeling of fullness along with it.

Zira didn't understand what just happened, but she didn't care. Her eyes filled with tears, and she plopped onto her side, sobbing once again.

Not Alone

"Where could she be?" Brianna asked, frustration boiling inside of her.

"I don't know," Sundown answered with a sigh, running a hand over his head. "I mean, we've checked all her favorite places, but there's nothing."

"Come on, guys," Faustina said confidently as she kept her eyes focused on the road. "The police are looking, her family's looking, our families are looking, and people from the school are looking. We'll find her; I know we will."

"But where haven't we looked?" Brianna asked.

"Wait, pull over," Haven shouted.

Faustina did as instructed and pulled into the nearest gas station parking lot. When she parked, she and Sundown turned to face the girls in the back. "Yeah, Shrimp?"

"Stop calling me that," Haven growled.

"Never, Shrimp," Faustina said with a sly smile.

Haven glared.

Brianna cleared her throat, bringing the group back on track. "Guys, Zira's missing. We don't have time for this."

The brunette shook herself out of it. "Right. I think we need to consider where Zira *wouldn't* go."

"What do you mean?" Sundown asked.

"I mean, Zira ran away. Clearly, she doesn't want to be found. So, what if she went somewhere we wouldn't expect?"

"Wait, but earlier, you said that most runaway kids want to be found," Brianna pointed out.

"And that's still true. Zira wants to be found, but she doesn't *want* to be found. Make sense?"

"No," all three said in unison.

"Whatever. I'll explain later—but let's think of places Zira doesn't like. I bet she's there."

They nodded in understanding, the car falling quiet as they thought.

"Outdoors!" Brianna shouted not even a minute later.

"What?" Haven and Faustina asked.

"Zira doesn't like being outside. She told me that when we first met. So, I invited her on our hike." Brianna could feel the wheels turning in her mind. "What's the biggest forest around here?"

"That would be Gunsmoke Valley," Sundown answered. "It's about an hour away."

"Then that's where we need to go," Haven said, her eyebrows furrowing in determination. "Drive, saint lady!"

Faustina shifted gears and started pulling out. "You know that's offensive, right?"

Haven smiled. "I know."

Off they went to Gunsmoke Valley, and three out of four of the passengers were praying to God that they would find Zira there.

"Here it is," Sundown said as he shut the car door. "Gunsmoke Valley."

"Even though it's a mountain," Haven remarked. "Why are humans terrible at naming things?"

"I don't know," Brianna said with a touch of impatience. She had higher priorities than figuring out naming conventions. She started walking to the base of the mountain, but Faustina stopped her.

"Whoa, slow down there, sis. We need a game plan first."

"Okay, well, what is it?" Brianna turned and placed her hands on her hips.

"I say we spread out and search for as long as we can," Sundown suggested. "We all have cellphones, right?"

Faustina and Brianna nodded, but Haven didn't.

"I kind of...left mine at home...."

"What?" Brianna shrieked.

"We were in a rush, okay? It was charging, and I thought we were going to stay together." She crossed her arms defensively.

Brianna made a frustrated noise, but Faustina interrupted her.

"It's okay. You can come with me. Come on—let's get going."

"Finally," Brianna huffed, then turned and headed into the woods. The other three went separate ways, and thus began their journey to find their missing friend.

"Zira," Sundown called out.

He had been walking for about two hours and was gaining a decent level of altitude on the mountain. He could see the whole town from there, and it was one of the most beautiful sights he had ever seen. He couldn't help but admire all the yellow, white, green, and red lights with the buildings sparkling around them and small splotches of forest green scattered about. As amazing as it was, he couldn't fully enjoy it. Zira was still missing, and if there was even a slim chance that she was on this mountain, he would search for days. He had to find her.

"Zira," he called out again, walking forward.

Nothing.

She's probably hiding.

Sundown walked for another half hour while calling out his friend's name at various intervals. He eventually stopped and sighed, whispering in a voice raspy from exertion, "Zira, where are you?"

Zira had only been asleep for a short amount of time when she was awoken by yelling. She looked around, wondering if she had dreamed it, but she froze when she heard it again.

"Zira."

It was a boy's voice calling her name.

The breath was taken from her lungs. "No...they found me."

The fire was already burnt out, so Zira grabbed her backpack and ran into the small cave. It hid her in the darkness with just enough space for her to fit. Whoever that person was wouldn't find her. She deserved to be alone in the cold woods forever.

"Zira."

Her heart rate increased, and her breathing quickened.

"Zira," he yelled, this time a bit louder.

She took quick, shaky breaths in an attempt at calming herself down. *It's okay. You're okay. You're getting what you deserve. It doesn't matter that they came all this way to look for you.*

"Zira!"

He was getting closer.

Zira's eyes filled with tears and sweat covered her body. She could feel the heat emanating from her.

Stop freaking out. You're in a cave; he won't find you. You're safe. If she was safe, why did it feel like evil was lurking just around the corner?

Footsteps approached. Zira covered her mouth with both hands, now breathing through her nose.

"Zira!"

The boy was in sight now.

Sundown? Her vision swayed. *Does he really care that much about me? He's probably been walking for hours. I don't deserve him. I don't deserve anyone.* Tears streamed down her face. All she could do was let them fall and desperately try not to make any noise.

"Zira?" Sundown exclaimed. "Zira, are you here?"

Yes, yes, I'm right here, she wanted to cry out. But she knew she couldn't—that she *shouldn't.* She had already hurt enough people. She would only continue hurting them if she didn't distance herself. Staying in the cave was for the best...wasn't it?

Why do I want to give in? I'll just hurt my loved ones over and over again, and the cycle will never end. I'll lie to them and accidentally hurt them with my magic. It's not worth the pain I would cause. She eyed Sundown, the worry etched into his face made her heart break, and the pressure behind her eyes increased as did the longing in her heart. *Is it?*

"Zira," he called out again, his voice breaking.

Zira felt all her emotions fall away, leaving her numb and empty. *He's right there and he wants* me. *And...and I want him. I want* all *of them. Why can't I just give in and show everyone how broken I really am?*

She removed her hands from her face and let herself sob into the night. *Please find me.*

"Zira?" Sundown asked, approaching the cave. "Are you in there?"

"Y-yes," Zira gasped out between breaths.

Sundown's face relaxed with immense relief, and he rubbed it with both hands. "Zira, I'm so glad I found you. Why did you run away?"

Zira wiped her face. "I— I hurt Ember. I had to get away be—before I hurt—someone—else."

Sundown raised his eyebrows, but his face quickly softened. "Zira, how did you hurt Ember?"

Zira attempted to take a deep breath. "We— We were arguing. I got mad and threw something. It wasn't supposed to hit her, but it did, and she fell back, and—and she was unconscious and wouldn't wake up. So, I ran. I couldn't risk hurting anyone else ever again."

Sundown's eyebrows knitted together. "Zira, you didn't mean to hurt Ember. It was an accident."

"I know! But how many more times will I *accidentally* hurt someone? How many more people will have to suffer because of my mistakes?" Zira's voice was groggy and congested.

Sundown was quiet for a moment. "Look, it doesn't matter if you accidentally hurt someone five more times or five hundred more times. If your heart was in the right place, that's all that matters."

"But my heart wasn't in the right place when I threw that thing."

"Yes, well, while that is true, it was still an accident. The best thing you can do with your mistakes is learn from them."

"So, I'll never be perfect," Zira said, the words finally starting to sink in

Sundown eyes widened slightly. "Of course not, Zira. No one can ever be perfect. That's part of being human. We make mistakes. But they don't have to be a bad thing. Sometimes they bring people together, like you and me. I'm not saying I wouldn't change things if I had the chance, but we may never have met if all this didn't happen. There's always a moon somewhere in the night sky, even if you can't see it sometimes."

Zira's breathing slowed down a little, though her tone was still frantic. "But how can I believe that when I've made so many mistakes that caused horrible things to happen?"

"Well, actions have consequences. Some are good; some are bad, but you can't be afraid of making mistakes. They're inevitable. We just have to respond to them in the right way."

"I don't know...." Zira trailed off. The tears were fading away, and her heartbeat was returning to normal, but there was still a heaviness inside of her.

"Come on. Let us show you. You don't have to do this on your own, you know." Sundown stretched his arm into the cave and offered Zira his hand.

She stared at it. He was offering to help her. Even though she had messed up so many times—even though she had caused his cousin so much pain—he still wanted to be there for her.

The Witch kept staring, unsure of what to do. She hated the fact that she needed help, but if the last few months had taught her anything, it was that help could save lives. Like when she helped Sundown in gym.

Zira exhaled deeply and gave in, taking his hand. When he helped her out of the cave, she collapsed into his arms.

"I don't want to be alone," she whimpered.

He hugged her tightly. "You're not alone. You have friends and family, and most importantly, God. He'll never abandon you, no matter what you do."

Zira let out a breath. "I think I like this God person."

Sundown laughed. "Yeah, me too."

They stayed like that until voices interrupted their peaceful embrace.

"There they are!"

A blonde female came running and slammed into them with a hug. "Zira, you're safe! I'm so happy you're safe."

Haven joined them a moment later, wrapping her arms around Zira and Sundown as she panted heavily. "Zira...you're...safe. Thank...goodness."

Zira smiled, fresh tears forming in her eyes. Her heart swelled with a love and a joy she had never felt in her life, and she wouldn't let anything take it away from her.

My Home

"Zira!" her mom called in relief at the sight of five people descending the mountain.

"*¡Mami!*" Zira called back, but a bolt of panic flashed in her chest, and she froze.

"What's wrong?" Brianna asked her friend, looking over her shoulder.

"What if they're mad?" Zira stammered. "What if they hate me?"

"Zira, if they hated you, they wouldn't look so relieved to see you. Go see them. Trust me: They'll forgive you even if they are mad."

Sundown nodded in agreement, as did a sleepy-eyed Haven whom he was carrying on his back.

Zira took a deep breath. "Okay."

She ran down the hill and stopped when she reached the pavement. Zira's family was standing only a few feet away from her. They stared at each other.

After a moment, Estelle ran over and hugged her daughter. "Oh, *mi amor,* I thought you were gone forever."

"I'm sorry, *Mami,*" Zira said, returning the embrace.

Estelle put her hands on Zira's shoulders and pushed her back, taking a good look at her daughter. "*Ay, mija,* you look so worn out. But you're safe, and that's all that matters."

David ran over and hugged them. "We were so worried about you, *princesa.*"

"*¡Hermana!*" Patrick yelled as he ran to his sister and tackled her. "You're okay!"

Zira smiled down at her brother, tears shimmering in her eyes as she hugged him back. "I missed you so much, *hermanito.* I missed you all so much."

The Flores family was back together—all except their oldest daughter, Destiny, but they knew she was there in spirit. It amazed Zira to know how happy everyone was to have her back where she belonged.

Mi hogar. Zira smiled. *My home.*

Zira sighed happily as she snuggled onto the couch, a wave of relief washing over her. She was finally home.

Nervousness soon replaced the relief as both of her parents came to sit in front of her. She cringed. *Here it comes.*

"So," her mom started out, "what happened? Why did you run away?"

Zira sat up and took a deep breath. "I hurt Ember. We were arguing and I had a prop in my hand. When I got mad at her...I threw it. I threw it so hard. It knocked her over and then she passed out." The teen looked up at her parents to see their reactions, but she couldn't read their faces. "I...felt like a monster. I had hurt so many people, and Ember was the final straw. She was my best friend and I—I knew everyone at school would be afraid of me. I thought you guys would be, too. So, I ran."

Her mom's posture fell, and tears came pouring out of her eyes. "I'm so sorry, *mija*. I had no idea how much you were truly hurting. I should've talked to you more. I wasn't paying attention." She wiped her eyes. "I promise, I'll be more present in your life from now on. But you need help, *cariña*—help we can't give you. So, we're going to find you a therapist. And I know it's scary, but we'll be with you every step of the way."

Zira paused for a moment. "I think you're right, *Mami*. I think I do need therapy."

Her parents smiled and looked at each other, tears still running down their faces.

David scooted closer to Zira and wrapped her in a hug. "I'm so happy to hear you say that, *mija*."

Zira put her arms around her dad. "I think I'm glad to hear myself say it too."

Her dad retreated, but he kept his hands on his daughter's upper arms. "Look at you. *Mi niñita* has been through so much, but you're still here, and you're still okay." He gave Zira's arms a squeeze.

She winced. "Ow."

David slowly retracted his hands. "Did that hurt? I didn't think I squeezed you that hard."

Zira put her hand over her gash, debating how to tell them she cut herself without revealing her powers.

"I... I...." She sighed. "I cut my arm a while ago on the way home from school. I didn't tell you because I thought I deserved the pain and lack of treatment."

Her parents exchanged looks as Zira took off her shirt to reveal the dirty bandages wrapped around her upper arm. The teen slowly unwound them, bracing for the pain as she did.

Her mom jumped forward and grabbed Zira's arm to look at the swollen, oozing, purple-and-red wound.

"Ow! *Mamá*, that hurts."

"I'm sorry, but Zira, this wound is infected. How long have you had it?"

Zira counted on her hand. "Um...maybe three weeks?"

"What?" her mother shouted. "Didn't you notice it was getting worse?"

Zira bit her lip. "Yes. But I thought I deserved to be in pain, that it was okay because—"

"Zira, it is *never* okay to injure yourself, nor let your injuries go untreated," Estelle said, staring into her daughter's eyes. "Do you know how many people wait to get things checked out and then it's too late? Or how many teens I've seen cutting themselves because of emotional pain? It never ends well. You're a person too, Zira. Hurting yourself is just as bad as hurting someone else, and you deserve every ounce of treatment as much as the kindest person on the planet does."

Tears welled up in Zira's eyes and her whole body started tingling. She could feel her magic buzzing on an entirely different level. *Hurting myself is just as bad as hurting someone else,* she echoed in her mind.

"I'm sorry, *Mamá.* I didn't realize..."

"It's okay, Zira, but we should go to the hospital to get you treated. You're lucky it's not worse." Estelle stood.

Zira followed her mom out the door. *Hurting myself is just as bad as hurting others because I'm a person too. If hurting myself was okay, then hurting others would be okay too...but it's not.*

This Means War

Ember woke up in a mental fog. A migraine instantly shot through her head, and she groaned, slowly opening her eyes.

"Ember?" a boy called out.

"Yeah?" she asked, reaching up to rub her forehead.

The boy grabbed her hand. "No, don't touch your head. You have a severe concussion."

She let him bring her arm down.

"What? How did I get it? And where are we, Ben?"

Ben, Ember's twin brother, held onto her hand. "We're in the hospital, Em. Something happened at school, and you hit your head really hard. You also have a wound on your stomach."

Ember raised her eyebrows. "What? How?"

Ben looked away, nervously bouncing his leg up and down. "We're... We're not sure."

"Ben, what aren't you telling me?" Ember could always tell when her brother lied due to his nervous fidgeting habits.

Ben sighed. "Look, Ember, you and your friend, um... It starts with a Z?"

"Her name is Zira."

"Zira, right. Well, you guys got into a fight, and Zira said she threw something at you which hit you and made you fall back. She took it with her so no one would know what really happened."

"What?" Ember asked harshly. "She's going to jail or something, right?"

"No, Mom and Dad didn't press charges." Ben took a deep breath. "I'm not saying I agree with them, but she is only thirteen, Ems, and she swears she didn't mean to throw it *at* you. She was just getting frustrated. She said she was really sorry when she came here yesterday to see you. Mom and Dad were still a little concerned with her anger issues, but her mother assured them Zira was going to start therapy soon, which would help with that. It wasn't on purpose, Ember. Let's move on."

Ember looked just about ready to explode. She yanked her hand from her brother's and tried to sit up, but it provoked her head pain, so she sank back down.

"She almost killed me, and you guys are going to let her get away with it?"

Ben's nervousness faded. "She didn't try to kill you, Ember. It was an accident. She only wanted to throw something to get her aggression out and scare you, not to hurt you."

"But she did hurt me, and that deserves punishment."

Ben stood. "Look, I know you have issues with people who don't like you, but Zira's not like that. She didn't intend to hurt

The Witch Chronicles: Unraveled

you. End of story." He made his way to the door of the tiny room.

"But she needs to be sorry for this," Ember said loudly. "I won't let her get away with it."

Ben only shook his head and sighed.

"Do you hear me? I will get her, even if it's the last thing I do," Ember shouted, but he just ignored her and let the door close on its own.

"This is war, Zira, and I hope you're ready to fight."

379

Almost Still Meant Almost

"All right, people—move it, move it," Mrs. Willow shouted at the kids setting up the musical decorations. "We have plenty of things to do, and I'm not going to do it all for you."

It was five days until opening night, and Zira couldn't contain her excitement to be in the musical. The story was something to which she could very much relate, and she could barely believe she was about to play its heroine. She felt as though she had been the villain for the last two years, so being the hero for once was a breath of fresh air. It made Zira's heart flutter just thinking about it.

"Geez, if we don't finish everything by tonight, I think Mrs. Willow's brain is gonna explode," Haven said with a smile.

Zira laughed. "I think you're right. We'd better hurry up, then."

"And before Mrs. Willow scolds us for talking," Brianna said, a hand cupped around the side of her mouth.

The Witch Chronicles: Unraveled

All three girls giggled, then they each picked up a box of streamers and headed for the stage.

"So, Bri, you excited for your first live performance?" Haven asked.

"I'm more nervous. I can't believe everyone is going to be watching me on this stage." She gazed ahead in awe. "It's too scary to think about."

Haven and Zira smiled, handing the streamers to someone who was hanging them up.

"It'll be okay," Zira said. "You have us."

"Yeah, we'll be cheering for you all night long," Haven reassured, "so don't even worry about messing up."

"But what if I do mess up?" Brianna exclaimed. "What if I trip and everyone laughs?"

"Then you play it off like it was supposed to be there."

"Yeah, and if you do trip, it'll be okay," Haven added. "It's one moment over hundreds of others. Do you think people are really going to complain about someone messing up in a middle school musical?"

"No," Brianna admitted, "but I'm still worried, okay?"

The brunette inched closer to Brianna and put an arm around her shoulders. "Look at it this way: If you do mess up, no one's gonna notice."

"Why?" Zira and Brianna asked simultaneously.

"Because you're already one big mess-up," Haven answered with a smirk, holding in her laughter.

Brianna's mouth gaped open. "I am not. You take that back."

"Nah," Haven said nonchalantly, her smile widening.

Brianna growled and lunged for the brunette, but Haven was quick. She dodged Brianna and darted for the stage stairs, disappearing behind the curtains.

Brianna ran after her, arms outstretched to catch her. "Come back here, Jackson!"

They both reappeared and ran up the side aisle.

"Never, Decker," Haven called back, already far ahead of Brianna.

Zira beamed. *I'm so glad they get along now.*

She looked around for something else to do, but then a voice called her name.

"Hey, Zira, can you hold this for me?"

Zira turned around to see Sundown by a metal ladder.

"Sure." She ran over to him and gripped the ladder firmly as he climbed up with white, sparkly streamers in hand.

"Thanks. I don't feel safe on this thing unless someone's holding it." Sundown began to tape streamers to a backdrop.

"I know you're afraid of heights, but I really don't think a ladder's that big a deal."

"You try being up here," Sundown said defensively. "It's scary."

"Trust me: I know scary, and that's...that's not that scary." Zira thought back to how scared she felt when she couldn't get Ember to wake up.

"We all have different levels of problems, Z; don't disrespect mine," Sundown deadpanned.

Zira pushed the thought of Ember away and rolled her eyes sarcastically. "Okay, I won't."

Sundown nodded with a satisfied expression. "Good."

After finishing most of the decorations for the musical, Mrs. Willow announced that it was time to go home. Mostly everyone was thankful for the reprieve from their exhausting tasks.

After grabbing her bag, Zira left the theater and waited for her friends by the lockers. While she was waiting, two familiar faces approached her.

"Hey, Hazel. Hey, Violet. What's up?"

"Nothing much," Hazel replied, a sweet smile on her face. "We just came to see how you're doing."

Zira was a little awestruck. "Oh, well, I'm doing much better; thanks. Therapy has helped a lot, and so has being honest with my family and friends."

Well, mostly, she thought as her mind flashed to magic. She talked about that with her therapist in a way that Zira wouldn't reveal herself, though. Now she almost didn't feel guilty for lying to her friends and family about her powers, especially since she had a stronger hold than ever on her magic.

But almost still meant almost.

"That's good to hear. Um, Violet and I—"

"We bought you a gift!" Violet interrupted, her brogue shining through. She was holding up a small velvet box.

Zira's face softened. "Aww, you guys." She took it from the brunette and flipped it open. It was a witch's hat necklace with the name "Zira" engraved into the purple. She gasped. "Oh my gosh, this is...perfect. How did you guys know?"

"Sundown mentioned how you like fictional witches. He finds it funny." Hazel chuckled.

"Well, I love it! Thank you guys so much." Zira said with a bright smile.

"Put it on," Violet urged, gesturing to the necklace.

"Right," Zira said. She took it out of the box and carefully clipped it around her neck. The charm fell a bit above her shirt, meaning it wouldn't be hidden. "It's perfect, guys. Thank you so much. What's it for?"

"A little musical good luck," Hazel said with a sly smile.

"Yeah, we'd hate for you to have bad luck during the musical," Violet said with a straight face. "That would be tragic."

Zira knew she was dead serious—which was why she didn't mention that she didn't believe in luck—but the gesture was still sweet.

"Well, thank you again. See you tomorrow!" Zira waved.

Violet and Hazel waved and started walking away.

"You're welcome, and I'll see you tomorrow," Hazel said.

" *Tá fáilte romhat!*" Violet called out.

Zira raised her eyebrows slightly. Violet had just spoken Irish in public. She had never done that before. *I guess everyone is making progress,* the teen thought with a smile, *especially on our* aislings.

Moments later, her friends came out of the theater.

"What took you so long?"

"I couldn't find my phone," Haven scoffed with an eye roll. "Why do I even need one anyway? I only use it, like, once a week."

The foursome started walking.

"Well, you could need it to get in touch with someone in case an emergency happens," Zira pointed out.

"Or to tell your dad you need a ride home from school because you missed the bus," Brianna commented, reminding everyone of an incident from a few weeks ago.

"Or to text your best friends," Sundown said, putting his hands on her shoulders from behind.

Haven rolled her eyes. "I usually use the home phone when I call you guys. What's the big deal about texting? The buttons are small, and you have to click on the same one multiple times to get the letter you want. Ugh, it's so annoying!"

"To you, maybe," Zira said, pulling out her phone. "I use mine to text all the time."

"Well, yeah, but that's because you're, like, magic."

Brianna and Sundown laughed, but Zira just smiled knowingly.

You know, Haven, you're not too far off about that.

Two Big Moments

Zira took a deep breath. The musical was about to start, and she could feel her heart pounding. She was more worried about poor Brianna, though, whose knuckles were turning white and whose fists were shaking.

"You'll do amazing," Zira whispered to her best friend.

"Easy for you to say," Brianna whisper-shouted. "You've been trained by a professional. This is just a hobby for me."

"That doesn't make me better than you," Zira assured. "Just trust yourself and try to stay calm. At the very least, you'll barely make it through tonight, but you'll still be amazing."

"I'll do my best," Brianna replied, no happiness present in her voice.

Then the curtain opened, and the music started.

The actors were nearing the end of the story, currently in the middle of the most important scene.

The family of Marigold—who Zira was playing—was trying to attack the evil ice witch who had captured Marigold and held her prisoner in her hollow ice mountain. Dramatic music played from the pit as Marigold sat on the side and watched the chaos unravel.

"Guys," she tried to call out, but no one heard her over the ruckus.

"Guys," she tried again, this time louder. Still, no one heard her. She huffed and stood, but before she could get a word out, the ice witch flung her grandfather across the stage. He hit the floor with a thud and rolled on the icy ground—which was just the stage floor with a bunch of large, light blue tarps strewn over it.

Marigold felt the anger rising inside her.

"QUIET!" she screamed.

As the music stopped, everyone turned their attention to her—even the witch.

She looked at her grandfather. "Poppy, are you okay?"

His wife helped him sit up. "Yeah, I'm okay. I was once shot back in my sheriff days. Nothing compares to that pain."

Marigold nodded to him, then looked back at her family and the witch. Everyone was still in hostile positions. The ice witch's hands were fogging from her powers—the fog was, of course, just white crepe paper—and Marigold's parents, played by Carlos and Brianna, had weapons pointed at the witch.

Marigold didn't hesitate to walk directly up to the villain.

Her mother gasped. "Mari, what are you—"

"Shh!" Marigold interrupted. "I want to ask the witch something."

"What is it?" she asked coldly.

Marigold stared straight into her icy blue eyes. "Who hurt you?"

The ice witch's eyes widened a little but quickly returned to normal. "Not this again, child—"

"No, who hurt you?" Marigold demanded. "Because the only way we'll resolve this without someone getting hurt"—she looked to her grandfather and back again—"is if we communicate our problems. There's no peace without that. So, I ask you again, who hurt you?"

The witch hesitated. She looked at each person on the stage, and then back at Marigold. Staring into the young girl's deep blue eyes, she knew she was sincere, and she couldn't hold back the flood of trauma anymore. The witch broke down crying. Everyone in the room gasped except Marigold.

The witch sank to the floor, and as she wiped her tears, Marigold knelt in front of her, placing her hands on the witch's shoulder.

The witch sniffed and looked up. She pointed to Marigold's grandfather, who was now standing and side-hugging his wife. "He did."

Another chorus of gasps reverberated in the theater, but Marigold once again remained silent.

"How did I hurt you?" Marigold's grandfather asked.

"When I was a little girl, my parents were very poor, and they stole food to keep us alive. On Christmas Eve, they stole money instead. You caught them and put them in jail. I didn't get to spend another Christmas with them again. You kept me from my parents. And after I acquired these ice powers"—she looked down at her hands—"I thought I could get revenge. So, I kidnapped your granddaughter a day before Christmas to make you feel the same pain."

Everyone was speechless.

"So, you don't actually hate me?" Marigold asked.

"Hate you?" the ice witch asked with a scoff. "You're the only one in over thirty years to ask me what was wrong."

Marigold gave her a gentle smile, and the witch smiled back.

"I'm sorry," Marigold's grandfather spoke up. "I'm so sorry. I had no idea they had a kid, and I had no idea how poor they were."

"What... What happened to them?" the witch asked, desperation in her eyes.

"I'm sorry, but...they died years ago. I would do anything to bring them back. Honest."

The witch looked down, her eyes wide. Everyone waited to see what would happen, and finally, she broke down again.

"I— I thought—I might have a—a family after all." She sniffled. "B-but I was wrong."

After a moment, Marigold got an idea. "You can be in our family if you want."

The witch looked up, still sniffling. "What?"

"You can join our family! We have plenty of room for another person, and I've always wanted an aunt." A smile grew on Marigold's face. She offered the ice witch her hand as soft, suspenseful music now began to play. "So, what do you say?"

The witch looked around at everyone to see if they really meant it. They were smiling, and then they all surrounded Marigold, each putting a hand on her shoulder to symbolize their acceptance of the ice witch into their family.

The witch's eyes welled with tears, and then she smiled. "I say...yes." She grabbed Marigold's hand and let the small girl help her up. Loud, joyful music started to swell.

"Group hug," Marigold's father shouted. They all surrounded the ice witch in a hug, but with so many people, she was perfectly invisible. And when they separated...

"Whoa, what happened?" Marigold exclaimed when she saw the ice witch's new appearance.

She had long, flowy dark hair that was all on one shoulder. There was a sparkly blue flower in her hair with shoes to match, and her dress now had a white laced top and a black, flowy high-low skirt. Her eyes were still the same icy blue they had been.

"I guess... I guess the dark magic I possessed to take revenge on you guys washed away when I reformed. But... I still feel..." She put out one hand above the other, palms facing each other. She focused, and then a snowflake formed at her will. Slow, awe-filled music played to distract audiences from the kid dressed in all blue holding a snowflake-shaped Christmas decoration in between the witch's hands. "I still have some magic! I guess it wasn't all bad."

"And neither are you," Marigold told her.

The ice witch smiled.

"Do you have a name we can call you?" Marigold's mother asked her.

"Oh, yes," she answered. "Eira."

"Welcome to the family Eira." Marigold's mother put her arm around the former ice witch, smiling at her.

"Alright, enough of all this chitter-chatter," Marigold's grandfather said. "Let's get home for Christmas!"

Everyone cheered, and the final song started up.

The curtain fell, and the crowd clapped. When the curtain went up again, the set had changed, showing they were back in the village.

The cast danced and sang their last song, all the main characters getting their own parts. Eira and Marigold were the centers of the stage though and dueted a lot throughout the song.

Once the last beat went off and the performers struck their final poses, the crowd clapped and cheered. As the curtain closed, they stood and cheered even louder.

"Wooo!" Estelle shouted.

"That's our daughter!" David exclaimed.

A more upbeat, instrumental version of Marigold's main song started playing, and then the curtain opened again.

The background characters came out and walked to the front, bowing. The crowd cheered for them. The secondary characters like Marigold's friends from the beginning came out and bowed. The crowd cheered even louder. Marigold's family—Brianna, Carlos, and the people who played her grandparents—all came to the front, taking a bow. More excitement from the crowd.

Last but not least, Zira and the girl who played the ice witch, Sadie, came out and met in the middle of the stage, taking each other's hands. The crowd burst into applause as the two girls walked to the front and bowed. The rest of the cast joined them, getting in a line, then they all linked hands and took a bow. The crowd went wild.

Zira didn't care about any of that. All Zira cared about were the reactions of her friends and family. She searched for their faces and found them all together. Hazel, Violet, Sundown, Haven, her brother, her parents, and Brianna's family were lined up in one of the middle rows. They were all smiling and cheering for her and Brianna.

Zira smiled brightly at them. She would never forget how blessed she was.

Zira walked up to a classroom door. The glass was blurry, preventing her from seeing inside, but it didn't matter. She was going in.

Zira took a deep breath and opened the door. She strode into the dark room and stood in front of the teacher's desk. She looked around the room until her eyes fell on a chair in the last row, and she stared at it like it would come to life at any second. After a moment, she lifted her hands, lighting them up along with two desks.

"*Reobicar,*" she said, and the memory came back to her.

The sound of the classroom as it had been in the past filled her ears, and she could hear all her classmates, their faces appearing in her mind. Zira closed her eyes and immersed herself in the memory.

She was sitting at her desk in the middle row, trying to focus, but everyone was too loud. The teacher helplessly tried to calm them down, but it didn't work. Zira looked up from her desk and around at the noisy kids, scowling. Then she paused the memory when it landed on a girl in the left middle seat of the back row. She was leaning on her right hand as she stared down at her book, a pencil in the other hand. Her brown hair covered some of her face, and a melancholy expression was glazed in her Caribbean blue eyes. It didn't even seem like she was doing any of the work.

As the memory faded, Zira could feel a sob in her chest. *I miss you.* She opened her eyes and wiped away her tears. *I'm sorry.*

There was a knock at the door as a figure appeared.

"Are you ready, Zira?" asked the voice of her mother.

She nodded at her mom. "Yep, I'm coming."

Estelle smiled at her daughter. "Good. We're waiting in the main hall."

As her mom walked away, Zira approached the door, putting her hand on the knob as she looked back at that same seat. "Goodbye...Sam."

She left, closing the door behind her.

Epilogue

Three Months Later...

Zira and her friends laughed as they strode down the town sidewalk. They had all gotten ice cream, and Haven was telling a story about a time her dad had an anaphylactic episode.

"Your mom didn't know there were peanuts in the ice cream?" Zira asked, taking a bite of her own ice cream.

"She swears it was an accident," Haven explained, licking the melted sweet treat off her hand. "It was one of those 'may contain peanuts' things. The funniest part was that since I was so young, I didn't understand what was going on. When he started to blow up, I just laughed and called him a balloon."

All of them burst out laughing.

Brianna almost choked on her ice cream. "Then what happened?"

"Mom got his EpiPen and injected him. She called an ambulance, and he was okay."

As they turned the corner, Zira looked into the windows of the stores. She passed by toys, clothes, and books, but when they reached an antique store display, she froze.

Sundown stopped when he realized Zira wasn't following anymore. "You coming, Z?"

She waved him off, staring at the large book on display. "Yeah, yeah, I'll catch up. I just need to go in there real quick. Here—take this." She handed him her ice cream cup. "I'll be quick. Don't wait for me; I know where we're going."

"Are you sure? I can go get the others and—"

"No," Zira hastily interrupted. "I mean, that's okay. This is something I need to do alone."

Sundown shrugged. "All right, good luck."

"You too," Zira said without thinking, already walking to the door.

She entered the shop, a little bell ringing as she did. She approached the counter and addressed the tan cashier with a bandana wrapped around her gray hair. "Excuse me, but what do you know about the book in the window?"

"Ah," the cashier said, walking over to the display and picking up the large, leather-bound book with the title *Magic and Mysteries* engraved in it. "You fancy this book?"

"Um, maybe. What's it about?"

The cashier walked back behind the counter and slid the book toward Zira. "It has many wonderful things in it. Spells and potions, for one. It was used by Witches, Warlocks, Enchanters, and even more back in the day. It is very old."

"Whoa," Zira said, her breath taken away.

"And most importantly," the woman added, her Latin accent shining through, "it solves the mystery of what happened to Merlin, the greatest Warlock of all time."

Zira raised her eyebrows in surprise. "Merlin.... I've heard that name somewhere."

The lady's smile widened. "I'm sure you have, *mija*."

"How much is it?" Zira asked, opening her backpack to find money.

The cashier thought about it. "Twenty-five dollars."

Zira almost fell over. "What? But I thought you said it was old...."

"Everything in here is old; this wouldn't be an antique shop if it wasn't. But you know what? I'm old too, and I don't think old things should go to waste. Why do you think I run this shop?" She gave the teenager a knowing smile.

"To give...old things a purpose?" Zira asked, cocking her head.

"Exactly. And in my opinion, a purpose isn't letting some rich person buy an item, and then it ends up living on his shelf for the next fifty years only to be destroyed one day. I can tell you will put this book to good use, so I'm letting you buy it for twenty-five dollars."

Zira smiled back as she pulled a twenty and a ten out of her bag. "I like that logic, and I will be using this book. I can tell it's special." She handed the cashier her money.

"But not as special as the person destined to have it," the cashier said quietly, opening the till and handing Zira her change.

Zira flinched at the statement but chose not to question it. A feeling in her gut told her she could trust this woman.

The lady pushed the book towards her. "It's all yours."

"Thank you, I will use it wisely," Zira said with an appreciative smile as she walked toward the door and out of the shop.

The lady's grin widened. "Oh, *mija*, I know you will."

The Witch Chronicles: Unraveled

Maggie Frost

Acknowledgments

Oh boy. Acknowledgements.

I honestly wasn't sure if I'd get here. But I did.

I want to go ahead and thank first and foremost God for giving me this story and guiding me in it. I never thought my weird self-insert daydreams of Trollhunters would develop into its own thing and become my main WIP series. Thank You so much for giving me this story and entrusting Zira's character to me. I hope You love this book as much as I do.

To my family, particularly my sister, Lexy, who alpha-read this book and gave some great feedback. Also for that 6am brainstorming session that gave me the name for the first saga and for making the peg-dolls goodies. Thanks to my mom for letting me publish and for paying some of the publishing costs; I couldn't have done this without you. And thanks to my dad, who solely inspired David Flores. I'm proud to spread your name around the world since you can't do it yourself anymore.

Thank you to Paris and Tatyanah, my other two alpha-readers! You guys help a TON and read this book when it was in such a messy stage. I'm forever grateful that you were honest with me and told me what I needed to hear. Also, thank you for all your chaotic comments. They made me laugh and smile a ton.

Thank you to my betas, McKenna, Emma, Kara, Savannah-Rose, and Elsa. First of all, McKenna, you are super helpful and are definitely my rock when I'm feeling stressed. I'm so glad to have a friend like you that I can always count on to be there for me. Thank you.

Emma, thank you so much for your feedback and critique. I'm glad I had you on my team.

Kara, thank you SO FRICKIN' MUCH for all your feedback and the multiple read-throughs that you did. You helped me change this book for the better and really helped fix plot holes and gave Zira a clearer motivation for why she became a bully. Also thanks for giving me the push to make Sundown Sam's cousin. This book is not the same as it was when the betas read it and you should know a lot of that is because of you.

Savannah-Rose, thank you so much for reading this book and drawing the map of Lionfield County. You brought my vision to life and were so patient with me and all the changes I requested. Thank you so much for your time and kindness.

Elsa, you did not read a whole lot of this book, lol. But I still thank you for reading it and giving feedback on what you did. And thank you SO FLIPPIN' MUCH for formatting this book. I probably would've lost it if you hadn't stepped up and offered your services. Thank you for saving me from those mental breakdowns.

Thank you to Miriam who helped me turn Zira's meanness level up a ton. The points you made were stuff I already had Zira doing, but off screen. You helped me put it in the book and just make things spicier. So, thank you so much my fellow Catholic artist!

Thank you to Abby who was the final person to read this book besides the editor. You gave me the calmness I needed to complete this book somewhat on time. I seriously wouldn't have been able to let a lot of details go if you hadn't read it. So thank you for making my life easier and my mind clearer. And thanks for helping with the blurb! You're a life saver!

Arianna Fox, thank you so much for editing this book. You helped a ton in the Spanish department and of course suggested edits that made everything SO MUCH BETTER. I'm so glad I chose you to be my editor and thank you for giving me that insanely kind discount. Seriously, without that this book would be very different and I'm glad it isn't. You helped so much. Thank you again, my birthday buddy and honorary younger sister.

Esther, thank you so much for drawing the cover. DOESNT IT LOOK FREAKIN AMAZING?! I'm so glad I found you and your talent before looking for a cover artist. Your style matched exactly what I wanted and the result speaks for itself. Thank you for your patience and suggestions that made this cover better. I couldn't have published without you and keep following your dreams and drawing your pictures. God blessed you with a real amazing talent and there's a reason for that. Keep following His will and I know you will go places.

And last but not least, thank YOU, my snowflakes, for reading this book. Without all your encouragement and enthusiasm, I may have given up. And I'm glad I didn't. The world needs this story for one reason or another, and maybe it really touched your hearts. All I can say is thank you for giving it a chance and coming along on the start of Zira's journey. She'd be very confused why anyone wants to read about her. But little does she know how amazing she truly is.

Now, who's ready for book two?!

Maggie Frost

The Witch Chronicles: Unraveled

Maggie Frost

The Witch Chronicles

Destiny Ignites Saga

Mirrors

Coming Soon

Maggie Frost

About The Author

Maggie Frost is an eighteen-year-old author who has been writing since a young age. She loves telling stories and learning how much she connects with each of her characters.

Her love for story-telling came from loving stories as she grew up; whether that was from TV shows, movies, or books, she couldn't get enough of it (and still can't). Noticing how much stories affected her own life and views, she came up with her own ideas for what should be in them. Now she writes them herself.

Maggie is a devout Roman Catholic and believes God has placed all these stories in her heart for a reason and hopes to spread His word through them.

When she's not writing, you can find Maggie drawing, watching TV, movies and YouTube (mainly the *Dangie Bros*), listening to music, singing, or doting over her two pets: a white boxer named Clover, and a leopard gecko named Nuri.

You can follow Maggie on her Instagram, *@thefrostedauthor*.